VIENNA

VIENNA

WILLIAM S. KIRBY

A TOM DOHERTY ASSOCIATES BOOK
New York

VIENNA

Copyright © 2015 by William S. Kirby

A Forge Book
Published by Tom Doherty Associates, LLC
175 Fifth Avenue
New York, NY 10010

www.tor-forge.com

Forge® is a registered trademark of Tom Doherty Associates, LLC.

The Library of Congress Cataloging-in-Publication Data is available upon request.

ISBN 978-0-7653-7583-4 (hardcover)
ISBN 978-1-4668-4795-8 (e-book)

Forge books may be purchased for educational, business, or promotional use. For information on bulk purchases, please contact the Macmillan Corporate and Premium Sales Department at 1-800-221-7945, extension 5442, or write to specialmarkets@macmillan.com.

First Edition: September 2015

Printed in the United States of America

0   9   8   7   6   5   4   3   2   1

For Kathryn
and
In memory of Robert Waldron Kirby:
father, teacher, friend

Much madness is divinest sense
To a discerning eye;
Much sense the starkest madness.
'Tis the majority
In this, as all, prevails.
Assent, and you are sane;
Demur—you're straightway dangerous,
And handled with a chain.

—EMILY DICKINSON

VIENNA

1

Brussels

Awake under a hollow sunrise, Justine Am sought cover behind a hangover that wasn't there. The previous night's drinking had consisted of two sips of vodka drowning in peach liqueur. She'd switched to tonic water well before the pink eyedropper of liquid ecstasy made its rounds. Not that she would've taken part. Boredom was cheaper and it unleashed the same chaos. Sprawled across a stranger's swaybacked bed, Justine still felt the subterranean echo of house electronica pacing behind her rib cage: *boom, boom, boom.* She'd fallen in with a post-tribal, post-trance, post-everything crowd. World-weary gods draped over the cherry and onyx pillows of Holler. They'd offered her a sucker's bet and she'd raised the stakes right into this bed.

Sketchy times since Prague. Pouring rain and the howl of police sirens; a lone separatist locked in the Dancing House with a vest of high explosives and a heart of rust. Security concerns caused a three-day delay, even though the standoff only lasted four hours. Local politicians didn't want to take chances of an A-list fashion model getting splattered across the electorate.

Then a two-night shoot for the Clay to Flesh project, set in front of the Národní Muzeum. City lights doubled across wet concrete. Justine in Dory McCallister's iconic drop-waist silks, posed next to a wooden manikin. She mimicked the statue's skipping stance, toes pointed and fingers splayed. The photographer's ancient camera whirred to life. Justine called up her world-famous smile, coy under lowered eyelids. Through the thin fabric across her legs, she felt the first breath of winter falling from blue-white stars.

Returning the following evening, it was bad enough Justine

thought the two-hundred-year-old manikin had shifted positions overnight; worse that she'd mentioned it to her agent. Nothing good had happened in the four days since, and last night hit magnitude nine on the nothing good scale.

And yet, the wooden girl had moved between the two sessions. It'd been such a certainty at the time. A subtle swing to a more rigid stance. The manikin's tupelo smile tightening to a sadistic leer. Justine had gone as far as calling up the previous night's photos, but the manikin had been backlit to the point of being little more than a silhouette. She'd tried pointing out what she saw to James, but the more she spoke, the more she sounded as if she were trying to convince herself. James had been at his most patronizing. "Pinocchio aside, I doubt wooden dolls come to life."

The episode had left Justine feeling idiotic. Fears barely controlled back in med school rattled loose chains. Echoes of children screaming at the pasty green cinder blocks of the Felton Gables Ward.

Am I becoming like them?

Justine opened her eyes. The yellowed plaster overhead was split by a lightning bolt fracture. She stared at the leading edge, anxious that her presence would somehow cause it to spread another quarter inch. After a few seconds, she realized someone had used a fine-tipped pencil to outline the crack with machine precision; as if cordoning off the defect. But sadness spilled over nonetheless, seeping down the ancient walls.

She remembered a rant from her Stanford bioethics professor: "Doctors don't save lives. Doctors only give life a chance. Learn the difference or get out."

Shit.

The thin breeze coming through the bedside window smelled of lilac. Where would such an ambitious flower grow in Lower Town's acres of eroded stone? Justine sat up, pulling a threadbare sheet with her. The bed springs released her 116 pounds in a chorus of squeaks.

She hunched over by the small window. Three stories down, a

fairy-tale church of arches and spires overshadowed a plaza of gray cobblestone. The building's walls were etched in soot, although a battered section of scaffolding suggested a minor restoration was underway. It looked like a hundred other churches Justine had seen, except for the doors: two massive slabs of burgundy under a Gothic arch. They told her nothing. Every other building in Brussels was a church.

The tortoiseshell glasses that had landed her here were folded on a plastic nightstand. She put them on in hopes they might allow her to read the small white-on-blue street sign posted on the church. There was no change looking through the spotless lenses.

"I need those."

Justine turned and saw the punch line of last night's tired joke. The girl's cinnamon-brown hair, shoulder length and of that extreme fineness that would tangle over a whisper. Stone-washed hazel eyes above expressionless lips. The nose was better, a modestly upturned anime arc soon to be consumed by the Frankenstein glasses. Her skin was clear to the point of unhealthy pallor, accenting her wispy frame. Her name was something cringe-worthy—a place name.

Vienna.

Even in the morning sun, she seemed nothing more than a lesser poltergeist. Bound to her forgotten crypt with no television, no computer, no MP3 player. No phone. Only a single stack of old hardcovers, their spines tight against the wall. Justine handed Vienna the glasses. *Why would anyone wear nonprescription lenses?*

"Do you want breakfast?" Vienna asked. Her British accent sounded like a cheap imitation. She'd looked a timid twenty in last night's glittering lights. Justine found herself praying for eighteen. *What was the age of consent in Belgium?* Followed by the most dreaded cliché in the business: *Did the blogs already have pictures?*

And when had Vienna drifted out of bed anyway? Justine felt the pinpricks of her flight reflex, kicking in eight hours too late. "What are you making?"

"Eggs, orange juice, strawberries, and tea."

It sounded harmless. "Do I have time to shower?"

Vienna nodded.

"Have you seen my BlackBerry?" Justine asked.

"You left it in the bathroom."

"I need to check for messages." Justine stood, the thin sheet falling away.

"Heather!" Vienna darted around the bed, averting her eyes and yanking the shade across the tiny window. Her movement was subtly stuttered—exaggerated in a way that suggested either phencyclidine abuse or a developmental disorder. Then she was gone, out to the small kitchen. Justine was left feeling unaccountably self-conscious.

Why did I give her my real name? She pulled the top book in the stack away from the wall enough to see the title on the spine: *Methods of Political Assassination in Nazi Germany.*

Justine kept her eyes open in the standing-room-only shower. As if Vienna might sneak in, wielding a knife like Anthony Perkins. It seemed fitting that the shower curtain was a perfect set piece. Flat gray, with no tropical fish, no blooming flowers, no unicorns. Justine looked closer. Not even a textural pattern in the plastic. It might have worked in modern design, but here, where a splash of color would have been blessed relief, it hung off the bar like a funeral shroud.

Water hissed against the plastic as Justine straightened. She closed her eyes and heard static pouring from her grandfather's ancient radio. Minor league baseball wavering over Montana from somewhere in Colorado . . . *hanging slider . . . out of the park . . .* Words lost in a crescendo of pops and crackles. Lord help you if you touched the tuner. A decade gone and it felt more real than this bleak apartment.

Justine frowned. More wicked Prague karma.

That stupid manikin.

Followed by an even more dreary thought: *I had sex with a woman last night.*

Well, sort of. Vienna had approached lovemaking like a blind girl playing connect-the-dots: every step planned and executed with painstaking attention that was endearing for two minutes and tedious the next forty. You would at least think another woman would know what worked and what didn't. *Another myth shattered.* It wasn't as if Vienna was a virgin. Justine had felt compelled to check after the first fifteen minutes.

And that's the extent of what I know about her. That, and the fact that Vienna didn't smell like anything. Not perfume, or deodorant, or shampoo. And not, thank goodness, the vinegar reek cultivated by a handful of Europe's old-school bathing deniers. Nothing. As if she had been scrubbed in an alpine lake and sealed in her black shirtdress. It didn't fit anywhere on Justine's organizational chart of social status.

Justine absently rubbed the sleek lizard tattoo on her left hip. A reminder of choices made, some worse than others.

Out of the shower, she took her BlackBerry from the tiny vanity. The first call had to be to her agent, still hanging on her shoulder. Making certain his prize mare wasn't losing her head; asking every five minutes if she was okay, or if she needed rest. Or if she was seeing any other statues move.

James Hargrave was his usual triple-espresso alert. Justine described the church—it had to be near the Grand-Place de Bruxelles, as they had walked through that ancient mall with the glass ceiling. There had been a sculpture of a well-endowed cat on a bicycle along the way.

James asked her what the hell she thought she was doing.

"I'm not your daughter, James. I'm fine. Go back to New York."

"I will when you stop seeing manikins dance around."

"It was a joke," Justine said.

"Uh-huh."

He said he would send a car when he had the church pinned down, and that there was a surprise waiting, and she had to be in the chair by 9:30 for the second day of the Brussels Clay to Flesh shoot, and she had to give Bernoulli an answer for his winter show at Carrousel du Louvre by three at the latest as she had already put him off once, and London called for a *Vogue* cover and they were offering an ungodly amount of money, but Sandra Bennet just had to have Justine Am for next fall's fashion issue and they already confirmed Smyth and Weston for hair and face, and they were going to be in London for the next stage of Clay to Flesh anyway, so why not do it?

Justine said fine and hung up; slipping into a Toni Frieze original that would pay six months' rent on Vienna's prêt-à-porter life.

The claustrophobic hall held the only art Vienna seemed to own. An elfish girl with jet-black hair and serrated beauty. Justine recognized it as a cover from one of Björk's early solo efforts. The bottom tenth of the poster, which must have held a track listing, had been trimmed off. The pencil had been used here as well. A nested frame of eight concentric rectangles had been drafted onto the plaster. Justine brushed her fingers over the lines, feeling shallow grooves etched into the surface. It seemed to her that if she found the perfect tension, the furrows would play back like old vinyl. A recording of whatever madness had set the pencil in motion.

A deep breath and on to the galley kitchen.

Vienna was dressed for a '60s Disney musical: white pinafore over a powder blue shirt. Faux mother of pearl buttons. Methodically clipping fresh chives over frying eggs. The girl looked up from her work, peering through the useless glasses. "Your hair is blond."

Brunette, but now wasn't the time to explain. "Yes?"

"It was blue last night."

Justine laughed. "Soluble dye for a last-minute promo. The ads are already printed and going up today."

"Promo?"

"A photo shoot for high-end footwear."

The girl's eyes pinched together. "You dye your hair blue to photograph shoes?"

"No, silly. People take pictures of me wearing the shoes."

"Oh. I thought it was a little odd. Sort of scary. Pretty though."

It finally hit Justine on a visceral level that Vienna had no clue who Justine Am was. It made her feel as if she'd drifted too far from shore. Reaching down with her toes and not touching bottom. "Thank you, I think." The involuntary gulp of mossy lake water.

Vienna nodded. "The eggs are ready, if you want."

Justine tried to remember the exact moment when any of this had seemed like a good idea. *Didn't you always say you wanted adventure?*

They sat at the table, white plates flanked by unadorned flatware. Justine was surprised how hungry the childhood smell of salt and pepper on eggs made her. Vienna served them sunny-side up, salmonella be damned. Justine didn't have the heart to turn them down. Poison or not they were delicious, and the macerated strawberries were dead ripe. Better add an extra half hour at the gym.

Justine ate in silence; noted that Vienna placed her own berries as far as possible from the eggs. Shepherding runny yolks away. Justine had observed such behavior numerous times during her internship. Seeing it repeated in this airless apartment made her queasy.

"I'll do dishes," Vienna said after she finished. She reached for the plates and Justine saw the girl's fingernails were chewed ragged. Justine had seen plenty of that back at Stanford as well.

Hurry up, James.

Vienna's black flats whispered over the floor; a sheet of white laminate running into the narrow hallway. The same floor in the bedroom and bathroom. Justine couldn't remember seeing a solitary seam breaking its nonreflective surface. How would such a large piece have been unrolled and installed? It must have cost a fortune. Maybe it was there before Vienna moved in?

It's none of my business. Justine sat in awkward silence before deciding conversation was the least of evils. "You're a student?"

"No."

"It's just the stack of books in your room."

Vienna paused. "I'm learning World War Two this week."

"Oh?"

"Hitler and Himmler. Goring, Goebbels, yeah?" She paused. "Bernie Madoff."

Justine laughed before she realized how odd it was to hear Vienna trying to joke. Even more astounded to hear the girl exhale a single sigh of laughter. As if she had at last been given permission to act human, only to forget how.

The BlackBerry interrupted with an oldie Justine's parents had gotten her hooked on. *The world was moving, she was right there with it and she was.* Vienna inhaled at the sound.

"Yes?" Justine said into the phone.

"Eglise St.-Jean-du-Béguinage," James said.

"What?"

"The church with red doors. We're in the courtyard."

"Be right there." She turned off the phone. "Vienna, I have to—"

"'And She Was,'" Vienna said. "Three minutes, thirty-nine seconds. Track number one of *Little Creatures,* by the Talking Heads. June 16, 1985, Sire Records. ID Number TAH-2. All songs by David Byrne unless noted."

"Excuse me?"

"Your ringtone. It's about a girl who took LSD near a factory that made chocolate milk."

"I didn't know that." Justine forced a smile. "I have to leave, honey. I have a shoot with Vincent Mathews this afternoon."

"Is he your boyfriend?"

"Matty? Hardly. Don't you ever watch TV?"

Vienna's voice was almost too soft to hear. "It's bad for me."

"Bad?"

"Because I'm broken."

"I'm sorry." *What am I supposed to say?* "I have to go."

"I can walk you down."

"You don't have to."

"I need to go to work."

Justine sighed. Whatever got her out of this broken-soul corner of the universe the quickest.

Out into Brussels's hazy October; sunlight spreading across the ash-colored city in a watery blush. A summer morning arriving three months late. The air already felt like dilute glue.

The limo was waiting, a glossy special effect projected in front of the medieval church. James would have the AC on full. Justine put on her sunglasses. "This is good-bye."

"Okay."

"Take care, Vienna." It almost sounded like an apology.

"Okay."

Justine was mortified when the girl followed her to the car, even more so when Grant stepped from the back. The surprise James had mentioned. Grant's Hermès jeans and black T-shirt looked painted on his surfer boy frame. His wavy brown hair cropped short. He smiled behind Oakley wraps. *Paint him white and snap off his arms and you would have a Greek statue.*

"I told you not to come, silly," Justine said. "I don't have much free time."

"We'll make do." He gave her an unhurried kiss. Nothing less than full on the lips for Grant. "Introduce your companion?"

"This is Vienna, an old friend I was visiting. Vienna? This is Grant Eriksson."

"A pleasure to meet you, Vienna."

"I'm not—"

Justine interrupted before Vienna could explain that a one-night stand didn't amount to being friends. "Grant's an old friend, too." Well, he'd lasted more than a night, anyway.

Vienna nodded. "Where are you from, Mr. Grant?"

Justine rolled her eyes, glad they were hidden behind her sunglasses' oil-slick lenses.

Grant smiled, he was too aware of being in public not to. "America—a small town in Nebraska."

In a frozen heartbeat, so quickly gone Justine wasn't sure she'd even seen it, Vienna's lips twisted into a leer of purest loathing.

"What town?" Her voice as empty as ice on a lake.

Grant looked at Justine, who could only summon a shrug. "Kearney."

"The elm trees there are lovely."

Grant smiled. "Especially in autumn." He glanced at his Breitling, reflections from the bezel skipping across the plaza. "We're running late." He nodded toward Vienna. "Good to meet you."

Grant guided Justine to the car. James Hargrave sat shotgun, wearing his annoyance in a gunfighter scowl. Doors shut. Justine looked back at the girl, standing alone by the church. Motionless as a statue. Or as motionless as any statue except that idiotic manikin in Prague.

Just get me out of here.

The limo turned down a canyon etched in the gothic landscape, and Vienna was gone.

I have to call Bernoulli this afternoon. Paris in the off-season sounds perfect.

2

And she was alone in the courtyard of Eglise St.-Jean-du-Béguinage, her shadow fractured across worn cobbles. *Why had Heather's boyfriend lied about who he was?* But then, Heather had lied, too. Vienna knew this because she'd stood outside the bathroom door after she'd heard the shower go off. Her ear to the hollow wood, the paring knife she'd used for the strawberries forgotten in her hand. Surgery syrup inching down the blade. The angry person on the phone had called Heather "Justine."

Would it have been so hard to tell the truth about her name? So hard to pretend it mattered? So hard to stay a little longer?

Vienna walked to one of the friezes that flanked the doors of the church, if only for the sake of appearing to be doing something. Other than crying.

Christ waited there, beseeching weathered apostles. The Agony in the Garden. There were words that went with the scene, written in italic red letters: *Watch and pray, that ye enter not into temptation; the spirit is indeed willing, but the flesh is weak.* Vienna had read the passage as a child, growing up near Bath. Scampering down the tomblike ruins of a Roman hypocaust when the world got too big and twisted inside her head.

Ironic to see the words here, outside a chapel dedicated to the widows of crusaders. But then, their flesh had been weak, too. Ripped apart by swords and trampled under horses, leaving behind only grieving lovers. Vienna's own apartment housed such a widow, centuries ago.

The architectural elements of the Béguinage in Brussels are unique from the standpoint of . . . Vienna closed her eyes, consciously letting the words go. *It's because my mind doesn't work right.* There was nothing new in the thought. *Then why cry now?* She wiped the tears away.

Footsteps; a shadow next to hers.

"I meant no harm," a man said. Vienna shied from the voice, turned, and saw a short, sandy-haired man. Jeans and a plaid shirt. Vienna's mind slipped into the patterned fabric. Endless tunnels of squares, hypercubes that shifted perspective every time the man moved. Ratios of sides and surface areas blossomed in Vienna's mind. It would take 172 of the large red squares to tile the uneven shape of the fabric, but some would be wasted. A better pattern would be . . .

She looked away, into fresh tears.

"They're replacing them all," the man said. "I don't know why. There's a good amount of gold inside, but not enough to pay my commission." He handed her a scrap of paper. She glanced at a nearly illegible scrawl:

Au 5 gm / Ag 3 gm
Au 3 gm / Cu 18 gm
Au 7 gm / Fe 21 gm
Au 11 gm / Pb 14 gm

"I don't understand," Vienna said. She felt a shiver of alarm beyond the whirling geometry of his shirt.

"Show this to her." His voice had a Scottish burr. "I was lucky to get measurements from the piece in Rome. They're paranoid of everyone."

"What do you mean?" she whispered. *Am I in danger?*

"I saw you with Justine Am last night. Your apartment was being watched—a Yank in dark glasses. I couldn't approach while the limo was here, they would have recognized me. You have to tell her."

"Tell her what?" Vienna kept her eyes away from the nightmare squares.

"What happened in Prague was my fault. Rush job when the

first one broke—lorry smash-up on the E50. She has to forget it."
His voice grew quiet and quick. "Andries is dangerous. They say
he murdered an art dealer a year ago in Munich. I've seen it in
his eyes. She has to let it go."

"I don't—"

"You have to tell her!"

The rough cough of a lorry echoed from the walls. Vienna
heard the man step away and then race across the plaza. She stood
for over a minute, carefully focusing on the frieze. What just
happened?

It's none of my business. Vienna crumpled the paper and threw
it in a rubbish bin at the side of the church.

She left the plaza by the same street Heather's black limousine
had taken—past a sign showing a car with a red slash through it.
Stupid Americans. A few turns and she entered the Galleries Saint
Hubert. She loved the spider web of iron and glass that covered
the long plaza, hung from the heavens with spectral grace. It was
so familiar by now that it rarely made her dizzy. And if it did,
there were always window displays to distract her. Chocolate
and shoes and watches and photographs of beautiful people in
beautiful places.

The stores had yet to open for the day, and the corridor smelled
faintly of bleach. Brussels had thrown its customary Saturday
night party, and the Sunday morning custodians had already en-
gaged the citywide hangover of garbage in the gutters and piss in
the alleys.

Vienna wondered why she'd tried to join the festivities. Cecile
had asked to meet her at Holler, though Vienna never expected
her to actually show up, and of course she hadn't. But Vienna had
been too hot and too afraid of another night lost in the sad memories of widows. She'd stepped out a few times before with no
harm coming from it. Only this time she was propositioned by a
woman with blue hair, cut in straight bangs down to liquid emerald eyes. Vienna had thought her beautiful, but maybe her
exotic appearance kept her from dating.

And she lied about her name.

As for the night, Vienna didn't like thinking about it. Cecile had suggested sleeping with a woman might be a good tonic for Vienna's shyness. Vienna wouldn't have considered it back in London. Her foster father would have been horrified. But here, sinking ever lower in the city's social strata, she didn't see any harm to it.

Still, it had been too overwhelming and too foreign to be anything other than shameful. Vienna hadn't known what was expected—had never been with anyone—though she knew in one respect her coworker had been right. With a woman, she at least knew the topography well enough to guess a route. The wrong one, apparently.

I should forget it happened. Now that was funny.

It was Christmas in Bath all over again. Gifts under the tree and everyone talking too loudly and eating too many sweets and lights blinking in discordant cycles and it was never anything she wanted anyway. It always passed in a blur, as if Vienna were missing some internal switch to reach out and experience it as others did. Which was true enough.

Anyway, maybe it was best to add sex to the list of useless things, because then it would be one less thing to worry about. She'd done it and now there was no reason for anyone to tease her about it. So she never had to do it again.

She cut across Rue des Bouchers, lined with cafés and salons. Briefly into the wavering sun before entering the Galerie de la Reine. There were words to go with this as well, set in the blurry ink of a manually typed dissertation. Her eyes traced across a phantom page:

The Galeries Royal Saint-Hubert comprise the Galerie du Roy, the Galerie de la Reine, and the Galerie des Princes. They were conceived in 1836 by Jean-Pierre Cluysenaer . . . It went on for pages. There was the barber who slit his throat over the structure's tangled property rights. And here was the aesthetic reason for the bend in the middle of the structure. Vienna didn't have the energy to

go back to the beginning and see who wrote it. If she kept walking, the words would slip away.

Coffee steam and the yeast smell of fresh pastries rose through
the air. The bells atop the massive Cathedral of Saint Michael and
Saint Gudule called the faithful to Sunday mass. Maybe she
would go after work.

The spirit is willing, but the flesh is weak.

Across Rue du Marché aux Herbes. Vienna relished the sound
of the French names, the way they tasted like spring. But after
four months in Brussels, she knew little French, or Flemish for
that matter. She recognized the sounds and some meaning, but
with no education in it she lacked any idea of syntax or grammar. Which had come as an unpleasant shock.

Into the Grote Markt—the Grand Place. Built in the twilight
of the Northern Renaissance, the town square was surrounded
by layers of baroque architecture. Vienna felt like a playhouse
princess lost on a stage of narrow steeples and filigreed stonework.
There was even an evil king, compliments of an encyclopedia
entry she'd read back in London:

*In 1695, King Louis XIV ordered Brussels to be bombarded with
red-hot cannon balls. The resulting firestorm engulfed the entire
Grand Place, with the exception of the Hotel de Ville . . .*

The same Hotel de Ville in front of her as she crossed the plaza.
Archangel Michael on the highest steeple, trampling a demon.
Vienna imagined Grant Eriksson under Michael's pitchfork and
immediately crossed herself. *Are ye not then partial in yourselves,
and are become judges of evil thoughts?*

She continued across the square, letting her thoughts dance
through words, even though her doctors told her never to do that.
*The Hotel de Ville was designed by a Flemish . . . The word Flemish
means "that which is flooded" . . . The deadliest flood in history was
the 1931 flooding of the Yanktze, Huang He, and Huai Rivers, in
which four million people were . . .* There was a picture there. Long
rows of dead children, stiff limbs twisted in mud.

She stepped up to a lemon-yellow door on Rue du Marché au

Charbon. A rustic sign, implying history where there was none, marked the Gelataria du Cygne. The store's window sported a deco golden goose in the upper left corner, leaving room to display a rack of stainless steel gelato bins. The sunshine was warm on Vienna's shoulders; it would be a busy day. She produced the right key from a small chain and unlocked the door.

By noon, she'd served 124 customers 186 scoops of gelato. She said the right phrases in French to collect euros, switching to English for British and American tourists. Vienna knew by late afternoon the day's heat would drive citrus flavors to the top of the chart she kept on scrap paper. She thought a lot of inventory might be saved with the information she was collecting, but the manager was a busy man and there never seemed a chance to get a word in.

At 2:17, two men appeared at the shoe store across the street. They removed the old poster for Versace and put up a new one for Step Out. It featured a girl who was nude except for a pair of white stiletto heels, straps set with diamonds. She was seated on white-blue fur, her body turned away from the camera, but her eyes gazing back over her shoulder. Her long, smooth legs were curled under her, showing the shoes to good effect. She was positioned in such a way—her closer arm behind her bottom—to avoid being outright pornographic. But the raw sensuality of her face was intoxicating. She had blue hair and emerald eyes and a small tattoo of a lizard on her left hip. The poster said the woman's name was Justine Am.

Pedestrians gawked at the image. Vulgar laughter over imagined bedroom scenes.

For the next four hours, Vienna served melting scoops of gelato under the poster's sensuous gaze. Her stomach twisted around a knot of anger. Easy enough to find words for Justine: *Their drink is sour: they have committed whoredom continually.*

No doubt the strange man wearing the shirt-of-squares had been a gently used article left by the wayside. He'd said something about "killer" and Vienna was certain the word was used in America to describe people of sexual prowess. "She's a man killer," and the like. Not that sleeping with Justine had been all that great. Or even great at all.

Everything had gone pear-shaped, and the more Vienna thought about it, the more it was her foster father's fault. Arthur Emerson Grayfield, Earl of Idiots and Knight Commander of Nothing Anyone Had Ever Heard Of. Titles or not, he was just a miserable old git in a miserable old flat. "It's time for you to make your own way, Vienna." As if he knew what was best for her, even though he wasn't really her father. "I have prepared a modest room for you in Brussels. I know you can do this." Because he didn't have the courage to say: "I never wanted you in the first place." And . . .

Stop being petulant.

But if she was petulant, then it just proved she was right about not being ready to be alone and Grayfield was wrong. A real knight would admit his mistake, and he would come and rescue her. And . . .

To complete the day Cecile showed up just before closing, suspended between aluminum crutches. Long, brown-gold hair that always looked better than Vienna's. "Sorry I didn't make it last night," she said. "I twisted my ankle."

"Okay."

"I heard what happened, Vienna. I'm so sorry. They had no right."

"Okay."

"They were paid to set you up by some wealthy perv, an American."

"Okay." It wasn't, really, but she only had herself to blame.

Cecile looked as if she wanted to add something more, but she only nodded and limped from the store.

Vienna closed the shop at seven, cleaned up, and locked the door.

Night came on and she was running back to Holler. She was going to tell Justine or Heather—or whatever her real name was— that even if she wasn't on any posters at least she wasn't a whore.

But the club was closed because it was Sunday and Justine was probably far away. Probably in another person's bed. And that was okay, because Vienna wouldn't have yelled at anyone. Wouldn't have even opened the door.

She was home by nine, crying into the sheets. Her doctors said that was bad, too.

Stop it!

Vienna peeled herself from the bed and went to the sole dresser she owned. In the bottom drawer, buried under shirts and folded jeans she never wore, she felt the smooth edges of her Apple Air. She pulled it out and plugged it in, connecting a thin cable to the room's phone jack. Dressed in its aluminum shell, the computer looked sleekly sinister. But it was safe to use it tonight. She didn't work on Mondays until noon.

The log-in screen was forest green, without a single icon marring its surface. Grayfield had set it up that way. His kind voice filling his London flat, his silver hair smelling faintly of cinnamon. Vivaldi playing on a real phonograph because Grayfield said it sounded better that way. Vienna looked at the composer's name and saw that he'd written his most famous works in a home for abandoned children. And it was just perfect, the way everything fit together.

With a theatrical sigh, Vienna pressed a key to call up hidden icons. She ordered the computer's ghost fingers into the net. The screen filled with ads and banners. *Don't look!*

A pointless reflex arriving far too late. *Fix your credit now! The secret to whiter teeth!* And she knew every word. *Earn 2,000€ a week! Your stomach can be this flat!*

Vienna closed her eyes to a squint and made certain the cursor was in the Google window. She typed out "Justine Am."

3

The Brussels Clay to Flesh shoot was set at the Atomium, a mansion-sized model of molecular iron left over from the '58 World Expo. Justine thought it looked like a chrome Tinkertoy on HGH, but she wasn't paid to think. She was paid to be in platinum hair, slate lipstick, silver nails, and the scratchy plastics of Dexter Collins's latest collection of highly textured, wildly popular, deeply symbolic crap. She fidgeted with the Velcro that anchored the towering shoulder pads.

The girl doing wardrobe looked increasingly suicidal—her big break shot to hell by the ludicrous getup. "Could be worse," Justine said. "You could be wearing it." The humor fell flat. If the session bombed, Justine was too valuable to take the fall. Scapegoats would materialize down the food chain.

A rising crowd flowed around the yellow tape cordoning off Heysel Plateau. Those in front waved glossies from Justine's recent projects. Careful not to upend the polymer subdivision on her shoulders, Justine scrawled her initials a few times while the lights and umbrella reflectors were being set up. As per recent instructions from James, she stayed near the cops who had been called in.

Justine could see Lower Town in the pastel distance. She heard cascading bells calling the faithful to Sunday morning mass. Was Nowhere Girl there now? Hypnotized by the threaded smoke of votive candles and praying that God might notice her at last? Long odds on that.

Justine turned back into the Atomium's latticework shadow. Mathews and his two assistants had the Brussels manikin decked out in a replica Coco Chanel little black dress. Bias-cut with full sleeves and a flawlessly proportioned V-neck. They'd sliced the seams and pinned it together over lifeless wood.

Mathews caught Justine's thought. "Our tupelo lady fetched the better designer," he said.

"Understatement of the decade."

Justine remembered from the Clay to Flesh media guide that this manikin's namesake was Duchess Joan of Someplace. A fourteenth-century warrior queen who tried to unify embryonic Belgium. Having failed to die horribly, she'd been largely forgotten.

Since Joan's creation a hundred and fifty years ago, some philistine had stained her blue. The caustic dye had distended the grain, giving her a corrugated appearance. She didn't even feel like wood anymore. The manikin stood upright, palms on hips. Below a flowing brunette wig, her expression was wistful, lips frozen in a sad smile. Her gaze downcast, as if surveying life's bitter defeats. Justine guessed that the sculptor—she couldn't remember his name—had been a hard-luck case.

Searching the manikin's dead eyes, Justine tried to untangle the Prague Weirdness. Had one of Joan's wooden sisters moved? Elizabetha had been carved in mid-skip—a motion capture of youthful energy. Over two days of shooting, Elizabetha's left arm had shifted down, or her torso had canted to the side, or her feet had spread farther apart. Something.

Or was it simply the manikin's dynamic pose suggested movement? Why was the obvious answer so hard to believe?

"We're ready, Justine." Mathews showed her the first position marks of the day. His boney hands shifted into constant motion, framing each shot. "Three quarters to the fan, smile . . . more pout . . . this light is for shit . . . tilt forward from the hips . . . You seem off today. Tired? That's better . . . If another pigeon wanders in frame, I want it fucking strangled. . . . Get the hair again . . . less happy, more smug . . . hand lower on your leg . . ." Justine thought Mathews sounded like someone who wanted to sound like a fashion photographer.

Five hours and six wardrobe changes later, Justine was left demoralized. The day had been too hot and too wet and her thoughts remained tethered to Vienna's gray shower curtain. The seamless floor and fractured ceiling. The broken spirit forever guarding strawberries from invading yolk. *I shouldn't have just blown her off.*

Guilt on a seven-hour delay. Wonderful.

Justine waved to the crowd and ducked into the wardrobe tent pitched to the side of the camera. By the time she emerged, Mathews was downloading pictures to his oversized laptop while his assistants finished stowing gear. Justine watched the images stream by, depressing in their rows of sameness.

"We have several excellent shots." Mathews pointed to a picture of her mimicking the manikin's pose, her absurdly padded shoulders towering overhead. "This is nice."

She knew his reputation enough to trust him. She signed off the final paperwork and said her good-byes.

Back to the hotel for an hour of cardio. A quick shower and a primal rendezvous with Grant. He moved with relaxed confidence, hands guiding her hips, his cool lips on her throat. Justine felt her body respond to his touch through filters of fatigue.

Off to rinse, adding a mental note to make certain all the water wasn't drying her skin. Dress in something expensively casual and spend the late afternoon on the phone. To Bernoulli in Paris: I'll be there. Adelina in New York: please double-check my London itinerary for the next stage of Clay to Flesh, and contact *Vogue* to see exactly what they want. A quick call back to Georgia. Mom fixing tea and fiddling with a new math curriculum. Dad out for a jog along the shoals.

"You check for wayward shopping carts?" Justine asked. An old family joke.

"Of course," her mother answered. "I take care of your father."

Conversation danced around the trivial. Justine tried to emulate her mother's tranquility. The genes had to be there somewhere.

"What's wrong, Sassy?" Her mother's ability to sniff out sulking was known to exceed the speed of light.

"Nothing major."

Off the phone and on to a radio promo—which was mental as she didn't speak French or Flemish. Then dinner with Grant at a place serving Lilliputian portions of perfect food. His cell rang three times. He kept each call short, but it annoyed her that he took them at all. Just another lesson from the biz: *show me the most beautiful girl in the world, and I'll show you the guy who's tired of doing her.*

I'm getting old. The thought was darkly funny.

Back at the Cosmopolitan, she watched the BBC for fifteen minutes and went to bed. Grant was on the phone again, talking to someone named Cecile. His fingers drumming on the table next to him. It was a disquieting mannerism from a man who made a conscious effort to eliminate offensive habits. Justine was asleep before the call was over.

She woke to timid knocking. A bleary glance at the bedside clock. Who would be here at freaking five on a Monday morning? Justine pulled herself from bed, careful not to wake Grant.

Too groggy to think, she pulled the chain without checking the peephole. And there was Vienna, direct from Planet Weird. Her face smothered by the ludicrous glasses; her hair at DEF-CON four, tangles flowing from a rat's nest over her right temple. She moved her lips silently, as if reading.

Justine wished for a replay button at the door chain. "How did you find me?"

"Ophiostoma novo-ulmi."

"What?"

"Your boyfriend is a dobbing poser, yeah?"

"Vienna?"

"He deviseth mischief upon his bed." Vienna's eyes scanned left to right over blank air. "He setteth himself in a way that is not good; he abhorreth not evil." Tears falling on her white blouse.

She spun on her heel and marched down the hall and around the corner without looking back.

Fine.

Close the door.

Double-check the chain is back in place.

I should call the police. And tell them what? That a deranged female was threatening her with what sounded like Old Testament brimstone? It was not, as James would say, an actionable transgression. The only reasonable response was more sleep.

When Justine woke two hours later, the incident felt like a sour dream. Down to the gym for Pilates, then to the spa with Grant.

They made love as afternoon faded. Justine knew it was a mistake before they began. She was distracted, Grant's finely calculated moves leaving her anxious to be alone. He didn't notice. Justine let him finish then prepared to ditch him for the evening.

"I came to see you," Grant protested. "Nothing will be happening on a Monday night."

"I'll be back soon enough, silly." She stepped to the bathroom for a final mirror check before takeoff.

"Okay."

"Just like that?" She grabbed her BlackBerry from the vanity—might need a cab.

"You don't call anyone but me 'silly.'"

"Oh?"

"I figure it's a sign of affection," he said. "That's good enough for now."

Into Brussels's molten copper twilight, lines of gray buildings retouched in sepia. The working girls, so pretty here; a pipe organ breathing diatonic scales; young lovers weaving fingers; blue neon signs over centuries'-old stonework. Seafood steam from street cafés.

She hit the clubs, surprised how they buzzed on a weeknight. Jeux d'Hiver, Fuse, Le Mirano Continental, with its irrationally revolving dance floor. On to Holler, still a hot spot a year after the death of Chadron Hite—whose inspiration for the place (so he claimed) came during a sexual encounter in Palermo. Maybe it was the one that killed him. It made a good story anyway.

By the time Justine reached Holler's stainless steel bar, she was tired of noise and smoke. She sat unfashionably close to the door, waving off advances from men and a few women. Thankfully the Brussels club scene was too self-absorbed to pay much attention to the celebrity behind the fashion. They just wanted the goods. Justine was left alone, nursing a glass of tonic water softened with a splash of gin.

Could I find her apartment? Justine traced a line through the condensation on her glass. Drops gathered under the streak and trailed down. Why bother? Go to bed and spend tomorrow getting ready for London.

Back into the night. Two random turns left her at the glass-covered mall, its arches of iron straight out of Dickens. It drew her in and left her on a narrow street. A sculpture of a cat on a bicycle waited on the far side, the feline's eyes wide in shock at finding herself there.

I'm not that far away.

Justine crossed the street and put her hand on the cat's garish pink top. *You're like me.* Sui generis. An oddity to note in passing. Look behind you and see the swelling bell curve of normal people.

Dear God, stop whining.

Justine heard static from her grandfather's radio, trapped inside for sixteen years. *Two outs in the bottom of . . . fair ball . . . digging for home . . .*

A final pat on the sculpture, then a call to Taxis Bleus de Bruxelles.

She entered her suite quietly, not wanting to disturb Grant. Black heels kicked off, hose removed in a high-stepping, heel-on-toes dance. She padded toward the bathroom. Across the tile floor, she stepped into something sticky and cold. Flashback to her family's Carolina beach house, back when they had cats. Stepping into a hocked-up fur ball during a nocturnal visit to the bathroom. She flipped on the lights over the vanity.

Grant lay sprawled across the floor by the sink. Most of what had been his head blown across the sauna tub. Justine looked down at the congealed blood on her bare feet.

She must have screamed, but afterward she no longer remembered.

4

The Monday shift ended at 7:00. Vienna fidgeted. Her coworkers were careless with portions and inventory was always off. She left before she could tell them to be more conscientious. Cecile had told her to stop doing that and she was the boss, having been hired three weeks before Vienna.

Diesel air trapped between buildings was still warm, but cross-street breezes held the coming winter. Justine's poster played to an enthralled crowd. *And upon her forehead was a name written, mystery, Babylon the great, the mother of harlots and abominations of the earth.* Vienna wanted to scratch it down, but couldn't afford to replace it.

She wandered through Lower Town, carried along the tourist stream, hoping the day's melancholy would ebb away because that was another thing her doctors warned her about. She found herself at the city's mascot, a small bronze of a boy peeing. The Manneken Pis stood peacock proud in the failing twilight, backdrop to countless photographs. Vienna wondered how many people knew it was a fake. The real one had been stolen by the French in the nineteenth century. Even that had been a copy of a fourteenth-century work.

Americans loved it, which Vienna figured went a long way toward explaining Justine Am. And there was the depression again.

She left the crowds on Rue de Bouchers, turning down Impasse de la Fidélité. Here was the female version of the Manneken. Jeanneken Pis was carved from a bluish-gray limestone that made her look sick. She squatted in a featureless cubby, locked behind iron bars. An angry scrawl of secessionist graffiti stained the wall to her left. Jenny's fountain was not working, for which Vienna was grateful. There was shame enough in her prison. Shame enough in being sick.

Vienna sighed. Her mind seethed in the alley's silence, thoughts jumping like sparks across frayed wires. Limestone. Calcium carbonate. Calcite, from the Greek word for pebble. Counting pebbles was called calculus. The first true calculus demonstrated the volume of a frustum. The frustum in the Great Seal of the United States of America was of Masonic origin. The earliest Masonic writing extant was the Regius Manuscript, dating from the thirteenth . . .

The world flowed beneath Vienna's skittering thoughts. Evening slipped into night. She didn't hear the rush of feet behind her. Wasn't aware she was no longer alone until two men grabbed her. She struggled until she caught a glimpse of blue police uniforms. She was hustled into a white and blue car. One of the policemen said something about what rights she had. The siren wailed to life.

Some mistake must have been made. Vienna worked a fingernail between her teeth. Unless . . . Maybe she had unknowingly witnessed an illicit activity, and the police were whisking her to safety. That happened in books all the time. Given the quality of her recent company, it wasn't even far-fetched. Maybe she would even be a hero and there would be posters of her. They would be better than Justine's posters. Vienna considered possible designs.

The car turned onto a ramp and descended to a subterranean garage.

All things come from the earth, and to the earth they return.

On foot through long hallways to a cube tucked within a glass tower. White walls and four pairs of fluorescents embedded in a tiled ceiling. Vienna sat in front of a desk, opposite a large man with blond hair. She thought he was handsome, but it was wrong to tell policemen things like that. He asked if she wanted to make a phone call, but she couldn't think of anyone to talk to. Then he asked questions in perfect English and made careful notes of her answers.

"Tell me everything you did today, from when you woke until you were picked up by the police."

Vienna knew from her reading that it was important to get every detail right. Except for visiting Justine's room. There was no reason to embarrass herself with that. "I made breakfast at 6:12. I had two scrambled eggs with chives and eight pieces of cantaloupe from the farmer's market on Place Sainte-Catherine. I wanted to get juice but it was expensive and—"

The policeman rubbed his left temple.

"Do you have a headache?" Vienna asked. "I have aspirin in my purse. Though I don't know where it is now. I would like it back."

"It will be returned after this incident is cleared up."

"It's from willow trees."

"What?"

"Aspirin. First synthesized in 1853 by—"

"Just tell me what you were doing every half hour."

"Starting every hour? Or some other time?"

"On the hour will be fine."

"I couldn't always see a clock, so I'll have to guess for some of it."

"That's fine."

So she told him what she had been doing every half hour. He didn't tell her what was going on, and she couldn't break his endless questions to ask. But this didn't fit her theory of being whisked away to safety. After an hour, the policeman leaned back. "You will be held until we verify your statement. If it is determined you constitute a flight risk you may be detained for up to seventy-two hours without specific charges. You should make your phone call now."

"Who should I call?"

"Surely you have a guardian?"

"No." *Unless maybe my old foster father in London.* There had been some paperwork about that on her sixteenth birthday. Now didn't seem the time to bring it up.

"A close friend?"

"I moved from London four months ago."

"Then someone in London?"

"No."

"That leaves the British consulate. I'll let you know their instructions as soon as possible." He left. Minutes merged into hours. An overweight woman knocked every fifteen minutes to see if Vienna was hungry or if she needed to use the toilet or a bed to lie down. Vienna shook her head, too scared to talk.

Three hours. Vienna slouched in the hard chair and stared at the tiled ceiling. Twelve tiles by fourteen. She saw that a twelve-by-twelve set would hold a progression of differently sized squares up to twelve squared: $1+4+9+16$ . . . It was an old sequence, safe in its familiarity. Then she realized the tiles were textured in six different patterns. Assuming the placement was random, it was possible to further sort the tiles by . . .

The ceiling unglued itself from the building, flowing to fit the numbers swimming in Vienna's head. The sensation made her want to throw up.

Stop it!

She screwed her eyes shut. Footsteps on the tiled floor outside the door. A sound from years ago. Vienna saw herself in the long, stone hallways of the Cart House. The telegraph click of her shoes as she ran past picture windows. Panes brushed with the rising sun; colored with kitchen gardens and calico cats and butterflies. Out into the Austrian woods with her arms curled around a heavy book. She never went far. She was too scared of ghosts by the lake and Uncle Anson always seemed to know where she was anyway. But she had her book; "CRC" written in gold across the cover. Pages of small print and charts and tables. Inside the book was the one hiding place no one could ever find.

Alone in the police station, she disappeared into it again, picking a page at random.

The preparation of bench solutions of sodium hydroxide as a reagent for analytical applications is a necessary skill for . . . The meaningless words closed around her in a numbing fog.

Four hours and twenty-three minutes after she was taken to the room, the door was roughly opened. A man in a black suit and dark gray tie leaned in. He was older, with a taut face and a razor-straight scar in front of his left ear. His steel-colored hair was cut military short, and his eyes were dark as spilled ink. And it was sort of witchy because it was Uncle Anson, just when she had been thinking of him.

He wasn't her real uncle, of course, but Grayfield wanted Vienna to call him that. Uncle Anson was the first one who took her to the Cart House. Showed her a path through the forest to a lake where pagan girls drowned themselves for their goddess. Vienna wasn't sure that really happened, but if it had, the forest had to be filled with ghosts. Even if she really didn't believe in ghosts.

" 'The graves stood tenantless,' " she whispered, " 'and the sheeted dead did squeak and gibber in the Roman streets.' " She'd always liked that about Shakespeare—the way he wasn't afraid to use childish words. " 'Squeak and gibber,' " she repeated.

She thought Uncle Anson and her foster father were old friends. They usually spoke in low voices she couldn't hear, and when they spoke louder it was always about how they hoped Tottenham Hotspur would finally march into Stamford Bridge and beat Chelsea straight into the pitch.

Vienna didn't even know Uncle Anson's full name. She never asked because he'd always sort of intimidated her even though he had never been anything but nice. And, looking at him now, it wasn't as if he were a muscle-bound Hercules. He was more like . . . "Jason of the Argonauts," she said aloud. Always in command. She saw rocks shifting to crush the Argo and there was Lord Byron: *Those waves, we follow on till the dark Euxine roll'd upon the blue Symplegades.* Euxine was the Black Sea, and . . .

"Vienna." Uncle Anson's voice was soft, but she was right. He was in command. *How does he always know where I am?*

She secretly called him Mr. Scar, although that wasn't very nice. His fingers were blue-white on the doorknob.

"Come with me."

She nodded and walked toward him.

"Hold," he said when she reached him. He pulled out a thin black phone, opened its screen like an army knife and showed her a phone number with a three-one international code. That meant the Netherlands. There were seven other threes in the number, for a total of eight threes. Three raised to the eighth power was—

"Have you seen this number?" Mr. Scar asked.

"No."

"Follow me." He turned and marched down a long, featureless corridor. Through a narrow window, Vienna saw a street below, dead in the night. Mr. Scar opened a door seemingly at random and held it for Vienna.

The room was dominated by a mahogany table. Five men and one woman sat on one side, dressed in dark colors. Two men in police uniforms sat opposite them. The policemen looked everywhere but across the table. They had rows of polished commendations over their hearts. Puffy circles around their eyes.

Vienna was surprised to see the woman was Justine Am. Her eyes were red and her hair, brunette this time, was in disarray. And still she was the most beautiful person Vienna had ever seen. *Why couldn't I have been more like her?* The men to her right sat in stony silence.

Mr. Scar held a chair opposite Justine and nodded toward Vienna. She sidestepped in front of the chair, studying the table's dense grain so she wouldn't have to look at Justine. *What's happening?* What was she supposed to do? Soft pressure behind her knees as Scar pushed the chair to her. "Take your seat," he whispered. "Everything will be fine." She dropped to the chair; she felt the brief weight of Scar's hand on her shoulder. He moved to the seat beside her.

The tall man next to Justine leaned over the table. "Rest assured I will be filing protests with both the Belgium and British consulates, as well as alerting the American authorities."

Mr. Scar canted forward until his face was inches away from the speaker. "You lot will explain, in plain English, what this person"—he glared at Justine for a fraction of a second—"has accused my client of. You will address my client respectfully as Miss Vienna."

The man swallowed and eased back into his chair. Mr. Scar backed away and sat next to Vienna.

The man cleared his throat. "Miss Vienna, my name is James Hargrave. I'm Justine Am's agent and lawyer." Vienna thought James Hargrave looked like a drawing of a cowboy. His face had those hard angles that cowboys were supposed to have, and he squinted, as if he had been looking at the sun all day. His eyes and his hair were the same shade of dark brown. He was very handsome, but then every man in Justine Am's world would be.

"Buckaroo," she said under her breath. "From the Spanish *vaquero,* from the Latin *vacca,* meaning cow."

"Excuse me?" Mr. Hargrave said.

Vienna shook her head once.

Hargrave cleared his throat. "I have little experience in international criminal law, but I have several associates to guide me." He gestured to the men next to him. "In order to proceed, I need to know what the police have told you."

"Nothing."

"Allow me to fill you in, as illegal as that doubtlessly is." Hargrave glared at the policemen. "Earlier this evening, sometime between the hours of seven and eight, Grant Eriksson was murdered in Justine Am's hotel suite."

Vienna looked wide-eyed at Justine. "I . . . am sorry." Was that the right thing to say about a murder?

Hargrave cleared his throat. "Yes. A tragedy."

"Why are you telling me this?"

"Because, Miss Vienna, it's natural to look for evidence—"

Mr. Scar interrupted. "They think you had something to do with it."

Vienna blinked. "How was he killed?"

Hargrave frowned at Mr. Scar. The older man waved away any concerns. "Tell her. Her alibi is unimpeachable."

"I'm not certain," said one of the policemen. He coughed. "In her statement, Miss Vienna neglected to mention that she had seen Justine Am the morning of the murder. A remarkable omission given the circumstances."

"I didn't think it was important," Vienna whispered.

"And we can be pretty damn certain Grant Eriksson was alive when she left, as your client stated he made love to her later that day." Mr. Scar leaned forward again. "Answer Miss Vienna's question."

Hargrave turned back to Vienna. "The gun used was a smaller civilian model; a Kimber or the like. I'm told these guns are often used by women. The ammunition was rimless .38 Super."

Vienna shifted, but the chair was uncomfortable no matter how she sat. "I don't own one of those. I don't know guns very well. You can look."

Mr. Scar folded his hands on the table. "The police have already been through your apartment, Vienna. A search was undertaken before I was aware of what was happening." He glanced at the stack of papers laid out before him. "They were present from nine to ten o'clock. The main cause for suspicion seems to be your laptop's browser history, which recorded several hours spent researching Justine Am."

Vienna looked at Justine. "Do you think I did it?"

James Hargrave quickly spoke. "Don't answer." He held his hands up, palms open. "Miss Vienna, despite Lord Davy's glowering demeanor, I will not apologize for your apartment being searched or for you being brought in for questioning. Given the circumstances, Lord Davy would have done the same."

Lord Davy? Uncle Anson was a member of the peerage? How

could that be? Did he have a periwig? How were such things assigned? Was there a ceremony—

"Miss Vienna?" Hargrave sounded impatient.

"You had to suspect me before you saw my computer," Vienna said.

"We did, for a number of reasons."

"I would like to hear them, if I may."

Hargrave exhaled. "First, a smaller gun was used. Second, you claimed to be a student of World War Two. Yet when my client asked what you were researching, you avoided the question with a joke. This led me to suspect you were lying. A small but clear strike against you."

Mr. Scar—Lord Davy—broke in. "Telling jokes is not a crime on this side of the Atlantic."

"Unlike this star chamber," Hargrave replied, "which most certainly is."

Lord Davy leaned back and he wasn't Jason of the Argonauts anymore. He was King Lear, full of anger. *I must have done something stupid.* Uncle Anson wore that smile people sometimes had when they weren't happy. "Name the first figure from World War Two that comes to mind."

"Julius Streicher," Justine said.

"I'm not familiar with the name," Davy said.

"I learned it in school," Justine answered. "Along with how to spot a wanker by the number of scars on his face."

Davy paled. A short, almost silent bark of air broke the silence. Vienna reflexively put her hand to her mouth. Too late. Everyone was looking at her. She rushed out a question. "Can you spell his name?"

"S-t-r-e-i-c-h-e-r." Justine's voice remained perfectly calm.

Vienna traced the letters on the desk with her finger. And there it was, next to a picture of a bald man with one of those scary Hitler mustaches. Vienna read the entry. "Julius Streicher was born on February 12, 1885, in the town of Fleinhausen, Bavaria. He was the youngest of nine children. As Streicher was to achieve notoriety as publisher of the virulently anti-Semitic newspaper *Der* . . . Vienna blushed. "I don't know how to pronounce the 'u' with the two little dots above it."

Justine tilted her head. "*Der Stürmer,*" she said. "It means *The Stormer.*"

Vienna nodded. ". . . the virulently anti-Semitic newspaper *Der Stürmer,* the impact of his early propaganda is often . . ." She stopped midsentence. "The rest is very dull." Her lips silently mouthed words. "I read other things about him." She was quiet again, not noticing Justine's puzzled look.

"From the unofficial records of the Nuremburg War Trials." Vienna took a deep breath. "Eyewitnesses reported that Streicher's neck was not broken when he was hanged. He gasped at the end of the rope until one of the executioners silenced him. To speed the process, the executioner added his weight to Streicher's. Several minutes passed before the man ceased struggling." Vienna slumped in her chair. "There's more, but it's not a happy story. I think he was a bad man."

"He was," Justine said.

"At any rate," Davy said, "there can be no question of Vienna's expertise."

Hargrave's answer seemed too loud. "An extraordinary demonstration Lord Davy, but you must admit—"

"I don't have to admit a damn thing—"

Suddenly the two men were yelling at each other. Vienna huddled deep inside herself, closing her eyes. *What have I done wrong?* Hot tears on her cheeks. Something brushed against her leg. She flinched and looked up. Justine was staring at her.

"You okay?" Justine mouthed the words silently.

Vienna didn't know how to react—no one else in the room was paying them the slightest attention. *Didn't she accuse me of murder?* Was it permissible to talk to her? Vienna looked down but knew Justine was still watching. "Symplegades." It came out as a whisper.

"Vienna?"

"I'm scared."

When Justine spoke her voice was not loud, but it somehow covered the strained conversation of Davy and Hargrave. It was the most remarkable trick Vienna had ever heard, to speak so quietly yet with so much weight. "Both of you shut up." She didn't sound angry or even interested in what they were saying. The men went quiet as if they'd been slapped.

Without turning from Vienna, Justine softened her tone. "Vienna, how did you know where I was staying?"

"When in Brussels, the scrumptious Justine Am prefers the classical comfort of the Cosmopolitan. . . ." She let the words trail off. "From an English fan site in Brazil." As if that meant anything. "They had a picture of you topless on a beach."

"How did you find my room number?"

"I told the man at the front desk that unless he gave me Justine Am's room number, I would tell management what he had been doing, and he didn't want that."

"What had he been doing?"

Vienna shrugged. "I don't know. I read a book where a private detective did this and it seemed like it might work."

Justine's eyes opened a fraction wider. "Perhaps the Brussels's police ought to look into this character."

Vienna glanced at the others, but they were intent on her and it was easier to look at Justine.

"Why did you track me down?" Justine asked.

"You lied about your name and you called me silly and it made me mad, like you didn't want me to know anything about you, like you wanted to get away as fast as you could. Like I was something to use and throw away." Vienna was horrified to hear her voice cracking, but she kept her head high. *Crying is well and good,* her foster father had once written in a note left on her pillow, *but it will buy you nothing here, and even less beyond these walls.* It took Vienna a long time to realize that he had written it so she would never forget.

Justine shook her head slowly. "I told you my real name. Justine Am is a pseudonym my first agent thought sounded exotic. You must have read that somewhere in your Internet search."

Vienna looked back through the images on her laptop. Knowing the shape of the words helped. There it was, on an English site from Tokyo. *Heather Ingles.* Complete with a biography. Justine's father, Robert Ingles, had a civil engineering degree from Stanford University. He'd played tennis until his feet got tangled in a cart at the market. Fall On Out-Stretched Hand. Vienna tried the acronym aloud. "Foosh." Justine's eyes opened wider. "Barton's fracture," Vienna added, as if to explain. Whatever that was, it required three operations. No more tennis. Justine's mother, Abigail Jefferson, also attended Stanford University, where she received a doctorate in twentieth-century British literature. Which was the stupidest thing Vienna had ever heard. Two older brothers, Jeff and Scott.

Vienna looked up and saw Justine—Heather—staring at her. Vienna quickly finished reading. "Your full name is Heather Abigail Ingles and your birthday is April fourteenth." And there was Justine's blood type: B positive.

"Correct on all counts," Justine said.

"Why do Japanese always go on about blood type?"

"What?"

Stupid! "I'm sorry." Her voice broke at last and she could hear herself inhaling loudly through the tears. "I didn't do anything wrong. I didn't kill anyone."

Justine held her hands across the table. "Hush. I know it wasn't you, and I'm glad you found me."

"Why?" Vienna kept her hands safely at her sides.

"When you came to the hotel room, you said a phrase. It sounded Latin. And then you said Grant—my boyfriend—was a poser."

Vienna nodded.

"What did you say?"

"Sometimes it doesn't work when I only say or hear things."

Justine frowned, pulling her hands back. "Then perhaps you read something that tipped you off?"

"He really was a liar?"

"Before he got his brains spilled at the base of my bathroom sink, Grant Eriksson was a bad boy. He'd never been to the Midwestern United States. He was born in Amsterdam, though he spent most of his life in San Francisco. He is—was—wanted in Munich in connection with the murder of an art dealer. His real name was David Andries."

Follow the shape of the word. After a moment, Vienna shook her head. "I don't know that name. I don't read much news. I don't like how it feels."

"But you knew he was pretending to be someone he wasn't?"

"Sometimes when I don't like people, I do mean things."

"What mean thing did you do?"

"When he said he was from Nebraska, I remembered the trees." Vienna paused long enough to roughly brush tears from her cheeks. She found the encyclopedia page she had seen earlier. "Dutch elm disease reached the United States in 1928, through a shipment of wood from the Netherlands to a furniture manufacturer in Ohio. From there it spread throughout the Midwest and South, annihilating entire populations of elm trees. The problem was exacerbated by a new strain of fungus, Ophiostoma novo-ulmi, which was recorded for the first time in North America in the 1940s."

"That was the phrase," Justine said. "Ophiostoma novo-ulma. I don't understand the connection to David Andries."

James Hargrave answered. "Dutch elm disease. When I was a child in Missouri I remember the elm trees dying. The leaves turning from orange to brown to gray. It was a disaster."

Justine leaned back in her chair, rubbing fingers over her eyes. "Grant said he loved the elm trees back in Nebraska, but they're all dead."

Vienna read further. "Not all, I think, but many. Growing up there he must have heard about it."

"He would have," Hargrave said. "The disease has been woven into the mythos of Midwestern culture."

Justine hissed between closed teeth. "Congratulations. You exposed him as a fraud in twenty seconds while I remained clueless the entire five weeks he was in my bed."

"Don't feel bad," Lord Davy said. "Vienna was faster than the Belgium police as well." The two men next to him shifted in their chairs but said nothing. "I believe that answers your questions, Mr. Hargrave."

"There is the matter of your earlier threats concerning Justine Am's career."

Davy stood. "I doubt my client will pursue this and I can't proceed against her wishes. If the police have no objections I hope we might be excused."

One of the policemen nodded, speaking in heavily accented English. "We have your passports. Affected parties will remain in Brussels. Given Lord Davy's word, I see no reason to issue bond for Miss Vienna."

"Then we will take our leave. Vienna, I can drop you off at your flat."

"No!"

"Vienna, we're finished here."

"I don't want to go."

"This is not the time—"

Justine interrupted, "She's exhausted and she's scared and she doesn't want to be alone. Can you blame her?"

"Then I must ask my colleagues in the Brussels police force to release her passport. I take full responsibility as to her whereabouts in London."

Vienna looked frantically at Justine. The model used her voice trick. "It's four in the morning. You can't put her on a flight or take her through the Chunnel. She needs a bed and security."

"You presume to speak for her?" Uncle Anson was doing that leaning thing again, only this time toward Justine. Of course she would agree to whatever he wanted.

"Someone sure as hell has to," Justine said. She stood and turned to Hargrave. "Where are we staying?"

"Radisson SAS—the closest place that had the room we needed."

Justine leaned right back at Lord Davy even as she spoke to Hargrave. "Get a room for Vienna."

Hargrave closed his eyes and took a quick breath. He let it go in carefully enunciated words. "Justine, you cannot take this woman with you. The press is poised to eat you alive. They see you with her and they will carve you up."

"I agree with Mr. Hargrave," Lord Davy said.

"Breaks my heart." Justine motioned to Vienna. "We have a car outside. Move."

Vienna scampered around the table to Justine's side. It seemed the safest thing to do.

5

James attempted several conversations from the front passenger seat. Justine refused to take part. She didn't need to be told her career was shot to hell and her life was in hot pursuit. But she couldn't force any reaction; sealed in a cocoon of murdered lovers and moving statues.

Vienna sat next to her, wearing the god-awful blue pinafore. Staring at shifting constellations of city lights. She spoke to herself in a rushed whisper. "Eleven, twenty-four, sixty-five hundred and sixty-one."

"What?" Justine asked.

"Three raised to the eighth power. It's the same as eighty-one squared. Bode's Galaxy."

"Vienna?"

The girl spoke louder. "Sixty-five hundred and sixty-one. Two sixes and a five and a one. Five plus one gives six, making three sixes altogether. 'Let him that hath understanding count the number of the beast: for it is the number of a man; and his number is six hundred threescore and six.'" The girl's eyes seemed to refocus. "Revelations." She flashed a pitiful smile, as though fully aware of her incoherent rambling but unable to find the brake. "It refers to Domitian, Emperor of Rome from 69 to 96 AD." Her sad smile faded away. "He banned mimes. He was afraid they would make fun of him." She rocked in her seat, her gaze fading from reach. "Mime is Greek but no one knows what the word originally meant. The Greeks . . ." Eyes scanning left to right. "Houses of dried reed. The flames of Sardis. Bodies rotting in the sun. They're all dead. Remember the Athenians. Remember the Athenians. Remember the Athenians."

Justine felt the hair on her forearms go prickly tight. She leaned toward her own window, ignoring the cold seeping in. *I should've let the scarred bastard take her.*

Three card keys were waiting at the Radisson's front desk. James led them past a closed restaurant at the base of an atrium. A glass elevator, pasted to the side of the cavernous space, slid up the floors. Empty tables below shrank to abstract patterns. James went to his room without a word.

"Your room is next to mine, Vienna." Justine pointed to the door.

Vienna didn't move. Her eyes were bright. "I'm not a child. I can take care of myself."

"I know."

"I don't want to be alone."

It sounded like a sexual gambit to Justine. Who knew what it sounded like to Vienna. Justine felt sticky sand in her eyes. Dead tears and no sleep and no patience. She put her hand over the lizard tattoo. "Come on then."

"I don't have bed clothes."

"I have a spare nightshirt—at least I think it was forwarded."

"I don't have a toothbrush."

"Ring the desk." It felt like a mistake the second she said it.

Vienna changed in the bathroom, emerging under a sleeveless cobalt tee that draped across her thin shoulders, down her modest chest to her knees.

Justine was surprised how handsome she was. Not dazzling, but well-proportioned for her lanky frame. Bookish in a way that many men found attractive. Large, clear eyes, freed from the hell glasses. Irises flecked brown-gold under the hotel's warm lights. Her tortured hair needed a machete and conditioner, but it had strong tints of red that could be accented. A little color for the cheeks—sunlight would do wonders there. Delicate wrists. A manicure . . .

Justine turned away. *I'm too tired to be codependent.* "I'm going to rinse off," she said. "Make yourself comfortable."

Ten minutes in the shower amounted to a technical knockout. *Weave and bob around the exhaustion all you want, but you won't be standing much longer.* Would Vienna expect sex? Maybe she's asleep? What if she isn't? *Doesn't matter.* Justine turned the water off.

Vienna was curled up on the left edge of the bed. Tiny under the king-sized spread.

Justine turned on the reading lamp before cutting the overhead lights. She knew she would never again cross any floor in the dark. Feet under the covers, she switched off the light.

"Did you really think I'd done it?" Vienna's voice was a scraping monotone.

Justine was too tired to construct acceptable lies. "I didn't know what to think. It was so wrong. So impossible. Like he'd been standing at the sink to shave or wash his face. And then someone just came in and shot him."

"But you told the police it might have been me."

"Yes."

Vienna was silent.

"I shouldn't have." Justine put a hand on Vienna's back. She felt the ragged breathing of tears. *She cries too much.* Was it Asperger's? Some of it fit—crying was often associated with autism—but Vienna failed to display several core symptoms. *The human condition is defined by having no definitions.* Another line from her med school days. "It's over. You need to sleep."

"Okay." The shaking slowly stilled.

Justine was left with the one thought she'd pushed away since Grant's murder. *You don't feel his absence.* She told herself it was because he turned out to be a liar and likely a killer as well. But that was beside the point. She was sorry he was dead, even if he was a bad man. But that was a long way from missing him.

Does that make me bad, too?

There was no answer, but finally facing the question somehow brought relief. Emotional knots loosened. Justine slipped into dreamless sleep.

She was alone when she awoke. The blue T-shirt folded at the foot of the bed.

"Other than that, how was the play, Mrs. Lincoln?" Her mother's wryest summation of bad news.

Justine showered and pulled an olive shirt and khaki capris from the closet. Urban camouflage for models. She was almost to the door when James knocked. "Going somewhere?"

"Yes."

"I wouldn't recommend it."

"Why not?"

"Your dead lover isn't even cold, and there's a woman in your room calling the front desk for a toothbrush. For added fun, the ex turns out to have a five-star police record. My favorite headline so far is, 'Lezzies Leave Loser.' Neanderthal elements of the British press have always been addicted to alliteration."

Justine glared at him. "Since when have you given a rat's ass about gossip columns?"

"Since your career started swirling down the drain."

"I need to go."

"Why?"

"I have to find her."

"Would you care to tell me and my splitting headache why?"

Impossible to explain. California sunshine washing over the lawns of Stanford; fear locked away behind a false smile. The children inside Felton Gables, imprisoned by something far more crushing than concrete walls. Justine's failure turning malignant, growing evermore bitter. "I don't have to justify myself to you."

"You don't know where she lives."

"You do."

James shook his head. "The four dozen reporters outside have clouded my memory."

"Fine. Go tell them I'll have a press conference at five."

"Wrong answer. You need to disappear for several weeks."

"Five o'clock. If they're waiting here they can't be following me. Square it with management."

"You'll never find her. You don't even know her last name."

"Don't ever sell me short." Justine pressed toward the door. Hargrave surrendered with a show of open hands.

Justine had long ago learned to access kitchen exits: *lady in distress, please help.* She stepped into an alley a block away from the front door, breathing through her mouth as she marched past reeking Dumpsters.

Vienna's pinafore was the answer. It wasn't a fashion meltdown, it was a uniform. Since Europeans preferred male waiters, Vienna would be working at a pastry counter or coffee shop. Someplace close, in the tourist haunts of Lower Town. Justine couldn't see Vienna taking the bus, let alone driving. Start in the Grand Place.

Success in under thirty minutes. Vienna inside a gelato store, a sign on the door flipped to FERMÉ. There was a man pressed against the stainless counter, a Nikon DSLR in his right hand; lanyard looped to his knees. An oily black tattoo lay coiled on the back of his forearm, showing a series of swept curves tapering to points.

Vienna cowered against the wall. It seemed so familiar.

I hear the only reason she got accepted into med school is she does her professors. No way her test scores are legit. What a skank. I've got a buck-fifty, ask her if she swallows.

The past twisted inside Justine in a jagged feedback of rage. Only now it was Vienna, defenseless against a storm she couldn't see coming.

Justine was inside before the man had a chance to turn from Vienna. She grabbed the dangling lanyard, jerking the camera from the man's grasp. He turned to her, recognition widening his eyes.

"Justine Am." He pushed his left hand through over-long brown hair, revealing black, triangular ear studs. Justine saw his thoughts—the prize he thought he had. Justine Am goes crazy, read all about it.

Justine opened the camera's side panel and ejected the memory chip. "Come out of there, Vienna, if this cocksack found you, others will follow."

Vienna sidestepped around the counter and with a quick skip stood beside Justine. Her voice was louder than Justine remembered. "He took my picture and asked about you and about our relationship and if you tied me up when we boffed or if I tied you up and I don't know what 'boffed' is supposed to mean."

"Nice." Justine smiled her hate. She dropped the Nikon's memory chip into her capris' oversized pocket.

The photographer's grin didn't slip. "You're sinking fast." His teeth were white and straight, but somehow too small for his mouth.

"You're one to be talking."

He shook his head. "Do you have the star?"

"Have what?"

"Once panic sets in, the dying won't stop. Give me the camera and we can talk."

"We don't have anything to talk about."

"Famous last words."

Sometimes when I don't like people I do mean things. Justine turned to Vienna. "He grabbed your shoulder, isn't that right? He kept reaching for your ass. Isn't that what you're going to tell the police?"

Vienna blinked while Justine prayed the girl was smart enough to go along. "Okay," she whispered.

"I saw it all," Justine said.

"I don't scare so easily," the photographer said. "My record is clean." His voice was too cavalier. A small push . . .

"Too bad we have your picture of her alone. Get a lawyer, asshat, because I've seen hers, and he has a real attitude problem."

The man's smile drained into thin, pale lips. He took a single step and jumped toward Justine. She was a kid again, back on the tennis court at home. Scott picking on her. She hadn't meant to hurt him so badly.

Justine stepped into the photographer. Oldest defense in the world. Her left knee connected with his groin. She felt air explode from his chest as he collapsed. She dropped the camera next to him, heard the lens crack.

"Vienna." She gestured to the door, even as the man began losing his breakfast. "We need a quiet place to talk, somewhere close."

Vienna nodded. "Vik's is on the second floor of—"

"Go."

Through medieval streets for three harried minutes before Vienna entered an alley. Up a creaking set of stairs to a coffee shop. It wasn't much beyond blue walls surrounding a few aluminum tables. The coffee cups were squat cylinders of uniform white. The archaic register sported a no smoking sign. The perfect hidey-hole for Vienna, who was likely asthmatic on top of everything else.

Justine took a corner seat away from the railed windows.

"I have to get back," Vienna said. "He might take something."

"I doubt he's off the floor yet."

"But—"

"Do you have the owner's phone number?"

"Yes."

"Does he speak English?"

"Yes."

"Give it to me."

Vienna repeated a series of digits in her flat voice. Justine punched them in her BlackBerry and waited for an answer. The conversation took five minutes.

"It's taken care of," she told Vienna.

"There was more to it than that—you spoke longer."

"He's seen the news. He knows it will get worse. You've been fired."

"I don't understand."

"It's my fault. When you called the front desk for a toothbrush last night, someone snitched. Word got around that a woman was sleeping in Justine Am's room. What a scoop to find her first. Others will follow."

"Others? Paparazzi?"

"Of course."

Vienna looked at the table. "What am I supposed to do?"

"Write your memoirs and get rich. Just make shit up. No one will care as long as it's juicy."

"Please don't joke. I don't want to go back to London."

"You won't have to. News is only worthy until the next scandal. Forget fifteen minutes, you'll be lucky with fifteen words on Twitter."

"I don't have much money."

"I'll pay the equivalent of your salary until you get back on your feet."

Vienna's face was as blank as her apartment's impossible floor. When she spoke, Justine strained to hear. "I wanted to, yeah? I didn't know what was expected and I didn't know how to ask and it didn't seem right the first time but maybe I could do better." She took a quick breath. "And now your boyfriend is dead and I know you're all big time and I'm so thick no matter what I do."

It took Justine a second to realize what Vienna was talking about. *What do I say?*

"I couldn't figure why you went to my apartment in the first place," Vienna continued. "Then I remembered who you were with at the club. A girl and three boys. I work with them. They dared you, didn't they?"

"I'm sorry, Vienna. It was cruel."

"They picked me because I'm ugly."

"Wrong."

"Don't be stupid."

Justine shook her head. "It was because I'm American—which means prude—and your friends thought that made the bet more clever. I was bored enough to go along with it." She realized how terrible it sounded, but Vienna gave no reaction.

"They were paid to do it," Vienna said.

"Likely by the same species of sleaze monkey that tracked you down."

"But wouldn't they have set you up with someone pretty?"

Justine frowned. "You read too much—especially too much written by lonely old men."

"What does that mean?"

"You think physical looks mean much in a crowd where half the tits and asses were ordered out of a catalogue?" She leaned forward and whispered, "Ninety percent of the men on that dance floor would have done you in a heartbeat, if only you looked ready. Attitude is everything to these people. You looked like a deer in headlights, so they thought it would be hilarious to send a Ferrari your way."

"I don't know anything about dancing. I can't help it."

"Yes, you can. You might need a little coaching at first, but . . ." Her voice trailed off. *You tried this back at Stanford, remember? You know it's pointless. Give it up.*

"Yes?"

Justine looked inward and felt the rage staring back. "When I was in third grade, my brothers fit a cardboard racecar body over a wagon. I wanted to be the first to try it down a steep hill near our house. I ended up with a broken arm. My father joked that while other people had angels and devils pitching advice from their shoulders, I had a dumb-ass."

"What does that mean?"

Justine tried again. "You know those bad ideas you got back in school, when the world was going to hell and you wanted to tell everyone to piss off?"

"I was taught at home."

"Then it's time you learned. I'm sick of worrying about things I can't control. I'm sick of feeling guilty for not feeling guilty about Grant. I'm doubly sick of being Justine Am without having any fun at it." Justine flashed a tight grin. "Besides, Miss Unemployed, neither of us have anywhere to go today and I'll be damned if I am going to sit in a hotel room and sulk."

"I have no idea what you're on about."

"Something shoulder-length. No ponytails; with your physique they would attract the wrong attention."

"My physique?"

"You would look fifteen in tails." Justine held up her hand to cut off a reply she knew would be self-derogatory. "We'll go sophisticated. Something sleek, assuming we can add body to your hair."

"You want me to get my hair cut?"

Justine laughed. "Not the phrase I would have used, but yes. And new glasses, something retro librarian. Smart is sexy. That's your first lesson. For attire, A-line full length, and flats or modest pumps. If we have time for something formal, maybe a knock-off Chanel. Shorter kitten heels to match."

"Is this an American thing?"

"Didn't you ever play dress-up with dolls?"

"I never played with dolls."

"Why not?"

"They told me bad things."

Miles of bad road there. "Well, you're in luck, because this year's black is black, and that's perfect for our studious girl."

Vienna shook her head. "I was just fired, yeah? I don't have any money."

"I do."

Vienna's eyes narrowed. "How much?"

"Your second lesson is to never ask about money. Shall we get your hair beat into shape?"

"They'll find us—the photographers."

"Paparazzi are like lions. They look threatening in a pack, but they spend most of their lives loafing in the shade."

Vienna remained quiet, waiting for explanation.

"Most will stay at the hotel," Justine said. "Why go on a wild goose chase when they can hole up at the nearest bar and get a picture when I return?"

"But one found me," Vienna protested.

"All the more reason not to go back," Justine said.

"We should hide," Vienna said.

"Wrong. No sulking in hotel rooms, remember? We avoid

busier tourist areas and only go into shops that won't rat us out and we'll be fine."

Vienna swallowed and brought her left hand to her mouth.

Justine closed her eyes. *I can't do this.* "No more chewing your nails. We'll pick up some clear polish. We don't want to draw attention to your fingers until they grow out." She looked at Vienna. An uncertain smile in answer as Vienna lowered her hand. And out of nowhere an utterly illogical thought: *maybe Vienna can.*

6

Outside Vik's, Vienna looked to the Palais de Justice de Bruxelles, looming on Galgenberg Hill. History flowed across her thoughts in a rainbow slick.

In the twelfth century, Galgenberg Hill housed a lepers' colony. The stench of rotting flesh . . .

On January 8 of 1360, the monarchs of Europe met on Galgenberg Hill to hold council over the Treaty of Brétigny. Knowledge of this event remains banned from public histories by order . . .

The city's gallows were later moved to Galgenberg Hill. Andreas Vesalius (1514–1564) collected human remains from the gibbet . . .

Cool air and the smell of turning leaves. Vienna breathed it in. Time unreeling in the low autumn sun. Cars and delivery trucks shimmered away in long shadows, leaving behind weeping fountains and stone columns. *I know the past more than I know the present.* As if Brussels's long story was hers alone.

Justine broke the spell, giving Vienna an address on Rue Bodenbroek.

"I don't know where that is."

"There's an information kiosk." Justine crossed the street to a slab of Plexiglas laid over a garish map. "We can find it."

Vienna looked at the map; saw its shape the same way she saw the shapes of words. Oriented on the Palais de Justice, she overlaid the map on the city. She had never tried anything like that. For a terrifying second, it didn't fit. A thick roil of nausea. She closed her eyes and willed the images to merge. When she dared look, she saw traces of sans serif italics, naming the streets before her. She stepped into the real-world map. Her foot stuttered across an uneven cobble.

"You okay?" Justine asked.

Vienna knew from weary experience it was pointless to explain. "Yes."

"We can rest longer. You've had a stressful morning."

It was so far from what Vienna felt she could only shake her head.

"Can you find the address?" Justine asked.

The map showed several lesser-traveled routes. "Yes." Vienna let the image fill her mind. "This way," she said, heading away from the Grand Place.

They ended up in front of a red storefront, modest even by Brussels's standards. A neon sign hung on the window said CHAT ROUGE, with no indication of what business went on inside. Justine opened the door and waved Vienna in.

The woman inside had one of those faces that was all angles. Her hair was unnaturally black. She must have known Justine because they embraced. Justine introduced Vienna. "We need something more refined than the current hatchet job."

The woman started by washing Vienna's hair, which was stupid as Vienna had already washed it at the Radisson. She spoke in a heavy French accent as she worked, tallying a list of sins: stressed hair and dry roots and split ends and the dire need for conditioners and nutrients.

Have I failed at growing hair, too?

Vienna was escorted to a different chair while Justine and the woman began discussing *bobs* (which the lady wanted), as opposed to *swept bangs* and *box-cut layers with a sculpted finish,* which Justine finally insisted on. Talk moved to length and ends. The soft breathing of scissors behind her head. Vienna tried not to flinch.

"Vienna, what do you know about that small park we passed on the way here, the one with the statues?"

Vienna was at a loss until she called up the ghost map. A small green square bordered their path. "Place du Petit Sablon."

"Yes."

Vienna searched for *Sablon,* unusual words being easy to track. "For those seeking a break from the city's pace, there is no better spot than the Place du Petit Sablon. This peaceful garden is noted for the forty-eighty statues, representing medieval guilds, guarding its perimeter. A large sculpture within the park commemorates Count Edgemont and Count Hoorn, sent to their deaths by King Philip II of Spain on June 5, 1658. Photographers will have the best chance of good light in early evening hours." Vienna frowned. "That's all I have."

"What about Edgemont and Hoorn?"

Pages from a yellowed book shelved in the Cart House's library. "They were members of the Order of the Golden Fleece." Handwritten ancestry charts hung on the library's gray walls, crowded next to photographs and old drawings and certificates and medals. The clutter scared Vienna until she studied each item and made certain it all fit inside her head.

"What else?"

Vienna found an encyclopedia entry, but it sounded too long for an American's attention span. She moved on. "There is a history of their deaths."

"This will take a while, Vienna. Let's hear it."

With newfound perception, Vienna understood that Justine wasn't really interested in the two martyrs. Then why? *Does she want to show the woman I'm not normal?*

"Vienna, are you okay?"

"May I have some water?"

"Of course." Justine filled a paper cone from the shop's watercooler.

Vienna drank it, noting as she did that the woman cutting her hair stopped. She'd forgotten that she needed to be still. And there was the real reason Justine wanted to hear the story. *Do I not move when I read?* Vienna felt rising shame, but refused to show it. Let Justine play her little games.

"Lamoral, Count of Edgemont, and Philip de Montmorency, Count of Hoorn, were executed by order of King Philip II . . ."

Vienna unfolded the story from memory. Not long in, she looked in the mirror in front of her chair and saw the woman glancing at Justine. Justine's only response was to raise her index finger to her lips. Vienna closed her eyes.

Count Hoorn was commending his spirit to God when the woman told Vienna she needed to open her eyes. Vienna looked into the reflection of a stranger. Her hair was the same brownish-red, but it was so shiny. It hung low on her forehead, swept to the left. From her temples to the back of her head, it fell straight and full and sleek to her shoulders. Like the beautiful pictures she saw in Saint-Hubert. She slowly reached up to touch it. *Feelings of corporeal dislocation are strong indicators of incipient seizures.* So her doctors warned.

"Do you like it?" Justine asked.

"It's pretty, I think."

"Me too."

Vienna turned her head from side-to-side, watching her hair catch the light. *Angle of incidence equals angle of reflection . . .* "How much do I owe you? I have twenty euros and—"

"Already paid," Justine interrupted. "And don't get comfortable in that chair. We're just getting started."

They stepped to the sidewalk and Justine gave another address. Vienna found it on her map and turned left. Justine followed without question.

She doesn't know where we're going! I could have gone the other way.

Vienna had always assumed that real lies—significant ones— were something she could never aspire to. That was part of how she was. But now . . . She detoured three blocks before meandering back almost to where they had started. Justine didn't notice.

She's so stupid.

Uncertain how to use her newfound power, Vienna resumed the correct course. They ended up at a shop that sold nothing but glasses. "Mikli unisex," Justine said. "Keep it black on the arms, and darker red for the frames." She requested several more pairs of glasses, creating an embarrassing pile of rejects on the table in front of Vienna. "I like the first pair," Justine said. "What about you, Vienna?"

"Okay." The lenses were narrow ellipses that curved slightly around her eyes. The geometry could be approximated in Euclidean space by . . .

"*Vous avez bon goût,*" said the young man helping them. "We require three days for the prescription."

"No prescription needed."

The man bowed slightly. "Then you may take them with you. The total is three hundred and eighteen euros."

Vienna felt a warm flush spread across her face. "We can't—"

Justine cut her off with a slice of her hand. "You're new here?" she said to the man.

"Oui. This week."

"You must learn it is distasteful to speak of money in public." Justine handed the man an American Express card, black with metallic swirls along the edges. It was not nearly as colorful as most cards Vienna had seen, but the man stammered as he took it. "Of course, mademoiselle."

"Please add twenty percent for your service."

The man nodded again. "Merci."

Outside, Justine took Vienna by the arm. "Our studious doll needs a timepiece. She has places to go, cops to outsmart, wars to study. We want classic and quiet. Something less ostentatious from Rolex."

"But those are expensive." At least Vienna had heard they were. She had no idea what a Rolex looked like.

"Not for girls who dye their hair neon blue, they aren't."

Vienna looked away. "I saw the picture they took of you when your hair was like that."

Justine smiled. "You don't approve?"

"How can you be nude while people take your picture?"

"That shot was taken by Flora Kierse. She is very sweet, on the far side of sixty, and has exactly zero interest in seeing females naked. Unless my gaydar is broken, her assistant has even less. You have to learn what people are after."

"Okay."

"Flora Kierse is trying to understand the human condition. Good photographers have that angle: Demarchelier, Biyan, Holt. Flora's fascination comes through in her pictures. It's what makes her a master. 'The proper study of mankind is man' and all that."

Vienna saw the words. "Alexander Pope, 'An Essay on Man.'" She read several sentences. "He published the first part anonymously."

Justine laughed. "You know it's okay to take Pope's advice." She nodded toward a knot of people standing at a gallery window. "See the man in the black pants?"

"Yes?"

"He is—as you would say—a poser."

Vienna looked back to Justine. "How do you mean?"

"Black Versace pants, black tee, and a black belt. Very swank. Did you notice his shoes?"

"No."

"Light brown," Justine said. "You don't spend that kind of money on clothes and get it so wrong unless you're a hack."

That made no sense. "Is this important?"

"Such observations lead to the most intricate puzzles."

"Puzzles?"

Justine hesitated before continuing. "What was Grant doing in the hotel bathroom when he was murdered?"

Vienna sighed. Why was talking to Justine so futile? "His real name wasn't Grant Eriksson. It was David Andries."

"He will always be Grant to me. That's all I knew him as."

Vienna shrugged. "What difference does it make where he was?"

"Our suite at the Cosmopolitan had two bedrooms with attached bathrooms, plus a small kitchen and great room. James told me there was no sign of a struggle; the assumption being that Grant knew his killer. But why was he in my bathroom? People go to kitchens to talk, or maybe the great room."

"He was running away?"

"That's what the police think, but it doesn't work. Grant was a careful man. Why run to the worst possible room? There was no way out. There wasn't anything there he could use as a weapon."

"But the bathroom door could be locked."

"Against a man with a gun? It doesn't take much to break through a bathroom door. Any decently strong man could do it."

"Maybe he was shot by a woman."

Justine exhaled. "Not Grant. He would never have run from a woman. Such an ignominious retreat was not in his genes. He may have been shot trying to sweet-talk a woman, but he never would have run."

"Then he was looking for something?"

Justine shook her head. "There was nothing in the bathroom except what is in every bathroom."

"Then I don't know."

Justine shook her head. "Neither do I. It doesn't make sense."

Vienna shrugged. "Neither does dying your hair blue and being starkers."

"Starkers?"

"Nude."

"Ah! Gotta love British slang."

"But why do it?"

"Because it beats flipping burgers for a living."

Vienna looked down. "I don't understand you at all."

"Good. I make my money by keeping them guessing." She patted Vienna's arm. "Now we have to be careful. This next shop is right next to the Grand Place."

Since Justine was being so mean, Vienna took another detour. But it all went wrong because in the end it didn't matter if Justine was lost or stupid. The truth was that she was placing her trust in Vienna. No one had ever done that before and Vienna didn't like it because what if she took a detour and they were crossing a street they had no business being on and a speeding car hit Justine and killed her? Even if no one else discovered the truth, God would know.

And now it seemed there was no way it couldn't happen.

Vienna stopped. Her throat tightened below the saliva that flooded her mouth.

"Vienna? Are you okay?"

No words would come.

"Vienna? It's okay. I'm here. Do we need to go back to the hotel?"

"I took a wrong turn." Not really the whole truth, but maybe enough?

"Are you lost?"

Vienna shook her head.

"Then no harm done. It's a beautiful day for a walk." Her voice was different somehow. *She knows!*

"I promise I won't do it again."

This time Justine was silent longer. "Vienna, this medieval maze has me completely flipped around. You're faring better than I am."

"I took a wrong turn on purpose."

Justine smiled, lifted her hand to Vienna's cheek, and brushed away a tear that Vienna hadn't even noticed. "I don't blame you for taking the long way. I'm excellent company."

And that was completely wrong and insulting as well. No one would want to be stuck with this boorish American. Vienna swallowed. *Unless they were brain damaged.* Which explained why it suddenly seemed that Justine was right after all.

She trusted me.

Vienna looked from the corner of her eyes and saw that Justine was watching her, a faint smile and no sign of impatience. That was something new, too.

"We need to cross the street and turn left and in two blocks we will be on the right street. But we have to be careful because sometimes people drive too fast."

"Lead on MacDuff."

Which wasn't what Macbeth said at all, but Vienna decided she could keep that to herself.

Another shop and Vienna was lost in cases of gold and diamond watches. Justine settled on one with a silver band and a dark blue face that Justine said was steel. It had roman numerals and a modest crown where "XII" should have been. Vienna loved it and since it wasn't covered in diamonds it must have been cheaper.

There were several routes to the next address, which Justine called, "One of those cute European boutiques that sell perfect clothes."

"Should I take a long way or a short way?" Vienna asked.

"I'm in no hurry."

Which maybe meant it was okay to take a longer way.

They ended up at a store that had more open space than inventory. Justine gave nonstop instructions in English. "Let's try a black A-Line, below the knees." And: "We need a belt, not dominatrix gear." Vienna thought the silk half bra and sheer panties that Justine chose hardly qualified as respectable, but the best option was to accept them without argument and get something over them.

Of course Justine was unhappy with the fit of everything. She ordered a small squad of clerks off with instructions for tailoring. "We only need one outfit to take with us," she said. "Forward the rest to the Radisson SAS under my name." The black credit card produced obsequious guarantees.

Vienna walked out wearing a new dress, soft and black. Whatever her underclothes were like, the dress covered everything from her neck to her ankles.

"Why is it you pose nude while I am dressed for mass?"

Justine started to say something, stopped, and then smiled. But it didn't look right. "Just luck, I guess."

Vienna was certain that made no sense even to Justine. Maybe it was one of those puzzles she had been talking about.

Back near the Radisson, Justine turned through a narrow ally that stank of rancid grease and fermenting fruit. She knocked on a battered door and was waved into the Radisson's kitchen. Up the elevator and into Justine's suite.

Her nasty agent was waiting for them. Vienna imagined him with one of those big, black cowboy hats. "You turned off your cell," he said. "Want to guess how many calls you missed? And in the unlikely event you had any doubts as to the score, Jordan Farquar flew in from New York last night."

"Tell him I'll give him ten dollars if he gets his mouth surgically removed. I'll be in the gym."

"Justine. You have to stop. We need damage control."

Justine did not turn to face him. "I've followed every word of advice you've given over the last two years. I've been a good client, made you good money."

"I would never say otherwise, but—"

"But nothing. I am going to do my Pilates. I'll be ready at five o'clock for the press. You have to be happy with that."

Hargrave shook his head. "This is a mistake."

"Not the last, and you've said nothing about Vienna." Which really didn't fit in the conversation at all.

Hargrave turned and gave a small nod to Vienna. "You look nice."

Silence was the better part of prudence.

"Now, if you could talk sense into Heather, we would all be happy."

"She hasn't made sense all day."

"I can see that."

Justine hissed like air leaking from a tire and walked to the bathroom. She came out a minute later in dark blue sweats. Her shoulder-length hair was gathered in a tight knot off her neck. "I'll be back in an hour. Take care of Vienna."

Hargrave held his arms wide in defeat as Justine left the room. Then he turned to Vienna. "I'm very busy. Is there anything I can get you?"

"A computer and Internet access, if that's okay."

Hargrave got her set up on a laptop and then was on the phone, handling ten conversations at once.

Jordan Farquar's homepage was full of ads for gold coins and homeopathy. A menu on the left side included a button for past columns. It was labeled: "From Where I Stand." Vienna clicked on that.

Three years of articles streamed by, every one starting with "From where I stand." Vienna initially thought the phrase was clever, but as the hour passed she saw it as a cheap gimmick. She didn't understand much of what she had read, but she knew that Jorden Farquar was a snake who only appeared to swallow the fallen.

That was okay, because Vienna had a plan. Something she never would have dared before the afternoon's detours.

7

The street fronting the Radisson was closed. Blue police lights swirling off the city's glass canyons. So often the final spotlights of celebrity.

Vienna had insisted on coming, her face clouding over when Justine objected. She'd spent an hour making certain her hair looked as good as it did when she'd left Chat Rouge. Her impulsive twirling of her bangs had played havoc with the salon's high-end sculpting gel. Justine raided her own travel kit and chose a darker base for Vienna's face, explaining that the lights would make her look pale. Then she helped Vienna put it on, as the girl had no clue.

A final wardrobe check and out into the surreal fireworks of camera flashes. Vienna put her hand low over her eyes. A murmur spread through the mob. There she is. That's the girl with Justine Am. Are they holding hands? Will they kiss? Is she really a retard?

Justine saw Jordan Farquar front and center and knew there was no chance of a happy ending. She was caught in the most hackneyed ritual of the biz. Break the rules; flame out at spin control. Pull a decade-long vanishing act and spend your declining years hawking off-brand eyeliner.

She stepped to the podium set on the hotel's landing, Vienna trailing in her wake. After the flashes died out, she saw several fans waving signs promising to stand by her. Sweet, but useless. A gaggle of society reporters with sleep-deprived eyes crowded closer. The curious and the bored come to see the show. Along with the sleazy photographer from Vienna's gelato shop, the tattoo on his forearm looking schoolyard cheap. Too much gel in his long hair; brown strings pooling on his shoulders.

Justine expected to be hit with his greasy smile, but he was looking away, taking pictures of the crowd. His finger danced on the shutter as he rotated the camera over his head. He wasn't taking background photos. He was making certain he marked everyone there. What the hell?

He turned to her. His lips were tight and his fingers fidgeted over the camera. He looked her in the eye and mouthed a phrase. "They are here," he moved his lips slowly, making certain she understood. "They are here."

Some ploy to cadge an exclusive? But he didn't look like he was scheming. Swollen eyes and washed-out expression.

"Justine?" Vienna whispered. "You're supposed to say something."

The opening lines James had so carefully crafted evaporated. Justine stammered the first thing that came to mind. "I understand some of you have questions."

Embarrassed laughter stirred the crowd. Where was the payoff? Where was the tirade about invasion of privacy? Where was the righteous anger at the press? Confused whispering rose from the ranks. Justine waited for silence. "Who's first?" Someone near the back of the crowd shouted derisively. Expense accounts were looking way out of line.

Jordan Farquar, thin as a bedroom lie, took charge. His anachronistic cherry-red notepad at the ready. He wore his trademark black T-shirt over those hideous mauve Slapdash jeans. The belt was exotic leather—komodo or some such. On anyone else it would have been absurd, on Farquar it was an open threat. A wakening northern breeze could not budge his perfect blond hair. The air smelled of cold rain.

Jordan flashed his wisest grin, gathering respectful silence. "The question foremost in our minds, darling, is how the lesbian experience is suiting you so soon after your boyfriend's murder." The skeletal hand holding the pad carved small circles through the air, already bored with whatever bullshit might be forthcoming.

No worse than expected. Justine readied the scripted denial.

She didn't get her mouth open before Vienna insistently pushed her aside. There would be no stopping her without a scene. The girl adjusted her glasses and calmly faced another wave of flashbulbs.

Oh yeah. This was going to be good.

I should have put her in tails after all. That would have given them something to talk about. Maybe a black choker.

Vienna's voice was quiet as always. Even with the mics, the crowd strained to hear.

"You are Jordan Farquar?"

Jordan offered a mock bow. Only unimportant people didn't know him.

"I read your articles this afternoon."

"A valuable use of time, I think."

A ripple of laughter stirred the mob.

"The world's shortest oxymoron," Vienna said.

"Excuse me?"

"You said, 'I think.' In your case, the world's shortest oxymoron."

Justine felt gravity quadruple. She looked at Vienna. The girl's face was polished marble behind the glasses. Her lips moved to text that likely floated in her vision like a heads-up display. The spinning wooziness in Justine's stomach spread to her head.

Jordan licked his lips. "I—"

Vienna cut him down. "Thank you for inquiring as to the particulars of Justine Am's sex life, even though the vicarious overtones suggest you need psychological help. I did sleep with Justine last night. Which is to say we slept in the same bed. I was scared and I didn't want to be alone." Justine saw expected tears slip down Vienna's cheeks. "I would have given more because I was confused and tired and she is beautiful. But she did not take advantage of me."

Dead silence. Not even the whispered click of cameras. Justine felt like a busker posing as a statue. *Look, mommy! It's Marie Antoinette!*

Farquar yipped his famous laugh.

The executioner's blade whistling through the October sky.

"I'm sure that's true, dear, but—"

Vienna's words cast a spell through the darkening twilight. The voice of an injured lady, demanding to be heard in its hush. "As you have asked a personal question, it is only fair that I ask one. How is it you sleep at night? Other than alone."

Justine remembered the jab from one of Jordan's first columns. A clever enough tactic, but Justine knew the edge tapering Vienna's voice was fiercely contained panic. Could she maintain control long enough to spring her useless traps?

Jordan's smile was intact, but Justine saw telltale hardness along his jaw. He opened his mouth, dramatically waiting for Vienna to cut him off. She only looked at him and again he appeared foolish. "May I speak without being interrupted?"

"Of course, Lewis. That is your real name, yeah? Don't you think Jordan is a bit affected for a man in your position? I mean, you lot really aren't journalists, are you?"

There was no mistaking the reaction this time. Jordan hated his real name and he despised anyone who questioned the validity of his profession. Score one for Research Girl. Jordan unplugged his smile. "It's hardly as pretentious as Vienna."

The crowd buzzed. Jordan never got suckered into trading quips. There might be a story after all.

Vienna sniffled at her tears. "Do you realize that hyenas are more closely related to cats than dogs? Isn't that odd?"

"What?"

"Many cultures thought they were hermaphrodites," Vienna said. "I mention that because you seem interested in sex and maybe you could use that in the future. Though I suspect you already know about hyenas."

Justine felt Vienna shaking. Too many people, too much anger, too many cameras. It needed to end.

"If we could return to the subject at hand," Jordan said, "I was merely going to point out, no offense intended, that as a woman with a past of mental illness, you're not who we came to see, honey. You need to let Justine speak at her own press conference."

Vienna flinched. Her hand moved toward her mouth. She froze and slowly lowered it. *Good girl.*

But the spell was broken. Justine sidestepped, set on scooting Vienna aside and giving Jordan all the headlines he could handle. She put a hand to Vienna, but the girl may as well have been cast from lead.

Vienna's voice went flat, as if dredging up one of her history lessons. "Your problem is that balmy people do crazy things and there is nothing you can do about it. And no, I'm not going to let Justine speak. Do you know why?"

"I'm sure we would all like to know, honey," Jordan answered, his tight smirk once again locked in place. He had his angle.

"Because you are a disagreeable child hoping to goad one of your betters into doing something stupid." Vienna tilted her head, a gesture Justine was certain she had studied. "And I am not your honey, or your dear, or your darling. Not for all the money in the world." She added one more line, in sterile perfection. "From where I stand, you are a miserable excuse for a man."

Justine saw a victorious smile spread Farquar's hollow face. She knew, as Vienna could not, that Jordan had achieved everything he'd set out to. Justine would be roasted alive. Jordan won again. He always did.

Amazing that it had almost been worth it. This wisp of a girl had lashed out as so many people hungered to, but never could for fear of destroying their careers. Before Justine understood the impulse, she was laughing. Cameras snapped to life, catching her laughter as tears stained Vienna's face. Perfect symmetry. They had each cost the other her job.

Vienna spoke again. "Lewis has had his questions. Are there any others?" Doubtless there were, but no one could frame a single syllable before Vienna offered a timid smile, wiping the tears from her cheeks. "Then we are finished. Good evening, yeah?" Even the slip into the strange syntax of backstreet English was perfect.

Vienna turned and was swept into the hotel's revolving door. There seemed nothing to do but follow. Justine took a last look at the crowd. The photographer from the gelato shop was gone. Near the back, she saw the scarred face of Lord Davy, his dark eyes radiating cold fury.

What the hell was he doing here? The door took her away.

Hargrave trailed behind, holding his anger until they reached Justine's suite. "I didn't sign on to watch you self-destruct."

Justine let herself fall to the bed. "I suppose we'll drop a few accounts."

"You're too optimistic. Simone from Carrie Limited called halfway through that debacle. They're claiming repudiatory breach of contract. Your two remaining TV spots have been canceled and they're considering filing for damages. By the time you wake tomorrow you will be out of work."

"What would you suggest, James?"

"Step one is to get rid of her." He pointed at Vienna.

She had never seen James so blatantly rude. "There's no reason to go down with the ship. Get out while the getting is good."

"You can't just throw it all away."

"A few days ago, I slept with a harmless girl on a bet. Her life will be a wreck for months to come. And then there's the creep I thought I loved, blown apart in my hotel room. I can't change that either. I'm tired, and I don't care what Jordan Farquar thinks. I'm going to bed. When I get up tomorrow, I'm getting my passport. I'm calling Adelina and booking the first flight back to Georgia. I need a break, a long one."

Hargrave steepled his hands and washed his fingers down his face. "Justine, I play this game to win. I don't care how egotistical it sounds. I can't—"

Justine cut him off. "You don't have to explain. I would wish you good luck, but you're too good to need it."

"Justine, we can still—"

"I'm tired of this, James."

Hargrave shook his head. "Apparently so." He turned away, closing the door behind him so softly that it didn't make a sound.

"What a day," Justine said.

She closed her eyes and saw Lord Davy's fury. *They are here.* Her anger slipped into apprehension. *He was there for Vienna, not me.* Why? What was so important about her?

Her thoughts derailed again, piling up against the previous night's fears: *would she expect sex?* Only this time the question warped back on itself. It never had been a matter of what Vienna wanted, had it? *Is that why I'm so scared?*

That whole karma thing again, and Justine figured it finally ran her over.

8

Justine's phone started with the Talking Heads song right after Justine disappeared into the shower. Vienna tried to ignore it, but the snippet of music just kept repeating. She hated that so she answered.

"Hello?"

A pause over the soft hiss of distance. "You must be Vienna." A woman's voice.

"Yes?"

"I'm Abby Ingles—Heather's mother."

Vienna knew exactly what to say. "Studying twentieth-century British literature is stupid."

A laugh crossed the Atlantic. "You might be right."

"Who did you learn about?"

"Mostly William Golding."

" 'Kill the beast! Cut his throat! Spill his blood! Do him in!' " That was from *Lord of the Flies*, by William Golding, published by Faber and Faber, September 17, 1954. It was a story about how children are vicious brats. Who needed a book to know that?

"That's the one," Dr. Ingles said.

"Okay." Having proved her point, Vienna had nothing to add.

"BBC America had a clip of you addressing that so-called reporter. Up on your high horse. I swear, you're just like Heather."

"She's in the shower."

"That's fine. She'll call back when she's ready. Send her our love."

"Okay."

"Good-bye, Vienna."

"Okay."

Vienna put the phone on the desk. *Just like Heather.* Famous and rich and happy. Exactly like that.

She shuffled to the bed and sat. The spread was silver-white, stitched in a diamond pattern. Diagonals drawn from each diamond's vertex formed eight different triangles, which could be used to form three different rhombuses the same size as the original. Endless permutations flowing through a complex cascade of angles and areas. Such geometries could make solid surfaces ripple like water. But now the shapes faded even as they appeared.

Vienna wasn't certain how, but she'd borked it all up. She'd planned to divert attention away from Justine. What difference did it make to her if the popular press thought she was stupid? She had no presence in their world. Wasn't it right that she took the lead, just as she had while navigating Brussels's winding streets?

She didn't want to think about it but she needed to know. When Justine stepped from the bathroom, draped in a white robe that covered her like a tent, Vienna screwed up her courage. "Can we talk?"

Justine folded a leg underneath herself as she sat next to Vienna, her free leg swinging slowly off the end of the bed. "It depends. I'm very tired, Vienna."

She didn't want to mention the phone call, but she'd told Dr. Ingles she would. "Your mother called. She said that she loves you."

"This is a test of the Abigail Emergency Broadcast System. Had this been an actual emergency, your father would already be on the line."

"What does that mean?"

"She's worried about me. You know, the dead boyfriend in the bathroom. The new girlfriend to be vetted. It's okay. They'll give me time to sort through it all—they've always been great that way. I'll call back when things settle down a bit."

Vienna gave up on whatever that was about. "She talked about horses and she said we're the same."

Justine was silent for several seconds, then a brief smile. "I bet she saw a video of you smacking Jordan around. Up on your high horse. She accuses me of that now and then. Taking on the world without caring about consequences."

Which at least was close to what Vienna really wanted to talk about.

"You haven't sat still since we returned."

"Anxious exhaustion."

Vienna decided that meant Justine was angry. "I didn't do well, did I?"

Justine lifted a hand and brushed it through Vienna's hair. "You did fine."

"I thought I could take the blame."

"There's no money in that. It's a much better story if Justine Am cowers behind a troubled girl."

"That's not how it was."

"Winners always write the histories." She took Vienna's glasses off, stretched up the bed to set them on the nightstand. "Anyway, you made it fun. I never expected that." She sat back up. "I thought Jordan Farquar was going to faint for a second. I was sure James was. It was no less than I deserve after dragging you all over town for my own amusement." She turned to face Vienna, pulling her leg up and under the bathrobe. "My turn to ask a question."

"Okay."

"When we were at the police station, you mumbled something under your breath. I caught the word 'buckaroo.' What did it mean?"

Vienna sighed because she knew where this was going, having been there a million times. "I thought Mr. Hargrave looked like a cowboy. The Spanish translation is *'vaquero,'* which became corrupted into the English word 'buckaroo.'"

Justine laughed, which wasn't anywhere in the script. "James does look like a cowboy. Can you imagine him roughing it on the open range, face-to-face with a longhorn? He'd piss himself."

She doesn't get it. "I have to find room for new things by attaching them to what I already know, otherwise I get anxious and sick even though everyone says that's wrong. It all has to fit together." Satisfied that would pull the conversation back to well-worn pathways, Vienna readied herself for *the speech* about how she needed to *try harder*.

"I think that's a beautiful way to see the world."

"You don't understand." It wasn't fair.

"Likely not, but I will try."

Vienna decided it would be less annoying to just give up and move on. "My turn to ask a question."

"One more."

"Why did you buy me glasses when you know I don't need them? They were very expensive."

"Because they make you comfortable."

"So why did you take them off?"

"One question too many." And now Justine's hand was over hers. The American continued in a whisper. "I would answer if I could."

Vienna felt the heat of a rising blush. "Will you try?"

"I don't know, Vienna. It might be because I am tired. Or because I am so alone tonight. Or because it's taboo back home and I am sick of rules. Or because what goes around comes around and this is a settling of accounts. Or maybe even because you are you and tonight I want to take the long way home."

Vienna spread her fingers under Justine's, letting them weave together. Was that being too forward? Or maybe not enough?

"What about you?" Justine asked.

"Me?"

"Why did you let me take them off?"

"I am like half the world."

"Now it is your turn to explain."

"I am like half the world, thinking I'm in love with Justine Am."

Justine nodded and Vienna felt the fool. How many times has she heard people say they love her?

"Why would you be in such a questionable state?"

"Because you are beautiful?" She hadn't meant it to sound like a question.

"So I'm told. Why do you find me beautiful?"

At least that was easy. "Symmetry."

For some reason that made Justine smile. "You lost me."

"Facial symmetry is the number one indicator of beauty. Followed by youth and clear skin." She looked over what little she had on the subject. "Though in the last decade, a flat belly has become more important."

"And here I assumed it was my ass."

Vienna considered this and decided to risk a less safe answer. "You read too many books by lonely old men."

That made Justine laugh aloud. "You're a little witch, you know that?"

Vienna couldn't make anything of that, except witches were bad, weren't they? Instead of explaining, Justine asked another question. "There were plenty of beautiful people at Holler that night. You said so yourself. So why me?"

Vienna felt the conversation slipping away. "I don't know," she whispered. "I don't know anything when you're like this."

"See? You understand perfectly."

That made no sense at all except just like that Justine was kissing her, her lips cool and soft. Vienna flinched back. "I don't—"

Justine held her index finger in front of Vienna's lips. Vienna expected her to say something, but Justine remained silent. After a few seconds, she leaned forward again and kissed Vienna a second time. Her teeth soft on Vienna's lower lip. Below growing confusion, Vienna felt a shift of intent. Justine edged closer. It was no longer a friendly kiss. It was insistent and pressing and filled with heavy, hungry tension. Vienna fought rising panic.

Here, invisible yet strong, was the taboo of the old life. That was William Golding.

The taboo of the old life.

I'll mess up again.

Justine shifted forward, pushing into Vienna. She felt herself turn to face Justine, as if Justine had her on a string. As if she had no choice but to answer.

To answer . . .

In an instant, Vienna knew why Grant had died in the bathroom. How his last desperate attempt to stay alive had failed. But there was no way she could stop what was happening. *The lust of the goat is the glory of God.*

Justine's hands undoing the back of her dress. Was this how it was supposed to be? *She moves and I respond without control? Does this mean something?*

"Shh," Justine whispered, even though Vienna hadn't said anything. "Sometimes you have to let the night breathe." The dress slipped off Vienna's shoulders. Justine's hand moved across her stomach. "Let me show you something," she said. Her other hand went behind Vienna. Once again, Vienna's body responded on its own, rising to meet Justine's touch.

Justine's hands moved further, and suddenly Vienna felt exposed. *Should I fight this?* Female lovers in books often did. Maybe it was expected, to prove she wasn't a harlot? Did it make a difference that she was with another female? She felt her muscles pull tight.

Justine pulled away. "Vienna? Do you want this to happen?"

Wasn't it a little late for questions? "Okay," she said, and that was all wrong. "Yes." Before she even had a chance to think about it.

"So much for going back to the States," Justine said. And that was sad and happy at the same time. Justine leaned forward again, her fingers shifted barely at all but it was enough to catch Vienna's breath.

Vienna closed her eyes, felt herself being pushed back. And at least that seemed right. She tried to hear music, because Cecile said she always did, but she couldn't hear anything except the susurration of fabric over skin and her own breathing.

Her clothes piled up at the foot of the bed, where they would get wrinkled. Justine's lips on her stomach. Warm and wet. Stimulus and response. All of her nerves suddenly running down instead of up. Vienna closed her eyes. Justine's lips trailing across her skin.

And that seemed right, too.

Let the night breathe. She repeated it to herself as a gentle mantra. Let the night breathe. And she was in that dark band of violet sky that always appeared between double rainbows. A place of profound quiet and light all around. And it was a little scary because there was so far to fall, but maybe that was how it was supposed to be. Time slipped away in a sensuous trance.

The feeling stayed with her even after movement slowed and ended, fading only as sleep came on. A soft voice there. "What you did was very brave, Vienna." It sounded somehow like love. "No worrying about tomorrow." But there was no way to know if it had been a dream or not.

Later, the clock moving through the small hours, Vienna seemed to catch the scent of sun-warmed pine trees. Her first visit to the Cart House, deep in the Austrian forest. The limestone mantel over the entry carved with the image of Nerthus, Mother Goddess of the World. The goddess was standing in a cart pulled by cows, surrounded by the young maidens who would drown when Nerthus returned to her lake. There was a Latin phrase below the carving, written by Tacitus. Uncle Anson said it meant days of celebration and happiness and that the estate should be called Nerthum Something Something but it was fine to call it Cart House, just as Gisella had a century ago. Whoever that was.

Then Vienna was inside the Cart House and there was fog everywhere. Pictures and paintings and diagrams covering the estate's endless hallways. They told her that David Andries, dead on the bathroom floor, had never been the target. It was Justine. And just like that, Justine was in Vienna's bathroom, shot in the face and so much blood streaming across the pure white floor. And Vienna had a pencil and she kept drawing lines around the invading red because lines helped her understand shape but there was so much blood and there was no way to stop it and there were girls in the lake, screaming as the water closed over them, and Vienna screamed too but there was no sound at all.

Vienna's eyes opened. Nothing but the shallow rasp of her own breathing. She reached back, her hand brushing low across Justine's side. *She's still here.* Vienna rolled to face her. In the clock's dim light, she watched Justine breathing. No sinister forest. Only the fading urgency of a nightmare.

It wasn't even a proper nightmare. It wasn't about how Vienna couldn't talk to people the right way or how the world made her sick. This dream had been about Justine.

Justine, who misquoted Shakespeare. Vienna closed her eyes. *William Shakespeare was baptized on April 26, 1564 . . .*

Othello to Desdemona: " 'She loved me for the dangers I had passed and I loved her that she did not pity them.' "

It all has to fit together. Vienna's fingers clinched tight around her pillow. It was impossible because even before they had sex, Justine had already done a million things differently than anyone else. Most of them wrong.

" 'I loved her that she did not pity . . .' " Vienna moved the words around, looking for a safe place to put them. She was still looking when sleep caught her again.

Vienna awoke at five. Justine was sprawled across the bed, her lips slightly parted in sleep. It took some effort to slide off without waking her. Off to the bathroom to take care of the morning. She took a long shower, not having any place to go. Nothing to think about except what had happened last night. *Did I do better? Does she hate me now? Am I a whore? Will we ever do that again? Was making love supposed to make you anxious?*

Thirty minutes in front of the mirror to get her hair looking right. At least that solved the mystery of why it took Justine so long to get ready every morning. Having only her old clothes and the new ones Justine bought, she slipped into her old ones, banging her arm painfully on the side of the sink when Justine's Black-Berry startled her with some internal alarm.

Justine was quickly there, shutting it off. "I have to work out, hun. Can you wait for breakfast?"

I'm starving. "Okay."

Justine was in her sweats and at the door before she looked back at Vienna. "I enjoyed last night, Vienna."

I need to tell her that I enjoyed last night, too. But different words came: "You can't quit because of me." Why was that important? Vienna looked away. Justine couldn't quit because the nightmare forest was somehow real and if Justine tried to walk away, the evil hidden there would lash out and find its true target. But there was no way to say that without sounding stupid.

Justine remained silent until Vienna turned back to her. "Contrary to available evidence," the model said, "I won't do anything reckless. Speaking of which, you better stay here. I imagine the press is still lurking around."

"Okay."

Justine paused as if to add something, but with a quick turn she was gone.

Alone, Vienna wandered around the perimeter of the suite, trailing her hand along the wall. When she reached Justine's closet, she pulled the double doors open. Four racks of clothes. There were the khaki capris she had been wearing at the gelato stand. *The photographer's pictures!*

Vienna reached into the pocket and grabbed the camera chip. Justine's Sony had a slot for it. Pictures filed onto the screen. Justine in front of the Atomium. Justine walking in the Grand Place. Justine entering the Cosmopolitan. Justine with her flawlessly handsome boyfriend. Vienna frowned and came up with his real name, even though she had never seen it written. David Andries. So what if he had been handsome? He was likely a killer so his looks didn't mean that much. Anyway, he was dead, which was just fine with Vienna. She returned to the images. Justine eating dinner. Justine with Mr. Hargrave. Justine at an interview. Justine up close. Justine midshot. Justine against a foreshortened background, likely caused by a telephoto lens. Justine topless with blue hair. Vienna noted that Justine's left breast was a tiny fraction smaller than the right.

That made her feel better.

Justine with blond hair. With brown hair. With black hair. Justine. Justine. Justine. And two final pictures of Vienna at the gelato store, looking dull and flat-chested and scared. The final three files were hiding behind icons Vienna didn't recognize. She was still trying to open them when Justine returned, a fine sheen of sweat on her throat.

"The man's pictures," Vienna said, rationalizing her uninvited use of Justine's computer.

"I'd forgotten them."

"There are three files I can't read." Vienna pointed at the icons.

"Video clips—use Cyberlink. I need a quick shower and then we'll get something to eat."

Vienna tried to ignore the growling in her stomach. *Might as well see the videos.*

The first one was of Justine striding on a catwalk. She had that walk, placing her leading leg unnaturally across the center of her stride, causing her hips to swivel with each step. Vienna was certain it wouldn't be easy in high heels, but Justine skated smoothly down the stage.

The second video was of Justine eating dinner with David Andries. A restaurant with cream walls and Art Nouveau woodwork. The third was of Justine posing next to a skipping manikin. Wet concrete below her, reflections of lighted buildings smeared across its surface. Vienna searched her memory and found the building's shape as a sketch in an architecture book. The Národní Muzeum in Prague.

The manikin was wood, old but exquisitely done. Justine had struck a pose mimicking the manikin, her hands locked behind her back, her shoulders tilted, her left leg forward, toes pointed. Both were dressed in the same short, lemon yellow skirt and cobalt blouse. Justine's stockings had a white chevron pattern with a white line down the back.

"Chianti Twor. First night of shooting in Prague." Vienna flinched and turned.

"I didn't mean to scare you." Justine laughed.

Vienna looked back to the computer. "It's very bright."

"Chianti loves her colors, but she pulls it off. I love her designs."

"You're beautiful," Vienna added.

"I know." Justine's voice was wrong, somehow. "Anything of interest?"

"He seems obsessed with you—the photographer."

"First line of the job description. What were the other movies?"

"Nothing important."

Justine started the second video before Vienna could close the window. David Andries and Justine eating. Vienna glanced back. Justine's face was frozen. *Does she still see him as her lover?*

They were seated at a table, looking away. Andries held a sliver of a cell phone to his right ear. Justine was stabbing at a pineapple dessert.

"Comme Chez Soi," Justine said.

"What?"

"The restaurant. Here in Brussels. That creep must have been sitting right beside us."

Justine pushed a key and the sound came up. Andries talking on the phone, barely heard above other conversations. "Weather isn't bad, and the food can't be beat . . ." His voice sounded unnatural in the laptop's tiny speakers. "Yes, that's it . . . inalienable artifact . . ." He laughed. ". . . how should I know? The advantages of being wealthy." He paused and then: "Right, we can do lunch next time." He hung up.

Vienna glanced back at Justine and saw she was quietly crying. But the image was already far away.

Inalienable artifact.

Follow the shape of the words.

9

Afternoon hours bled into melancholy haze. Justine called the American embassy for her passport, but hung up the first time she was put on hold. However bad things were here, they would be worse in the States. No reason to drag her family into this. Even if they would stand by her. Even if she would be safer there. Even if she looked at Vienna every few seconds.

An e-mail from Hargrave contained documents for severing their business relationship. A lengthy attachment showed legal forms from canceled contracts. As Hargrave had foretold, Justine lost all seven of her endorsement deals. The possibility that she was involved in murder was of no concern. The possibility that she was sleeping with an Unmarketable Person of the Female Persuasion was too dodgy. *Vogue* made new plans for their summer feature. Bernoulli no longer required her for his show; Paris bleaching away like a distant dream. Friends evaporated as fast as delete keys could be pushed.

Except Igor Czasky: "My intention is to retain you for the Clay to Flesh project. Three sessions left. Everyone else can go to hell." Justine saved the note and moved on.

On the bright side there was a slew of new offers. *Hustler. Penthouse. Vivid. Digital Playground.* The offers were impressive if she appeared with Vienna. Dear God, Vienna in a nudie shoot. *"I don't understand. Why would I put my hand there?"*

Martyrdom being the order of the day, Justine went to Jordan Farquar's site. The picture of her laughing while Vienna cried was predictable, but Farquar had plenty to add.

Justine glanced at Vienna, sitting on the bed, slowly rocking back and forth. She'd spent the morning whispering to herself.

Justine had caught a few minutes of dreary monologue concerning the fractional distillation of aldehydes.

"Have you seen this Vienna?"

Vienna blinked her eyes open. "Seen what?" Justine was certain Vienna would spend the rest of her life indoors if she had the chance.

"Jordan Farquar's rant."

"No."

"Come look."

Vienna unfolded from her crossed-legged perch and glanced at the computer before turning back to the bed. "Why are you bothering?" she asked.

"Aren't you going to read it?" *Gotcha.*

Vienna froze, her stance rigid in dawning panic. "I see," Justine said. She turned the screen away from Vienna. "Read it to me."

Vienna retreated to petulance. "You're making fun of me."

"No, I'm not."

"Don't be mean." Her voice brittle.

Justine shook her head. "Not going to work, Vienna. Read it to me."

Vienna's voice went hollow, her eyes scanning across empty air. "'From where I stand, Justine Am's true colors have finally shown, and let me tell you, darlings, they are not at all in fashion this year, assuming they ever were. That she would let a troubled young lady speak for her indicates reprehensible cowardice at worse, and a complete lack of moral fiber at best. I am certain her erstwhile promoters are scrambling to disassociate themselves from this shameful—'"

A loud bang on the door cut her off. "No one's home!" Justine answered. Vienna performed her most theatrical sigh and went to the door. At least she was smart enough to look through the peephole. Not that it helped. The Furies in the guise of Lord Anson Davy.

I should have gone back to Georgia.

Davy possessed the immaculate fashion sense of truly powerful men. Justine couldn't guess the designer of his black and ash-gray ensemble, but the subtle Asian tones would part any crowd. She felt the murky pull of his sexuality.

"Vienna is returning to London," he said. Justine wondered if alpha males could be measured by vocal tone.

Justine closed the computer. "Isn't that for her to decide?"

"Despite having reached England's age of majority, Vienna still has a guardian. She signed the requisite forms as per the judgment of an appointed family proceedings court. The documents are available at the East Finchley public records, under the heading of Grayfield. You will find she granted her foster father consider-able leeway. Her flight leaves in two hours."

Vienna started to speak, but Justine held up her hand. *Get in the wagon and find the steepest hill.* "Explain Vienna's condition."

"What condition are you referring to?"

"Don't be a jackass. Whatever paperwork you have in England, this hotel room is under my name, not Vienna's, and you are here without my consent."

"After yesterday's performance, I doubt you would fare well should this become a legal matter," he said.

"Speaking of yesterday, what were you doing at the press con-ference? Did you know your picture was taken? How embarrass-ing for your Finchley client if I accuse you of stalking me."

Lord Davy's thin lips almost turned up. "So the legendary stubbornness of American women surfaces at precisely the wrong time. Do you think your request is appropriate?" He nodded toward Vienna. "Whatever her condition, I'm assuming Vienna can hear us talking."

"Would you rather I talk behind her back? If I'm asking ques-tions about her, she has the right to know."

Davy's eyes opened a fraction wider. "I seem to have misjudged the situation?"

How does he turn the tables so effortlessly? Justine swallowed. "I'm on uncertain ground."

"Well, that's brilliant. How did this come about?"

"I'm not certain it has. She just . . ." Justine turned her hands up in resignation of ever being able to finish the thought.

"I see. The pundits may have finally gotten something right."

"What are you talking about?" Vienna asked.

This time Lord Davy did smile. "Let's start at the beginning." He gestured for them to sit. Justine sank back into her chair while Vienna stepped over to the bed and curled her legs under her.

"Be specific," Davy said to Justine.

Another flawless change of topic. Justine rolled with it. "Vienna saw my laptop screen for two seconds and can recite the complete image. Getting her hair done she quoted from what had to be a Brussels tourist guide, and then she had some stodgy history that sounded nineteenth century. I'm willing to bet she was quoting it word-for-word."

"A safe wager."

"Such feats are the domain of autistic savants."

"Not all savants are autistic."

"Don't be disingenuous. She spent the entire morning in a trance."

"You weren't doing anything either," Vienna accused.

"I was moping, silly. There's a difference." She turned to Davy. "Surely her guardian has taken her to several doctors."

"I go to doctors all the time," Vienna said.

"They give you tests?"

She nodded. "Sometimes with pictures that change a little bit and sometimes asking how I make friends. Sometimes London postal codes, as if I care. But I learned them anyway so I could get them right. Stupid stuff like that, yeah?"

Justine looked at Lord Davy. "Well?"

Davy walked to the bed and sat next to Vienna, looking out of place in such an informal pose. "Our girl Vienna was left at the SOS Children's Village at Hinterbrühl—an orphanage in the Wienerwald outside of Vienna. With no name to work from, one of the nurses named her for the city. I must say it's fitting. Viennese can present a difficult exterior, but when times are bad they

show great tenderness. If by the light of day they are gloomy business, in the gentler tones of night they possess rare beauty."

Justine nodded, knowing that Vienna had not heard Davy's
warning shot. He thought of her as more than a client. *This just
keeps getting better.*

"It was clear that Vienna was special," Davy continued. "She
had yet to speak at four years. By six—living in a country estate
south of Bath—she still hadn't uttered a single word, though tests
showed no physical issues. And then, on Christmas Day, she
started talking in complete sentences. Though no one understood
what she was saying." Davy offered Vienna an encouraging smile.
"After a number of experts had been consulted, a local war vet-
eran came to the rescue. Vienna was speaking in mispronounced
German. We discovered she was reading verbatim from the
Einheitsübersetzung—the German Roman Catholic Bible. She
hadn't seen a German Bible since leaving the orphanage three
years previously."

"Because I'm broken," Vienna said.

She makes a better martyr than I do.

Davy smiled. "Broken in an extraordinary way. Most notable
is hypoplasia of the corpus callosum, which means—"

"Fewer connections between the hemispheres of the brain,"
Justine said. "Vienna was born prematurely?"

"A full month, according to the heavily redacted records left
with the orphanage's medical staff. It made her susceptible to
asthma, among other things. How did you know?"

"Hypoplasia is often caused by premature birth. In more extreme cases, often associated with third trimester injury to the
fetus, periventricular leukomalacia can be found. This does not
seem to be the case here." *Chew on that, Lord London Hotshot.*

Davy's left eyebrow arched, but he calmly continued. "So I've
been told. Vienna's physical neurology is often associated with
prodigious feats of memory, though no one knows why." He
paused. "Unless there has been some discovery on the far side of
the pond?"

"None that I know of," Justine said. "It's a complex situation, accompanied by irregularities of the forebrain. Perception poorly filtering stimuli. Subjects often display unnatural focus to the exclusion of emotional awareness."

"Which explains why Vienna has an extraordinary facility with geometric patterns. She would be the devil's chess player."

"Chess is boring," Vienna said, her voice forecasting an increasing chance of downpours.

"What else?" Justine asked.

"Two further medical items. The first is a complex partial seizure preceded by an aura of depersonalization. The effect lasts minutes or in bad cases an hour. Vienna's thoughts depart while her body carries on a familiar and highly repetitive motion. It's frightening, but transitory."

"Also found in some autistic cases. Has the trigger for these episodes been discovered?"

"Vienna has tried to explain."

"The world doesn't fold together the right way." Vienna spoke over an absurdly long sigh. Best get this finished.

"What else?"

"A physiological condition related to involuntary retinal scanning. The explanation is fairly technical. Saccades happening too frequently, which I gather results in a visual stutter of sorts. When Vienna was young, it pushed optometrists to distraction. It amounts to an unconscious, obsessive stall over written words. She can't not look at them, so to speak."

"And once she sees them—"

"She memorizes them, apparently forever. I believe that for the first six years of her life Vienna was drowning in sensory overload. It's a miracle she conquered her environment at all." Davy set his hand on Vienna's shoulder. "There was, as you guessed, much discussion of autism spectrum disorders."

Justine shook her head. "I did work in the field. It doesn't fit. There are symptoms though."

Vienna's patience evaporated. "Are you finished yet?"

"I haven't even started. But I know enough to see that our knighted guest is full of horseshit."

"Justine!"

"It's quite all right," Davy said. "While I take issue with Yankee vernacular, I understand the essence. The question is if she knows why."

"I don't," Vienna said.

"This was not your test to take," Davy said to her. Looking at Justine, he added, "Let this go, for now."

"For the sake of your snobbish East Finchley client?"

Davy's eyes hardened. "You're a woman around whom men make mistakes." He brushed an imaginary wrinkle from his slacks. "I said too much, but then, not many Americans are familiar with London neighborhoods."

"East Finchley is the richest section of London. It may yet be the wealthiest locality in Europe. Is your client embarrassed by Vienna?"

"I assure you this is not the case. We have only Vienna's interests at heart."

"Then we're finished here."

"Almost." Davy stood up. "An offer was delivered to Vienna's patron, requesting rights for a video staring Justine and Vienna." He turned to Vienna. "You can guess the theme of this film?"

Vienna shook her head.

"They want to tape us having sex," Justine said.

Vienna crossed her arms in front of her. "Derpy. According to Austrian law, two women are incapable of having sex."

"Nonetheless, they are willing to pay three million euros to see you try," Davy said. "Would you do it if Justine asked you to? If she needed the money?"

"She has a lot of money. She would never ask."

"That was not the question."

"And I am not very good at it. No one would care. She knows."

Davy's face flushed, the razor scar showing white. "That was not the question either."

Vienna looked at Justine, and nodded once.

"Now we are done." Lord Davy stood.

Vienna stood behind him. "Are you taking me away?"

"Do you want to leave Justine?"

Vienna kicked at the floor. "The pattern on the bedspread doesn't matter."

"Perhaps you can explain with a touch more clarity," Davy said.

"She gets in the way," Vienna said.

Davy looked at Justine. "Are you satisfied with that?"

"I want to fly back to Georgia," Justine answered. "She gets in the way."

"I'm worried that I almost grasp the feminine logic involved." He reached out to shake Vienna's hand. The girl responded out of reflex. "I will not lie. Your guardian has a more traditional view of relationships. But it seems we have little choice." He turned away. "Should you have any further insight concerning the death of David Andries, contact me at once. Given Vienna's choice in partners, I want the issue resolved."

Justine spoke as Davy reached the door. "The white picket fence and the two-and-a-half children were never going to happen."

"I suspect not."

"Anyway, she lied."

"Lied?"

"She's soft rain in the spring. Quiet in all the noise."

Davy raised an eyebrow.

"Vienna is no longer a child," Justine continued. "Her guardian needs to know that."

Davy nodded. "We feared she would never find . . ." He took a deep breath and opened the door. "I will speak on your behalf." There was a trace of a smile. "Godspeed." And he was gone.

If nothing else, it was clear that Lord Anson Davy cared deeply for Vienna.

That makes him one of the good guys, right?

10

Vienna stomped across the room. "Why did you talk about me like I wasn't here?" *Who wouldn't be pissed right off the end of the pier?*

"I had to show him I could be with you."

"You could have just told him."

Justine walked over to the bed, putting her hands on Vienna's waist and easing her down to sit side-by-side. "He had no reason to believe."

"Believe?"

Justine raised her hand to Vienna's cheek. "You don't get half the world to love you. Only one."

Vienna studied the words; pieces from a thousand different puzzles. She tried to think of something to say, but as usual messed up. "Why?"

Justine shook her head. "No clue. But I dealt with your nasty lawyer; that must mean something."

"I'm sorry."

Justine smiled. "I know what you want to say next."

Was that true? Vienna changed course. "What was the porno yack?"

"I need to start writing down British slang." Justine brushed Vienna's tears away. "When someone in my line takes a dive, the next step is usually nudie pictures."

"But why ask me?"

"Because he wanted to show me you would do it."

"Because I am still like half the world." Vienna grabbed at the bedspread. "But it's wrong because you're so frustrating and anyway one of us is supposed to be male and I don't know . . ." She let her voice trail off, embarrassed.

"That will do, for now," Justine said.

"But it was wrong. I can tell."

"Not wrong for you."

"At least I try to answer. Why did Uncle Anson ask if I would have sex with you on video? Answer me."

"He asked so he could show me that you would follow my lead."

"Because I'm broken."

"Ah, you said it anyway," Justine said.

"That's borked. Most people would love to have sex with you, video or not. Why am I different?"

"Because you're broken."

Vienna wanted to scream, but somehow this was one of those tests her doctors made her take. "You're just as bad as I am, only with people instead of numbers. You turn them inside out."

"Then we're broken together."

Vienna considered this before discarding it as evidence of Justine's callousness. "How do you know so much about autism?"

Justine looked down.

She looked away when something bad came up. Did everyone do that?

"Tell me."

Justine paused. "You already know the answer. Foosh."

Vienna blinked. "Fall on outstretched hand."

"Father's tennis career was cut short by a compound fracture of his right wrist. It happened eight years before I was born, but I was inconsolable when I understood what had happened. It wasn't fair. Daddy was the most greatest man in the whole world. I decided I would become a doctor and fix his wrist so he could play tennis again." A short exhale. "By the time I was old enough to realize how irrational that was, I was too invested in the idea to back out. Being a doctor was a good thing even if I couldn't help Father."

"Okay."

"So I was the perfect student all through school. Got bumped up two grades. Collected pre-med credits from UGA. Went to Stanford. I was going to be the best." Justine's right index finger drew fitful circles on the bedspread. "My first semester in med school, I was following a friend to a party. A utility truck burned a red light and sideswiped her Audi. By the time I reached her, there was blood everywhere. Handfuls of her hair had been ripped out by the headrest." Justine looked up. "She was laughing. Can you believe that? I knew it was shock, but it was so wrong. Her body was still there, but her mind was gone. We feared brain damage. She turned out fine—though she never remembered what happened. Post-traumatic amnesia. It scared me so much. I had nightmares about losing the ability to think. Of being trapped inside my own skull." She shrugged. "Anyway, I decided to face my fear. Isn't that what they always tell you to do? I went to work with severely autistic children."

"Did it help?"

"No." Justine barely breathed the word. "They cried so much, and they couldn't tell me why and I couldn't help no matter what I did. I was terrified, but I had to bottle it up and pretend everything was okay."

"You see some of this in me, that I am trapped inside myself?"

"Much worse."

"How can it be any worse?"

"I began to think it was contagious, that I would become trapped as well. Absurd, but I couldn't stop the fear. What was I supposed to do?"

And this couldn't be love because lovers would never make you feel so hurt and angry.

"I never told anyone that before," Justine whispered.

That only made Vienna more angry. "Of course not. Is it hard being perfect?"

Justine turned away, tears in her eyes for a change. "It is, but as you can see I'm very good at it."

Vienna knew she'd missed everything important. Why was Justine so upset? She wasn't the one with the problems. It had to be more than kids crying. Something deeper. Vienna tried to work it out, but it was impossible how Justine said one thing and meant something else. Was this something beautiful women did, or just Americans? She gave up and went back to Davy's visit. Tears or not, that's what they were supposed to be talking about.

"Why did you slander Lord Davy? He's a member of the peerage."

"Because he avoided the most important aspect of your childhood." Justine pulled a small mirror from her nightstand and gently daubed her fingers around her eyes.

"You're wrong. I was there, yeah?"

"So girls who are suspected of being at least mildly autistic are pulled from orphanages in Austria and moved to country estates? They are important enough to warrant house calls from language experts?" The pocket mirror was returned to the nightstand and Justine looked the same as she always did. "And these girls go on to live in East Finchley, where they are represented by one of the top barristers in London? Oh, yes, I looked into Lord Anson Davy. He is a man of considerable power at Ten Downing as well as Buckingham. Does that sound normal to you?"

Vienna blinked. "But that's how it happened."

"It's very Dickensian, don't you think?"

"Like Pip. I remember . . ." She trailed off.

"Then you remember that Pip's having a hidden benefactor wasn't all frosting. I'd love to see your family tree."

Was my childhood a lie? Unfamiliar pathways and shadow worlds never considered. Reasons and purposes lost in the white noise of physical reality.

Blood seeping across a bathroom floor.

"It can wait until we find out who is trying to kill you."

"Kill me?"

"Your boyfriend was in the bathroom because he was looking for your BlackBerry."

"The cops would have seen it. . . ." Justine paused. "Wait. I thought I might need to call a taxi."

"It wasn't there for the police to see."

"You can't know—"

"Where is your BlackBerry now?" *Why is she being so slow?*

Justine looked to the empty nightstand on her side of the bed. "In the bathroom."

"The focus of where he was. You told me he had gone to the sink, like he was brushing his teeth, yeah? But the killer thought he was stalling when there was nothing there."

"But there's nothing on my BlackBerry."

Vienna's laugh was tentative as always. "Then why have it?"

"It's useless. Most of my contracts have been canceled."

"Most?"

"I still have the Clay to Flesh series for Igor Czasky."

"What's that?"

"You saw some of it, when I was posing next to the manikin. Clay to Flesh has me next to a set of wooden models carved by Christian Bell. The manikins in historic dress and me in modern."

Christian Bell. There he was: *Gentlemen of Business, Volume One*, fifth edition, Royal Printers, London, 1889. There had been a copy in Grayfield's den. Pages 335 and 336. "The subject of our next portrait is Christian Bell. Mister Bell was born in Glasgow on September 3, 1837. His father, John Bell, born June 13, 1803, was employed most of his life at Dixon's Blazes, a large ironworks located . . ." Her voice trailed off.

"That's him," Justine said.

Vienna felt shame flushing her cheeks. *This is why she thinks I'm trapped inside myself.*

"Hey." Justine put her hand under Vienna's chin and lifted her head. "No pouting over life's quirks, okay? Besides, I like having a personal Wikipedia." She stood up and started for the bathroom. "Keep reading."

Vienna smiled, offended that Justine could make her do that when she didn't want to. "Okay." She read more of the entry to herself. Justine returned with a brush and sat behind Vienna. Vienna felt the soft tug of having her hair combed.

"Is my hair wrong?"

"No."

"Then why are you brushing it?"

"Because it needs it."

Vienna frowned, but Justine had no way of seeing.

"Please continue our history lesson."

Vienna constructed a scene where she turned around and told Justine that teasing was childish. Justine was sorry and she apologized and said she would never do it again. But Vienna knew Justine would never get her part right.

"Christian Bell carved ten life-sized female figures from tupelo." She paused, her thoughts arcing to other sources. "Elvis Presley was born in a place named Tupelo. It used to be called Gum Pond because . . ." Vienna let the thought go. The world was all connected and it was beautiful, but she could tell this wasn't what Justine wanted. "Bell couldn't get big enough blocks of wood for a complete figure, and so he used a series of pieces for each work. It's sort of appropriate, because tupelo is from the genus Nyssa, which means nymph." The brush stopped and Vienna saw an image of Justine silently laughing. She rushed ahead to a diagram she had seen in the hallways of the Cart House. Labeled in perfect block letters: MR. BELL'S LADY, which hadn't made any sense at all until now. "Each piece of tupelo was cut to be interlocking, like a huge puzzle box. The manikins are hollow." Vienna studied the diagram. "It's very clever," she said.

"You know more about it than I do. What else?"

"There was a fire in Bell's workshop. The oils he used for treating the wood were inflammable. Bell saved seven statues— amazing considering his age. They each weighed fifteen stone." She remembered that Americans never used stones and found a conversion table. "Over two hundred pounds. Returning for the eighth, he was overcome by fumes. He died in the fire, August 4, 1888."

Vienna went to another source—an obituary from one of Bell's descendants. It had been clipped and placed in *Gentlemen of Business, Volume One*. Who would have done that? "The remaining statues were kept in Bell's family for a generation. David Bell, Christian's eldest son, inherited them along with his father's considerable wealth." Vienna skipped ahead. "David was an anarchist—traveling to Budapest, which was a hotbed of radical thinking. He fell in love with a woman named Lina Zahler." Another line of words from an old history book. "Zahler was connected, through a man named Pozzio, to Luigi Lucheni, the man who killed Sisi, the Empress Elisabeth Amalie Eugenie . . ." She slapped at the bed in frustration and jumped back to the less interesting story. "Lina spurned Bell, and he returned home a broken man." She paused. "Broken?"

"Rejected by his true love. A much more serious condition than you have."

Vienna dismissed that. "He sold his father's statues to Harry Gordon Selfridge in 1910. Selfridge used them in his London department store to display clothes. After World War Two, the collection was auctioned at Christie's to collectors across Europe."

The brush stopped. "How much for one?"

"Between twenty and thirty thousand pounds."

"Not a huge amount, even in the fifties."

Vienna's lips kept moving as she read from an art collector's book. "All the statues had a woman's name stamped on the underside of their left feet. These names represented famous women connected to the great cities of Europe. The manikins ended up in private collections within their corresponding cities." Her eyes opened wider. "There is a Vienna."

"Is she broken, too?"

Vienna spoke without thinking, an odd phrase she heard back in London. "Who elected you high snarky bitch of parliament?"

Vienna was horrified but Justine was hugging her, laughing. "There you go," she said, as if that explained everything. A soft kiss on the back of Vienna's neck. "The Clay to Flesh project started in Budapest," Justine continued. "The manikin there was named Gisella—after an Austrian princess I think."

Vienna didn't know how to spell the name so she skipped over it. "What does any of this mean?" She turned to face Justine.

"My ex-boyfriend mentioned Budapest. He said he never wanted to go back." Justine set the brush on the bed. "I met David Andries two weeks after the project was announced. How long do you suppose he had been living under the name Grant Eriksson?"

"Do you think he knew about the manikins?"

"He knew art."

"But the manikins aren't worth that much," Vienna said.

"Everything goes back to them. Budapest to Paris to Rome to Prague to Brussels. I thought the statue in Prague moved between sessions. I joked about it and James flew out to see if I was okay. I understand that; he has millions tied up in me. But then Grant came to see me here in Brussels. I wonder if he knew about Prague."

"The statue moved?"

"It seemed different the second day; I couldn't say why. We looked at the pictures from both nights and they were the same."

"Do you still have the pictures?" Vienna asked.

"We can check the dailies folder in my portfolio."

"Do it now."

Justine laughed. "Yes, master." She moved to the desk and called up the Prague photos on her Sony. She selected two that showed the skipping manikin. "Here. The one on the left is from the first day, the right one from the second. They're the same."

Vienna clapped several times and laughed. "You're blind!" She skipped around Justine. "Blind, blind, blind."

"What?"

Vienna stopped and pointed at the images. "The one from the second day is smaller."

Justine squinted. "I don't think so—"

"Blind and stupid." She fell to the bed. "They aren't the same.

Your shape is the same both days, it fits within itself. The statues don't."

"How can you be certain?"

Vienna enunciated her words, as if speaking to a child. "I put the second one in the first one, and the first one overlaps all the way around. Just like your right breast is larger than your left."

"Well, there's more information than I bargained for. Maybe humidity caused the change? I mean in the manikin, not my breast."

"No. They are not the same statue."

"Vienna, they look—"

"Stop being stupid!" She realized she was shouting and that was wrong because the doctors told her shouting might hurt the person she was shouting at. She lowered her voice. "Any tosser can see they aren't the same. The left arm of the smaller one is lower by a centimeter. They. Are. Not. The. Same. Show me the others."

It took Justine thirty minutes to call up pictures for each statue, one from the initial setup and one from the following photoshoot. Vienna looked at each paired set of images.

She doesn't see it! "They all changed overnight."

Justine shook her head. "It makes no sense."

Delight in the discovery faded. There had to be a reason. A purpose that followed Justine from Budapest to Brussels. *It's here. It killed David Andries.*

She wanted to tell Justine but she didn't know how to explain and when she started talking all the wrong words came out, like they always did with Justine. "Why did you tell Lord Davy that love with me was like rain?"

Justine put her hand over Vienna's. "Where I come from, spring rain is like heaven."

"In London, rain is cold and tedious. And anyway, it's supposed to be private."

Justine answered so softly that Vienna barely heard. "He needed to know you are not so broken after all."

And then the words Vienna had meant to speak at first suddenly were there. "I'm scared and I don't know why."

"We'll be fine."

Vienna remembered her foster father in London saying, as clearly as if he had written it: *You must learn to know what people are hiding behind words.*

11

Their passports were returned by spit-and-polish representatives from the American and United Kingdom embassies. Justine tossed hers in her carry-on bag. With more resignation than anticipation, she called Adelina and rescheduled her London itinerary. Running home now would be one defeat too many. Or at least that made a good rationalization.

She reserved a seat for Vienna on British Air and made certain the girl was registered at the Savoy. Two beds, because that seemed prudent. Or prudish. The amount was too trivial to worry over even if Vienna decided to stay. Which seemed likely. The girl remained anchored to the bed, rocked side-to-side by undercurrents of eidetic memory.

Shepherding her through airport security would be a thrill.

Justine sat at the suite's table, searching for the kill switch to whatever machine was hell-bent on shredding her life. She could almost see whirring gears. The original Clay to Flesh proposal mentioned that the Budapest manikin had long ago been vandalized. Giselle's name scratched out and replaced with "Lina." A complete mystery according to the owner. But Vienna's stuttered history made David Bell the number one suspect, pining away for his anarchist girlfriend, Lina Zahler.

Vienna had also said Zahler was connected to the murder of someone named Sisi. The name was vaguely familiar, but Justine was too distracted to dredge up the memory. Google had it anyway. Elisabeth of Bavaria, Queen of Hungary and Empress of Austria, assassinated on September 10, 1898.

Headlines over a century old. There had to be something more relevant.

Three hours of paging through the BlackBerry failed to find it. A hundred names and numbers, useless now. A note from Simone Dyer, contracts attorney for Carrie Ltd. Justine opened it, expecting legal threats she had no way to fight.

> Heather:
>
> You are stronger for facing the cameras while I remain hidden. Not sure why there would be any questions about your new direction, but if there are, do not hesitate to call me, as a friend if nothing else.

Justine recalled meeting Simone at a party in Tribeca. The lawyer had the exotic allure of Mediterranean blood tempered with cold-weather genes—Scandinavian or Russian. Pretty and witty enough to draw a sizable crowd of male admirers. Apparently not what she wanted.

I know the feeling. Note Exhibit V, staring at the ceiling in a hyper-focused trance. Squeaking nonverbals and pounding the bed every fifteen minutes. Hair reverted to a fractal weave of tangles. *What the hell was I thinking last night?*

Love never used to be so complicated.

A moot point because here she was obsessing over Vienna again. Justine tried to rationalize the sexual pull as collateral damage from her career. Vienna didn't demand fireworks with every kiss and Justine had so often been victimized by such expectations. But that wasn't it.

She would do anything I asked. The exact warning Lord Davy had come to deliver—a truth as perilous as the sun setting. *And didn't you always know the scariest monsters came out after dark?* Was the damage already done?

Performances Justine had witnessed in L.A. and Bangkok made her session with Vienna look banal. Quiet exploration in a world where high velocity and higher risk had become the preferred mode of bedroom communication. Perhaps Vienna's innocence remained unscarred? But it was the most dangerous kind of lie; one that told the truth for all the wrong reasons.

Justine forced herself to refocus on the BlackBerry. Had Vienna been right in thinking Grant died looking for something here? Even as the thought came, Justine paged across her favorite picture of him. They were on a sailboat off a private island in the Caribbean. Sun-filled turquoise water so pure it was as if light itself provided buoyancy. A triangle of lemon yellow sail to the side; a contour of white sand behind them. A sleek GPS in Grant's left hand, and Justine snuggled in the arc of his right arm. Grant hadn't known a thing about sailing, but his Greek sailor's cap and tanned chest worked well enough for Justine. He'd titled the picture before sending it to her. "My wonderful mermaid, captured at N48º 14'079; E 16º 15'031." God, he was beautiful.

Justine turned the BlackBerry off. If Grant pretended to be nice to her, didn't that mean, in a way, that he really was nice to her? She missed him after all. His easy confidence. Never angry or upset. It would be so perfect now.

As compared to Vienna, who hadn't said a recognizable word in hours. Misery: the world's oldest sexually transmitted disease.

Fed up with the day, Justine went to the foot of the bed. "Vienna, come here." The girl obeyed without objection, sitting cross-legged. "Tell me what's wrong."

Vienna shrank down. "Something happened and I can't remember but it's important and I don't know what to do because you'll think it's stupid."

Justine wound her way through the words. "Happened when?"

"A long time ago but it has to do with what David Andries said."

The use of Grant's real name was still a shock. "What did he say?"

"Inalienable artifacts."

"And?" Irritation at being swept up in the girl's wandering thoughts.

"The words aren't right."

"But they're connected to you?"

"Not to me." Vienna exhaled and stiffened her back. "There's this villa next to a lake, yeah? Three stories of gray limestone." Her hands framed large blocks. "The ground floor was rusticated, like Raphael's House except much larger." Her arms spread wide. "Palladian style with attached wings and jade moss spreading in the shade. Tiny white flowers." A breath of silence. "Piano nobile." Whatever that was, it triggered the ghost smile. "There used to be a room just for me that overlooked the courtyard fountain and formal gardens. The kitchen and medicinal gardens were off the south wing so I couldn't see them so well."

Suddenly conscious of her hands, Vienna hid them under her legs. "Fenugreek," she said.

"Vienna?"

A sharp intake of breath. "Uncle Anson took me there several times when I was younger. He said it had once served as a summer house for the Habsburgs and he said I should call it the Cart House because above the door there is an engraving of a Germanic goddess riding a cart."

"Not what I picture as divine transport," Justine said.

Vienna's gaze slipped away. "It's a very nice cart, pulled by four oxen. Nerthus returning to her lake, surrounded by maidens." This was cause for a frown. "Days of celebration and happiness." Tears turning her eyes glassy.

"Hey, it's okay." Justine put her hand on Vienna's knee. A quiet gesture that had somehow eluded Justine back in med school.

It was enough to reset the girl's thoughts. Vienna pushed on. "There's a chapel in the north wing, with a huge telly. Men watch football matches and even bet on them, so maybe it isn't a real chapel anymore. It has seventeen huge windows with red and blue glass. Ruby glass used to be made with gold. . . ." Vienna gave a soft, toneless hum, already a recognizable sign of attention wandering away. "Johann Kunckel." She sighed. "There are glass-covered bookcases with lots of books in English, but some very

old, with the spelling wrong, yeah? 'Bleffing' instead of 'Blessing.'
I saw . . ." She cut the words off.

"Keep going."

Vienna's jaw clinched. "A unicorn."

Justine realized it was the perfect setup for a cherished family
joke, honed over years of visiting her grandfather's ranch. Every
project, from clearing snow to erecting a barn, seemed to call for
an eight-ton capacity loader. The claim had morphed into a
maxim for dealing with unwanted realities.

*I'm having an affair with a girl who thinks unicorns had some-
thing to do with a murder.* Gonna need an eight-ton capacity loader
for that.

"Unicorn?"

"And a plate, and a star," Vienna said.

"These things are related to what Grant said?"

"I can't remember!"

"Well, we know it was something you heard and not something
you read."

Vienna brightened. "That's true."

"But it fails to account for why you set up camp as far away
from me as possible."

Vienna inhaled and let out a rush of words. "If you see too
much of me you'll get bored because my body is stupid and sick
and you'll leave."

Predictable, which didn't help. "Strip down, and we'll time
how long until boredom sets in."

Vienna looked at the bedside clock and her hands went to the
top button of her blouse.

Justine winced and took hold of her fingers. "Vienna, with you
avoiding me, I thought you no longer wanted to be with me."

Vienna shook her head once and pitched herself forward in an
awkward hug—arms held stiffly behind Justine. "You know that
isn't right!"

Justine was left queasy at the effortless manipulation. Vienna
shifted closer and Justine understood her want, probably better

than she did. *Not now.* She disentangled herself. *Maybe not ever again.*

"Business before pleasure."

Vienna's gaze lowered.

"Don't give me that. You're the one who got me thinking I might be in trouble. Time to find out."

"How?"

"By being a pain in the ass." Justine pulled her BlackBerry from the table. She navigated past Igor Czasky's secretary in record time.

"Mr. Czasky? . . . Fine, all things considered . . . yes . . . she's with me now . . . no, no, nothing like that. Given recent events, I don't feel it would be right to hold you to our contract for the Clay to Flesh series. . . . I appreciate that, Mr. Czasky, but I'm not certain I can face work, with the death of Grant . . . I see . . . No, that won't be necessary. . . . well, then I accept. Thank you . . . yes . . . good-bye."

Justine turned the phone off. "How unsettling was that?" she said to Vienna. Vienna's face went blank, and Justine couldn't help smiling. "You're cute when you're lost. Free of the world's worries. I like that."

"You're making fun of me."

"Do you know why?"

"No. It's mean."

"It's something you have to discover for yourself." She set the BlackBerry down. "Czasky added a huge bonus for staying on. What do you make of that?"

"He's nice?"

"Not in this business."

Vienna swirled a lock of hair in her fingers, adding another layer of tangles. "The manikins are in private collections, yeah? Getting permission to shoot them must have been hard."

"Agreed."

"If there's a tight schedule, bringing in a new model might ruin that?"

"Every girl strutting every catwalk under the sun would be on a plane inside thirty minutes for a payday like this. Something else."

"Maybe it's important that you and no one else keeps the schedule?" Vienna asked.

"That's what I was afraid of."

"Then why are the manikins being replaced?"

"We aren't certain they are."

"Don't be thick. Someone made a mold of the statues, using sand since that would produce a smaller replica. Then maybe a polyvinyl chloride polymer with kaolin clay and—" She paused. "Kaolin means 'high hill.'" She blushed and added a slight shrug. "Get the chemistry right, paint it like the original, and the texture would pass for polished wood. The mass would be off though."

"I don't buy it. How long would it take to make a duplicate? A week? A month?"

"Wrong, wrong, wrong. You don't know anything. Polymers set within two hours. The rest would be finishing work. Maybe three days if you worked really hard."

"That's a day less than the project requires for each manikin. Clothes need to be fit and crates need to be constructed for carrying everything to location." Justine shook her head. "But still pointless. There isn't any money in it."

"Then for another reason. How many are left to photograph?"

"London, Reykjavík, and your namesake."

"They haven't found what they are after, or else they wouldn't be in such a hurry to keep going."

"They?"

"Czasky and whoever else is interested in your work," Vienna answered.

Justine folded her arms in front of her. "Including you?" Vienna shook her head, a cold front gathering in her eyes. Justine pushed harder. "In fact, you top the suspect list."

"Stop it!"

Just can't help yourself, can you? "Might have to search you."

Vienna froze. Vanishing inside herself, trying so hard to think her way through such transparent innuendo. "Okay?" was all she finally said. Far too shaky for what had already happened.

"For now, we need to—"

There was a solid knock on the door. Justine unfolded herself from the bed. She glanced through the peephole and opened the door in surprise. James Hargrave. *Vienna's right. He does look like a cowboy.*

He held out his hand. "James Hargrave, Hargrave International Talent."

Justine hesitantly shook his hand. The black face of his watch caught the light, the small travel chronometer already set one hour behind for tomorrow's trip to London. Hargrave S.O.P. to make certain he set his watch to local time after travel.

"I would say I'm a sucker for hard-luck cases, but the truth is that as a skilled parasite I still sense money." He tilted his head as if appraising art. "Besides, I've grown fond of you and all your thorns. I would like to come back."

"There isn't much left to represent."

"Enough to rebuild. You're still the best there is. I couldn't bring myself to do anything other than delete all the crap I sent you."

Justine looked at Vienna. But she was gone, wrapped inside herself as she rocked gently on the bed. Her gaze as distant as Elvis back in Tupelo.

12

London

Out of the jet fuel chaos of Heathrow and on the Tube. Mind the gap. When the rails were above ground, Vienna saw blue sky flash through fences. She'd expected cold fog, so now her steel-colored culottes and dark top were too warm. They were pretty though. One of twelve tailored outfits that had followed her here, carried on a cushion of Justine Am's wealth.

From the Charing Cross Station on foot to the Savoy. The Thames beside them as dark and primal as Gihon flowing from the Garden. Vienna saw words from an American named Emily Dickinson. *Eden is that old-fashioned house we dwell in every day; Without suspecting our abode, until we drive away.*

"Why didn't you take the car with Mr. Hargrave and our luggage?" she asked. She didn't feel like walking through the ghosts of London. The home she had before Grayfield forced her out.

"It's too nice to be in a car."

"But you're filthy."

"Filthy?"

"Rich."

"To paraphrase you, rich people can do whatever they want and there's not much you can do about it."

"That's completely off the tracks."

"Said the broken girl."

Vienna went silent.

"Anyway, I don't like taxis here. Something you'd drive over the end credits of classic film noir. Cagney behind the wheel and a blonde stuffed in the trunk." She smiled. "Boot, before you ask."

Vienna had no idea what that was supposed to mean. Before she could make anything up, she heard footsteps from behind.

"You owe me a Nikkor 17-to-55 stabilized zoom."

Vienna turned and saw the long-haired photographer from the Brussels gelato shop.

"You owe me for sucking air that actual humans might use," Justine said.

"If that's the best you have, keep your day job." His eyes were pinched like he was looking at the sun, and his voice was quiet. The tattoo on his forearm ugly and mean as a scab.

"Why are you following us?" Vienna asked.

The man shook his head, stringy hair brushing across his forehead. "Something going down here. It'll play out big."

Justine exhaled through her teeth. "You know, after Di's death, they don't much like your kind in London."

"Don't be so precious. Without my kind, your kind wouldn't exist."

"Newsflash, asshole: I don't care. Go spawn in someone else's slime trail."

"Harsh words from someone who used to be a pressroom darling. Why the vitriol?"

Justine glanced at Vienna.

"So it's true. You've fallen for the wind-up toy? Beauty and the bizarre. You want a medal? I couldn't care less who you sleep with."

"Then what do you want?"

"I want to know why David Andries is dead."

"So would the police. Ask them."

"They gave me the usual runaround, but the truth is they have no idea."

"So shoot yourself and ask him in person."

"I would rather find answers from this side of the grave."

"And have you?" Vienna asked.

He turned to face her. "Your coworker, Cecile Doren, identified David Andries from a set of photos I showed her."

Why would Cecile know him? "What else?"

"David Andries's father had several friends within the Order of the Golden Fleece. There was a time when he was very well connected."

"Was?"

"Ostracized several years ago. David was deeply bitter over his father's disgrace."

"Get him a shrink," Justine said.

"Justine, please," Vienna said. "Why was David's father driven out?"

"Have you heard of the Star of Memphis?"

Vienna followed the words. "No."

"A shame. It's an interesting story."

"What does it have to do with David Andries?"

The man's greasy smile returned. "What can you offer for my hard-won knowledge? It didn't come cheap."

"Vienna, you can't deal with this pig."

"You can't stop me. Tell me what you know."

The photographer gave a mock bow. "We'll settle later."

"With what," Justine demanded.

"Exclusive with Vienna. My choice of venue."

"No deal," Justine said.

"If what you say helps us, I agree," Vienna quickly said.

"Good. You're staying at the Savoy?"

Vienna looked at Justine. "We are," she said.

"Then we'll meet at the American Bar at five o'clock?"

"You haven't given us a reason," Justine said.

"That's for Vienna to decide."

Justine turned to her. "I don't want you doing this, okay?"

Vienna thought that was stupid, but people were already looking their way. Not that Justine would care. She would keep arguing until her feet took root and drained the Thames. "Okay."

Justine's smile was tight-lipped. "Game over."

The man rubbed his thumbs across his fingertips. "Did you know Andries was in Scotland before he came out to see you? His destination appeared to be Glasgow, but he went to a place named Dumfries, not far from Lockerbie." He put his hand into a nose-dive. "My source in Glasgow suspects David had a bonnie lass stashed away, but I don't buy it."

"Why not? He lied about everything else."

"Because there was no percentage in it, and Andries never did anything unless he had an angle. You've heard rumors connecting him to the murder of a German art dealer?"

"Never proven," Justine said.

Why would she defend him?

"All the same, I looked for artists in Dumfries. Came across a gent by the name of Julian Dardonelle—clearly not from a local family. I gave him a call." Small teeth flashed. "He wasn't home. The day after David Andries was shot, Julian washed out of the Schelde."

Vienna tracked the name down. "The river that flows through Antwerp."

"The same." The photographer spread his arms wide. "The police have no reason to connect the two deaths."

Justine closed her eyes. "Meaning?"

He shook his head. "Five o'clock, American Bar."

"If we aren't there by five-oh-one, we aren't coming."

The man nodded. "Till then." He turned away.

"Wait," Vienna said. "What's your name?"

The man gave her a puzzled look, as if he hadn't expected to be asked. "Gary Sinoro."

Another two blocks and they were inside the art deco Savoy; up to a top-floor suite. Leather chairs and two queen-sized beds guarded by a squad of mahogany posts. Vienna looked down at the Thames. Lord Davy would be somewhere in the city. As well as Arthur Grayfield, his smile warm and comforting. Just another lie.

Vienna found nothing better to do than fidget while Justine inspected her wardrobe. *The most expensive dress in the world is thought to be the diamond-laden spider web worn by Samantha Mumba at the premiere of . . .* Boring.

After series of calls from her BlackBerry, Justine spent thirty minutes in the adjacent room talking with Hargrave. When she returned she went to her closet. "What is it, Vienna?"

"Does there have to be anything?"

"Yes."

"We have to see Mr. Sinoro."

Justine sighed. "We are, after all, professionals."

Vienna felt the sticky irritation that crawled through every conversation with Justine. "What does that mean?"

"All that reading and no Hunter S. Thompson?" Justine gathered her workout clothes.

"I don't know what you're on about."

"It's impossible to understand Americans unless you read Hunter S. Thompson. He was our inner rage and our finest muse." She started changing clothes. "I have a Kindle here. . . ." She dug into one of her bags and handed the e-reader to Vienna. "*Fear and Loathing in Las Vegas.*"

"Does this mean we'll meet Sinoro?"

"It does." Which was unfair because Vienna had practiced several arguments and now she didn't need them.

She turned her attention to the e-book and paged through the contents. *Fear and Loathing in Las Vegas.* What a stupid title. She read the introduction and saw that Hunter S. Thompson committed suicide by shooting himself. Which was as American as you could get.

"I have to do my Pilates, be back in ninety minutes. And Vienna? Don't leave the room."

"Okay."

Vienna began reading, impatient with how slowly the machine turned pages. It started sort of funny, in that way that never made you really laugh, but then it got mean. And then terrifying. But it couldn't be true, could it? It was just a stupid story. Vienna was using the Sony to search for the definition of "sunshine blotter" when Justine returned. "What did you think of the book?"

Vienna gave the rehearsed answer. "Strange."

That made Justine laugh. "Not as strange as reality. But I see you have other concerns."

Vienna closed the laptop. "What do we do now?"

"Preliminary Clay to Flesh session tomorrow at the Eye." Justine started stripping down as she talked. *She's comfortable being naked in front of me.* So? She was comfortable being naked in front of everyone. Vienna didn't want to think about that.

"Will Mr. Hargrave be there?"

"He's more of a behind-the-scenes operator."

"Do you think he's involved in replacing the statues?"

"He's making a great deal of money representing me. It's in his best interest that this goes smoothly. And despite his joking, I think he does care for me."

"You should refuse to do any more."

"Why so jumpy?" Justine was nude, letting her hair down. Vienna thought the sheen of sweat was pretty, but Americans were fussy about such things. *She would be upset to know what I am thinking.* Best not to look.

Vienna turned away, shifting into uneasy suspicion. Maybe Justine Am didn't care if people saw her naked because Justine Am wasn't real. "Prosopon," she whispered. A mask.

"Vienna?"

Vienna dragged herself back to Justine's question. "Sinoro mentioned the Order of the Golden Fleece. They include the ruling monarchs of Europe and a good portion of Asia."

"That's more than mildly alarming."

Why were Americans so ignorant? "The Order of the Golden Fleece is an honorary title started in 1430 by Philip the Good." Vienna saw that Philip captured Joan of Arc and that her fate had been sealed years before with the assassination of John the Fearless by the Dauphin. "Dauphin the dolphin," Vienna whispered. But dolphins didn't matter because Justine was looking at her, and she didn't look angry or impatient like everyone else did. Vienna felt herself blushing, which was thick as two short planks, so she went on with what she'd been trying to say. "You can look up every living member online. It's a trinket rich people get to add to their names. It's not like they all get together in a secret lair and don black robes and decide how to run the world."

"Perhaps I've seen too many James Bond movies."

"A complete tosser. Besides, we were told that Andries's father was associated with the order, not that he was a member himself. There are numerous ancillary organizations."

"Filled with wealthy individuals?"

"I assume so."

"Paranoia aside, powerful people rarely get that way by mistake. They see a different world than we do." Justine walked to the bathroom, talking over her shoulder. "Still, it's worth remembering that Sinoro's idea of a solid source is the nearest gossip blog." She paused. "Vienna? Why did you turn away?"

"I didn't want you to be embarrassed."

Justine stopped moving. *What is she thinking, behind the mask?* "I have to shower," Justine said. Which told Vienna nothing. "Then we'll see what Sinoro has."

By the time they left the suite, Vienna felt the greasy anxiety of Thompson's book leaching through her. *We are, after all, professionals.*

The oversized leather chairs of the American Bar threatened to swallow her. Justine had some trick that kept her afloat. They waited three hours, but the photographer failed to show.

"Typical," Justine said. "Bedtime. Tomorrow will be a busy day."

13

Justine thought Boadicea was an odd name for the London manikin. Hadn't the Warrior Queen burned the place to the ground?
Or had that been the Romans? Vienna would know the story,
footnotes and all. Better not ask with anything under fifteen
minutes to spare.

The statue had a round face and dark bourbon eyes under a
Japanese hime cut. Hardly expected coiffure for a barbarian, and
the one-off eye color meant contacts for Justine. Early on, some
genius from Czasky's publisher thought it would be clever if
Justine's eyes matched the manikins'. An obscure meta-statement
on reality versus image that would be exploited by intellectuals
as an excuse to buy the book. Heaven forbid the real reason ever
be mentioned.

Boadicea had been one of the more difficult shoots to arrange.
The statue was on loan from Franklin Court, a livestock magnate
who kept the manikin in storage near his Mayfair flat. He had
little tolerance for fashion or photography but greed was always
in style. Czasky flashed enough money to free Boadicea during
one of Franklin's many vacations to the Canaries.

Now there's a man with a Spanish lover stashed away.

After the shoot, the manikin would vanish back into storage.

The London Clay to Flesh photographer was George Holt, a
young gun Justine had worked with once in Italy. Despite his age,
he'd racked up the hottest portfolio in the business. He'd even
obtained his own measure of celebrity after a 4chan hacker released dozens of pirated images from his unpublished early work.
The Internet's hive mind appended a wistful soundtrack and the
pictures went viral.

Tall and on the lean side of athletic, Holt let his brown hair run free range, flopping down over his eyes. His face was so smooth Justine figured he had a doll's chance of growing a beard. His dazzling talent was punctured by almost crippling shyness. He worked like a fire dancer, always at the edge of his subject.

"I would like to have the ascending portion of the Millennium Wheel serve as the background for the initial medium shots, if that is okay, Miss Am. I see the concept of ascension as crucial to the premise." Holt bit his lip as if he were asking her on a date. The last soul in the business not jaded by beauty. Justine wondered if that's what made him so good.

"It's fine, George." She liked working with him.

Holt nodded. "Good. We need the manikin in the foreground on a narrow focal plane, maybe even fake a tilt-shift in post, and you medium distance in soft focus. Then we'll progressively reverse the field in keeping with the theme of life from the inanimate. We can start with darker wardrobe to contrast the sky."

George took few photographs but gave copious notes to his younger sister, Emily, who served as assistant and business manager. Emily's dishwater blond hair was held in a high tail by a twenty-cent band of blue elastic. Razor thin arcs for eyebrows and a dusting of light base on her cheeks. Melanin deficiency had left her eyes pale blue; stunning hand-me-downs from Slavic ancestors charging across windswept tundra. Wasted on a tomboy who didn't know what to do with her angular beauty.

She helped Justine with wardrobe, though they were only testing a few pieces before the next day's full shoot. "So, what's it like beating around the bushes?" she asked.

"More difficult than pole dancing," Justine answered.

"I can imagine. What's she like?"

"Spookier than moonlight shadows in the woods."

"Yeah? How did she set her hooks in you?"

"She doesn't believe in any of this." Justine waved at the clothes. "It reminds me there is more to life."

"A little young for philosophy, aren't you?"

"Young is a relative term in the biz."

"Point taken." Emily paused behind a questioning look.

"Yes?" Justine asked.

"One of us has changed since Milan. You said all the right things back then, which was boring as hell. Now here you are, performing this agonizing, slow-motion implosion, in full sight of the public no less. It's wonderfully cathartic. I like it and I want to meet the girl who caused it."

"I'll bring her tomorrow. She needs to get out more."

"Does she really have . . . you know . . ." Emily tapped her temple.

"You just say what's on your mind, don't you?"

"George never will, so I have to."

Justine smiled. "She isn't what I would call normal—whatever that means. You'll have to see for yourself. You have to do me a favor in return."

"Yes?"

"I want pictures of the manikin from every angle. I need them today."

"Why?"

"That's not part of the deal."

"A mystery then? I love mysteries."

"If you solve Vienna, tell me. She makes me want to scream ten times a minute."

Holt had the shooting schedule blocked out by mid-afternoon. Justine prepared to leave as Emily was convincing her brother to take pictures of the manikin. Justine turned to her. "Do you know a photographer named Sinoro?"

Emily was silent while she thought it over. "Don't think so. Why?"

"Another mystery," Justine said. "See you tomorrow."

Back in the suite, Vienna sat on the bed, wrapped around herself. She insisted they eat at the Savoy. "Mr. Sinoro still might show up."

Justine gave in, escorting her to the American Bar. "What did you do with the day?"

"I used your laptop. Mr. Sinoro was right about David Andries's father. Jorgan Andries was an architect working out of Oslo. He liked Byzantine design." Justine caught the familiar delay of derailed thought. "Squinches," Vienna said. A shift of her eyes and the original discourse resumed. "I think he was a distant relation to the northern branch of the Habsburgs, but no one online is certain. He was a member of the Order of Rahab."

"Rahab?"

"Her house backed the great wall of Jericho." Vienna rocked forward. " 'Your terror is fallen upon us, and all the inhabitants of the land faint because of you.' "

Justine gave what she hoped was an encouraging smile. "Never heard of knights called that."

"One of ninety-three recognized orders of knighthood in Europe. They became allied with the Order of the Golden Fleece in 1728 when . . ." Vienna's voice trailed off. "Anyway, modern members tend to be wealthy. I couldn't find much about them."

"Why was Jorgan Andries booted?"

"His son David was involved in a scandal. There were accusations of stealing books from an estate near Groisbach. I couldn't find anything about that either." Vienna turned away. "Why did you ever date such a chav?"

"Assuming a chav is a bad thing, my only defense is that he smelled good and had perfect teeth."

Vienna shrugged. "I tried to find more about the Star of Memphis, but I either got Tennessee or the ancient capital of Upper Egypt." She sat up schoolmarm straight. "The Greek translation of the ancient name for Memphis is what gave us the name 'Egypt.' "

Justine smiled at how this scrap of trivia brightened Vienna's face. "Anything else?"

"No."

"Thank you for looking, but that's enough computer time. I want you to come with me tomorrow. I need help with wardrobe changes."

Panic sifted through the girl's features. "I don't know anything about that, and you have someone there who can help, don't you?"

"A girl named Emily."

"Get her to do it!"

So much for jealousy as motivation. "I would be more comfortable with you."

Vienna spun a 180 without missing a breath. "I'll help, if you want."

Justine's BlackBerry cut in with the Talking Heads. Holt's number came up. Justine remembered her frustration with Grant taking calls. "It's from my photographer. Do you mind if I take it? Or should I wait?"

Vienna looked as if the fate of the world hung on the decision. "It might be important."

She nodded. "Hey, George," she said into the BlackBerry.

"It's Emily. I sent the manikin pics."

"Thanks."

"One more thing."

"Yes?"

"You mentioned a paparazzi goon named Sinoro. Gary Sinoro?"

"Yeah."

"He wasn't a friend, was he?"

"Hardly—wait, what do you mean?"

"He made the BBC. His corpse got hung up on the Surrey Docks last night. Details have just been released. He was shot in the left temple. Small caliber gun."

No protection in his thug-life tattoo or triangle ear studs. "I didn't really know him," was all Justine could think to say. She hung up after a quick good-bye.

"What was that about?"

"We can talk later, in our room."

Justine felt a familiar weariness by the time they were back in the suite. It still amazed her how much energy a session took. *Self-pity is the crutch of failure.* Advice from her first manager. He'd been great until he fired up his Porsche in his Santa Barbara garage and asphyxiated on his lifestyle.

"We have to talk," she said to Vienna. The girl nodded and stepped to the bed farthest from the window, sitting Indian-style on its foot. Justine sat next to her.

"Sinoro was shot last night. His body was dumped in the Thames."

If Vienna felt any remorse, she didn't show it. "Do you think it's a coincidence?"

"No."

"I was worried you would be gasping for explanations, yeah?"

"What do you make of it?"

Vienna looked down. "I'm not a detective—I don't know about causes of death or what might be learned from a body that has been under water for a day."

"That's extraordinarily unhelpful."

"I'm sorry, Miss Perfect."

Justine clinched her jaw. "Let it go. We should take it to the police."

"And tell them what exactly? Don't be daffy."

"They might be able to make something of it."

"Stupid times ten." Vienna was almost screaming. "The police would make reports, and those would get passed into the hands of people with real power and they would know we've become suspicious and our bodies would be the next ones rotting in the Thames."

"Vienna, the real world doesn't work that way."

"Don't patronize me," Vienna snapped. "It has always worked that way. Do you need proof? Operation Kratos and the slaying of Jean Charles de Menezes in London. The police did him right in and tried to cover it up. And the Redfern Riots—"

"Vienna, shhh. It's okay." Justine realized the girl was terrified, her memory doubtless filled with numerous examples of lethal force employed by those in power. "We can't sit and do nothing."

"Yes, we can. You're not the true target or you would be dead. It's not you."

"The manikins," Justine said.

"I already told you but you never listen."

Justine swallowed an angry reply. "And when the photo shoot is over? When they suspect we might know something? What happens then? They let us go?"

Vienna shook her head. "I don't know. . . ."

"Now who's being disingenuous?"

Vienna slapped at the bed. "Why do you keep asking me? It's not fair." The girl sped through the words. "I don't see that you have any ideas. I'm doing all the work and all you do is smile for a camera."

Justine felt the muscles in her chest go tight. "Like your sorry ass is in a position to judge me." That was just for starters—the opening shot in a host of responses carefully locked away. Every drop of poison she'd collected in the California sunshine.

Vienna was oblivious, wrapped in her own anger. "I don't care and it's true anyway."

Damn you!

"Anyone could do it," Vienna added.

Justine closed her eyes, searched for anything to hold the words back. Heard her brothers laughing, out in the woods behind the house. Shaking cans of cheap pop and hitting them with hollow points loaded into Granddad's old rifle. It happened impossibly fast. The can was there, sweating in the Georgia summer, and then there was nothing but aluminum confetti pushing through a fog of orange soda. Her turn. Father's hand on her shoulder. "Don't anticipate the shot. Partial exhale, straight back on the trigger." And the can was gone.

Justine let the images distract her. Partial exhale. She found her bedside manner. "Vienna, it's okay. We have time to think this through. We can panic later."

"How can you joke?"

"Coping mechanism from med school."

"It's stupid."

"If things get bad, I can always bail out." It worked well enough back in California.

"That won't stop what's happening."

"Maybe." Temper slipping away again. Talk about something else. "I had Emily take pictures of the London statue. Do you want to see them?"

Vienna was silent, staring blankly ahead.

"Vienna?"

"Do you know a man in a plaid shirt?"

"What?"

"I didn't see him very well. His shirt was a long tunnel of surface area and hypercubes."

"What are you talking about?"

"In Brussels. A man in a plaid shirt spoke to me after you left. He said to forget about what happened in Prague. I thought he was a rejected lover."

"Prague?"

"Where you first noticed the manikins changing, yeah? Sinoro had a picture of you in front of the museum there."

"Why didn't you tell me? What did this man look like?"

"I couldn't look at him; his shirt wouldn't let me!"

Justine saw the girl was on the ragged edge of tears. *I'll always be in retreat with her.* "It's okay. It might make sense later."

"I'm no good at all, just useless. I don't understand anything that's happening." The tears came. "No wonder you hate me, just like everyone else does. Bog off! Leave me alone."

Justine felt her fingers clinch. The nightmare of Felton Gables all over again. "Forget it. Let's get some sleep."

"I want this bed to myself. Go away."

And there was the grand sum of Saturday night in London. The most exciting Saturday night Vienna would ever know. The most exciting Saturday night Justine could hope for as long as she stayed with the girl. From fashion model to babysitter in one step.

Off to bed, but not sleep.

All you do is smile for the camera.

Justine closed her eyes and saw Georgia sunlight passing through window sheers. Her mother sipping chai and working on lesson plans. A Ph.D. in literature from Stanford and she was teaching second grade in a nowhere school outside of Athens. Finger paint portraits and a pastel alphabet strung over the chalkboard. Such an unexpected door for shame to walk through.

Upstairs, tucked away in the hall closet, the brittle glue in Dad's college scrapbook slowly letting go of the past. Every picture and every article crowning John Ingles as the best young player in America. Maybe in the world. He'd toss the ball high and his racket would whip around and he would dance like a fencer. Another match point for John Ingles.

There had to be times, late at night, ice in a pool of Scotch, when he railed at what had become of him. Sunday afternoon tee times and shooting pop cans with his kids. He'd amassed a fortune since his fall, but what was that next to what had been lost? Even his children deserted him. Jeff off to Michigan for a degree in marine engineering. Scott gone a year later, headed to Annapolis. All those lazy days spent tinkering with the boat, magically transformed into smooth confidence.

Eighteen months after Scott left, Heather was bound for Stanford. Two years ahead of schedule. Nothing but blue sky. And when it came crashing down, it wasn't just the children at Felton Gables. It was the drunk shivering in the ICU. The stoic child with the lethal blotch on her sagittal MRI. The laughing grandfather with the separated shoulder. An endless succession of story problems.

Justine's own condition was easily identified, unforeseen, and terminal to her career. Outside of a textbook, she didn't want to see abscessed toenails or middle-aged men with the clap. There was nothing deep or mysterious about it. She hated every second of it. Late in her third year she compressed the entirety of her misery into a single thought: I could always run away to some shithole town and teach second grade.

Halfway across the world and still losing sleep over it. Justine heard Vienna get up and walk to the table. Saw the blue glow of the computer screen. Closed her eyes.

The final act had been brilliant. Returning home for Christmas and helping Mom clean out the hallway closet. Dad's scrapbook sitting on top of three manuscript boxes. Each box stuffed with cards and printed e-mails from kids Abigail Ingles had taught over the years. "I had to tell you how much I appreciate everything you did for us." Lawyers and truck drivers and programmers. "You had a huge influence on my life." Page after page.

Justine had three days of contemplating how petty her world had become before it was back to Stanford for the spring semester. That didn't pan out either. Prior to Christmas, she'd done a local-access commercial for a friend's secondhand furniture store. A rep from a Frisco talent agency happened to see it while flipping through channels. He'd been waiting at her apartment. The money wasn't great at the start, but it beat working on the latest case of fecal vomiting. Justine left school three weeks later. Headed for the top after all.

All you do is smile at the camera.

And the only person with the guts to call her bluff was too messed up to see the nerve she'd hit. Because it wasn't as if Justine could win a tennis match, or design a ship, or inspire anyone enough to write back fifteen years later.

The soft tap of Vienna's fingers on the keyboard.

A week before Justine quit med school she asked her father if he was bitter.

"For a time I was," he answered. "But 'if only' gets boring mighty fast."

"But you might have reached number one," Justine said.

John laughed. "Tell me, who won Wimbledon in, say, 1991? It wasn't that long ago."

"I don't know."

"How about the Australian Open five years ago?"

Justine was silent.

"When is my birthday?" John asked.

"August third."

"See? I have all the fame I can handle."

And the funny part? The perfect ending to the whole mess? There was every chance that the befuddled girl sitting a few feet away knew exactly who won Wimbledon in 1991.

Justine drifted off, only to wake two hours later. Vienna was still sitting at the suite's table, staring into the Sony. She was reading from memory, her lips moving. Justine walked to her, arms crossed as a tight shield in front of her chest.

At first Justine couldn't decipher the screen. Then she realized it was one of Emily's pictures. George had tilted the manikin while Emily had taken a picture of the bottom. The soles of the statue's feet almost filled the picture. The word "Boadicea" was stamped on the left foot.

Justine thought Emily had been too literal in carrying out the favor. Then she saw what Vienna was staring at. Three symbols had been carved on the inside of the arch of the manikin's right foot. A seven-pointed star, the concentric circles of a plate, and a unicorn head topped by a glorious horn.

Justine swallowed. "Vienna?"

The girl's voice rose from silence. ". . . . and he searcheth after every green thing. Will the unicorn be willing to serve thee, or abide by thy crib? Canst thou bind the unicorn with his band to the furrow?"

The girl was dredging up every passage she'd ever read about unicorns. No room for anything else. Nothing beyond the wretched ghost in Brussels. The endless white floor. Justine kept her distance.

"Vienna!"

She turned to face Justine, but kept reading. Her gummy eyes bloodshot.

The week came crashing down. *I already did my time!* Anger shot through jagged nerves. Lord Davy was right. This wasn't what she wanted. It was senseless to go on pretending it was.

Fuck the moving manikins and the sleazy photographers and the mentally ill girl sitting in front of her.

Whatever love was left would never overcome this. She looked at it for what it was: pretense to cover a suddenly lonely life and a shattered career.

Skip the dénouement and roll the credits.

14

It felt like good-bye—like hollow rage. Justine was leaving. Vienna knew it in the way the American avoided her look. In the way she sat at the table, silently waiting for their breakfast of melon and eggs. In the way her lips were tight and her face held nothing except tiredness.

Vienna wouldn't have noticed a week ago. She cursed Justine for giving her new awareness. She wanted to scream, but it was safer to seal her heart in ice. She would face isolation as she always had. There was nothing new here.

Breakfast was served, Justine pushing the food across her plate without eating. She finally slid her fork down to the table.

"Vienna . . ."

"Bog off."

"I never meant—"

"Bog off."

Justine nodded. "Will you be okay? I can give you some money."

"I don't want your bloody charity."

"I understand. I'm going to call Holt and cancel the shoot. I'm firing James and going back to the states. Getting away from all this."

"Okay."

Justine drew a sharp breath, but kept her voice low. "I've paid for the hotel suite for six weeks. That should give you time to get back on your feet. I know Lord Davy will help you. Sell some of the stuff we got together if you need to. It will bring good money. More than you would have made working for a year."

See what happens when you tire of playing dress-up with your dolls? "Okay."

"I can't stand long good-byes. I want you to know that you're not broken at all." An obvious lie or she wouldn't be leaving. And why ever hope Justine would be different from anyone else anyway? Justine gave a mimed kiss because who would give a real kiss to someone who was sick. She stood from the table. Walked away.

There were words for this, too, of course. From Ovid long ago to Circe: *Love settled deep in your unwilling heart. You could change men into a thousand shapes, you could not change the commands of your heart.* Vienna realized the words were not written in sorrow, but in numb, powerless rage. To be tricked by desire is to forget that desire meant nothing at all. She sat alone until the wait staff asked her to leave so they could make preparations for lunch.

She walked to the Millennium Bridge, standing to the side as tourists flowed behind her.

In 1996, the Financial Times announced a competition to design a pedestrian bridge to span the Thames . . .

The river's oily current flowed below her, devouring sunlight. *And this also has been one of the dark places of the earth.* She knew the words were from *Heart of Darkness,* and she knew what they really meant because she had read about symbols. *Am I like Marlow?* So helpless, in the end, to see what is really there?

High, thin clouds arced overhead and the breeze smelled of cold water.

She put her hands in the pockets of an expensive skirt Justine had brought for her. Her fingers curled around the credit card shape of the hotel key. She took it out and bent it between her hands. It was surprisingly flexible. More pressure, until the plastic went white at the fold. She bent it back and forth until it snapped in two. Looked at the pieces from a great distance, as if having no memory of how they had come to be in her hands. She wanted to be rid of it—to throw it to the river below. Let it find its own dark place in the earth. But some inner voice begged her not to add to the river's misery. She shoved the pieces in her pocket.

The ice from her heart spread through her body, until she stood in suspended animation. Motionless and thoughtless while the world moved around her. The sun slid across the universe in time-lapse. Clouds grew from white patchwork to gray sheets. The afternoon went dull and cold. She didn't move. She no longer seemed to be breathing. The clouds burned umber, then faded to indigo. The lights of the great city came up and she was alone on a stage of towers and castle walls.

Her thoughts unexpectedly settled on the man with the shirt of squares. He had a northern accent. An artist from Dumfries. Julian Dardonelle, trying to warn Justine about the manikin in Prague. *I saw him just before he died. Just like I saw Mr. Sinoro and David Andries before they died.*

There was no one to tell now. Justine was back in America.

Accepting the truth shook Vienna from her stasis. She was aware of being cold on an autumn night. Of being hungry and of the tiredness in her legs and the demands of her body. She turned away from the river and collided with a person standing too close behind her. She looked into the exotic green eyes and newly blond bangs of Justine Am.

"You're an idiot," Justine said.

Adrift in some strange way from her body, Vienna waited for her own lips to move, just to see what words they would shape. For long seconds, nothing would come. "What?" she finally said.

"It's okay. So am I."

"What?" All the words she'd ever read, reduced to one. "What?"

"In the Brussels police station, you didn't know how to pronounce 'Stürmer.' You know the words but you don't know the language. I can't believe I missed that."

Vienna could only shake her head.

"You've been searching your memory for a unicorn. A picture you saw as a child. But you never saw a picture of a unicorn when you were small."

"I did so."

"You couldn't have. You were in Austria. There are no unicorns in Austria. According to Babel Fish, there are einhorns. That's the word you saw by the picture. In German, not English."

"Einhorn?"

"Give me your hand."

Vienna held her hand up. Justine took it, and with a pen from her bag, she wrote "einhorn" on Vienna's palm. "That's the word you've been searching for. Can you find it?"

Vienna took her hand from Justine's and looked at the word. It was there, lost in a stream of words she didn't understand. She set them aside.

"Why are you here?"

Justine gave a small, sad smile. "I don't want to talk about it."

Vienna felt the ice in her chest again. "That's not fair."

"Do you want me to leave?"

Vienna's anger told lies. "Yes."

"Too bad." She offered her hand.

Vienna looked away. "How did you find me?"

"The hotel purser said you hadn't checked out. I knew you were close. It was only a matter of looking. Are you okay?"

"Surely Cupid has crept in and skillfully wounded me with secret art."

"That's a little melodramatic, isn't it? Who is it?"

"Publius Ovidius Naso. He was banished to Tomi—a frontier town on the Black Sea. It's where Jason landed with the Golden Fleece." Her eyes moved across unseen pages. "Poetry makes me see things a certain way. And I hate you."

Justine's smile was still tired, but somehow less tense. "I was expecting Sappho."

Vienna had no idea who that was.

"S-a-p-p-h-o."

She blinked and followed the word, pages of poetry unfolding before her, from an oversized book in Grayfield's flat. " 'What in my mad heart was my greatest desire; Who must feel my allurements; Who was the fair one that must be persuaded; Who wronged thee Sappho?' "

"There we go. Much more appropriate, don't you think?"

Vienna read on. "According to legend, she threw herself from a cliff out of unrequited love."

"I wouldn't recommend it. The Thames looks chilly and none too clean."

"Why do you tease me?"

"Self-defense," Justine said.

"I don't understand."

"This wasn't supposed to be my life."

"It doesn't have to be."

Justine sighed. "Sometimes, you have to stop analyzing every rational outcome. Quit assessing every permutation and flinching from every fear. Foot on the gas, tires squealing. Find what you think is true." She raised her hand slightly, reissuing the invitation.

"Your hair is blond again," Vienna said. "And shorter."

"Asymmetrical bob in layers. Do you like it? It's supposed to be sexy."

"I liked it when it was blue. It was bright and no one else had hair like it."

For some reason that made Justine laugh.

Vienna slipped her hand into Justine's. "I've been here all day," she said.

"I know, hun."

"I have to pee."

"Then we better hurry back." They marched through pools of lamplight cast on the walk. Justine so poised and not separating from Vienna when others walked by. Even when they stared.

"Vienna? Didn't Boadicea burn London down?"

"Who?"

"The woman's name on the manikin's foot."

Vienna saw it. "Yes. After the Romans killed her husband and raped her daughters." There wasn't much more to the story. "The Romans won in the end and Boadicea committed suicide, just

like Sappho. Does this have something to do with why Mr. Sinoro died?"

"No. It has to do with you."

"Me?"

"No Twitter drivel or Facebook angst. Just poetry and history,
even if it's gloomy." She purposely bumped her hip into Vienna,
knocking her steps out of rhythm. It didn't seem like a nice thing
to do. "That's part of why I came back, since you asked."

They turned to the hotel entrance. "I don't have my key."

"It's okay." Justine still had hers.

Back in the suite, a quick stop in the bathroom and a shower
to stop the chills. Out to the suite's main window. The Thames
visible as a wide, black rainbow against the brilliant city night.
Vienna saw herself hiding in the darkness. Let everyone pass by
on bright sidewalks and statue-lined boulevards.

She felt Justine behind her. She decided she was still angry, or
at least she wanted to be. She kept looking out the window.

"If part of why you came back was because you're worried
about me or because you thought I might get into trouble, then
I want you to leave."

"Technically this is still my hotel room."

"Then I'll leave," Vienna said.

"I would like you to stay."

"And you won't say why."

"Please listen for a few minutes? Before you leave or demand
answers?"

Vienna felt the broken hotel key in her pocket. There was nothing else there. She nodded.

"In a month or two, we might reach the point where we have
to work at things. Where we have to take everything apart to see
how we fit together. But it's too early for that—too much work
right now. This is new to us both. It's late and we both have had
a long, bad day. I don't ask for much tonight. Only that you sleep
in my bed, close enough I can feel you breathing."

"If I had been the one to walk out the door would you take me back so quickly?"

Justine closed her eyes. "No."

"Yet you expect it of me?"

"Yes."

"Why?"

"Because I spent four hours moping around Heathrow, another hour fretting whether or not to call home, and two more hours wallowing in depression while an insanely gossipy man twitched over my hair. Because I've walked out so many doors over the last four years, and I've never returned through any of them until tonight."

"That doesn't make it any better."

"I know."

"Did you call your parents?"

"No," Justine said.

"They hate me."

"You mean because you're a woman or because you're not right in the head?"

"All of it."

"Vienna." Justine's arms were suddenly around her, arms crossed in front of her chest and hands on her arms. "They don't care."

"Then why didn't you call?"

"I love my mother and father, but they would have offered all sorts of good advice and I don't need that right now."

"Codswallop," Vienna whispered to herself. But what else was there to do? Go back to Brussels? Back to Jeanneken Pis in her locked cage? Back to long dead widows and the vacant church plaza? Vienna sighed loudly enough to make certain Justine understood how upset she was.

Of course the night had no chance of unfolding as Justine had said. After room service delivered dinner with wine and a small plate of ice cream, Vienna ended up nude, on her back with her legs wrapped around Justine's hips.

She found it odd, this position so finely evolved for male and female. She expected to feel some connection missing, some lack of current that would have come to life had there been a male above her. But trying to force the feeling did nothing. She didn't want anyone else. Right or wrong, male or female didn't even enter into it.

But Justine had to feel the lack. This would be a break, maybe even a pleasant one, from what she was used to. A temporary change of pace. Best keep that in mind.

Abruptly Vienna snapped back to the outside world. Justine was looking at her. "What?" The stupid word came out as a whisper.

Justine didn't answer. Instead she shifted her weight, pressing down slightly harder on Vienna. The motion was small but the effect was immediate. Vienna felt the response her body wanted to make. Resented being so inexperienced that she couldn't find it.

She looked to Justine as if to apologize; saw her faint smile. And then it happened, Vienna moved the way her muscles told her was right. Her knees shifting upward, her hips rocking open.

She would have thought such a purely biological signal would have little effect. She was wrong about that, too. She closed her eyes and tried to release her body—let it respond to the slow dance of instinct. Let the night breathe. But it wouldn't. Justine gently took both of Vienna's wrists and pinned them above her head. Vienna panicked as she realized that now her breasts looked small. *She will see I am so much less beautiful than she is.* But Justine only lowered her lips to Vienna's left ear. Her body pressed tightly over Vienna's. She was warm. Vienna had never thought of temperature as a sexual quality.

"I'm sorry for what I did," Justine whispered. "It was horrible."

"It's okay."

Justine bit her ear, almost enough to hurt. "It's not, but it was something I needed to think through."

"I understand." It was a lie but maybe it sounded right.

Justine laughed. "Then you'll have to explain it to me."

Were people supposed to talk during sex? It didn't seem right. Justine didn't care. She just kept right on. "Do you like this?"

The question was impossibly vague. "As opposed to what?"

Another bite on her ear. "As opposed to not making love. Or as opposed to you being up here and me being down there.

Vienna considered the question. What she wanted to say was that having her wrists above her head made her horny, except she wasn't certain what it meant, although it probably referred to men and erections, which meant it wasn't the right word at all. "It's warm with you there." She paused. "Except . . ." She suddenly realized that she was going to say too much after all.

"Except?"

"Nothing."

"You have to tell me."

"No I don't."

"It's part of the rules."

It seemed pointless to ask about that. "I'm listening to my body like Cecile told me to and it's saying that I'm not so fragile. Is that okay? I'm not trying to be mean."

"Danger, Will Robinson, danger," Justine answered.

More nonsense. "Does that mean you're upset?"

"Just nervous. You have to tell me if you get uncomfortable, promise?"

"Promise." *If it makes you shut up.*

Justine widened her legs inside of Vienna's. Vienna inhaled at the adrenaline rush from the increased exposure. Still, she decided that her body liked it, even if it was a little scary. And after the first, wild, sensation faded she realized that Justine was being careful so it wasn't really scary after all. But maybe it was okay to pretend it was, just a little.

Anyway, it felt good to have Justine's hand sliding over her stomach. And since maybe Justine expected to talk during love, Vienna thought she needed to say something. She remembered leading Justine through the streets of Brussels and how Justine had followed without question, and for once she knew what to say. "I trust you."

It must have been right, because Justine was less hesitant, and the next bite was soft on the hollow of Vienna's throat. That was good too, because it was like they were doing something almost illegal and at least Justine couldn't talk like that. Except . . . Isn't that how people got those red marks on their necks? Everyone would see it! Vienna flinched.

"Shh," Justine said. "We aren't in junior high. I know you that well."

And it had to be true because Justine didn't leave any red mark at all. Vienna felt deeply tethered fears snap. She could move with Justine now, if she dared.

Justine's hand shifted and Vienna felt her body kick free of words and worry. She let them go, feeling only what immediate sensation told her. The warm brush of Justine's lips. The smell of her hair. The sound of her breathing. The feel of her smooth skin.

She knew at last that Lord Davy had been wrong about sensory overload, because it was happening now. Every nerve overflowing. *You can move.* And despite what the doctors had said over the years it didn't feel dangerous. *Move. Do it now.* Vienna arched her back, pushing against Justine.

And just like that, Justine was catching her breath for a change. Maybe it wasn't so hard after all. *Maybe I know her, too.*

Later, with sleep muddling her thoughts, she heard Justine softly humming. It sounded like the old recordings her foster father listened to. Her thoughts flowed into long chains. George Gershwin. A hundred pianos playing all at once. Tin Pan Alley. Ancient alchemists used tin with copper to form bronze: 18g Cu. Eighteen grams of copper, recorded on a slip of paper by a dead man with a Scottish accent and a shirt of squares. *It has something to do with the manikins, but you never listen.*

Thoughts slipped into dreams.

She looked into Sinoro's dead eyes, open under the cold river. His mouth slack. The sun fading as he sank deeper. He was screaming, his lungs filling with black water. His long hair tangled in the muddy riverbed.

"Shh. Vienna, it's only a bad dream. I'm right here."

And she was in the foyer of the Cart House. The smell of pine resin. There were no other children, only a few men, dressed in red hunting caps and tan breeches. Old rifles, hinged open at the breech, muzzles to the ground. One of the men tussled her hair as he left with his comrades. She didn't recognize any of them except Uncle Anson, looking over her shoulder as she played with a set of wooden blocks.

He had always been with her, the razor scar on his face. And Vienna knew that part wasn't a dream at all.

15

Autumn's waning sun lost its hold on the sky. A frozen hook of low pressure kicked whitecaps across the North Atlantic and reached down to embrace London. The Thames faded to a band of tarnished silver; the buildings of Piccadilly Circus growing hazy in the heavy air. George Holt loved it. "Far more intense than yesterday. See how we still have enough ambient light for natural dark tones? Bring out muted highlights and step up saturation and we have London as chiaroscuro." He set up his camera within a forest of reflective umbrellas.

Emily and Justine sat at the edge of Jubilee Gardens. The London Eye rose behind them, hoisting tourists into the clouds. "Look! Behind the fog is where Big Ben is!" Emily cycled forms across a foldout table, every page highlighted where Justine's signature was required. Promo rights, copyrights, insurance to cover every catastrophe from torn garments to death.

"We thought you were finished," Emily said.

"Seemed like a good idea to kiss it off."

"So why are you still here?"

"I hope staying the extra day wasn't a hassle."

"We have been well compensated by your employer. So why are you still here?"

"Might as well finish the job."

"For a beautiful woman, you're an ugly liar. So why are you still here?"

Justine glanced toward Vienna, standing out of earshot. She was staring across the river, toward the tired ramparts of the Ministry of Defense. Her right wrist moved through an endless loop, fingers curled around nothing. A scratched mind stuck on a familiar song: Vienna on the banks of the Thames, scooping Brussels gelato from foggy air. Justine followed her gaze, felt the poisonous geometry of the ministry's facade.

"One moment." She walked to Vienna and took her hand, stopping the unconscious motion. Vienna made no move. Justine stepped in front of her.

"Vienna? You have to stop."

"Sierpinski Carpet."

"Vienna?"

"The left wall is cut by six groups of nine windows. Divide the space between the windows into nine equal squares, and remove the central one. Repeat this recursively an infinite number of times. The result has an infinite perimeter but an area of zero."

"It's the Ministry of Defense. You can't expect much."

Vienna's lips moved a few seconds longer. Her hand stopped pushing against Justine's. But there was no shelter here. No blank shower curtain. No unbroken floors. No pencil lines to hold back widening fractures in heaven.

Vienna focused on Justine. "In 1938, Queen Mary requested that the wine cellar of old Whitehall Palace be saved. The entire structure was moved by hand and is now located in the basement of the Ministry of Defense."

"I didn't know that."

"It's true, according to *Uncle Scrooge's Guide to Modern London*, published by Thomas Doring Press, third edition, page twelve. The cellar was built for Henry VIII in 1536." Vienna smiled in apology. "Henry's last words were 'Monks! Monks! Monks!' Isn't that odd?"

Justine sensed, at uneasy distance, how foreign Vienna's world was. Every written page and every shape an assault on a defenseless mind. How was it possible to function with that slithering through your skull? *Get her away from it.*

"We're about to start and I need your help with wardrobe."

Vienna nodded. "Okay." Which caused a blush that Justine was surprised to feel herself returning.

"Let's go."

Vienna hesitated. "It really isn't contagious, you know."

"I'm prepared to risk it."

Vienna's lips moved as she said something to herself. A second later, she spoke the words aloud: "I'm pretty sure Anne Boleyn thought the same thing." Her hushed laughter raced by in a single breath. She nodded toward Holt. "He's waiting for you."

Justine could only follow in stunned silence.

As always, George Holt was a sideways experience. Although when he got wherever he was going, he knew it. "Almost forced perspective! See that, with the wheel? Industry! We can use that." Justine wondered how he could see anything through his curtain of hair. "Harmony of texture against shape. Pure evolution of the standard. We encompass progress in a single image." Whatever that meant. "Face the smallest fraction left."

The matte black Fuji would apparently shoot a million pictures, but Justine was never certain. George used a remote for the shutter, and he'd removed the digital clicking sound from the ghostly quiet camera. "Women are prettier when they don't know they're being photographed," was his explanation.

The predictable crowd of onlookers manifested, but George had closed off several shooting angles. A pair of London bobbies were enough to assure good manners. Between shots, Justine noted as many fingers pointed at Vienna as at her.

Any publicity is good publicity, right?

Vienna was oblivious, hunched over a computer with Emily. The first array of pictures had been wirelessly downloaded and Emily was weeding through obvious rejects. Smothered giggles as a bad photo came up. Justine found herself on the business end of jealousy.

Wardrobe changes were done in a North Face expedition tent

behind the camera. Holt was more interested in protecting his models' modesty than his models were. He'd had the tent's rain fly coated in a white paste that wouldn't pass a shadow even under a full spot. It smelled of camphor.

A shame current circumstances rendered privacy more provocative than nudity. Whenever Justine and Vienna stepped into the tent, the crowd reacted with enthusiastic cheers. It didn't help that the clothes, Ian Deckard's goth-punk skirts, came with enough straps for a delivery truck. Each change took several minutes longer than expected. The cheers grew louder.

"They like you," Vienna said, working on a herd of clasps that would have scared Houdini.

"They think we're feeling each other up."

"There isn't time." Delivered with as much heat as a January blizzard. Justine found the comment delightful. *No one outside has a clue.* How little there was left to prove, here in the tent with Vienna.

"You're right."

Justine fell into the semi-meditative state long ago adopted for photo sessions. It was like driving. Stop at red lights, make correct turns, switch lanes, and suddenly you're home without knowing how you got there. Toward late afternoon, she caught Emily's gaze long enough for the assistant to flash an enthusiastic "okay" circle with her right hand. Emily knew enough of her brother's business to know what was working.

The rains came on the final planned set. George and Emily scrambled to get their equipment stowed. The manikin was rushed into a white delivery van even as Justine ran to the tent. The clothes had to be kept dry. *If they shrink, I'll suffocate.*

Vienna joined her in the tent, accompanied by the expected chorus of cheers. Justine popped out her contacts and squeezed a small stream of saline into her eyes. "I hope the next manikin has green eyes."

Vienna hung clothes while Justine changed into her own shirt and slacks. The girl managed to get everything repacked in their original garment bags without resorting to Justine's usual stuff-sack approach. *So now who's the immature one?*

Emily met them at the rain fly's opening. "You have quite a following." She handed Justine an umbrella.

The crowd had tripled despite the rain. Justine spotted an additional five policemen pacing the taped boundary. "Vultures circling the kill," she said.

Emily tilted her head as if listening. "Perhaps. We need you in the van to sign off our end of the deal."

"Can I have the umbrella?" Vienna asked. "I don't think the lorry has enough room for us all."

Justine handed the umbrella to her. "This will only take a few minutes."

Inside, Justine saw a few images as George scrolled through them in the back. "Excellent. Very ethereal, as if you are a ghost as much as the manikin. Reminiscent of Schumann's musical spirits." He hummed several atonal bars.

Justine glanced at Emily for explanation, but Emily could only offer a shrug. "I was right in thinking the change did you good," she said.

Justine refused to take the bait, making a production of reading the final form. Not that there was any need. James had already looked them over. Thank God he'd stayed.

"George will be impossible to talk to for at least a week," Emily said after they exited the van. The rain had paused, though the sky was darker. The real showers had yet to begin.

Justine looked behind the van. "Where has that girl gone to?"

Emily looked further away. "There." She nodded toward the crowd.

Justine saw Vienna's back, sheltered by the umbrella. She was against the tape barricade, talking to the crowd. The Eye towered over her in a turning mandala of steel and fog.

"Well shit." Justine started across the grass.

"Wait," Emily said, holding Justine's arm.

Justine looked at her.

Emily gave a small shrug. "She seems to be doing okay. The police won't let anything happen."

Justine saw two policemen flanking Vienna. It was hard to tell, but they seemed to be smiling. "You don't know her. She can find trouble in a second."

"I know more than you might think about people who aren't right with the world." She gave a barely perceptible nod to the van.

Justine gave her a surprised look.

Emily mouthed three letters. "OCD."

Justine nodded in return. Obsessive compulsive disorder was easy enough to hide from casual acquaintances, but it could be murder on long-term relationships. If it was serious enough, it would explain why George ended up with his sister looking out for him.

"See what happens," Emily said.

"The crowd will be all over her."

"I don't think so. Have you ever heard of *volksgeist*?"

"No."

"An old German psychiatric term, warped into heinous racism. It means the spirit-soul of a given people. No one much believes it anymore, the world is too flat from Starbucks and Walmart. But I swear I feel it as we travel."

"And?"

She pointed to the dark sky. "The English are heavy weather people. A once great empire that understands hard times. Perhaps Vienna has a few issues—made one or two naive statements. Yonder Brits won't hold that against her."

Justine glared toward the crowd and tried to think calming thoughts. It wasn't working.

"So things are that serious," Emily said after a minute.

"Last night . . . well . . ." Justine's voice trailed off.

"Yes?" Emily's sky blue eyes opened a fraction wider in challenge.

"Too much information."

"No fair starting and bailing."

"It just worked is all. As much as it ever has. I mean, not any better, you know, but as good. I don't have to be anything for her." A flash of upturned hands. "I don't know."

"Have you told Vienna any of this?"

"Telling her would be the same as admitting it fully to myself. On some level I'm not ready."

"Us Yanks tend to be inflexible."

"Our *volksgeist?*"

"More so since 9/11."

"I suppose." Justine willed her muscles to relax. "How many other German words do you know?"

"Four years in school. *Ich bin ein schneller Student, mein Freund.*"

"Are you leaving London right away?"

"No."

"Care to meet us for dinner?"

"Count George out. He won't pass as human until he has brooded over the pictures."

Justine rubbed her hands together to ward off the damp chill. "I used to have a table at the River Café. Not so sure now, especially on short notice."

"The natural arc of fame. You have my cell? I would just as soon get out of the hotel tonight."

Justine nodded. "I better collect Vienna. *Volksgeist* or not, the rain will start again soon."

The crowd grew louder as Justine approached. Fragments of commentary reached her. "Batting for the opposition," was obvious enough. But what was an aviation blonde?

Vienna was speaking in her characteristic whisper, forcing a hush. Justine wasn't certain what she expected, but Shakespeare wasn't high on the list. ". . . but it's true. Romeo and Juliet deserved what they got. They had no faith in each other. It's an insipid story, below Shakespeare's skill."

Justine braced for a riot, but the laughter seemed good-natured rather than derisive. How had she gotten away with mocking the country's greatest hero? Did being raised in England allow such criticism?

"What does the Yank think of that?" a younger member of the crowd asked. The question held a definite edge. Justine parried.

"The Yank is wondering why Lord Anson Davy is here." She nodded to the rear of the crowd. Faces turned and Justine heard a cascade of whispers. Americans might provide simple amusement, but Anson Davy was part of the royal obsession.

Davy gave a thin smile, the scar below his temple pinching the skin. "I was passing by and was taken in by Miss Vienna's exposition upon the nature of love. Her feminine critique reminds one that it is always prudent to give an ear to the other side, however irrational the other side might be."

This brought forth good-natured camaraderie from the men. "Hear, hear!"

How does he always have me on the defensive? "And what have you learned?"

"This young lady has the nerve to question Shakespeare. Parliament shall take action. Heaven knows the bloody sods have nothing better to do with their time." Davy again scored with the crowd, most of whom didn't expect informal language from the peerage. "Furthermore, she's in love with a denizen of one of our trans-Atlantic colonies. The name escapes me—such a trivial place after all." More cheering. "As a knight of the British Empire, I must ask Justine Am as to her intentions."

Justine didn't hesitate. "I was thinking of plundering away."

This brought a wild roar from the crowd. *Take that.*

"Yes, well, you Americans have a reputation for disposable romance."

"It's a colonial thing. It's why we left you in the first place."

Whatever else, the crowd was having a fine day.

"I see." Davy was silent for longer than Justine thought he needed. When he spoke, the banter was out of his voice. "I received word that you went to Heathrow yesterday. I want to know why."

"Knight of the realm or not, it's none of your business."

"Granted, my lady. Just the same."

She had to be careful. Davy was popular and he had all the cards, Justine's battered reputation would sink under the softest murmur of bad press. "Miss Vienna drives me to distraction. Her presence is a constant annoyance. She destroys my plans, she wrecks my morning workout, she spoils my alone time. She cries too much. She is in all ways the most infuriating creature I have ever met. She gets angry when I tease her. She misses my best jokes. She's hell on my career. There's only one reason I'm still here."

Davy played along. "What would that be?"

"I had a ticket home. I think you know the answer."

Davy gave her an accepting nod, and then turned to face Vienna. "Miss Vienna?"

"Yes?" Confusion in her wavering voice.

"Causing misery to Americans is God's work. Carry on."

Another ovation from the crowd. Davy turned, and the crowd parted before him.

"Lord Davy?"

He stopped and turned back to Justine.

People with real power will find out!

Her mouth suddenly dry. "It's . . . nothing."

He gave her a questioning look before stepping away.

Justine leaned to Vienna. "The rain is coming again. It's time to go."

Back in the Savoy, Justine called the River Café. "We never pay any attention to the press," she was told. She reserved a table for three at seven. Two hours until the limo picked them up.

"Vienna, off to the shower. We have to get ready."

"For dinner?"

"Yes. Casual, but formally so, if you know what I mean."

"No."

Justine caught the tone of her voice. "You were hurt by what I said to Davy."

"You had no right to say such horrible things. And thank you for saying them in public. I hate it when you're smarmy."

Justine stepped to her. "I know sometimes we don't connect. And I know some of it is because of the way you are, and the way I am as well."

"I don't understand, except you're saying I'm not right in the head and trying to be nice about it and failing."

Justine shook her head. "I'll make a deal with you."

"What?"

"Lord Davy is a man of considerable popularity. My guess is our exchange will garner some society press. I want you to hold off judgment until you see what they say."

"But you can't stand them."

"Do it for me anyway, okay?"

She sighed. "My period is coming."

"Has this been happening since we met?"

"Justine!"

"Shh. A bad joke. It's okay. You'll likely miss it, so be ready."

"How can you know that?"

"I'm psychic."

Vienna blinked twice in quick succession, but plowed ahead. "I want to stay home."

"You saw yesterday's pictures of the manikin. Was she the same today?"

"She was smaller, just like the others. I don't think it was a good job. It really didn't feel like wood, though the colors were good and the wig was the same."

"I agree. Had the Holts been open to the idea of a copy, they surely would have spotted it. At least we know why the quality dropped."

"We do?"

"Julian Dardonelle's body in that river near Antwerp. They had to get someone new to craft this replica. Someone not as skilled." Justine's hand passed over the lizard on her hip. "I want you to come with me. We might learn something."

"Why is it I always do what you say?"

"Because I'm a spoiled pain in the ass."

"That must be it."

"You need to get in the shower."

Vienna kicked at the carpet and turned away.

"Wait a second, hun. Whose idea was it that you go out on the night we met?"

"Cecile's—a friend at work."

"Who happened to know Grant."

Vienna said nothing.

"Grant gets one of your friends to meet you at Holler. He knew it was my favorite club in Brussels. He knew I would stop there."

"Except Cecile hurt her ankle."

"Maybe."

"She was using crutches."

"Which proves she knew where to get some. Either way, Grant paid your friends to dare me to sleep with you. They said exactly the right things to goad me into going along with it. They were perfectly coached. I should have realized that the second they started."

"But why?"

"I don't know. I almost see it, like reflections in a mirror. Shift your position a single step, and you see something new. Grant was after something related to the manikins. He wanted to meet you."

"He couldn't have known I would walk outside with you that morning in Brussels."

"But he was there just in case. If that failed, he could have stopped by your gelato shop with me in tow. We would have exchanged greetings and he would have had a proper introduction. After we spent the night together, he had several options for meeting you through me." So why hadn't he just seduced Vienna? There had to be more to it. "But things went wrong. He expected a one night stand, and instead he got you, all red in tooth and claw."

"Lord Alfred Tennyson," Vienna said. "'In Memoriam of A.H.H.'" Vienna's eyes scanned over words. "Arthur Henry Hallam," she continued. "He died in Vienna." Her face took on a soft blush of delight at the connection to her name. But she quickly grew stormy. "Why did you say that? That I was red in tooth and claw?"

"You set Grant up and ran him over with dead elm trees. I saw the devil in your eyes. I know when a member of my sex has her fangs out, Vienna."

"I didn't like him, and I was right not to."

"You were, but you didn't like him the second you saw him. Why not?"

"I don't want to talk about it."

Justine smiled. "Fair enough."

"You aren't mad?"

"We both know the answer." She stepped to Vienna and brushed her fingers through her hair. "For all his planning, my dear boyfriend never would have counted on anything happening between us." *Or on having his handsome, scheming face blasted off.*

"If he'd lived, you would be with him, and I would still be in Brussels."

Justine remembered her dissatisfaction on that last day. "I don't think so."

"That's a nice thing to say, but it's wrong to lie." Vienna turned again to the bathroom.

"Vienna?"

"Yes?"

"Last night was perfect. I wanted you to know."

Vienna considered this for several seconds. "Does it bother you that my breasts are so small?"

"They're perfect, too."

Vienna's hands went to her chest, covering herself. After a minute, she ventured an uncertain smile. "The average bra size in

Great Britain in the 1940s was 30B. So I would have been closer
to normal."

Vienna's deepest prayer lay bare. Closer to normal. But the window closed even as the words were spoken.

"Three hundred and sixty poppy seeds," Vienna whispered.
"Between the crosses, row on row."

Justine had no idea what it meant.

16

Vienna had what she always wanted only now she didn't want it so much anymore. She was always making mistakes or getting lost in Justine's words. Worse, there was the endless geometry of so many new places. Shapes twisting inside the compulsive topology of her mind. She imagined the chain anchoring her to safe places fast playing out against the onslaught of Hurricane Justine.

There was no reason to put herself through this except that she couldn't help herself. But then, maybe that was what Justine told Lord Davy. That she couldn't help herself either. Vienna wanted to believe it, but she couldn't fool herself that much. Beautiful people didn't work that way.

Dinner was in a restaurant on the Thames, further east than the neighborhoods Vienna knew. White chairs and blue carpet. It was absent of the clutter of most public places. Vienna glanced at Justine. *For me, or coincidence?*

But nothing hid the people pointing in their direction. Laughter over imagined bedroom scenes. Vienna knew she had been right about staying at the hotel.

Emily appeared in a dark green sweater against the chill that played through the rain. Her hair was still in a tail, which didn't seem right given how well-dressed other diners were. Emily didn't care. No one else did either. Just like no one cared that Emily's eyes were that blue color because of a genetic defect. No one made fun of her. "You appear to be the subject of many a dinner conversation," Emily said as she sat.

"Our fifteen minutes is about up," Justine said.

"An overly modest or overly naive assessment," Emily answered.

Justine ordered four courses of fish and soup, without a strand of spaghetti in sight. So it wasn't even real Italian food, despite what the menu said. Vienna wanted to eat in silence, but Justine would probably die if she stopped talking. Conversation centered around trivial aspects of fashion until Emily spoke.

"I spent the afternoon trying to connect the death of a paparazzi stooge to pictures of a Christian Bell manikin." She sipped her wine. "And let's not forget my knowledge of German."

"I need paper and a pen for the German part," Vienna said.

Justine supplied both from her black handbag.

"There are lots of words," Vienna said, "but most are small. I think they are like 'the' yeah?" She printed out *"Mit ihrer Spannweite von 76 cm ist sie die größe. gemmoglyptische Schale der Welt"* and handed the paper to Emily.

The woman frowned. "It's about a special bowl, the largest one in the world. Not certain what kind. I've never seen the word *'gemmoglyptische'* before. I could Google it if you want."

Vienna sighed. "I don't know it either."

"I didn't realize you spoke German."

"I don't."

Emily and Justine smiled, and once again Vienna had made a fool of herself.

"We can check later. Is there more?" Justine asked.

"I want to go home."

"I know you do, Vienna. Is there more German?"

Vienna grabbed the paper, slapping the table loud enough for more people to stare at them. In block letters: *"Wegen dieser Bedeutung, der einzigartigen Größe des Steines und seiner meisterhaften Formgebung wurde die Achatschale (zusammen mit dem 'Ainkhürn,' dem Stoßzahn eines Narwales, welchen Kaiser Ferdinand I. von König Sigismund II. von Polen als Geschenk erhalten hatte) im Erbvertrag der Söhne Kaiser Ferdinands I. 1564 als unveräußerliches Erbstück des Hauses Habsburg bezeichnet."*

"Ainkhürn" is a unicorn horn, just like *einhorn*," Vienna said. "And I don't know how I know that, so I must have heard it

somewhere." She was speaking too loudly, but she didn't care because it would embarrass Justine.

Emily spoke in her normal voice. "You did this from memory in a language you don't speak?"

Vienna felt heat in her face. There was no reason to be mean to Emily. "It might be wrong."

"The spelling and grammar are flawless." Emily shook her head. "Most of the tabloid biographies have you leaving Austria while still a child. How young were you?"

"Six."

Emily was silent for a few seconds, distracted by some thought process Vienna couldn't follow. A slight narrowing of the eyes that doubtless conveyed paragraphs to Justine.

I hate this.

Emily turned her attention back to the writing. "It's about the bowl. I'm certain *'achat'* "—she pointed to the word—"is agate. So we have an agate bowl. A masterpiece and, as we already know, the largest one in the world. It says this bowl, along with the tusk of a narwhal—once thought to be the horn of a unicorn—are in possession of the Habsburgs. The horn was a gift of King Sigismund II of Poland. The bowl and the horn are considered inalienable heirlooms of the family and as such can never be sold. They're on display in a museum in Vienna."

Vienna began to speak, but paused when she felt Justine's hand on her leg. Uncertain, she went on. "Those are the same words that—" Justine's hand closed tighter around her leg. "Ouch!"

Emily laughed. "Not exactly subtle."

Justine sighed. "What do you know about narwhals?"

That hadn't been what Vienna was going to say. *Why did Justine change the topic?* She felt Justine's fingers move across her leg. Two distinct motions. A "T" shape. Was it some form of shorthand?

Emily shrugged. "Not much. A whale or dolphin with a horn."

"What about you, Vienna? Did you have time to read anything about narwhals before mastering World War Two?"

Vienna printed the word.

" 'H' after the 'W,' " Justine corrected.

It was different enough to follow. "There is an entry in the *Encyclopedia Britannica*, Eleventh Edition, 1911, Cambridge, England . . ." She stopped and put her head on the table; cradled in the crook of her right arm. "Bog off." Her voice was muffled in her ears.

"Does the encyclopedia have anything of interest?" Justine asked, as if nothing were wrong.

Vienna looked it over in the darkness of her arm-tent, resisting the habitual urge to read aloud. She tried parsing the entry into partial sentences, adding only a few words. "The scientific name is *Monodon monoceros*. . . . They have a single horn, which is actually the left incisor. . . . They are arctic whales. . . . In medieval times, when the horns washed to shore after a narwhal died, they were thought to be the horns of unicorns." She paused. Another squeeze on her leg. "And you can stop pinching my leg. I don't like it." She went ahead with the article. "These often found their way into 'cabinets of curiosities,' which were collections of artifacts outside contemporary scientific expertise." Vienna read on, her lips moving silently, rejecting most of what was there. "The word 'nar' comes from Old Norse, meaning corpse. It might refer to the creature's pallid skin, or to the fact that narwhals often swim upside down. That's all I know and I don't care what you think."

"That's more than I knew," Emily said.

Corpse. Vienna sat up.

It wasn't a "T." It was a boneyard cross. Sinoro had been killed—maybe because he knew something he shouldn't. If they told Emily, maybe she would know something she shouldn't. That was Justine's signal to change the subject. She had been trying to help. *And I acted like a spoiled baby.*

Vienna didn't like that because it was true. *I'm tired of myself.* She didn't like that for the same reason. "Are you going to leave me again?" Because she was sure she would if their places were reversed, though maybe she shouldn't have asked while Emily was listening.

Justine leaned toward her and whispered in her ear. "In a few days, when you feel better, I'm going to shove you into bed and bang you till you can't see straight."

Vienna felt the color drain from her face. They were in a public place! And she was going to have her period. "*. . . according to the days of the separation for her infirmity shall she be unclean . . .*" And only creepy people spoke in that vulgar way to begin with.

Justine leaned back. Her out-loud voice hadn't changed. "So, we have a narwhal horn and an agate bowl. Does it mean anything to either of you?"

"No," Emily answered.

She turned to Vienna. "Do you have anything more?"

Vienna tried to mimic Justine's calm. "It would be in German, and I wouldn't know what it meant." And shoving someone into bed had to be rude, even for an American.

"Where does all this come from?" Emily asked.

"Something my ex-boyfriend said before he was killed." Vienna wondered at how Justine managed to say something that sounded meaningful, yet contained no information at all. *How many times has she done that to me?* Vienna decided worrying about that was like worrying that the world was round.

Soup was delivered, and Vienna made a game of eating all of one kind of vegetable from the broth. Celery, then beans, then carrots . . . For once Justine let her be. Conversation drifted to other topics as a new set of plates appeared. The food was delicious, served without the layers of sauce and cream that Vienna assumed expensive cuisine had to have.

So maybe this was how it was supposed to be. She was in a beautiful place with beautiful people. But it still wasn't right. There had to be transformation; that was the most important part. She imagined herself conducting conversation, witty and bright. Crescendos of laughter at exactly the right moments.

Painful to see the truth. That it wasn't her. That it never would be. *I left no room in my dreams for myself.*

But maybe it didn't matter anymore. She looked at Justine.

Even now, when they couldn't be together, she had whispered a possible future. Pushing Vienna into bed. Clothes piled on the floor. That was real. It could happen without Vienna morphing into implausible perfection. *I could move with her again.* Tangled in the sheets. *I could be laughing.*

And even that wasn't the important part, because Justine had said that other people in Holler would have made love to Vienna, too. Something more. *She was going home and she came back for me.*

"Why didn't you go back to the United States?"

"The weather in Georgia is terrible this time of year."

The air in Vienna's lungs turned to lead.

Justine's voice went soft. "Vienna, you're in London, not Georgia. I wanted to be with you." Justine smiled. "Peach sorbet for dessert?" she asked. As if nothing had changed. As if the future was right there, tangled sheets and walking side-by-side on the Thames even if people were watching. Cool air and the lights so bright off the river.

"I would like that," Vienna answered. *I would like that.*

After the order was placed, Justine started talking about the statues again. "What do you know of Franklin Court?"

"Never heard of him."

"The owner of the London manikin. From what James told me, Court is into Yoruba religion—precursor to voodoo."

"That's more than I know. We never met."

"How did you pick up the manikin?"

"Czasky's people handled it."

"Is that usually the way things are done?"

"Depends." For the first time, Vienna saw Emily hesitate. "The thing is, Justine, you and I live on the same planet but different worlds."

"Meaning?"

"Damage to the manikin could reach seventy or eighty thousand dollars for a total loss. It wouldn't come close to breaking us, but it would affect future business. We aren't living on an elite model's income. We're happy to let Czasky take liability for as long as he's willing."

"Makes sense." Justine paused while the waiter served dessert. He winked at Vienna when only she could see. Why did he do that? Justine thanked him and turned to Emily. "I suppose all photographers handle it the same way?"

"I would assume so." She leaned back in her chair. "You going to tell me what this is all about?"

"No."

"I didn't think so. So I started looking into it myself." Emily pointed at Justine with her dessert spoon. "In merry ol' England, if you go to the police, they assume you're trying to help. I suggested that I knew Sinoro and asked if there was any way I might be of assistance."

"What did they tell you?" Vienna asked.

Emily smiled. "You must learn to hide interest in things your girlfriend wants hidden."

"She's never happy with what I say anyway," Vienna said.

Emily paused. "Perhaps what I have to offer is valuable. What do you have to trade for it?"

"Sinoro asked her the same thing."

"And got himself dead for it," Emily said.

"We don't know that," Justine said.

"You suspect it," Emily answered. "Which means you cut a deal. What did you offer?"

"Vienna promised a photo shoot."

Emily looked at Vienna. "He would have had you bare ass to the sun."

"I'm not pretty enough to be of interest that way."

Emily looked at Justine. "Is she serious?"

"Apparently so."

Emily turned back to Vienna, her voice low and harsh. "Sinoro would have asked you to pose nude. And when he was done, he would have expected to screw you. You're exactly his type."

"Type?"

"Innocent as a wet kitten. It's a trick a lot of women try to pull, but the harder they try the less it works. You don't try, so you succeed brilliantly."

Vienna felt the edge again, tottering over some new realization, something logic would tell her was true, but she couldn't make sense of inside. She looked at Justine. "I feel that way to you?"

"Our love life is a private matter."

"It wasn't a private matter when you were talking to Lord Davy about rain."

"The situation—" She stopped and took a breath. "It affects me differently."

"I feel it," Emily said. "Not enough to putt from the other side of the green, but I do."

"Differently?"

Emily's hands took up part of her conversation, moving sharply with her words. "If men are aroused by the thought of taking innocence from a girl, women are often wired the other way. To protect. And protect can easily transform into possess."

"I don't understand."

Emily inhaled to speak but Justine cut her off. "Give it time." She turned to Vienna. "And before you say anything, just know that you are doing better in my world than I am in yours. Sometimes I glimpse what you see and it scares me to death."

"I don't believe you." Vienna looked at Emily. "I would be a model, if I was like that."

Emily patted the air with her hands. "Slow down, scout. You aren't a model because you would be dreadful." She leaned forward. "Justine Am's looks are far above average, but what sets her apart is the ability to project the essence of female form. Not just tits and ass, but psyche as well. It's a profoundly strong archetype that provokes an equally strong reaction. Even if you were her twin, you lack her ability to step outside herself." Emily scooped out a small crescent of sorbet. "A camera points our way and we take a self-conscious heartbeat to decide what image to present. That forever excludes us from the realm of Justine Am."

Justine smirked. "You make it sound rather lackluster."

"My brother once told me his talent is seeing the exact moment when a woman is more math than biology. He says topology is erotic to the hindbrain. It appeals to primordial pattern recognition and survival instincts." Emily sipped the sorbet from her spoon. "Whatever the case, there are usually fifteen or sixteen worthwhile pictures from a given shoot. With you, George agonizes over thirty."

"Out of hundreds taken."

"Thou too are mortal."

"I just want to know what the police said about Sinoro." Vienna's voice sounded pouty to her own ears, something else she was learning to hate.

"He had a room at the Airport Ibis. In that room, he had a notepad. And on that notepad, he had written: 'J.D. 4:30, Ruben's House, Antwerp. Joan: Hg—.247 ounces. Au—.035 ounces.' Does it mean anything to you?"

Vienna shook her head. "No." *J.D.—Julian Dardonelle!* The connection came a second after she spoke.

"Since you would be a worse liar than your girl, I believe you," Emily said. "Sinoro had also written a large block of uppercase letters. Perhaps a code or just as likely a random doodle. The London boys couldn't make heads or tails of it, so they gave me scratch paper and let me play with it for a while. I gave up after a couple of hours but somehow pocketed a copy."

"Illegally," Justine said.

"You going to turn me in?"

"Do you have it with you?" Vienna asked.

"Yes."

"May I see it?"

Emily reached down to her plain bag and pulled out a folded sheet of paper. She opened it just long enough for Vienna to see a large block of letters. "You can study it all you want if you tell me what's going on." She folded it closed.

Justine remained silent, and once again Vienna felt a gentle squeeze on her knee. The way seemed difficult, but Vienna came up with a way to change the topic like Justine was always doing. "I may have made a mistake with Sinoro."

"No 'may' about it. But given that one photographer is already dead, this might affect me more than you."

"I don't think so," Vienna said, gaining confidence. "A lot of people photograph Justine. Only one has been murdered."

Emily looked at Justine. "You know this is no fluke."

"Then let her protect you in her own way," Justine said.

"I'm going to keep digging."

"Why risk ending up like Sinoro?"

"I'm too smart."

"Smarts don't help breathing under water. Let it go. We aren't in any direct danger."

"Why are you keeping secrets?"

Justine smiled. "You know that fairy tale about London cops casually letting you see evidence from an ongoing murder investigation? Never happens this side of Hollywood."

Emily's spoon dipped into the sorbet again. "But it sounded so good."

"You have your own secrets."

"Bet mine are more harmless," Emily said.

"Bet Gary Sinoro would agree," Justine answered.

Back at the hotel, Vienna felt the weight of the day. Every breath a prelude to a yawn.

"Did you get it?" Justine asked.

"Get what?"

"Emily's letters."

"Yes. But I can't make anything of it. It may not be in English," Vienna said.

"I think it is. Sinoro certainly understood it, or some of it anyway."

"It's a code then, and I hate codes."

"Could you put it on my computer?"

"Not tonight."

Justine closed her eyes for a second. "There will be time later."

Vienna turned her thoughts inward. An agate bowl and a unicorn horn in a museum. But no star. There was a reason, but there seemed no way to rediscover it. Caught between exhaustion and Justine's verbal tricks and the onset of cramps, she gave up and went to bed.

Emily's square of letters flickered through layers of REM. Vienna was in the Cart House chapel with ruby sunlight coming through stained glass. The room was empty except for her and Uncle Anson, and for once the telly was off. Laughter drifting in from a distant corner of the Cart House, where men often played cards. She was showing the block of letters to Lord Davy. They had been written on a single piece of paper and put in a huge, boring book that was written in that old-fashioned style where every "S" was an "F." She thought the book was about prayers you had to say every hour so that God would like you.

"What does this mean?" She held the loose paper up to Uncle Anson.

"Why are you reading such boring tomes?" He took the paper from her. "There are more exciting things for our little princess to look at. Here we have a history of knights in shining armor. Isn't that more fun?"

She inhaled warm pine resin, drifting from sun-washed trees beyond the windows. Birds singing in the formal garden. Davy's oversized book was heavy in her lap. It opened to a picture of sixteenth-century plate mail made in a place called Styria.

Salet, Bevor, Pauldron . . .

She turned the page and there was that picture of Justine, skipping next to the manikin in Prague. And Justine was looking at the camera so she couldn't see that the manikin was moving behind her. Wooden arms reaching out, fingers curled into hooks.

17

Midnight left two e-mails on Justine's BlackBerry. The first from Emily:

> I'm cheering for her, but don't go mental trying to fix something you didn't break.

Justine glanced over at the bed; Vienna curled in her fetal tuck. Hair falling from her temple to her eyes. On cue, Vienna's body spasmed tight in the grip of a nightmare. How terrible must this have been when she lived alone in Brussels? Justine went to her side, brushing her hair. "Shh. I'm here. It's only a dream." Vienna's muscles went limp and she took a deep breath. "It's okay, Vienna." Her breathing steadied.

Emily was right; Vienna's troubles weren't going to simply fade away. Justine thought of Simone back in Tribeca. Still the obvious choice and still the wrong one.

More and more, she didn't want to think about it. She returned to the table.

The second e-mail had a URL of alphanumerics. A week ago, Justine would have deleted it. Now there wasn't anything else to look at.

There was no salutation.

> There comes a time in an old man's life when fear of his foster daughter's dating is overshadowed by fear that she will wither away in gray spinsterhood. If the old man is powerful, he has the means to see this does not happen. I was employed as one such means.

We sent her to Brussels, believing it a healthier environment for a young woman than Berlin or Paris. Far enough away to force her to begin her own life, but close enough to come to her aid. We forced her to find employment in an attempt to draw her from seclusion. When that failed, we began sending well-healed men in her direction. The girl is pretty enough and her excessive shyness is considered fetching by some. Inevitably the situation soured. Failure to elicit a response, even a negative one, is the worst form of assault upon the male ego.

I suggested she might prefer women. My patron was not amused, but as months passed, anxiety overcame objection. The results, while different in degree, were identical in substance. Women found her as boring as Parliament.

We retreated to getting her involved in any social arena at all. She would meet the most caring of her peers, Cecile, with the hope that some bond of friendship might form. Best laid plans and all. Cecile kicked up a loose cobble, leaving her less altruistic companions to meet Vienna. In what I gather was a moment of youthful spite, they sent you headlong into our project.

We assumed the rich model would move on. But after our clash in Brussels, I looked into the matter. I hardly expected to find top marks at the Stanford School of Medicine, despite being admitted at the age of sixteen. Nor that a term short of graduating you would suddenly depart.

It was bad enough that you were a woman, unthinkable that you were American, and distasteful that you were a creature of the mass media. Such is our well-deserved reward for meddling.

Given the girl's clinging desire for your company, my patron has made peace with circumstance. I leave you with a final plea on the girl's behalf. In the course of maturation, there lies a sharp distinction between *want* and *love*. I understand how harsh this must sound, but her heart can

break over merely wanting a thing. I don't think yours can.
If you must leave, the sooner the better.

As you have guessed, there is money behind our girl.
Her foster father is Arthur Grayfield, of whom you can discover everything you might wish by checking his founda-
tion's website. For now it is enough that he is wealthy and
that a portion of that wealth will be used to assist Vienna as
my patron sees fit. If you wish to contact me, you have this
address and she has my number. I wrote it for her once and
I doubt she has forgotten it.

I remain,
Your humble servant;
Lord Wanker

So Lord Davy was the hidden general, sliding Vienna to Brussels like a plastic marker on a battlefield map. He put her in Holler the night they met. Didn't that make him the enemy? Justine
looked at the letter again. No obvious connection between Lord
Anson Davy, Knight Companion of the Garter, and David Andries, Minister of the Cheap Scam. Hard to imagine them shar-
ing dry martinis at the bar; the murderous con man and the . . .
whatever Lord Davy was. Something beyond the event horizon
that separated the ostentatious from the powerful. *I could ring
Davy up and ask.*

Justine sat up. Call Davy. No, not Lord Davy. David Andries.

Andries, at least in his Grant Eriksson persona, believed
three was his lucky number. He'd worked eight of them into
his phone number. Justine was certain it had surfaced since his
murder. Someplace it shouldn't have been. Had Davy mentioned it?

The more Justine pushed, the more distant the memory became. She gave up when the BlackBerry's clock hit one. Vienna
was still curled up, unaware of the strings that had looped themselves around her. *What should I do with you?*

Any pretense of a typical relationship, even allowing same sex standards, was out of the question. *Was it even moral to be with Vienna?* Lord Davy publically accepted it, even joked about it. He should know, shouldn't he? Assuming he was on her side, which looked more questionable by the second.

Eight threes . . .

Justine stripped down and stepped into the shower. Off to Iceland tomorrow evening. Three days there, and then to Vienna. Then, one way or another, it would be over. She let blood-warm water run over her as sleep came on. Willed it to wash away the fear she had soaked up from Vienna.

By morning, London was finally London. Gray streets under gray buildings under a gray sky. A shadow-girl at the laptop. Justine couldn't help a smile at the unaffected charm of Vienna's concentration. Useless but oh-so-stylish glasses and fingers mussing her hair. Her nails carefully trimmed.

"What are you working on, lover?"

"Lover?" Vienna's panic meter jumped to wounded impala at a lion convention.

"Isn't that what we are? Lovers?"

"But, I can't! I'm sorry."

Justine wrapped her arms around the girl. "You're being silly."

Vienna's breathing slowed. "After what you said at dinner I thought . . . I can take medicine so I never have another one, if you want."

"I do not want. Your hormones are part of you. Drugs that stop them are not."

Vienna frowned. Her voice was heavy. "It's harder not knowing the right questions than not knowing the right answers."

"Questions and answers will come." Justine released her. "What are you working on?"

"The block of letters that Emily got from Gary Sinoro's room."

Justine looked at the screen.

```
MOEEEXLHWTCIESXKQTKTTHTIOEKRBZIQVAMMOIAPMCXVJCMSHMLS
FWYUKKICXATALWTKZOYWSHIDTALWPEDEMOIXIMSNYIDWFAKAATXT
TALWFRMNWPRELQOKKICSRTALTWEZEMZEYHMLPHCDEETALTWEZEMZ
QZZQOGLXZQQALBVPHUSMHRNIANXASXIMSNYIEMYEBUXSIOIMF
SQXTEPOMEIIAESWOMPMXUIDAQAKAMPWFAKVJSSDULHVZYZ
DAPWYIOKAPWASIEKPWZYDSWVASEFTAVYHMXTILENINRH
ALPVEAGKWTWFEKZFPPUEOLEWPYIZOXMIYAWLPPZQL
```

Words surfaced from the random background. "Lenin," she said, pointing to the end of the sixth row.

"What?"

"You know. Vladimir Ilyich? Famous revolutionary and dictator of the Russian persuasion? Maestro of the Red Terror? That has to be important."

"The word 'vase' appears ten letters before. Are we going to look for suspicious flowers next? Don't be daffy." The change in temper came breathlessly fast.

Justine snapped back. "Vienna, it can't be coincidence."

"Yes it can. Any idiot would see that."

"Well, thanks for your support. What do you make of it?"

"It's a code."

"You think?"

Sarcasm was lost on Vienna. "The underlying pattern is too strong for chance."

Justine looked at the letters. "I don't see it."

Vienna's voice took a brittle edge. "The sequence 'TAL' appears five times, each repeating letter separated by fourteen, then twenty-eight, then twice by twenty-one letters." She took a quick breath, rocking back and forth. "The letters 'MOI' appear twice, forty-nine letters apart. 'KKI' is separated by sixty-three letters. 'VJ' is also duplicated once; 196 letters apart. The longest repeating string is 'TALTWEZEMZ,' which is separated by twenty-one letters."

"I can't see all that."

Vienna slapped keys to put the letters in lowercase.

```
MOEEEXLHWTCIESXKQTKTTHTIOEKRBZIQVAMmoiAPMCXvjCMSHMLS
FWYUkkiCXAtalWTKZOYWSHIDtalWPEDEmoiXIMSNYIDWFAKAATXT
talWFRMNWPRELQOkkiCSRtaltwezemzEYHMLPHCDEEtaltwezemz
QZZQOGLXZQQALBVPHUSMHRNIANXASXIMSNYIEMYEBUXSIOIMF
SQXTEPOMEIIAESWOMPMXUIDAQAKAMPWFAKvjSSDULHVZYZ
DAPWYIOKAPWASIEKPWZYDSWVASEFTAVYHMXTILENINRH
ALPVEAGKWTWFEKZFPPUEOLEWPYIZOXMIYAWLPPZQL
```

"And the pattern to this?"

"The gaps between groups are divisible by seven. But it doesn't always work. Some two-letter combinations break the relationship."

"What does it mean?"

Vienna stood as if she'd been kicked. "I don't know! I hate codes! They hurt and you don't care. You use me and then make fun of me when I can't help. Bog off!" She stepped around Justine, headed for the bedroom in full stomp. Her face already drenched in tears.

I ignored the signs.

"Vienna, stop." Justine's voice was as calm as she could make it. Vienna froze, resolutely not looking back. Justine walked to face her and then put her arms around the girl.

"I didn't mean to hurt you. I wasn't thinking." She brushed her fingers through Vienna's hair. "We have a flight to Iceland this evening. You need to shower and start packing. Okay?"

"What about the letters?" Her voice stuttered by shallow breaths.

"I have a few ideas."

"You think it's my period."

"No. I think your mind works too fast and sometimes it fills your head with too much information. I think it's very scary when it happens."

"Are you leaving me?"

"Only if you aren't ready to take off this evening. You better get going."

The girl stood still.

"Vienna?"

"Sometimes I see how stupid this is, yeah? All this sobbing and carrying on like a child. A part of me hates it—screams at me for it. But that only makes me cry more. It's the only way I know to make things stop. It takes all my energy to cry so I can't hang on to whatever is happening. It lets me break away." She sniffled. "And you were right anyway because that's just an excuse and I'm trapped inside myself just like you said."

Justine inhaled. "I feel the same way sometimes—more times than you would believe. I just keep it hidden."

"You aren't going to tell me to find other ways to make it stop? All the doctors tell me I should do other things."

"If you need to cry, then cry. But if we keep talking like this, then I'll be crying too and that won't get us anywhere."

Vienna nodded and with a deep breath walked to the bathroom. After she was gone, Justine collapsed into the chair in front of her Sony. Several minutes after hearing the water come on, she was still staring at the washed-out sky.

Carrying on like a child.

Justine shook her head. There were more important issues at hand. At least, they should be more important. Top of the list was whether or not Lord Davy could be trusted.

Start at the beginning, in Budapest. The manikin there had been vandalized, "Gisella" crossed out and "Lina" added. Young David Bell scrawling his love for Lina Zahler. The same Lina Zahler who, according to Vienna, was connected to the assassination of the empress of Austria.

Justine Googled the name and came up with a solitary hit, found inside a history book published in 1911. She skimmed dense paragraphs covering the Long Depression. Europe's masses falling to poverty while royalty toured the countryside in gilded coaches. Bejeweled knights, soon to be buried in the stinking trenches of World War I. The golden age of cloaks-and-daggers. Radical newspapers printed on clandestine presses; hushed meetings in dark cellars; chemical formulae for poisons and explosives passed in furtive handshakes. There was an element of romance to it—until words became action.

Luigi Lucheni rising from Parma slums to bury a shiv in the chest of the empress of Austria. "I hope I have killed her! Long live anarchy! Long live the revolution!"

Lina Zahler, who had supplied the knife, vanished as quickly as she appeared.

Secret societies and coded messages. Had Sinoro come across a relic from Zahler's world? What would Lord Davy make of it?

"Let's see which way you jump," Justine whispered.

She entered Lord Davy's e-mail address, and added a prayer.

> I suspect for Vienna love may never be more than mimicking what she thinks it should be. I know it can bring her happiness, but that's not your deepest concern is it? I can't answer that yet, being as confused as she is.
>
> Meantime, we came across a code in one of Vienna's memory books. It's from the turn of the last century, written by an anarchist. It looks like a block of random letters to me, but Vienna sees a pattern: groups of letters (usually three) repeated in multiples of seven. Does this suggest anything to you?
>
> We are headed to Reykjavík early this evening. Vienna seems content with this, though her crying spells have not decreased and may in fact be increasing.
>
> The woods are lovely, dark and deep,
> But I have promises to keep,
> and miles to go before I sleep.
>
> Yankee Invader

She wondered if she'd read the man correctly. Poetry with alpha males could be dicey. After a second's hesitation, she sent the note off.

Her inbox, once filled with invitations and praise, had turned into a reservoir of spam. Only one entry of any interest; a Thailand firm that made custom cases for high-end gaming computers. Hot Dragon. The website link showed Deco streamlines in high-gloss car enamel. The lowest price was 1600 euros. Apparently there was a demand for such things and apparently Justine Am's fall from grace was a marketable otaku meme. She would discuss it with James.

She was still looking over reviews of Hot Dragon when the Sony gave an e-mail beep. A reply from Lord Davy. The speed with which he'd replied was unsettling.

As you know, there are numerous behavioral and cognitive therapies that might help, but I would spare Vienna something she considers disgraceful. Then there are physiological treatments. The list is long and tiresome: methyphenidate, dextroamphetamine, and clonidine, for focus; mipramine and amoxapine for depression; fluoxetine and peroxetine for compulsive behavior. Some seemed to help, but they left her not herself. So you are now the sole drug and therapy.

Given the choice between unwarranted crying and the automaton haze left by the drugs, I would opt for the former. I trust female intuition can separate true anguish from habitual weeping. I have begun to consider this an advantage over a more traditional relationship. Forgive me if that sounds calculated.

The code is a strange question, not because it poses any issues, but because codes always sent her on one of her downward spirals. It is almost certainly a Vigenère cipher. The uneducated long considered such systems unbreakable, but as Vienna has demonstrated, it is nothing of the sort.

Encipherment begins with the selection of a keyword. In your case, the keyword is seven letters long. Given the source, I suspect it will be something inspiring to the radical mind. Next a Vigenère Square is constructed. This is a stack of twenty-six staggered alphabets. You can find examples on the Web. Encryption entails repeating the key word over the plain text. If the key word is "dissent" and the message to encrypt is "The first thing we do, let's kill all the lawyers" then our rebel would write:

DISSENTDISSENTDISSENTDISSENT**DIS**SENTDIS
thefirstthingwedoletskillall**the**lawyers

Encrypting the first letter, "t" is a matter of going across the top row of your Vigenère Square until you hit the "T" column, and then descending until you hit the row beginning with "D." The letter that appears at this intersection is the encrypted result. By luck, "the" appears twice under the same "D-I-S" of the keyword. It will be encoded in identical letters with a gap of twenty-eight letters between. Since the keyword is seven letters long, such repetitions will appear in multiples of seven.

Occam's razor suggests at least one of your three-letter groups is "the." With more letters you will be able to guess the keyword, at which point you possess the solution.

As for your fears, if I may answer your great Frost with a poet of our own:

Lovers and madmen have such seething brains,
Such shaping fantasies, that apprehend
More than cool reason ever comprehends.

Lord Wanker

The cipher explanation was clear as fog, but at least Justine had been right about the poetry. She found an entry for Vigenère ciphers on Wikipedia, complete with a square of alphabets and a description that unraveled Davy's hasty explanation. The algebra-heavy text made Justine wonder how Davy knew so much about codes.

"I'm packed." Vienna stood in the doorway, her eyes swollen. Justine hadn't heard the girl so much as squeak a floorboard. Vienna looked self-consciously down at her clothes. "Why are you staring at me?" she asked.

The cipher was essentially mathematical. *She'll tear it apart if we can get past her fear.* "I'm not staring at you. I'm staring at the teacher's edition to a math problem."

"What?"

"I sometimes used teacher's editions to cheat on homework when I was in high school. I found them at the University of Georgia campus in Athens. Come here." Vienna stepped to her and Justine fussed over her clothing and hair. Vienna's face grew cloudy.

"None of that," Justine said. "This is one of my joys."

"Making sure your doll doesn't look stupid?"

"I don't want you to embarrass me."

Vienna's eyes went wide.

"Hush," Justine said. "If you always assign me evil intentions, I'll never escape them. Now, what rule of human behavior were we on?"

"One jillion," Vienna said in her flat persona.

"Then rule one jillion and one is: people in relationships often find excuses to touch their partners. I find the sensation reassuring. Does it bother you?"

Vienna's long pause was expected. "Why would one of the world's most beautiful women need reassuring over anything? You always get me to do what you want anyway."

Justine leaned over to Vienna's ear and whispered, "That's lesson one jillion and two. People surprise you all the time."

Vienna's eyes moved across unseen words. "Touch may increase oxytocin in humans, particularly females, and may increase feelings of trust and generosity."

"There you go." *Feel the words instead of speaking them.*

"Oxytocin was first synthesized by Vincent du Vigneaud, who won the Nobel Prize in Chemistry in 1955."

Justine closed her eyes and gathered Vienna into her arms. The girl made no response, her lips giving silent voice to endless streams of words.

"We have to get going," Justine whispered.

They met James Hargrave for supper. He would not be joining them in Iceland.

"You have everything under control," he said, "and I need to get back to being an agent. Easier to do in New York than Reykjavík. I do have twenty-three other clients."

"When are you leaving?" Vienna asked.

"Tonight. Red eye to JFK on a triple seven."

"At least we don't have to put up with your suitcases," Justine said.

"Suitcases?" Vienna asked.

"Metal, hacked together from a Vietnam-era portable first aid station."

"That's balmy."

"Welcome to the world of fashion," Justine said.

"It's a guy thing." James smiled. "But they do raise eyebrows with security." He folded his arms on the table.

Justine read his black and silver watch: 6:04. Twenty-six minutes before they had to leave for the airport.

Justine closed her eyes against sudden disorientation. The watch's geometry was wrong; there was no other way to put it. It didn't fit reality.

Was Vienna's sickness contagious after all? *Is this the price of my sins?*

Justine blinked her eyes open. Girard-Perregaux / Manufacture. The minute hand approaching the "1." The hour hand pointing almost straight down, through the inset travel chronometer and matching the hour hand there. The left-side timer set at zero. The hands were on time and perfectly arranged.

What did that even mean, that the geometry was wrong?

She has stolen me from myself.

18

Iceland

Iceland was tethered to jet stream clouds, indigo and umber layers pearl-smooth in the lengthening shadow of the world. Fifty minutes from Keflavík. Vienna sat on the window side of the first-class section of a British Airways Airbus. The sea below was finished in icy blues. The colors turned her mind inward, walking lonely places she didn't want to see. Presents under the tree and the lights all wrong.

She burrowed deeper under the thick blanket the steward had supplied. She should have started her period, but the cramps had eased and nothing had happened and now it seemed she would miss it, leaving her worried and somehow stretched out.

How had she known?

Justine sat in the next seat, bent over her laptop. Vienna saw the American was working on Mr. Sinoro's code. She wanted to be too tired to care what Justine was doing.

Vienna tried to clear her mind, but succeeded only in noticing a faint oscillation in the vacuum roar of the engines. The jet sailed through the gathering night, as smooth as a leaf on a lake. The oscillation was actually two separate wavelengths transposed on top of each other.

A discrete Fourier transform is used for analyzing differing waveforms . . .

Jean-Baptiste Joseph Fourier was orphaned at the age of nine. His father had been a tailor. . . .

. . . where Hans Christian Andersen wrote The Emperor's New Clothes *. . .*

The discordant sound seemed to grow louder.

Make it stop, make it stop, make it stop.

Vienna pulled the blanket over her head, as if it would save her from the crash she was certain was only seconds away. In the darkness she saw the image from Justine's laptop.

```
12345671234567123456712345671234567123456712345
MOEEEXLHWTCIESXKQTKTTHTIOEKRBZIQVAMtheAPMCXVJCMSHMLSFW

671234567123456712345671234567123456712345671234567123
YUKKICXAtheWTKZOYWSHIDtheWPEDEtheXIMSNYIDWFAKAATXTtheW

45671234567123456712345671234567123456712345671
FRMNWPRELQOKKICSRtheTWEZEMZEYHMLPHCDEEtheTWEZEMZQZZQOG

234567123456712345671234567123456712345671234567123456
LXZQQALBVPHUSMHRNIANXASXIMSNYIEMYEBUXSIOIMFSQXTEPOMEII

712345671234567123456712345671234567123456712345671234
AESWOMPMXUIDAQAKAMPWFAKVJSSDULHVZYZDAPWYIOKAPWASIEKPWZ

567123456712345671234567123456712345671234567123456712
YDSWVASEFTAVYHMXTILENINRHALPVEAGKWTWFEKZFPPUEOLEWPYIZO

345671234567
XMIYAWLPPZQL

Possible keyword: the***a
```

Vienna compared the changes Justine had made with the memory of the original. Why was it so hard to see the patterns? She struggled with a trick that one of her first doctors had tried to teach her: *focus on one thing at a time.*

Whenever "MOI" originally appeared, it was under the numbers "123." "TAL" appeared under the numbers "712." Justine had replaced both with "the."

A new geometry laid itself out before Vienna. Letters shifted like cascades of sand down the face of a dune. Given a loop of alphabets, "T" appeared nineteen letters before "M." Shift every seventh letter nineteen spaces.

She saw it behind the numbers. The Star of Memphis. But there were too many choices. She felt her heart racing in the hollow of her throat. Alphabets sliding with each set of seven letters, taking parts of her mind with them. Nauseating dislocation.

"Vienna."

A modulo twenty-six series reeled across Cartesian coordinates.

"Vienna."

René Descartes was born on March 31, 1596. The impact he was to have on Western thought, particularly in the fields of . . .

"Stop." Justine's whisper was soft but intense. She pulled the blanket from Vienna's head.

"Britain was still using the Julian Calendar in 1596," Vienna said. "So that date wouldn't be right for London."

"Vienna."

The grid of letters collapsed. "It was there!"

"Shh. What was there?"

"The code. Why did you stop me?"

"Because ladies sketching on their seat trays when they have no pen chip their nails." Justine gently held Vienna's left hand. Vienna saw the nail on the index finger was broken.

"I saw your computer screen. The pattern isn't so hard."

"It is for me." She used a clipper to trim Vienna's broken nail. "You stopped chewing your nails."

"You told me to."

"Was I the first?"

"No."

"Good." Vienna felt the dissonance of Justine's pronouncement, but Justine was already back to the encryption.

"Too slow," Vienna said. "Give it to me."

Vienna let her finger move across the keyboard. She lost

herself in the mechanics of motion, not daring to think over the changes that appeared.

```
thEEEXloWTCIEseKQTKTtoTeOEKriZeQVAmtheAPMceVJCMShteSFW
YurKeCXAtheWTKZofWSHIDtheWPEDetheXIMsuYeDWFarAATXTtheW
FRMndPRELQorKeCSRtheTWEZetZEYHMlwHCDEEtheTWEZetZQZZQon
eXZQQasBVPHUstHRNIAneASXIMsuYeEMYeiUXSIOitFSQXTewhMEII
alSWOMPmeUeDAQarAMPWFarVJSSDusHVZYZdhPWYIOkhPWASIerPWZ
YDsdVASEFthVYHMXtpeENINroALPVEanKWTWFerZFPPUeveEWPYigh
XMIYadePPZQl
```

"That's amazing," Justine said.

"By which you mean amazing for anyone not an autistic savant." *Why does she piss me off every time she speaks?*

Justine smiled. "I'm not so sure. You created an algorithm to solve the problem on the fly. Savants often have issues with such things."

Vienna shrugged. "Twenty-six modulo algebra. The first element is shifted by nineteen, while the seventh has no shift at all. Surely you saw that when the 'T' in the sequence 'T-A-L' remained unchanged in the word 'T-H-E'."

"Obviously," Justine said in that weird voice she sometimes used. "Although it still doesn't look like much."

"You're wrong and not very smart." Vienna let the letters spill through her. She could track patterns almost in the same way she could track whole words. But now the choices had been narrowed to the point where she could see options without getting tangled in them. She was startled to see two words emerge from the chaos. "Look at the sequence at the beginning of the second line." She pointed at the screen and retyped the letters, replacing the unknown ones with spaces: **_ur_e_** "How many words have this pattern? I see 'burned,' 'buried,' 'burden,' 'cursed,' and 'curved.'" Vienna shifted in her seat. "'Nurses' also fits . . . 'purred' too, I guess."

"Maybe it's a code for cats," Justine said.

Vienna looked at her. "Or a starfish collector seeking pure echinoderms."

It took several seconds for Justine to see the pattern. When she got it, she seemed genuinely delighted, leaning over to kiss Vienna's right temple. "I bow to your wisdom."

Vienna sighed. "Can we be serious again? There is one other word that has a 'UR' in the middle and then an 'E.'"

"Murder," Justine said.

Vienna blinked, feeling that Justine had manipulated her. "You knew?"

"I may not be broken, but I'm reasonably bright."

Vienna let it go. "The "HTE" that appears just before it is an odd combination of letters, yeah?" she said. "I can think of only two words that fit in the nine-letter space we have. One is 'tightened,' which makes no sense."

"And the other?"

"Righteous."

"Righteous murder," Justine said.

"I think so." She gave the laptop back to Justine. "I don't like your code."

"I don't either."

"Where do you think Sinoro found it?"

"I don't know. But 'righteous murder' sounds like something an anarchist would threaten."

Vienna saw words from a poet named Yeats. *Mere anarchy is loosed upon the world.* She didn't say them out loud because they'd always scared her, and she didn't think poetry was supposed to be scary.

The steward stopped at their seats. "I'm sorry, miss, you have to shut off the laptop. We're close to final approach. Please stow your tables."

"I can get more of it," Justine whispered as she folded the laptop closed. "You have to promise me not to think about it."

"Okay." *She's afraid I'll go eppy before landing.*

It was dark by the time they stepped from the Keflavík airport into the SUV limo waiting to take them to Reykjavík. Justine gave the name of the hotel to the driver, another Radisson SAS.

"Pierre-Esprit Radisson's explorations of Hudson Bay in 1668 formed the impetus for the Hudson's Bay Company," Vienna said. The words came as the thought did—something that seemed to happen with Justine. *Because I'm not ashamed when she hears?*

"More important, they have a good restaurant."

The car drifted through sparse traffic. Vienna saw little from the windows, except that once outside Keflavík there were few lights breaking the night. A series of isolated crofts, calling out their presence. It seemed unnatural after the yellow-white brightness of London and Brussels.

Estimating the car's speed from highway signs, Vienna saw that their car traced bases of shifting triangles that reached to each light. Distances and angles flooded through her. Calculus as perfect trigonometry. She closed her eyes tight, but she was so tired and her thoughts were trapped.

"I'm here, Vienna."

"Do you see the sliding triangles? Distances in the lights, derived by speed. That's all there is."

Justine reached into her bag and pulled out what looked like an oversized phone with a large screen. She turned it on. "Show them to me."

"You're supposed to say they aren't real. That's what my doctor in London always said."

"I'm betting your doctor was wrong." The screen lit up and a map appeared. Vienna realized it was a GPS.

"One of Grant's old toys," Justine said, showing a half smile that vanished as soon as it formed.

Vienna looked at Justine. "If you can't see them, how do you know they're real?"

Justine pointed to a distant glow. "How far away is that light?"

"It will be easier when we're even with it."

"Tell me when we get there."

Concentrating on a single light, Vienna found the pain receding. When they were level with it, she said, "One-point-three kilometers. Assuming our speed hasn't changed and the road has been straight and the land is flat between us and the light. I'm using that bright star for a background, so I suppose its apparent movement caused by the Earth's rotation should be taken into account."

"Miles, hun."

Vienna found a conversion table. "Just under point eight—but it's probably way off! I need more time to get it right."

Justine smiled. "The GPS shows a structure zero-point-seven-four miles away. How can I say your triangles aren't real?"

Vienna felt calmness enfold her. A trick Justine could somehow turn, even when doctors could not. The triangles faded, as if they had nothing left to prove. "It's flatter than I thought it would be," she said.

"There's a delta on the southern coast so flat that you can't tell where the land ends and the sea begins. Ships used to run aground there."

"How did they fix it?"

Justine laughed. "They put up a lighthouse."

Vienna blushed. "That was a stupid question wasn't it?"

"It was a delightful question."

"But the answer is obvious."

"So is the fact that pickles come from cucumbers."

Vienna thought that over but could make no sense of it. "What?"

"I didn't realize pickles came from cucumbers until I was nineteen. Until that moment, I assumed there were pickle bushes."

Vienna found herself laughing before she could help it. With a start, she cut it off. "That was mean."

Justine shook her head. "It's a secret lovers share."

Why would you purposely embarrass yourself in front of someone you loved?

"Anyway, Miss Almanac, I need your help."

Vienna let the jab go. She was building a new idea wherein being in a relationship meant ignoring some of the things your partner said. Or even most of the things. "Yes?"

"I need a seven-letter word that begins 'T-H-E' and ends in 'A,'"

"Does this have to do with the code?"

"I've been thinking about the keyword—a shortcut that might make the path easier for us both. We almost have it."

"I need to see the letters."

Justine fished in her bag for a scrap of paper and a pen.

"I'm sorry," Vienna said as Justine whispered in frustration looking for paper.

"No reason to be sorry. I keep forgetting how differently we see the world. I make mistakes," Justine said.

"I don't understand."

"Lord Davy told me the halves of your brain don't communicate well with each other. Speaking and writing are not the same for you as for me. I should have remembered and written the letters to begin with."

Vienna gave up on the whole ignoring idea. "Everyone else avoids talking to me like that, just so you know."

"Ah, but have they slept with you?"

"Does that give you the right to demean me?"

"Did I demean you?"

"You said my brain doesn't work right."

"I said it was different and that I made a mistake, not you. Don't expect me to overlook how singular you are. Now, I want you to consider something."

"Okay."

"Maybe that difference is part of why I am here with you."

Vienna tried again to sort through the words, but it was

easier to let Justine choke on her own medicine. "At least the halves of my brain talk to each other enough to figure out pickles." She marveled at the light tone of her voice—how the words had just come out that way. She wasn't sure what would happen.

Justine laughed so loudly the driver looked briefly back through the glass that separated them. "Very good," she told Vienna.

"You're not mad?"

"I'll make you a deal. You don't tell anyone about the pickles and I won't tell anyone you're broken."

There was so much wrong with this reasoning that Vienna started to object. She caught herself and settled for a nod.

"Good! Now, look at this." Justine found a crumpled receipt and wrote on the back: THE_ _ _ A.

Vienna looked at the letters, saw the shape of words. "Thecata, thecoma, thelema, themata, theorba, Theresa."

"Remind me to talk to you next time I try a crossword puzzle," Justine said. "At least I know the last word."

"The first two are medical terms. I don't understand the definitions."

"Skip them for now."

"Theroba is an old type of musical instrument."

"Unlikely to be our key. What of the others?"

"A themata was an administrative unit of seventh-century Byzantine."

"That has to do with government, so keep it in mind. Was that all?"

"There was thelema." Vienna searched for the word, finding it in several places. "It means 'will.' It first came to prominence in the works of a sixteenth-century monk named R-a-b-e-l-a-i-s. I don't know how to pronounce that."

"Me neither. What did he say about it?"

"He named a town after it in one of his stories. It's associated with the phrase 'Do what thou will.' The Hellfire Club of England nicked it in the eighteenth century. It was a hedonistic society led by Sir Francis Dashwood." Vienna looked over several drawings associated with the text. "The society's 'nuns' were prostitutes." She crossed herself.

"Old as the hills and not what we're after."

"The word was used again in the nineteenth century by various anarchist societies."

"Now we're cooking."

Whatever that was supposed to mean. Vienna looked again at the code, seeing groups of seven that Justine had numbered. Shift each letter in the code by the letters of "thelema." "A" was the first letter of the alphabet, so there was no shift for it. That explained why letters in the seventh position stayed the same. "T" was the nineteenth letter . . .

She felt the acid seduction of the pattern, flowering in her mind like a virus. Night faded away under a shifting matrix of letters. There had never been anything else—never would be anything else. *Stop, stop, stop . . .*

"Vienna. What do you see?"

She couldn't answer. The message was there, she knew it but she couldn't say it. Her thoughts swimming in pain. She felt her hands being grabbed by someone.

"Write it out, Vienna. You have paper and a pen. Don't speak. Just write."

She felt the pen set in her grasp. As if controlled by a mad genie, the hand with the pen stuttered across the paper.

thatalloppressedmightonedayrisefromtheplaceofrighteousm
urdertothesignofpowerthesearethemeasuresstartwiththesun
andintheorderoftheplanetsandalwaysastheplanetsmoveoneto
measuredistanceonetomeasuretimeinthecityofthewhitewalls
didmeneswearthestarofhorusaroundhisneckhispowerisours
dowhatthouwiltpeacebrothersandsistersbelieveallmightbema
delevel

The lights of Reykjavík slid around them, blurred through tears. She was afraid and tired and she felt very far from home, but then she really didn't have a home, did she?

"Damn it." Justine's voice, so soft. "Vienna, it's okay. Let it go. I'm here. Let it go."

It's a thing lovers share.

The lights compressed into a tunnel with a bright spark at the end. A lake where girls drowned themselves for their goddess. A villa of limestone and dusty halls. *Palladian windows comprise paired pilasters upon which rests an entablature . . .* Vienna smelled the musty scent of old paper. She heard music, echoing from stone walls. Bach, she thought. Arpeggio. Lord Davy, eyes closed, conducting a phantom orchestra. Behind the musical scales, the sound of wind through trees.

"Will she be okay?" The accent was strange.

"She needs to sleep." Arms around her.

"There is a hospital nearby."

"It's a seizure, but not a serious one. A hospital would only increase the chance of recurrence. How many more miles to go?"

In miles, hun . . .

Americans didn't use metric. Should have remembered that.

.247 ounces Hg and .035 ounces Au. Emily Holt's copy of Sinoro's notes.

Seven grams of mercury. One gram of gold.

But you never listen.

Lord Davy sitting in an old chair, reading a book. The hushed light of the Cart House.

She saw that the high window above the massive television was a gothic rose of twenty-seven elements. It depicted Christ as the Sower. His disciples looked on in confusion while all around them grains and fruit sprang from the soil. The pagan goddess Nerthus imagined as a man. *And he said unto them, Know ye not this parable? And how then will ye know all parables? The sower soweth the word.*

And her head hurt so bad and they were in one of the Cart

House's long hallways, Vienna pointing at a small drawing. "Ah," Lord Davy said. "Here is a work by Sophia of the Palatinate. I am not one hundred percent certain what it depicts. Men fishing in the distance? Dinosaurs fighting?" Vienna laughed. "Sophia was a great patron of the arts," Davy added, "but a lesser practitioner."

Below that was a painting of a white unicorn, a green plate, and a rose star. Set in faded colors and in that old way where angles didn't work with perspective. "What does this mean?" she asked Uncle Anson.

"The shame of a forgotten prince. It's a very boring and very old story and it has no proper end anyway." He scooted her a step down the hall, to face a glass cabinet holding a tattered strip of leather. "A hunting crop said to belong to Edward the Black Prince," Davy said. "Though it just as easily might have been the property of Stanton the Unknown. Much of what is in the Cart House was put up during moments of great revelry or great melancholy. Neither is conducive to preserving truth."

"Then what is the point, if you don't know if any of it is real?"

Davy gestured the length of the hallway. "The Cart House is not a museum, Vienna. It's . . ." He smiled. "It's an echo. And like all echoes, it can be hard to tell where it originated. But always there is a tiny bit of the original sound left."

"Okay." Though it didn't explain anything. She pointed to a diagram of a steam engine fit with gears and levers that seemed to be employed in steering a horse-drawn carriage.

"I have no idea what it is," Lord Davy said, "beyond ambiance."

"You have to take it down, if you don't know! You can't put it up if you don't know what it is!"

"Enough," Davy said. "Time to be outside. The oak trees are pretty this fall, don't you think? Leaves of gold."

And at first the trees were pretty, but then she was alone. Lost in the nightmare forest and the ghosts of drowned maidens called to her and—

"It's okay, Vienna. I'm here." The words somehow fit inside her, and Justine was walking beside her along the Thames.

You're just like her.

And the nightmare vanished into deep sleep.

19

Reykjavík was built in classic Lego, red and blue triangles over white squares. A rocket ship cathedral claimed the city's highest hill, flanked by walls of descending stone hexagons. Justine saw it through Vienna's eyes: trying to overlay the walls to see if they matched. Fearful symmetry.

Instead of the usual European scrawl of political graffiti, here were trippy aliens sprayed to life on powder-blue cinder block. A half-mocking self-portrait of strangers in a strange land, laughing over a bite of hákarl before beaming back to the stars. Above the aliens, square windows marched across square walls. Sheets of glass streaked by rain.

The rigid geometry would be murder on Vienna. *Should have left her in London.* Justine checked for the hundredth time that Vienna was sleeping easily. Then back to the note Vienna had scrawled out. Justine had separated the words and entered the text on her Sony.

> That all oppressed might one day rise. From the place of righteous murder to the sign of power, these are the measures: Start with the sun and in the order of the planets and always as the planets move. One to measure distance, one to measure time. In the City of the White Walls did Menes wear the Star of Horus around his neck. His power is ours. Do what thou wilt. Peace, brothers and sisters, believe all might be made level.

No mention of Lenin. Frustrated, Justine went back and added multiple exclamation points to the end of each angst-filled phrase. She worried that it read better that way.

Google said the City of White Walls was *inbw-hdj,* an ancient name for Memphis. King Menes was the semi-mythical founder of the city. Apparently, the Star of Memphis was given to the king by the god Horus as a token of divine favor. Wikipedia seemed to have missed that part.

Hours of empty guessing and nothing beyond rising irritation. But as heavy clouds brightened with morning, Justine realized she'd overlooked the most obvious part of the message: *it's in English.*

Had Grant managed to decode it? Did these words somehow reach across a hundred years and put a bullet in his head? How much did Lord Davy know? How had Emily gained access to the code?

Then there was the man at the airport. Coal black hair in a regulation buzz cut and steel blue eyes. A cop with a generous helping of broad shoulders. If his arms were around you, you would know it. He spoke into a silver phone as they left the airport. Meaningless until Justine glanced back as their limo pulled away from the Radisson. The driver on a silver phone of the same make. Probably coincidence. Probably.

And because that wasn't enough to worry about, there was a tattered career to face. The penultimate Clay to Flesh shoot was in two days, near Gullfoss. Justine would be in Al-Begushi's sheer silks. It better be warm out. Gareth Kendal would be shooting. A stand-offish ass-hack with a habit of snapping his fingers at every flighty change of mood. He would cram the shoot into one day and depend on the skimpy wardrobe to cover his lack of talent.

"Heather?" Vienna's voice was unsteady.

"I'm here." Justine stepped to the side of the bed.

"Where are we?"

"The hotel. You had a mild seizure and slept through the night."

"Shouldn't I be in a hospital?"

"You needed rest, not emergency room chaos."

Vienna rubbed her eyes. "On the plane I said you weren't very smart. That was a bad thing to say."

"It's only fair that I make you want to scream now and then, too."

Vienna sorted that out in silence and dealt a new topic. "Have you read the message?"

"You shouldn't worry about it."

Vienna's ghost smile turned her lips for a breath. "Does it mean anything to you?"

"Other than being more purple than a broken nose, no."

"More purple?"

Justine snagged a chair leg with her foot and pulled it next to the bed. " 'That all oppressed might one day rise!' "

"I have no idea what you're on about."

"Vienna, no one talks like that anymore, assuming they ever did." Justine looked back at the message. " 'His power is ours!' " She mimicked a strident infomercial voice-over. "And it can be yours with no down payment." She raised her arms in resignation.

Vienna's expression froze into baffled emptiness.

"Come on, Vienna. Are you certain we aren't being trolled?" Justine continued before Vienna could ask. "Internet lingo meaning someone is pulling a spiteful joke. We have this astounding secret code, so important people are dying to see it, that reads like the opening monologue of a high school play."

"You think it's a sham?"

"I don't know. Would you ever write something like that?"

Vienna shifted. " 'Let all be made level' was an anarchist motto used before the Great War. No more rich kings and poor peasants, yeah? If the royal families wouldn't step aside, they would have to be killed. Not just Sisi, but Marie-Francois Carnot in France, and Alexander II in Russia, and William McKinley in the United States. They were all assassinated by anarchists, so that all might be made level."

"Not a good time to have a recognizable coat of arms. What of the rest?"

"I think the anarchists were terrified of what they'd become."

"What do you mean?"

"Every assassination and every bomb plot weakened the old order. The center could not hold. They felt the war coming—I see it in their books. So they pretended to speak from science and history, as if claiming ties to respected disciplines would somehow bring calm."

"That fits with the allusions to astronomy and ancient Egypt," Justine said. "But why so strident?"

Vienna gave a small shrug, hummed a single, short note. "Horace," she said. "He was the one who talked about words being purple. It's because purple dye used to be an extravagance." The timid smile. "We're stupid to solve a code and not understand it."

Justine rearranged the blankets around Vienna. "It doesn't seem fair."

"But some of it is real. It mentions the Star of Memphis."

"I have no idea what that is."

"I remembered it in my dreams."

"It can wait a few hours."

"I'm tired of sleeping.

Justine sat. "When I was in the third grade, I caught pneumonia. I was in bed for four weeks. Bored to tears but my parents wouldn't let me do anything. I swore I would never put anyone else through that."

"Now would be a good time to start."

"Except my parents were right."

Vienna sighed. "The Holy Grail: the vessel that caught the blood of Christ. You know the tale?"

"Vienna, there are vast sections of cable wasteland that make a living by revealing the shocking truth about the Holy Grail. Is this important?"

"I'm just trying to help."

She's beautiful when she's all business. The thought came before Justine had a chance to amend it with something safer. "Apologies, oh Master of History. Please continue."

"Several Eastern Christian traditions hold that the Holy Grail was a plate. In the eighteenth and nineteenth centuries, many people thought this plate resided in the treasury of the House of Habsburg. It was carved in ancient Rome from a single piece of agate, over half a meter across. It passed to the House of Burgundy after it was plundered from Constantinople in 1204." Vienna sighed while switching tracks. "The Fourth Crusade. Three days in April. Constantinople burned. Did you know that?" Her voice grew soft. "The city's treasures plundered. Blood so thick in the streets that horses lost their footing. The stench of rotting flesh. Girls raped while their fathers were forced to watch."

This is what it is to never forget. The nasty flip side to idyllic dreams of reincarnation. Justine gave Vienna's shoulder a soft squeeze. "So you think you've found the Holy Grail?" she asked, afraid of the answer.

"Don't be daft. Historians catalogue it as a fourth-century ornamental plate commissioned by a Roman aristocrat. But even that's something special. The craftsmanship has never been duplicated, and the legends only add to its value. The bowl is one of two recognized Inalienable Heirlooms of the Habsburgs. It's on display in Vienna. I saw it when I was small, an emerald surface polished to hold light. All green, in a million different hues. It appears very deep, as if the stone isn't really there at all, just the color. It's priceless."

Justine exhaled. "Grant mentioned inalienable artifacts, didn't he? Priceless ones at that."

Vienna nodded. "The other publicly known Inalienable Heirloom is a unicorn horn. Well, the horn of a narwhal, yeah? It's on display as well. I thought it was depressing." She rubbed her hand across the bedcover. "Anyway, there was a museum guidebook. That's the German I remembered."

"So far so good."

"But it's wrong. There was a third artifact. It was lost, or maybe stolen, in the nineteenth century. The only place I saw it was in a painting when I was younger. A unicorn horn, a plate, and a star, just like on the bottom of the statues."

Justine nodded but said nothing. She was no longer thinking about plates and stars.

A long time since colonial history, but the pieces were there, lying in the bed next to her. King George III. Not really a British king at all. He represented the House of Hanover, a German family brought in to replace the Stuarts. His Majesty had been a prince of the Holy Roman Empire, just as the Habsburgs had been before him.

The mirror shifted and she saw a new reflection. A handicapped girl left in an Austrian orphanage. The workers there had no idea who she was—Sir Davy had mentioned redacted records. But others had been watching. In light of her asthma, Vienna was taken to the clean air of southern Wales. When her health improved, she was fostered by an English gentleman living in one of the world's wealthiest neighborhoods. Centuries'-old ties never forgotten. Vienna's family name would be something familiar.

"Justine?"

"What?"

"I said the star disappeared in the 1880s. That's when the manikins were made. Maybe the star is hidden in one of them?"

"I don't think so, or chances are they would have found it by now. Or gone after it way before this. We already know they're willing to kill." Justine rubbed her hands over her face. "I'm in your shoes. Too many facts I can't put together and a pounding headache for my efforts."

Vienna fidgeted. "What do we do?"

"Follow the girl."

"The girl?"

"Lina Zahler."

"Who is . . ." Vienna's eyes tracked through memory. It would be much harder without seeing the name written. She found it all the same. "David Bell's girlfriend in Hungary. The woman who helped plan the assassination of Sisi."

"Almost girlfriend." Justine paused. "Girlfriend."

Realization hit so fast Justine was caught between laughter and disbelief. Crossed signals triggered a minor bout of coughing.

"Are you okay?"

"Nerds in love."

"What?"

"The code—it's a love letter. Rich boy falls for a girl from the wrong side of town. Bell's social standing would amount to nothing in the eyes of Lina Zahler. So he puts his fine English education to use by writing a cipher. He's a clever boy and he has studied the jargon. He knows how to do a proper job. You see? He's trying to impress her."

"How can you know?"

"Nothing generates pretentious language faster than a hard-on."

"You're only guessing."

"It's as flawless as your geometry. The code was written in English, and the timing is aligned with the star vanishing. Somehow Bell ended up with it."

"How?"

Justine shook her head. "No idea. But Zahler was an anarchist and Bell had something valuable to help her cause. He hid the star and dreamed up an elaborate code to prove his bona fides as a True Believer. If Lina wanted the star, she would have to deal with him." Justine leaned back. "She must have thought it hopelessly juvenile. At any rate she never answered Bell's passion. Bell returned to England. He carved his love's name into the sole of his father's Budapest manikin. He must have carved the unicorn head and plates and stars as well. A final reminder of his deeds for the cause."

"But they died over a hundred years ago. How can you know what they did?"

"Love comes and goes, but people never change."

"Okay." Vienna looked away. "Do you think I'm a nerd, too?"

"Of course. But you wear it with panache."

"And that makes you the mean woman who thinks everyone is juvenile?"

Justine closed her eyes for several seconds. "You give me too much credit. I'm going to pull the trick Lina refused to."

"What trick?"

"Pretend love where there is none."

Vienna's face clouded. "What do you mean?"

"Do you know why I tease you sometimes?"

"I think so."

Emily's right. She's a terrible liar.

Justine spoke just above a whisper. "For what we have to do next, you have to turn off what you think and trust me."

"What do we have to do?"

"In Brussels you said the manikins were puzzle boxes. Could you take one apart and put it back together?"

"The diagram I saw was very old. It was hanging on the wall of the Cart House."

"The same villa my dear dead lover was booted out of for stealing books. The same one where his father first came across the code. God only knows how Sinoro got it. I suppose Grant got careless in his haste. That would be like him."

"That's not right. Andries was rich and he was friends with members of the Golden Fleece. I'm a nobody."

"The Cart House was in a forest, wasn't it? You remember trees."

Vienna seemed to shrink within herself. "Yes. Uncle Anson took me there on holidays. Sunset clouds the color of cherry wine. I didn't think much of it then, but it was beautiful. In winter, the trees shimmered under snow. My foster father once took me for a ride on a horse-drawn sleigh. When I think about it sometimes I feel like crying because it was so perfect. Does that make sense?"

"Yes. It sounds like a wonderful place."

"The walls had all these pictures and things, dusty and sad. I asked Uncle Anson about it, and he said sometimes it was important to remember the way things used to be. And even if things used to be arrogant and wrongheaded, it was okay to be proud of your past. I'm not sure what that means. But outside it was peaceful, no one for miles around. Only the lake where Nerthus was supposed to have ridden her cart."

"Lario's Cove."

"What?"

"Two hour's cruise out of Nadi Town in Fiji there's a little island. You can't find it in guidebooks and maps show it as off-limits as an historic preserve. Lario pretty much owns the place. Crazy old islander, but sweet as any man you will ever meet. Unless you step on his island uninvited, then he starts talking native rights and lawsuits. Scary stuff."

"I don't understand."

"Lario's Cove is a playground for the famous. It's a chance to get away from the crowds. Drink too much and talk even more. It's blessed freedom from celebrity, but there are many unwritten rules. Privacy and respect above all else. Overstep the bounds even once and you're gone for good. There are several such places scattered around the world: Takachiho Spa; Marten's Ranch near Jackson Hole; St. Bessel on the Aegean."

"There was some drinking at Cart House," Vienna said. "And hunting and card games and a huge telly with football. There were seven old pinball machines in one of the old servant's houses. Uncle Anson kept them in perfect condition. He was very good at playing them." Vienna's finger's flashed as if she were working pinball paddles. "Lots of different men were there. Not as many women. I didn't recognize any of them, but they all seemed to know each other."

"Europe's gentry. Likely all related, however distantly. People from families that can trace their ancestry back for centuries. Dukes and counts and margraves. Titles that were once prestigious but now serve as fodder for gossip blogs. I can see why they hold on to their history. I would, too. I would love to see the inside of your forest villa."

"Why can't you? You're famous, yeah? More famous than any of them."

Justine smiled. "Same planet, different world. We Americans don't have the genealogy for it."

Vienna shrugged. "A few times I was there, they were dancing. Men in uniforms and the women in beautiful gowns. Everyone smiling and laughing. I didn't recognize many of the dances, but they always came back to waltzes. Chopin and Strauss and Haydn. It's like a painting." Vienna sipped at her water glass. "But I think you're right. If anyone made a commotion, they would never be allowed back." She went silent for several minutes before finding the original thread of the conversation. "The first time Uncle Anson took me to Cart House was seven months after I recited the German Bible in Bath. How could you know about the forest? I don't think I told you about that."

So Lord Davy was in the picture from the start. Big surprise.

"But you did tell me that Grant's troubles started near Grois-bach. I looked it up. It's on the edge of the Wienerwald, not far from your orphanage. I didn't see your fairyland estate on the map, but it's there, hidden in the forest." Justine bit her lip. "That's probably where Grant first saw you, a decade ago. He would have been about eighteen. You would be easily remembered, a single child in a house of adults. He discovered you were in Brussels and he found a way to introduce himself. You still have access to the estate and everything there. He could use you." She held up her hand before Vienna could repeat that she was a nobody orphan. "We can talk about it later. For now it's enough to know that the schematic for assembling the manikins is either rare or hidden. Can you follow it?"

"The big toe on the left foot is held with a wooden pin. Take the pin out and the toe drops. The ankle shifts down . . ." She swallowed. "Yes, I can do it."

"But only with one of the originals. The copies would be a single piece of resin, made to replace destroyed originals."

"Yes."

"We need enough time to take a real one apart without the owner knowing it."

"If the star isn't inside, then what is?"

"Christian Bell didn't craft exquisite puzzle boxes to leave them empty. Maybe love offerings of some kind. His anarchist offspring replaced them with something significant enough to get people killed, even after all these years." Justine clinched her jaw against another yawn. "Though none of this works unless the manikin puzzles are difficult to solve. Otherwise, why go through the destroy-and-replace cycle?"

Vienna's hands twisted over air, manipulating imagined pieces of wood. "The seven key pieces are small, three in the foot and four in the hip. The rest are larger. Without knowing about the small ones, you would have to split the wood. Once it was splintered, you would never discover the trick of taking them apart."

"Then we know what's happening, but not why."

"Or why Andries was killed in the first place."

"Because he believed you might provide answers. Once he had the solution, he wouldn't have to share the spoils. His seeking you out was a betrayal of whoever was working with him." Lord Davy.

"Then why not meet me at the gelato shop? He knew I worked there."

"He was scared."

"Scared of what?

"Dear Uncle Anson." It felt too right not to be true.

"But to know any of this for sure, we have to see inside an original manikin?"

"Exactly. The statue in Vienna is owned by an older woman. She's a huge fan of mine—or so James tells me—though not likely susceptible to my charms. But the Iceland manikin belongs to a musician—Haldor Stefansson. He's into New Age Nordic schlock. Fancies himself an international lady's man."

"You know him?"

"I read everything I could find on him over the last five hours. Wish I had your memory. Still, I know his discography, from *Northland Roar* to *Dawn of the Old Gods*. I called him before you woke. We're meeting him today." Justine tried to keep worry from her voice. "How long do you need to take the statue apart and put it back together?"

"Two hours, if it's like the diagram."

"I was hoping for fifteen minutes, but if it were easy, they would have figured it out. I can get you three hours."

"How?"

Here we go. "A disgraced fashion model and a niche musician who fancies himself the gods' gift to women. Surely he will be able to work his magic on me."

"Magic?"

"Love."

"But you're with me?"

"He doesn't have to know that."

"It's in the news."

"That means nothing. Men of a certain type believe that women of a certain type need men of a certain type."

"I don't understand."

"I know, Vienna. It's important that you listen, okay?"
She nodded.

"To make this work, I have to lie. It's not fair to you. Or to him, or to me, for that matter. But I'm scared. The police haven't connected the dots, but we have and they're all being murdered."

"What sort of lie?"

"That I don't love you and that I might be convinced to love him. You need to understand it will be a lie."

"Why would you do such a thing?"

"To get him out of the room so you can work. He lives north of Selfoss. I have a rental car waiting outside. We have to leave in two hours. Will you be okay?"

"Yes."

"Good. We need to get some protein in you, and fluid as well."
Vienna sat up. "You didn't sleep last night, did you?" she asked.
"I'll be fine for one day."

Justine helped Vienna choose clothes, picking the most unflat-
tering skirt and pulling a mismatched blouse. Vienna would
never notice. As Vienna started her shower, Justine went online,
tracking down a quote she'd heard back in school. Then a quick
text to Lord Davy:

> I know Shakespeare as well:
> "Let us sit upon the ground
> And tell sad stories of the death of kings."
> Which sad story am I sleeping with?
> Yankee Invader

Keep pushing and see what breaks loose. Isn't that what they
always did in the movies? She shut down the BlackBerry, ordered
a large breakfast for Vienna, and took her own shower. By the
time she was out, the BlackBerry had Davy's reply.

> Richard II is all well and good, but there are kings and then
> there are Kings. Try Deuteronomy for explanation:
> A bastard shall not enter into the congregation of the LORD;
> even to his tenth generation.
>
> For further enlightenment ask our girl for the history of Em-
> peror Franz Josef. She has a circumlocutious entry that we
> traced to a 50s encyclopedia. Heaven knows where she
> came across it. Time her recitation. She is nothing if not a
> creature of precision. Seven minutes in is the rest of your
> answer. Some genes carry true. As for a family name, her
> descent is strictly paternal. Few people know. Keep it that
> way.
>
> Lord Wanker

Justine erased the message. She'd expected Davy to evade her question. One more piece that didn't fit.

Out of the Radisson to the rental. The air smelled of wet pavement and winter. Rain coated the car's windshield. The sky was the color of seawater, as if the North Atlantic had been suspended overhead and was slowly seeping back to earth.

Justine wound through the Reykjavík traffic with recklessness copied from other European cities. Highway 5 was four lanes of asphalt that would rate as a minor artery in Atlanta.

"How are you doing, Vienna?"

Vienna pointed to a long row of white apartments. "Curtained windows and reflections like a captcha." It sounded bad, whatever it meant.

"Would it help to be distracted? Back at the Brussels stylist, you read local history."

"I don't know the history of Reykjavík. Except that part about throwing high-seat pillars—whatever those are—overboard and following them to see where they beached."

Justine resisted the impulse to follow that. "Then how about European history? Say, Franz Josef." It was such an awkward shift she worried Vienna would balk. But the girl fell into search mode.

"The emperor of Austria? He was very famous in connection with his beautiful wife." Her voice grew more animated. "Empress Elizabeth, that is to say Sisi, who was murdered by one of Lina Zahler's friends."

"Let's stick with him for now." That was all it took. Justine timed Vienna's recitation on the car's glowing blue clock. Seven minutes and twenty-one seconds in:

". . . Franz Josef was renowned for his ability to recall the names of people he had seen only once. He applied the same prodigious memory to written works, reading even the longest state documents and instantly memorizing them. . . ."

Justine expected Vienna to stop her recital long enough to consider such provocative lines, but she continued on, lost in the words. Vienna of the House of Habsburg, albeit by way of a bastard.

Not that her regal ancestry made any difference to the forest of corpses being planted at her feet.

20

Vienna took distant note of her surroundings as she read to Justine. They climbed a long hill out of Reykjavík. Geothermal plants tapped spigots from hell, sending roiling clouds of steam across the road. Beyond landscaped yards, there were no trees, only twisted channels of volcanic rock covered in emerald moss. The green looked overly saturated, as if backlit by elvish enchantment.

Selfoss passed in a huddle of wet buildings and long greenhouses. Justine took several turns under direction from her GPS. The result was a narrow, all-weather tarmac leading inland. The terrain became more rugged, waterfalls marking basalt scarps. The road resorted to roller-coastering over hills and around pitched gullies. Everything was green tundra and roiling water and silverblack gravel.

A band of white appeared in the distance. Vienna thought it was a cloud.

"Glacier," Justine said. Her voice didn't sound right.

Haldor's house was at the end of a long side road. A geodesic dome painted bright yellow. "Great," Justine said. "How are you with Fuller Domes?"

"They're boring," Vienna answered.

"Boring?"

"In Bath, my foster family had a geodesic greenhouse. I saw it every day, and they're all the same." She felt Justine wasn't convinced. "This is a third-order geodesation of an icosahedron, yeah?" She hoped she pronounced the words right. She'd never heard anyone actually use them.

"Naturally," Justine said. "So how many small triangles are there?"

Was she joking? There was no way of knowing except by asking, and there didn't seem time as they were almost in the driveway. Vienna spoke quickly. "The number of triangles is found by taking the square of the number of times a line of the original icosahedron is cut. A third order geodesation would result in 180 small triangles. But this isn't a complete sphere. I'm not sure how far it goes down in the back."

"Let's say ninety and call it good."

It would be more than that, but the car was stopping.

Haldor Stefansson was a nice-looking man, Vienna thought. Barrel chest and a full, red beard. Sandy-red hair and deep brown eyes. "Go than dragon," he said, or at least that's what it sounded like.

Justine reached out to shake hands. "Good afternoon," she replied.

"It's rare to greet such beauty at my doorstep," he said. His accent was Germanic, stretched over long, liquid vowels. His voice was deep and intimidating.

"Thank you." Justine nodded to Vienna, "This is Vienna."

"The Brit I've read so much about."

"Rumors fly."

The man smiled at this. "My sanctuary is yours."

The interior was a clutter of heavy timbers and thick furs. So much wasted space. Vienna rearranged the room in her mind, throwing a third of the furniture away. Starting with a gaudy two-handed sword in its polished stand—an ornate stage prop with no basis in history.

Lady Hildur, the Icelandic manikin, stood in the middle of the great room floor. The tupelo girl wore a wig of jet black. Her arms were folded under her breasts. She looked forlorn—like the poster of the girl Vienna had in Brussels. Haldor had left her nude, and Vienna was left to wonder why Christian Bell had taken the time to carve nipples on his statue's chest. Had he been embarrassed while he did it? At least the manikin had green eyes, so Justine wouldn't have to wear contacts.

Vienna placed the sculpture over the Cart House diagram, just as she'd placed the map over Brussels. She saw the shape of each piece. Unless you looked closely at the toes, you would never figure out how to get inside. She enjoyed her secret knowledge.

"She's amazing," Justine said. Her voice had the soft blush Vienna was familiar with from Justine talking too much during lovemaking.

"She's spending the night here after a week of getting fit for her new wardrobe," Stefansson replied. "I'm glad she's back." *The duplicate has been made.* "I had to have her, as she is named for the queen of elves. She has a very Icelandic spirit."

"Your country does have a magical temper, as you noted in your last CD. I can see how it inspires your music," Justine said. "A shame about the rain, I would love to explore."

"There's much to see close by; more beautiful in the rain than sun."

"One hundred and twenty-seven," Vienna said. It was all she could think of to draw attention to the fact she was being excluded from the conversation.

"What's that?" Justine said, not even turning around.

"The number of triangles in the dome."

"Yes, Vienna. That's a good girl." Justine kept her eyes on Haldor. Vienna sensed everything had changed but didn't know what it meant. Except that Justine was meaner than she ever had been and that was saying a lot.

She couldn't see Justine's face, but Haldor was smiling. "Perhaps we could explore together?" he asked.

"That would be wonderful." Justine paused. "We can take our car. Vienna can squeeze in the back."

"Or we could take my Porsche," Haldor said. "I wouldn't want to trouble Vienna over much. She looks tired and she would be more than welcome to stay here."

"A great idea," Justine said. "Be a good girl and don't get into trouble, Vienna."

"There are a few English channels on TV," Haldor said. "Mostly

BBC, but one or two from America if you want to hear people screaming at each other."

"Perfect," Justine said. "She loves watching the news."

And then, arm-in-arm, they were gone. Just like that. Vienna stood motionless. She felt her pulse thrumming in the back of her throat, driving shame through her body. Scattering her thoughts and leaving her mouth dry. Memories of men who'd come to her door in Brussels. They all left, too.

"Stop it!" she shouted into the empty room.

Deep breaths, like her doctors always wanted. Talk it through inside your head. Justine had said she was going to trick Haldor into believing she might care for him. And isn't that what she'd just done? It's okay. That had been the plan.

"It's okay."

Vienna tried to remember exactly what Justine had said, except now she got stuck on Justine's parting comment about watching the news.

"You didn't even remember that I don't like the telly," Vienna yelled at the empty house. "I've only told you a hundred times and if you really cared you would have remembered." And before Vienna could be still or do any of the things her doctors were always on about, she saw another truth. Justine had admitted that Haldor knew a lot about women. So how could he have been fooled by the flimsiest of pretense? Unless it had been no pretense at all.

"It's okay," she repeated.

What were they doing right now? Kissing? Were his hands already on her?

"It's okay." Because this had been predictable. *How many times did I tell Grayfield that moving out was a bad idea?* Of course Justine was the same as the men who had come to Vienna's door. Bleak satisfaction in being right.

"She already left me once." And that was true, too.

Tears everywhere.

I want to go home.

There had to be some way to Keflavík, and then London, and somehow to Brussels. Doubtless it could all be arranged with money, which Vienna didn't have because she didn't have a job thanks to Justine.

Lord Davy!

If the Cart House really was a hideaway for rich people, then Lord Davy had to be wealthy. He'd even said he wanted her back in London, and he never liked Justine, so it worked perfectly. He could call her a taxi and pay for it with a credit card number. Or maybe he had his own plane—one of those ones from the military that didn't need a tarmac. It could land close by and then fly right to London. That would be best, especially if Justine saw it. Vienna imagined herself waving out the window as the plane took off.

She pulled out her cell phone, relieved to find she had coverage. Davy answered on the first ring.

"Hello, Vienna. How are you?"

She spoke through her crying. "Justine left and I want to go home."

There was more of a pause than distance could account for. "Tell me what happened."

"She wanted to come to this man's house to look at this stupid manikin from her pictures and she said she wanted me to take it apart and see what was inside and she doesn't even remember that I can't watch TV and I am tired of her being mean and I want to go home."

Another long pause. When Davy spoke, he used that calm voice airline pilots used when they told passengers to fasten their seat belts. "I want 'yes' or 'no' answers. She said you liked television?"

"She told him I liked watching it, and she knows—"

"You are alone with a manikin from one of Justine Am's Clay to Flesh projects?"

"In this puke yellow geodesic dome in Iceland with nowhere—"

"Vienna. I'm trying to think, and I'm not sure how much time you have."

"Time?"

"Justine wanted you to take the statue apart? I didn't know they could be disassembled."

"It's a simple—"

"How long for you to do it?"

"One hour to take it apart and one to put it back."

"And she wanted you to find something inside?"

"Yes, but she doesn't know—"

"What did she suspect?"

"She didn't say. Maybe something about the Star of Memphis. I don't care anymore. I hate her. I want—"

"Vienna. Take the statue apart and see what is inside. You must start now."

"Why?"

"You have to trust me. Please, I need you to do this. Promise me."

"I don't—"

"Vienna. Promise me now."

"No."

"Vienna." He used that voice that meant he had lost the argument but he was going to get his way anyhow.

The back of Vienna's throat hurt, like it did just before she threw up. Everyone hated her. "I promise."

"Do it now and don't tell Justine you called me. It can be your way of getting back at her."

Vienna closed the phone without saying good-bye and went to the statue. Everyone asking her to do things and no one ever giving anything in return and it had always been that way. She thought about breaking her promise, but it was clear Uncle Anson wouldn't help because in the end he was just like everyone else. And now Vienna had to take the statue apart because he bullied her and people who broke promises went to hell forever. Where they could meet Justine Am when she ended up there.

Vienna was able to tip the manikin to the floor without letting it drop too hard. A plate, star, and unicorn horn tattooed in the left foot. The wooden holding pin in the big toe was almost invisible. She pulled it with an anticlockwise twist, and the toe popped loose. The fourth toe slid forward. That was enough to release the big toe. Vienna yanked it out and threw it across the room. The ankle dropped revealing a grooved track of wood, and now the foot was loose. She rotated the knee joint clockwise until the foot loosened further. Push the outside ankle in. Rotate the heel. Pull the small toe all the way out and the foot dropped free. Vienna threw it across the room as well.

Didn't you ever play with dolls?

Vienna worked her way up to the chest, throwing each piece as it came free. Behind the left breast there was a small box of red wood. It was not on the diagram. How had Justine guessed its existence?

Were all women like this? Things hidden away? Could the Star of Memphis be inside? Justine hadn't believed it, but she had to be wrong sooner or later.

Vienna slid the rounded lid off. Inside were two small cylinders of metal. One golden and the other dull gray.

Not golden. Real gold. It had to be—the weight of it and the way it caught the light. Maybe ten grams. Enough for a plane ticket. Vienna sat still for several minutes after cylinders found their way into her skirt pocket. *They belong on Julian Dardonelle's list.* The slip of paper he'd shown her back in Brussels. Gold and silver, gold and copper, gold and iron, gold and lead. He must have pulled each pair from the shattered remains of manikins in Rome, Paris, Budapest, and Prague. And somehow Sinoro had the weights of gold and mercury from the Brussels manikin. It didn't make any sense, and anyway if Justine thought Haldor was so much better than she was, let him figure it out.

I'm going home.

She scampered across the floor, collecting the manikin's scattered anatomy. She lined the pieces up and slid them into place as quickly as she could. It went together faster than she'd predicted. One hundred and fifty-three minutes since Justine left. If

Justine stayed out for the three hours she promised, she would not be back for another twenty-seven minutes.

Vienna spent several frantic minutes trying to set the statue back upright, but her arms shook under the weight. She gave up and ran out the door. Across a mosaic of moss-painted lava.

The rain had retreated to the clouds. A strip of blue stretched in a broken ring around the horizon. It seemed like a good sign.

She kept running until she could no longer see the house.

21

Vienna was gone when they got back.

Should have expected it.

The manikin was tipped over, glass eyes contemplating the tragedy of faux-Viking interior design. Justine sighed. "I'll pay for any damage."

Haldor easily righted the statue. "It looks fine. Will the girl come back? She seems a nuisance."

No wonder she hides away. "She likely panicked after pushing the manikin over. I better fetch her. Thank you for a wonderful time." If nothing else, Haldor had behaved the true gentleman, overriding an obvious desire not to.

"It was enjoyable, even taking into account your antiquarian ideas of courtship."

"Our national hang-up."

"Nonsense. Americans are fine people when you stop trying to convince everyone you are." He favored her with a condescending smile. "I shall attend your photo session and hope for more luck on a second date."

Justine forced a tight grin. "Fair enough. For now, I better get the girl."

"How will you find her?"

"Never sell me short."

Zoomed out, Justine's GPS showed a loose web of roads around Haldor's dome. Vienna wouldn't be on any of them. She'd take the shortest route to Reykjavík, calculated along a straight edge of tears and anger. No time to consider lava escarpments or glacial runoff. Justine called up the GPS's topographic overlay and saw a nightmarish maze of contour lines. The closest town was

Hveragerdi, a collection of geothermal greenhouses that may as well have been on Mars for all the chance Vienna had of reaching it before dark.

Justine chose the first road intercepting Vienna's path, a washboard of dirt that nullified her rental car agreement inside ten yards. She found a high point near Vienna's projected crossing and stepped from the car.

The evening grew temporarily brighter as the sun raked the bottom of tarnished clouds. Sitting in the warm light, Justine felt lost in a Van Gogh landscape. Rocks and waterfalls rendered in uneven layers of brilliant color. Even the smallest tundra flowers seemed to vibrate with life. The only thing missing was Vienna— her unassuming beauty captured in fretful brushstrokes.

The sun dipped and the landscape dimmed to muddy watercolors. "Come on, Vienna."

A lone figure topped a serpentine gravel bank south of Justine's vantage point. The only person Justine had seen since stopping. "There we go."

Exhaustion and the mousetrap terrain exposed Vienna's abridged motor skills. Every other step required stop-motion overbalancing to prevent a fall. Justine backed up fifty yards to intercept Vienna's asymmetrical march.

The dust-streaked trails left by tears were expected, but the smears across Vienna's glasses were somehow more painful. The girl's hair had achieved new levels of anarchy. She had a cut on the underside of her right forearm as a firsthand lesson on the sharpness of basalt. Her skirt was wet along the bottom, evidence of a stream crossing. Goose bumps on her forearms.

Vienna glanced at Justine then looked away, set on walking.

She tries so hard to keep everything together and it blows up anyway. It wasn't a condition you could diagnose or dissect. It was the sunny lawns of Stanford.

I've got this one.

She spoke just above a whisper. "Stop."

"Bog off," Vienna said. She stopped all the same.

"Not going to happen."

"I hate you."

"Then why walk all this way to get my attention?"

"I don't care what you think."

"I think I don't hate you at all. Tough luck for us both, huh?"

The girl had no end of ability to make tears. Justine quashed a sudden image of her shriveling like a mummy to supply her waterworks.

"You left me."

"I warned you."

"You said you would . . ." The girl's face drained of expression. "You didn't even remember I don't like the telly."

"I remembered perfectly. I suggested it to let you know I was lying. It was something Haldor wouldn't know, but you would."

"I don't care."

Justine saw the girl fitting pieces together, reaching the obvious conclusion hours late. *It happened too fast, even though she knew what was coming.* No time to find emotional equilibrium. "Vienna, you instantly recognize geometrical relationships that I might never see."

"So what?"

"Sometimes I'm quick to see patterns, too. I see what will move people in a direction I want. I saw what would move Haldor and I used it."

"Do you do that to me?"

"Yes."

"You have no right," Vienna sniffled.

"I have every right. This is my life. I'll take what I can. If I want you, I'll use every trick to get you."

"Like David Bell wanting Lina Zahler."

"Except he failed."

"What trick do you use to move me?"

"Honesty."

Vienna looked down at her feet. "Why haven't you asked me what was in the statue? You know I took it apart."

Back in Montana all those years ago. Once in a long while, Granddad's old radio came in crystal clear. *There's a hanging slider in the wheelhouse* . . . "You first, everything else second. Isn't that how your books say it should be?" . . . *and she's gone yard!*

Without looking up, Vienna ran the short distance to Justine and stood before her. Justine understood the oddly incomplete motion and enfolded Vienna in her arms.

"Do you hate me?" Vienna asked.

"No."

"It's not fair that no matter what you say, I end up going along with it."

"You're better off than I am. You don't say anything at all, and here I am waiting."

Justine was startled to hear muffled laughter. "I'm not going to cry anymore."

"It's okay, Vienna."

"And you lied back in London."

"I did?"

"You said you wouldn't come back if I left you, and here you are."

The Hollywood rejoinder would be a slow-motion kiss. An inexcusable mistake with Vienna. *My feet are muddy! There's blood on my arm and dirt everywhere! Don't kiss me! You'll leave again!*

Justine released her hold. "I came back because I want you with me."

Vienna smiled, caught herself, then let the smile through anyway. A short sniffle. "There were two cylinders of metal in the manikin. I think one is gold."

"You took them?"

"I know it was stealing. We can take them back."

"With this mess, all bets are off. I'll make amends later."

Vienna hesitated. "Then you don't like him?"

"The man lives in Iceland and drives a ragtop 911."

"Ragtop?"

"Convertible."

Vienna stood motionless as the seconds passed. "The average annual temperature of inland Iceland varies between zero and five degrees centigrade." She nodded, as if satisfied with a long chain of deductions.

Justine removed the girl's glasses and carefully brushed the lenses on her sleeve. "Didn't I tell you smart is sexy?"

"A smart person would have understood why you left with him."

"A smart person would have figured out how to get inside the manikin without seducing him in the first place." Justine led Vienna to the car. "I act within my limitations no less than you."

Vienna fell asleep within minutes of sitting in the car. The difference between the real world and the Euclidian landscape that filled her head must have come as a shock.

A lot like med school.

An hour later streetlights reached to the sky, glowing off the aluminum outliers of Reykjavík. A shimmering city on the edge of the world. Venus chasing the cobalt postscript of sunset.

You always said you wanted adventure.

"Wake up, Vienna. We're almost home."

The girl stretched in her seat. "The city is very pretty."

"It is."

A quiet hum, and then "Kubla Khan."

Justine found herself delighted to follow the simple link in Vienna's thoughts.

Back at the Radisson, Vienna went straight to the shower. She emerged thirty minutes later, mummified within one of the hotel's oversized towels. She held two cylinders of metal.

"The small one is definitely gold," Justine said. She ran a damp cloth over Vienna's arm, pulling away dried blood Vienna had missed, revealing a long but shallow cut. "Eight ounces maybe." She poked Vienna gently. "Enough to buy a ticket home."

"I never thought about that."

Justine laughed. "Liar." She wiped a film of antiseptic gel over the cut. "Foosh."

Vienna smiled. "I'm as clumsy as your father."

"I think he has you beat." A last check to make certain the cut was clean. "No scratching, okay?"

"Okay."

Justine picked up the larger of the metal cylinders. "Any idea what this is?"

"Silver?"

"Not enough luster."

"Tin?"

"As good a guess as any," Justine answered.

"What does it mean?"

"I don't know."

"The density of tin is 7.287 grams per cubic centimeter. The volume of a cylinder is pi radius squared by height." Vienna's pale eyes lost their grip on the room. "If this cylinder is .5 centimeters in radius and just under ten centimeters in height, then it contains fifty-seven grams of tin."

"I'm no good with the metric system. Does it feel like fifty-seven grams?"

Vienna's face clouded. "I'm not sure about weight, but I think the radius and height are pretty close."

"The hotel kitchen will have a scale. What about the gold one?"

"How did you know I would miss my period? I feel stretched apart and I don't like it."

Justine brushed her hand through Vienna's hair, working out tangles. "It's not serious, unless you think I got you pregnant."

The confusion on Vienna's face ended in the same exhalation of self-conscious laughter Justine had heard back in the Brussels apartment. "I don't think so," she said.

"I have a question." Justine said.

"Okay."

"How did you get from metal cylinders to telling me you missed your period?"

"You knew there would be a hidden compartment in the

manikin. You knew where to find me when I left that man's house. You knew I would miss my period."

"All guesses."

"Then tell me how you guessed."

"You've been under constant stress since your friend Cecile invited you to Holler. Anxiety plays havoc with hormones. Not enough estrogen is produced and before you know it: hypothalamic amenorrhea. Ovulation is missed."

"It would be a lot less stressful if you . . ." Vienna let the sentence fade away.

"If I treated you like a sick girl?"

"I didn't mean it that way."

"I'm not going to cut you any slack. You don't need it and I make a rickety crutch." The final truth of her days at Stanford.

"But when two people love each other, they help each other."

"When two people love each other, they depend on each other to hold the howling wolves at bay."

Vienna looked away. "Why do I never understand you?"

"I think you do." Justine read the exhaustion in Vienna's eyes. "For now, back to the cylinders."

"They're the same radius. The density of gold is 19.32 grams per cubic centimeter. The cylinder is less than one centimeter long. Nine grams of gold."

"Tin and gold. Does it mean anything to you?"

"I have the *Chemical Rubber Company Handbook of Chemistry and Physics,* Sixteenth Edition."

"Not exactly light reading."

"There was a copy in the Cart House. I hide there when I'm scared."

"Does it have anything for us?"

Vienna's lips moved. A minute later she shook her head. "Both elements have been known since antiquity. Tin is the ancient alchemical symbol for Jupiter. When you bend it, it is said to cry as the crystal structure breaks. Under thirteen degrees centigrade it forms an allotrope of gray dust. It bonds with gold under certain conditions."

"Hardly earth-shaking."

Vienna's voice went more quiet than normal. "I betrayed you."

The melodrama would've been comical coming from anyone else. "What happened?"

"I called Lord Davy. I told him you left and I told him why and he said to take apart the manikin."

Shit. "Was he surprised to hear from you?"

"I don't know." She looked down. "He said not to tell you about the call."

"Why did you?"

"I think this is one of those things lovers share?"

"It is. Give me a second to think." Justine rubbed her hand over her tattooed lizard. "Lord Davy holds rank even within the powerful company he keeps."

"Maybe."

"No doubt about it. He bent the rules enough to get an orphaned girl into a forest mansion that very few people ever see." She paused. "I want you to text him tomorrow and ask him where the place of righteous murder is."

"The phrase from the code."

"Yes."

"Why?"

"Lina Zahler. Never forget her."

"I don't understand."

"My guess is the place of righteous murder is where Sisi was killed by Zahler's friend. I bet Davy knows it by that name. Your note will test if he is hiding things from us."

"It's inappropriate to deceive a member of the peerage."

"It's something we have to do. I assume you know where Sisi was killed?"

"Yes."

"Will you save me the trouble of looking it up?"

"Don't you trust me to do this?"

"I do, but I expect Davy to e-mail me the answer. His way of telling me not to drag you into doing my dirty work. Whatever happens, he will protect you." *Not so much me.*

"How do you know?"

"The floor in your apartment. No patterns, no seams. No geometry to poison your mind. He has been watching over you, Vienna."

Vienna shrugged, as if to say she didn't think much of his efforts. "Empress Sisi was stabbed on the promenade of the passenger piers of Lake Geneva. September 10, 1898. She didn't die until she was on the boat. Her corset was so tight it staunched the flow of blood."

"Europe certainly has its share of exciting history."

Vienna's lips pinched. "I'll ask the American Indians about that should I ever visit your country."

She was too tired for this. "Touché. Vienna, it's late, and you had a long day. Bed time."

The girl's expression immediately changed. "You're not mad? I did okay?"

"You did great."

Vienna tugged at her bathrobe. "Why didn't you yell at me when you picked me up? Everyone else would have."

"It seemed like too much effort."

"I really hate you, sometimes."

"I know."

"It doesn't bother you?"

"Hate is not exclusive of love. When you get bored, then it will be time to worry."

Vienna shook her head. "You're spinny."

"Whatever that means, I agree."

"It means strange. Why did you leave medical school?"

Where had that come from? "I fooled myself into believing some very stupid things." After all this time, the simple truth.

Vienna nodded. "Just like hiking across the lava. I didn't think it would be so hard."

Absolution, so easily given. "I know."

Vienna silently tried out her next thought. With a sigh she went ahead. "What stupid things did you do?"

The extended version would take all night. Justine settled for the short form. "I fell off my high horse."

Vienna's hand covered her mouth to hide an abridged giggle. "You know that's the wrong answer."

"I suppose so."

"But not for you." A shy smile and a trip to the bathroom to replace her bathrobe with the blue nightshirt. Then to bed without another word, the day's emotional fireworks apparently forgotten. She was asleep within minutes of lying down, her knees in her arms.

Left alone with her thoughts, Justine's mood soured. She went to the hotel's kitchen and asked to use a food scale. One metal cylinder weighed fifty-seven grams, and the other weighed nine. Tin and gold.

22

Justine's photo shoot was on an exposed tongue of rock above a cavernous waterfall.

Gullfoss (Golden Falls) owes its ferocity to fractures in ancient lava flows. The mighty Hvita tumbles over a series of . . .

Vienna watched the river charge over a wide fall, make a ninety-degree turn, and plummet into an implausibly straight fault line. The deep-throated roar resonated inside her lungs with every breath. Hypnotic patterns braided the laminar current above the cataract. The point of no return where turbulence flattened to deadly force. Spray fogged Vienna's glasses. She flexed her muscles as if to step forward. Looking for secrets under the quick-silver surface.

The Nykur, Iceland's mythic water-horse, is often depicted with reversed ears and hooves. It is said to lure girls underwater and hold them until death. . . .

Vienna settled for standing statue-still, like one of Justine's wooden manikins. *Girl Not Riding a Nykur,* she named herself.

Justine was posed at the end of the stone jetty, a bare ten feet from the torrent. If someone wanted to kill her, this was the place. A push and she would vanish forever. Like Sherlock Holmes over Reichenbach Falls: *"deep down in that dreadful caldron of swirling water and seething foam."*

Mist surrounded Justine, cutting through the thin fabric she wore. The backs of her hands were pearly blue-white and she hugged herself between shots. Yet every time the camera clicked, she was smiling.

Why didn't she ask to have the pictures taken some place

warmer? Vienna wanted to shout at the photographer, but she was held silent by the appearance of Haldor. He stood as close to Justine as the rope boundary allowed. Vienna was surprised he didn't go into the tent to help her change.

Disgusted with the day, Vienna retreated from the center of attention. Closer to the onlookers, but as far as possible from Haldor. Fingers pointed her way, whispers rippling through the crowd. Vienna wondered if Justine could interpret what it meant—decided she could—which shifted her depression to a whole new gear.

It's the way I am.

Carried forward by familiar self-assessment, Vienna stepped to the crowd. Little to prove and less to lose, because after she had been so stupid about running away she thought maybe Justine would be happier with Haldor. *If I loved Justine I would set her free and all that.* Except she didn't want to, which only proved she wasn't really in love in the first place.

This crowd was different from the one she'd seen in London. It wasn't just the strange language. People seemed less willing to talk to her, or even look at her.

Icelanders are self-reliant to the point of xenophobia. They are the kindest people you will ever meet, but also the most reticent. Remember your manners and you will be rewarded. . . .

"Hello," she said quietly. A few people returned her greeting in heavily accented English. No one added anything to the conversation. "I'm sorry. I can't speak your language."

"You're speaking mine," a young man called out to a few quiet laughs.

Vienna took a step back. This wasn't according to the guidebook at all. "I don't understand."

"Are you still with the American, or did the great Haldor steal her away?"

Vienna felt warmth in her face. What seemed so certain when Justine was beside her seemed so doubtful here. But this time she did exactly what she was supposed to. *Talk it through inside your head.* One fact above all others. *She came back to me.* "She's with me." Maybe that was saying too much in public?

"If she changes her mind, I'll take you," said a female from the back. Vienna saw smiles in the crowd. *Are they making fun of me?* She recalled that Iceland had elected the first openly lesbian prime minister in Europe. Her throat had the tight feeling of not knowing what to do. Why were they laughing? She took a step back. Someone behind her. She whirled to bump into Justine.

"You okay?" Justine asked.

"Are you finished?"

Justine laughed. "These clothes aren't exactly street wear for Iceland." She was dressed in the sheerest of pale pink fabrics.

Why had they planned the photographs where such thin fabric would get wet? Vienna saw the crowd staring and decided the question answered itself. Except it was all wrong. Vienna saw a deeper truth without seeing the steps that led to it. *They are intimidated by her.* How could that be?

Vienna stepped forward to shield Justine. "They're asking if we're still together."

Justine answered loud enough for the crowd to hear. "Which way is Reykjavík?"

Vienna pointed to the southeast.

"Is she right?" Justine asked of the crowd.

"Dead on," an older man answered.

"Why is this important?" Vienna asked.

"I knew you would have your bearings." Justine put her hand on Vienna's cheek. Vienna was shocked at how cold Justine's fingers were. Justine leaned close and whispered in Vienna's ear, "It's another one of those things lovers share." She turned away. "I have to get back to work," she said over her shoulder. Vienna watched her walk back toward the falls. Amazed that for once she knew what Justine's words really meant.

"I have to help." Vienna curtseyed (*remember your manners!*) and ran after Justine. She was embarrassed to hear a few shouts of laughter from the crowd. But they were speaking Icelandic, and she couldn't guess what they were saying.

The photo shoot dragged on for another three hours. When the camera wasn't clicking away, Justine's smile vanished into exhaustion. The photographer snapped his fingers at her and she smiled again. But it only looked like a smile.

"Prosopon."

If I try, I can see how she really feels. Like seeing a taste or smelling a color.

The afternoon waned before the last of the equipment was being packed away. Vienna watched the manikin being carried up the sweeping trail from the falls to the parking lot. Into a white lorry. The movers slammed the doors shut and the lorry pounded through gears in a cloud of blue diesel.

Not the original manikin, but the duplicate. It had to be that way because when the photographs were published in Justine's book, they would show the fakes. That way, if the fakes were discovered, the photographs could be enhanced and used as evidence that the copies predated the project, and questions would be directed elsewhere. Still, they had to use the real manikins until the last possible moment because every minute would be needed to perfect the duplicate.

Vienna was on the verge of telling Justine this when she realized it wouldn't work. The change from real to duplicate had been recorded within the photographer's portfolios stored on Justine's computer. The computer's memory would have to be destroyed. And even that wouldn't be enough if the killer discovered that Justine knew the truth. She would have to be destroyed as well.

It was the nightmare all over again: Justine's blood spreading across a white floor and no way to stop it. But Vienna had to take care of it herself because words could be bent into something less true and she never got words right anyway. She stepped closer to Justine, wondering if that counted as an apology for keeping secrets.

"You're warm," Justine said. Vienna liked that.

Haldor stayed until they were ready to leave. Justine took him to the side and spoke to him for several minutes. He turned abruptly away and went to his car without a word.

"What an absolutely, amazingly crappy day," was Justine's only comment.

Vienna touched Justine's shoulder. Was that right for something like this? People were watching. She tried to keep words from rushing by like water over Gullfoss. "Now it's my turn to tell you to go to bed?"

Justine leaned forward until their foreheads were touching. "Home and a quick dinner and I shall follow your advice." People were taking pictures but it no longer seemed important.

Morning brought the newly familiar routine of sneaking out of bed while Justine slept. Vienna went to the hotel's restaurant. Rain turning the windows bottle green. The morning paper had a picture of her and Justine, standing together, their foreheads touching. *Everyone can see it!* Except . . . the picture didn't look so bad. Vienna didn't look stupid or ugly. Maybe a little skinny behind her glasses, but that sort of looked okay. Justine was dazzling, of course. Vienna went through the paper, looking for more pictures.

The breakfast waiter spoke as if Vienna was an old friend. "How are you today, Miss Vienna?"

"Fine, thank you."

"Let me know if you need anything."

Something different behind the short exchange. Vienna didn't like it.

Justine appeared as Vienna was still eating; an early arrival for her. "Good morning." Her voice was light.

"Hello."

"I don't suppose you checked the blogsphere this morning?"

Vienna shook her head.

"Jordan Farquar once again turned his jaundiced gaze in our direction. He blasted Igor Czasky for keeping me in employ. From where he stands it is a gross mistake."

"Will you lose your job?"

Justine shook her head. "Jordan should have had a little chat with Emily Holt before setting fingers to keyboard. If Americans love seeing their heroes cut down, they'll never stomach a cheap shot against the innocent. Jordan was doing fine smacking me around, but last night he called you a degenerate."

"Why?"

"Because he's a vicious leach and too arrogant to realize his mistake. It's early morning in the States but by sunrise, hating Jordan Farquar will be a national obsession."

"Why didn't this happen before?"

"Because now his victims can stand behind poor Vienna, who isn't quite right in the head. Congratulations, you're a hero."

"I don't want everyone talking about me."

"There's no stopping it."

"You have to!" The newspaper picture didn't make up for this!

Justine shook her head. "The media possesses remorseless momentum. *Frontline* is doing a segment on the science of autism next week. Pushed up the schedule by a month."

"*Frontline?*"

"A news show in America."

"What should I do?"

"Accept it in good grace. Heaven knows it would be a welcome departure from the norm."

Vienna felt anger stirring again. *Why is she so flippant?*

Justine laughed quietly. "Poor little Storm Cloud. But your Brussels apartment with its seamless floor will never do. If bad things happen outside, at least you're free to feel them."

"I want to go home anyway."

"Too bad. I want you with me."

"That's kidnapping."

"Vienna, I can't physically keep you here if you really want to go."

"I have no money."

"I can call Lord Davy and transfer several hundred thousand euros into an account under your name, if you wish."

Vienna set her fork down too loudly, then took a deep breath. "If I asked you to skip the last pictures for the Clay to Flesh book, would you?"

"Yes, if you had reason."

Vienna thought this over. It fit the morning's newly minted Special Theory of Justine. *Use every trick to get what I want.* "I sent an e-mail to Lord Davy, like you asked." *I can play that game better than you.*

"We should hear back soon."

Vienna was on the verge of explaining that Justine's methods were unnecessarily complex when four men entered the dining room. Policemen with tired, sad faces. She knew in an instant who they were looking for.

23

Haldor Steffansson had been shot an inch under his left eye, the bullet entering at the precise angle to bisect his left internal carotid artery. His life tapped out; a thickening pool flowing around a flamboyant, two-handed sword.

His manikin had suffered a similar fate, her carved beauty ripped apart. In the drying blood and splintered wood, the police saw a line running from David Andries to Haldor Stefansson. It passed straight through Justine Am.

After a short account of the murder, Vienna was taken to a separate room. Two officers remained with Justine, embarking with little enthusiasm on three hours of questioning. Justine was too worried about Vienna to pay any attention to their bullying and begging.

Eventually Vienna was ushered back in, apparently with the idea the women might be induced to trip over each other's story. Justine was amused to see how exasperated Vienna's questioners looked.

Within a few minutes, the broad-shouldered man Justine had seen at the airport entered the room and took up the battle. Clean-shaven with a jaw like Clark Kent stepping from a phone booth. His black, crew-cut hair stood at attention. A good deal of rank was pinned to his chest. The top of a tattoo peeked from the collar of his uniform sweater; a ship's silhouette. He introduced himself as Olifur and apologized for the questioning. "It's required by the paperwork drones." He held up a form as if to prove the point, but Justine had no doubt he'd read every word.

"There are a woman's prints on the manikin pieces," he

continued. "Even the inside." His English was more American than British.

"Justine left with Haldor and I took the statue apart," Vienna said. "I didn't hurt it."

"But it's possible you did something to the statue that led to Haldor's murder. The way it was torn apart points to something placed inside."

The half accusation flirted with the truth, but under pressure, Vienna's rigid thought process could only target the direct question. "If I had something of value, why hide it in Haldor's house?" she said. "I was unlikely to ever go there again. And if I had anything valuable, I would have been the easier target."

Vienna rocked in her chair, unimpressed with her own line of reasoning. "It would make more sense that I became jealous of Haldor and arranged to have him killed." Her face brightened. "You see? My assassin was told to take apart the manikin in order to remove my fingerprints. But after shooting Haldor, the killer panicked and left." She smiled.

Jaws clinched around the room, although Olifur appeared ready to return Vienna's smile. "You have no money and you've never been to Iceland. You would hardly know how to contact an assassin under such circumstances."

"Then maybe something was inside the statue and I stole it," Vienna said.

Holy flipping shit. Justine's heartbeat had to be loud enough to hear.

Olifur did smile at that. "Then Haldor would have been killed long ago. He has owned the statue for eight years. There would have been plenty of chances to break into his house while he was on tour."

"But—"

The chief held up his hand to cut her off. "You're not a suspect, Miss Vienna, and neither is Miss Am. Miss Am was seen in the hotel kitchen last night, and your rental car's engine was too cold to have traveled in the last eight hours. Nonetheless a man is dead, and no one believes it's coincidence after the death of David Andries."

Justine let a silent breath slip between tight lips. Either Vienna had just gotten unbelievably lucky, or she'd played the cop with virtuoso skill. Time to commandeer the conversation before another heart attack twist. "There's another possibility."

"Yes?"

How much was safe to say? "Perhaps I have picked up a stalker who doesn't appreciate competition."

"The thought occurred to us as well as the FBI and Interpol. It explains much, with the glaring exception of the unharmed woman sitting next to you."

Justine shook her head. "I don't mean to sound sexist, but the fact that Vienna is female might make all the difference in the world. Most men would consider a second woman as fantasy fulfillment rather than competition."

"Also something we considered; with the conclusion that if this theory is correct, Vienna is in considerable danger. It's possible she's being saved for some sexually violent act, likely carried out in your presence. Computer profiles predict such behavior."

Justine looked sharply at the man. *Why is he trying to scare me?*

Olifur leaned back in his chair. "You should know that Lord Anson Davy is worried as well; hence our exchanged glance at the Keflavík terminal." Olifur waved to an underling in a gesture Justine interpreted as "coffee." "Davy doesn't accept the stalker theory, though I think it's probable."

"How do you know him?" Justine asked. *How closely is Davy having us watched?*

"Lord Davy is an old friend." Which told Justine nothing. "He mentioned by way of helping establish Vienna's alibi that Vienna had sent a curious e-mail last night. Problem is, I don't like curious things when a man has been killed." He showed a tight smile when Vienna jerked forward to listen. "He shoots, he scores. Now then, Miss Vienna, what did you ask him?"

"I asked where Empress Sisi was murdered."

The man's eyes narrowed. "He acted as if you'd been spying on the queen."

"Does Lord Davy have reason to be worried?" Justine cut in. "Were we followed when we entered the country?"

"If you were, it was either by someone with great skill or someone who knew your itinerary well enough to give you a long lead. I don't think it's likely." Black coffee appeared on the table beside him. "I'm tempted to revoke your passports until we know the score." He sipped at the steaming cup.

"Davy is the one keeping secrets. Vienna told you the truth about the e-mail. I can retrieve it if you wish."

"I get the feeling Lord Davy would be upset if it were passed around the station."

"If you cover for him, you have no grounds to detain us."

"I could make something up, based on Miss Vienna's fairy tale if nothing else."

Justine shook her head. "We're leaving for Austria the day after tomorrow. After that we will not be your concern."

"My concern might extend beyond my jurisdiction, all the way to the safety of two women caught in a bloody tangle."

"We've told you everything. We don't know who killed Haldor or Andries." Or Sinoro. Or Dardonelle.

"I believe you, as far as that goes." He paused. "I'd bet my pension something has you scared." Another long sip. "If you are being coerced by threats to a friend or family member, we can protect your loved ones. Playing this game will only get more people killed."

"No one is being threatened."

"Then I don't understand. . . ." The man's voice trailed off. He tapped the table with his index finger. The sound of rain blowing against windows. Olifur's finger stopped and Justine looked up to see that he was staring at her. "It's us, isn't it? The police. Despite the fact that we only just met. How can that be?" His eyes widened. "Not the police. Higher up. Conspiracies between powerful people."

Justine tried to keep her gaze level, but it wasn't enough.

"Lord Davy's kind of power. He has no authority here, but our friendship has you shadowboxing."

"Can we leave now?"

He ignored her. "Anson Davy is the finest man I know. He's also the toughest son of a bitch I've ever met. He ever tell you how he got that scar on his face?"

"No."

"Do yourself a favor and never ask. Lord Davy has done difficult work for queen and country, but he would die before putting Miss Vienna in jeopardy." The finger resumed its metronome tapping. "Of course this is exactly what I would say if I were covering for him. How can I gain the trust of strangers under such circumstances?"

"I can't think of a way. If you have no further questions, we will—"

"We will not." He turned to address his men. "Miss Vienna, Miss Am, and I will be stepping out to clear the air. We are not to be followed or in any way observed." The men nodded without comment. Justine had no doubt that all of Olifur's instructions were followed without deviation or hesitation. "In a public place," she added.

"Ah, so you don't trust me. Yes, in a public place."

The same cold rain was drifting over Reykjavík. Drops so small they amounted to little more than fog, saturating the air with a penetrating chill. Justine wondered if it were ever dry here.

They wound through twisting blocks to an old wooden building with red awnings. SHALIMAR: INDIAN AND PAKISTANI CUISINE. Olifur held the door and gestured them in. The dining room was full, locals in huddled conversation. Olifur led Justine and Vienna up a narrow staircase. The upper level sported several vacant booths. The policeman took one in the far corner.

"Alone, but within shouting distance for help," Olifur said. He slid into the booth. "Most tourists aren't used to Icelandic spice blends. Sadly, after four years at Quantico I acquired a barbaric taste for heat."

When the waiter appeared, Olifur ordered in English without opening the menu. "Masala nan for starters, two murgh madras curry, and one prawn tikka." The waiter nodded as he wrote the order. "The food is excellent and easily shared," Olifur said as the waiter left. "I stayed away from the more volcanic concoctions. I find most women prefer something less threatening."

"Especially when you want them to trust you."

"Especially then." He had the hard but compassionate persona going full blast. He wore it well. "I have a solution to our problem. Vienna, does your cell phone have a conference mode?"

"I'm not sure."

"Here, hun, let me check." Justine held out her hand as Vienna dug her phone out of the small handbag Justine had given her. Justine paged through the menu until she found the speaker. "It's on."

Olifur nodded to Vienna. "Call Lord Davy."

Davy picked up on the second ring. "Hello, Vienna," he said.

"And friends," Olifur spoke before Vienna could answer. "You're on speaker, Lord Davy. Your audience is Miss Vienna, Justine Am, and myself."

"Tell me, Dizzy, why do you sound involved on a personal level?"

"I have a soft spot for damsels in distress," Olifur answered.

"Soft spot? Is that what they're calling it these days? I didn't realize irony was in style. What can I do for you?"

"You can answer Vienna's e-mail. She stated for the record that she asked you where an empress with the improbable name of Sisi was murdered."

"That wasn't the question," Lord Davy said.

"What else would it have been?" Justine asked.

"A matter of honor."

Olifur's voice went hard. "Are you joking? This isn't Camelot.

Would you allow Vienna to be harmed for the sake of your honor? I'm asking as a friend. Don't make me ask as a cop."

"I could guarantee Vienna's safety if she returned to London."

"She isn't going anywhere without Miss Am."

"Justine would be welcome as well."

"They don't trust you, Anson, and from what I'm hearing, I don't blame them."

"I should have known you would end up siding with the long legs."

"The e-mail, Lord Davy. This is me asking as a cop."

"Vienna, or I should say Justine acting through Vienna, asked where the place of righteous murder is. The truth is, I don't know. No one does. But it doesn't refer to the murder of Sisi."

"Then what?" Olifur asked.

"An old scandal with no connection to Iceland."

"Please," Vienna said.

"Bloody hell."

"Language, Anson. There are ladies present," Olifur said.

"If they retain that state of grace after being with you, you're losing your touch." There was a slight pause. "I know you too well to ask the obvious favor."

Olifur nodded. "I'll do everything in my power to keep this between the four of us. It's important, old friend. I feel quicksand steps."

The phrase seemed to mean something to Davy. "If I must compromise my honor, you might as well be in on it. Lord knows it would make a pleasant reversal of our usual arrangement."

"Bravo, as your peers would say."

Davy ignored that. "Vienna, what do you have on Sisi's son, Prince Rudolph?"

Vienna's gaze went blank. "Archduke Rudolph was born on August 21, 1858. The son of Emperor Franz Josef I and—"

"That's the one," Davy cut her off. Vienna blushed and looked away. Justine took her hand under the table. "What do you know of his death?" Davy asked.

Vienna swallowed and looked inward again. Her lips moved, but she remained silent. Olifur stared at her in increasing amazement. "He died with his lover, Marie Alexandrine von Vetsera." Vienna paused and repeated the name in a cheap vampire movie accent. "von Vetsera." The ghost smile. "Erzsébet Báthory, bathing in blood." Her hand tightened briefly over Justine's. "Voivode." She shifted and sighed.

"Cause of death?" Davy asked.

"Rudolph shot Marie and then himself. The murder-suicide was provoked by the emperor's demand that the lovers end their adulterous affair. Their bodies were discovered at a hunting lodge in Mayerling."

"A convenient lie," Davy said. "The emperor had long been aware of his son's infidelity. Hell, he was having his own affair at the time."

"But suicide makes no sense as a lie," Vienna said. "The emperor had to beg the papacy for his son to receive last rites. Besides, the prince wrote a note for his wife: 'Dear Stephanie, you are now rid of my presence and annoyance; be happy in your own way. Take care of the poor wee one—' "

"It wasn't a suicide note."

"Then what was it?" Justine asked.

"A damn soap opera."

"Turns out I have time for one," Olifur said. "Keep going."

"Emperor Joseph and Sisi were terrible parents. Rudolph grew up starved for attention. In the spring of 1884, he fell in love with an anarchist named Lina Zahler. Promises were made, likely buried under layers of flattery. Zahler persuaded him to raid the royal treasury. He pilfered a stone called the Star of Memphis. He thought it would be sold to further the cause of the working man. Revenge against his mother and father."

Olifur leaned toward the phone. "That's it? That's your shameful secret? My nana has better stories. Let me guess the ending: Zahler blackmailed our hapless prince."

"She did, but you haven't heard the complicated bit. With cash in hand, Zahler beguiled several impressionable men. Among them a young radical named Luigi Lucheni."

"The man who killed Sisi!" Vienna said.

"The complicated bit," Davy said. "Zahler originally told Lucheni to assassinate Philippe, duc d'Orléans. Do you know the name, Vienna?"

"The Pretender of the French Throne?"

"Another in a growing list of ex-lovers and blackmail victims, I assume," Olifur said.

"Likely."

Olifur crossed his arms, elbows on the table. "So we have a se-ductress with sharp fangs and less restraint than a cockroach in a kitchen. Sad but hardly unique. What's the catch?"

"After Prince Rudolph fell in love with Marie von Vetsera, he no longer cared if his theft became known. Zahler's blackmail lost traction and the prince had to be silenced. She caught Marie and Rudolph alone in the Wienerwald. The prince was granted enough time to write his enigmatic note before he and his lover were gunned down."

"Why was all of this kept secret?" Vienna asked.

Davy was silent.

"I have the feeling this is the good part," Olifur said.

"Uncle Anson? Are you still there?"

"Politics, Vienna. In stealing the Star of Memphis, Rudolph had unwittingly offered to finance people who planned—for whatever private reasons—to assassinate Philippe. Europe was already on the edge of chaos. If the truth had come out, France would have ripped Austria to pieces. It would have accelerated World War One by two decades."

Olifur cleared his throat. "Isn't that a little over the top? All of this angst over one man?"

"Stupid," Vienna said. "After Prince Rudolph's death, his cousin, Archduke Franz Ferdinand became heir presumptive to the throne. Ferdinand was assassinated in 1914. Do you remember what happened next, or do I have to tell you?"

Olifur's eyes opened wider even as gentle laughter came over the phone. "I stand corrected, young lady," Olifur said.

Davy continued. "The suicide story was the perfect dodge for the very reason Vienna mentioned. Once admitted, few could imagine any truth more painful. It was a clever stroke by Sisi."

"But not clever enough to save her own life," Justine said.

"Sisi made an appointment with Zahler, hoping to buy the star back. Zahler sent Luigi Lucheni to take care of it. He caught Sisi at Lake Geneva, with the sad result Vienna alluded to."

"What became of the Star of Memphis?" Justine asked.

"Unknown. One tale has Lina Zahler passing away of old age in Bratislava, babbling of her one true love and of the star being hidden among the planets. An equally probable story has her clutching the star to her breast and jumping off the Széchenyi Lánchíd into the Danube."

"And the place of righteous murder?"

"Rudolph's murder occurred a mile into the Wienerwald. Near the Dornbach—a small stream in the forest. No other details remain. There was only Lina's scrap of a confession, couched in anarchist babble: 'The royal line is ended, here at this place of righteous murder. Let all be made level.' Given the circumstances, it was quashed by the royal family."

"And if this Star of Memphis were to surface today?" Olifur asked.

"It is one of three inalienable treasures of the House of Habsburg. The Austrian government would pay millions to have it back."

"Strange how this story comes to light the day after a murder. I'm not a believer in coincidence, although I can't see Haldor having such a thing. What was it, exactly?"

"Nineteenth-century royal catalogues refer to it as bixbite, a form of beryl called scarlet emerald," Davy said. "The stone was listed as an uncut, roughly hexagonal crystal. It was said to have come from the ancient city of Memphis, a gift of the gods. How it got there is anyone's guess, as bixbite is only found in the southwestern United States. In Sisi's time, the star was considered a piece of heaven fallen to earth. Some hocus-pocus based on Old Testament prophecy."

Vienna sat up straight. " 'The appearance of the wheels and their work was like unto the color of a beryl,' " Vienna quoted in her reading voice, " 'and they four had one likeness: and their appearance and their work was as it were a wheel in the middle of a wheel.' " She paused and gave her apologetic half smile. "Ezekiel's vision of heaven."

"That's the one," Davy said. "Nineteenth-century mystics thought it had something to do with the machinery of God."

Olifur glanced across the table. "Miss Am, it seems you were familiar with parts of this story when you had Vienna e-mail Lord Davy. Is it possible you might know the location of this star?"

"If I knew, I would tell you to be free of this." *Assuming I could be certain you weren't part of the gang putting bodies in rivers.*

"But you think the star is tied in with—"

"Olifur," Davy interrupted. "She's cognizant that Vienna might be placed in jeopardy by this thing. I am finally wrapping my brain around the notion that she is hopelessly in love with our girl."

"How do you know?" Vienna asked. The hurt in her voice was unmistakable. *She wonders how everyone recognizes so easily what she struggles to see.*

"I'm a spy, Miss Vienna. It's my business to know."

"I'm not joking," Vienna said.

"Neither is he," Justine answered.

"Stop teasing me!"

"My apologies," Davy said. "The inference is simple. No sane person would spend fifteen minutes, let alone five hours, in Heathrow. Only extreme agitation could account for Justine Am accomplishing this questionable feat."

"Agitation?"

"The original synonym of love, Vienna, as I suspect you are discovering."

"I sense a good story," Olifur said, "but it will have to wait." The officer leaned back into the booth. "I think we can agree that Lord Davy has been truthful."

"I have been."

"I appreciate your help, sir," Olifur said. "I will contact you with any developments."

"Please do." He paused. "Ladies, good day." The connection went dead.

How many wheels would Davy set rolling now? Justine handed the phone back to Vienna.

"I hope that clears up any misunderstandings," Olifur said.

"Not even close. Next time you talk to your pal, ask him why he has David Andries's phone number on his phone, and why he used it to set Vienna up the night we met."

"I find it impossible to believe you have seen Lord Davy's phone."

"Vienna told me."

"I did?" Vienna asked. "But I've never seen David Andries's number."

Justine exhaled. "We have to work on our partners-in-crime routine."

"I'm sorry."

Olifur's tone dropped. "I don't know why you tried to lie—"

"Vienna was shown the number in Brussels. I didn't show it to her and I doubt the Belgium police did. They would have already checked her phone records and seen that she had no contact with Andries. But Lord Davy saw her just before I did. He showed her a phone number, I suspect asking her if she recognized it."

Vienna's face brightened. "That's right! But I never told you."

"You did, in your own way." Justine turned to Olifur. "Lord Davy had someone watching me at Heathrow and at Keflavík and he certainly is holding his own secrets. I accept that Haldor was killed in part because he spent time with me; I'll spend the rest of my life dealing with that." She paused as the waiter delivered their dinner and departed. "I would give anything to change what happened. But I can't, and I don't believe you can hold us."

"Not as a member of the police. But as a decent man I am asking you to stay here until we get this sorted out."

"No."

"Why in God's name not?"

"Because there's one manikin left, owned by an old lady in Austria. I don't want her hurt."

"And Vienna? Will you risk her as well?"

Justine looked at the girl. "She should return to London."

Vienna answered in full pout. "You sound like one of those stupid monster films."

"I do?"

"Leave the helpless woman behind while you go do whatever it is you are going to. I hate that, and so would you."

Justine turned to Olifur. "What was it you said about this not being Camelot?"

"Bad timing," Olifur answered.

24

"Once upon a time there was a farmer with a beautiful daughter," Justine started. She paused long enough to smile. "Of course that's how it begins," she added.

"Of course?" Vienna asked.

"In America, every story starts with a beautiful farmer's daughter."

Vienna had read dozens of novels from America and none of them even mentioned farmer's daughters. She accepted Justine's explanation as one of those occasions when people lie for no reason. It happened a lot more than you'd think.

Justine went on to explain that the farmer's daughter attracted the attention of two men who lived across the wasteland. When they came to court the girl, the farmer made a bargain. If the men cleared a bridal path, he would give his daughter's hand in marriage. As the wasteland was filled with warped pillars of volcanic stone, the task looked impossible. But the men flew into a rage, throwing massive boulders as if they were handfuls of grass.

"In a single day the path was cleared, and the stronger of the men demanded the daughter's hand," Justine said. "The farmer agreed and offered the men use of his sauna to soothe their aching muscles. As soon as they were seated, the farmer collapsed the room, killing them both. At least that's the legend."

But if it was a myth, why were there fragments of a path through the Berserkjahraun? Vienna stood in one such clearing, wondering how the mossy lane had come to be. It looked too artificial to be an accident of nature.

"Several years ago an ancient grave was discovered near here," Justine said. "It contained the remains of two large men."

"Then the story is real?"

"No more or less real than a unicorn horn."

"Unicorns aren't real." Vienna frowned.

"But they are. One is considered beyond value by one of the grandest European empires."

"Like the Star of Memphis. But it's not real either."

"How do you mean?"

"I looked. Red beryl only occurs in the United States, just like Davy said. How would one have gotten to ancient Egypt? It's impossible."

Justine laughed. "It's impossible we are together."

Vienna tried to think of a way to teach Justine not to be so smug. *Hopeless.* "Why are we here? It's a long drive back to the hotel."

"Fresh air."

"Aren't you afraid?"

"A little."

"You're daffy."

Justine waved at the jumbled towers of emerald moss and onyx lava that defined the Berserker's Field. "What geometrical patterns appear?"

"It's chaos." Vienna turned a full circle where she stood. "There is nothing man-made."

"How does it feel?"

"I'm not sure. More free than the city."

Justine stuck out her tongue—a ridiculously childish gesture. "Then I guess you know why we're here."

Vienna chose the easiest refutation. "I don't know anything. I don't even know how you guessed Lord Davy showed me a telephone number back in Brussels."

Justine seemed disappointed with the question. "You told me during the ride to the hotel."

"I did?"

"You were speaking to yourself. 'Six-five-six-one,' you kept saying. You added the five and one and put it next to the other two sixes and came up with the sign of the beast."

"I don't remember."

"I wouldn't have either, except that I thought it was so creepy. The other numbers you mentioned were eleven and twenty-four. Three plus eight and three times eight. Six thousand five hundred and sixty-one is three to the eighth. I checked it out this morning, though unlike you I had to use a calculator."

"I still don't understand."

"Lord Davy said you exhibit obsessive behaviors. Grant's phone number had eight threes in it. Someone showed you the number and it started spinning cookies in your skull. Who else but Davy?"

"Spinning cookies?"

"The numbers got stuck there."

"You must think I'm clueless." Play yourself the fool, never be disappointed when others see you that way.

"Pretty much," Justine said.

The answer came like a slap. Tears gathered before Vienna could stop them. Justine was smiling, but it wasn't right. Her lips were too tight.

"It's the rain, you know," Justine said. Her voice was quiet and Vienna didn't know what it meant.

"Rain?"

"Research from a few years ago, in Seattle, I think. A study uncovered an apparent link between developmental disorders and rain. It always rains in Europe."

Familiar confusion closing in. *What do I say?* She remembered Justine in the silk clothing, freezing from the spray of Gullfoss, still smiling. "Sometimes, you smile when you're not happy?" Her voice turned upward in a question.

"Sometimes."

Something was wrong. *She's almost in tears.* Vienna didn't stop to wonder how the knowledge came to her. "What is it?" she asked.

"I'm not sure you and I—what we're doing is right."

Vienna sorted through the words. "I know two females

together is not accepted in America, and it's little better here
but—"

"Not that."

Vienna sighed. Always so impossible. "Then what?"

Justine looked away, remaining silent. *Afraid of what she wants
to say.*

Vienna was back in Bath. Christmas Eve and the anxiety that
meant nothing. She wanted to scream in frustration, but she
didn't like looking childish in front of Justine.

And there was her answer. Childish. *She believes that she has
committed an unforgivable sin. How could I convince her otherwise,
with all she has seen?*

"When I was ten," Vienna said, "I was sent to a hospital in Edin-
burgh. Men in white smocks showed me yellow cards covered
with marker tics. They asked me how many I saw. So I told them,
one after another: 'two hundred and twelve,' or 'three hundred
and fifty-six.' Each one was up for a second, maybe two at most.
I thought it was normal, yeah? I thought anyone could do it." She
stepped closer to Justine. For once, the right words were there,
overheard from countless doctors. "I'm not a creature of my own
design. Slipping from viral thought to the world's blank physi-
cality. Sometimes there's no connection at all; sometimes too
much."

Justine remained silent.

"You see how I interact with the world, and to you it makes
no sense. So you see one mistake after another, and you're embarrassed for me. You see me cry like a child and you twist love
into the worst of crimes."

"Vienna—"

Vienna held her finger to Justine's lips—an exact copy of Justine's motion for silence. "A string of genes that almost worked."
She considered this. "Or worked too well. I see things instantly
that you might never see." She smiled at this new thought, though
maybe her smile was as sad as Justine's.

"It's more than that," Justine said. "When we're together . . . I can't tell if you like such things. Or if you are ready for them." Justine rushed on. "You're readily compliant, but maybe only because I ask."

Vienna remembered Davy talking about the porno video. *Would you do it if she asked?* Not so much a hypothetical question now. "I'm used to you guessing things right and now you're so wrong."

"I am?" Justine asked.

"Does it displease you when I am compliant?"

For the first time Vienna could remember, Justine was blushing. "That wasn't what I was getting at."

Vienna fought her way through the tortured words, knowing she was missing something vital. Why did Justine blush? "This is flippy."

Justine's lips turned up slightly. "Do tell."

"I know what my body wants. I know what loneliness is. I know that the whitest floors hide ghosts that no one will ever see but me. I know you're warm and I like your touch. I like hearing you ask for mine. I like how you breathe when I get it right. It makes me feel as if I can do it."

"It's just—"

"I don't think it's broken to want to feel wanted."

Justine took Vienna's hands. "You find your own answers better than I do."

Vienna shook her head. "Only with you. I don't understand any of the rest."

The half smile. "Such as?"

"Why would Lord Davy have David Andries's phone number?"

Justine frowned. "Andries was a scheming bastard, but Davy is an old-fashioned, cast-iron, dyed in the wool, alpha wolf."

"He scares you?"

"Right down to my toes."

"He used to take me shopping along Regent Street, yeah? I remember once, three boys in black leather bumped into me. They made several sexual suggestions. Davy took them to the side and a few minutes later, each one apologized. I think they were frightened."

"I bet."

"So what do we do?"

"We go over everything in my BlackBerry to find what Andries was after when he died."

Vienna bit her lip. Hadn't she said that days ago? "I can do it tonight if we start back soon, it will be dark before long."

"That's the idea. I borrowed a few heavy blankets from the hotel and had a dinner made up as well. It's in the trunk."

They spread blankets on the path that was part myth. "I don't think we're supposed be here after dark," Vienna said.

"They can chase us out easily enough."

They ate a small dinner under the impossibly wide sky, found enough privacy for a lav. The temperature dropped quickly after the rolling sun finally set.

"No posters with tic marks when I was young," Justine said. "Instead, I had a grandfather who lived in Montana. Baseball on the radio until evening turned to night. No lights for miles. The Milky Way so bright you almost could read by it."

They pulled the heavy blankets to their chins and lay as close together as they could. It took over an hour for the first star to come out.

"That's Jupiter," Justine said when Vienna pointed to it. "It doesn't count."

"Count?"

" 'Star light, star bright, first star I see tonight. I wish I may, I wish I might, have the wish I wish tonight.' Jupiter isn't a star, so you can't wish upon it."

"What would I wish for?"

Justine laughed. "You can't tell anyone or it won't come true."

Jupiter. The alchemical symbol for Jupiter was tin. . . . A star lost in the planets. Isn't that what Lina Zahler had said?

"There!" Justine pointed up. "See it? Bluish-white. Vega. So low. Fall is growing old. Now you can make a wish."

Vienna couldn't think of one, so she remained quiet.

"Do you know the constellations?" Justine asked.

"There's not much to see from London or Brussels."

"That will not be a problem tonight."

It was like nothing Vienna had ever seen. The stars awoke in pale hues of blue and red and yellow. Vienna lost count—too many appearing too quickly. *He telleth the number of stars; he calleth them all by their names.*

For a few breathless moments, her mind drew lines between the brightest stars; shapes defining areas. . . .

"Let it go, Vienna. Your triangles really are an illusion here."

Vienna yanked her eyes to the dark silhouette of Justine. "How did you know?"

"Your breathing was shallow. But we can do this." Justine pointed, her arm easily seen in the glow of the stars. "Do you know the big dipper?"

"I've seen it in London." It took her a few seconds to find the familiar shape in the profusion of stars.

"Look at the second star of the handle. What do you see?"

"It's just a star. Wait. There are two stars, very close."

"Alcor and Mizor. The horse and the rider."

"They're beautiful."

Vienna felt Justine's hand over hers. "Now from the arc of the Big Dipper, we could find Arcturus if we were further south. We have Cassiopeia though."

Justine told her Cassiopeia's story, even though Vienna already knew it. And that would have been okay, except as the storytelling spread to other constellations, Vienna began to wonder why they weren't having sex. *Surely she knows I can tonight.* Vienna wanted to, out here under the stars. Cecile said it was the best. *Am I doing something wrong?* Her fear spoke before she could stop it.

"Why aren't we making love?"

"We are."

Vienna was surprised less by the answer than by how it made perfect sense. "This is the part of you not in the photographs."

"You could say that."

"Did you share this with Andries?"

Justine was silent for a full minute before answering. "No."

"Good," Vienna whispered.

"I heard that."

"I'm sorry."

"Lovers are allowed to be selfish."

Vienna was certain she'd never read that. *Am I supposed to share my life, too?* "I always wanted to learn how to waltz," she said. "Like the beautiful women in the Cart House." That seemed to fit.

Justine started to say something, but suddenly stopped and started over. "We'll have to do something about that."

"I don't want other people to see!"

"We can talk about it later. And one more thing."

"Yes?"

"You really did need one more night, maybe two, even if you don't feel it. Your body needs to catch its breath. Any other time I would have forgotten all the cutesy crap."

"And felt guilty?"

"Lust always trumps guilt."

"I was beginning to wonder."

Justine laughed and squeezed her hand. "Can I ask a question?"

"Yes?"

"What did the dolls tell you when you were young?"

Vienna remembered the comment she had made in Brussels. "That I was flat and my hair was bad and I didn't fit in."

"That's a relief."

"Excuse me?"

"I thought they might be telling you to kill people or set houses on fire."

"I'm not that broken."

"Proof that I'm a prisoner of my fears no less than you are."

Vienna sensed unspoken meaning. It wasn't anything she could have believed a few days ago. "What did the dolls tell you?"

"That I was one of them."

And that was sad, even though Vienna couldn't pin down exactly why. It was wrong anyway. "You don't fit that way."

"Vienna?"

"How everything fits together. You aren't that way."

"How do I fit?"

"Everywhere." She let the words rush out before they were lost. "That's why it was hard to see, yeah? I thought it had to be wrong, because nothing fits like that. But I think that's the way it's supposed to be."

Justine rolled to her, arms tight around her. "Thank you."

Vienna was ashamed that she'd once believed this moment could be described in a book. She held her breath. *Let this last.* But her thoughts raced on. *When we fit together this way, it keeps my feet warm.* She wanted to scream because that was stupidly out of place and it was all slipping away. But then everything turned around, and time did stop. The stars frozen in the Icelandic night. Easy to imagine Justine mentioning cold feet, even at a time like this. It was exactly the sort of snarky remark she would make.

Even now she's inside me.

Vienna took a deep breath; shifted in just the right way to make Justine hold her tighter. And the universe came unstuck but it didn't really matter anymore.

Vienna slept most of the way home, the car's heater blowing at her feet. She woke once to see Justine driving, her hands softly tapping the wheel in rhythm to a silent song. The dying moon, cold and silver overhead, reflected from endless pools of water along the road. She closed her eyes again.

Breakfast at the Radisson was a buffet that looked familiar but didn't taste right. Vienna missed eggs made exactly the way she liked them. It was depressing even before everyone decided they needed to talk to her.

"Is the food okay?" "Is Justine a nice person?" "How do you like Iceland?" "Can I have Justine's phone number?" "If I ever see that Jordan guy, I am going to kick his ass so hard he'll be chewing toenails for a month." That from a big man with an American accent. It reminded Vienna of Hunter S. Thompson.

The questions stopped when Justine came down.

"Good morning, Little Storm Cloud," she said.

"Why do you call me that?"

"You show your feelings in your eyes. What were you thinking about?"

Vienna decided on a new tack. Instead of trying to figure out every angle of conversation, she would answer with whatever came to mind. "You always look beautiful and I don't."

"You want to know a secret?"

"Okay."

"I'm not a creature of my own design either. I like hearing that you think I'm beautiful though. You can say that all you want."

As if being beautiful equated to seizures. Vienna took a deep breath. "Why did you book an extra day in Iceland? You're always in a rush, yeah?"

"Back when the project got underway, I wanted to be here on a Friday night for the runtur. Adelina—she handles my travel— knew this, so she kept the extra day in our itinerary. I was too distracted to notice."

"Runtur?"

"The Reykjavík pub crawl. Legendary craziness. We'll do something more quiet though."

"Let's go out." Justine raised a single eyebrow, which Vienna thought of as a question. She answered. "When other people see me with you, they can be jealous instead of me."

Justine smiled. "You are red in tooth and claw. I like it. I'll look my best."

After breakfast Justine worked out for two hours. "I should

have been born twenty years ago, when anemic was in," she said when she got back. "Though I'll pass on cigarettes and the Technicolor yawn." Not even worth guessing what that was about.

Then Justine was on the phone for over an hour. "I can't get James, which means he's working." Another two calls and then: "An offer from Madrid. What about a week in Spain?"

It amazed Vienna how Justine casually mentioned such a huge undertaking. "I would like to see the Plaza de Cibeles, there's a statue of Cybele." And because this seemed incomplete, she added a touch of history that had always eerily fascinated her. "Males castrated themselves before her to appear more female."

"Bravo! I'll forward the request to James. A small show on December sixteenth, some up-and-coming accessories designer I've never heard of. Hardly Hong Kong or New York, but I'm not out of work yet."

Then she was off to get the right clothes, even though she already had enough for a Shakespearian company.

Vienna had two hours alone to play with Justine's Kindle. She read Mark Twain, having heard he was as American as Americans could get. He liked cats, which surprised Vienna as she thought Americans preferred dogs or snakes or whatever. He was supposed to be funny, but Vienna saw his writing as a plea for compassion in a world where it was already in short supply. She decided Twain had been broken in a sad but beautiful way and that maybe she could be, too.

Little Storm Cloud.

Justine returned with a handful of bags. "It stopped raining, if you can believe it. Off to the shower. Tonight's mode will be semiformal party."

Over the next hour, Vienna was again transformed into the girl that was not quite her. "You look great," Justine said. "My turn. New Jimmy Choos tonight." Which must have been exciting news.

Justine ended up in a modest dress that somehow showed off everything she had. The fabric was heavier against the cold night, black fading to dark gray at the collar. Her makeup was different—slightly shaded around her eyes, though nothing near as dark as what Vienna had seen her coworkers wear. She was as beautiful as a fallen angel.

Vienna wanted to ask how Justine could forget all the terrible things that had happened long enough to enjoy the evening. But she knew she wouldn't understand the answer anyway.

Into the cold Icelandic night, where the taciturn populace had gone insane. People singing and shouting. Some of the women wore next to nothing despite the cold. One was pressing her bare chest against the window of a pub. And maybe Vienna would be expected to do that and she didn't really want to. She was about to suggest turning back when Justine took a proprietary grip on her hand. There was no mistaking it for a friendly clasp.

I will take what I can. It bothered Vienna because she wanted it so much—to be with Justine. To belong to her? Was that okay? It wasn't a question you could ever really ask anyone.

Justine sailed through pubs, crowds materializing around her. A man had the poster of her with the diamond shoes. Justine signed it with a laugh.

There seemed little dancing and a lot of drinking. Justine let Vienna have two cocktails, called cosmos, which made everything swirly bright. "No more for Vienna," she said when the second one was gone. Something in the way she spoke made everyone ask if Vienna was okay, or if she needed water or something to eat. She accepted water and noted that even Justine drank less than she seemed to, despite the fact that everyone was buying her alcohol. Another one of her tricks.

All this in a whirling cyclone of perfume and cologne. Mock squeals of distress and staccato peals of laughter. Rugby on the telly; mud and muscles and crowds cheering. Vienna skated on the thin film of sexual tension, feeling it tear under her.

Midnight came and went. Olifur appeared at a discreet distance just after one thirty. If Justine noticed, she didn't say anything. The decibels rose another notch. Justine rode the wave of noise and light, poised at its highest curl.

Vienna snuck another drink, something she could have sworn the bartender called "black death." It tasted terrible, so she drank it all at once. And suddenly she was outside her head and floating inside a pub with a shoulder-tight crowd of Icelanders. Looking from disembodied distance, she saw again that no one was comfortable around Justine. They wanted to talk to her and be seen with her and sleep with her and that didn't leave any time to just be with her. Those who kept their distance hissed poisonous envy. Vienna wanted to slap them.

I will not ruin her night.

And she didn't, though she worried when Justine's new clothes ended up in a wrinkled heap on the hotel room floor. So much for waiting another night. And because Justine would feel guilty, Vienna encouraged her to just do what she wanted. Which only made Justine talk in tedious length. Finally it was too much.

"We are like the two stars. A horse and a rider." Which was the most vulgar thing Vienna had ever said, and she wasn't even certain the context was right given they were both female.

At first it seemed like a mistake because Justine slid off the bed and walked to the pile of clothes and pulled out Vienna's blouse. She put it on Vienna, which seemed the opposite of sex until she started taking it off again. The second Vienna's hands were overhead, Justine grabbed the fabric and twisted it in some way so that Vienna's wrists were tied together.

"A trick I saw at a show in Berlin. Crazy town," she said. "Last chance to run."

Vienna decided that under the current circumstance, she could hardly be expected to make any choices. Which was perfect, as long as Justine would just shut up.

"Vienna, I . . ." blah blah blah until the stars went cold.

Vienna defaulted to returning one of Justine's gestures. She stuck out her tongue.

It must have been the right reply. Justine straddled her hips and leaned over until her nose just touched Vienna's.

"Your turn," she said.

"My turn?"

"To tell me you love me."

And there was the alcohol back again because she couldn't think and it was so unfair. So unfair to be alone in a tiny apartment in Brussels. Unfair to stare at the same crack in the ceiling every night. Unfair that she wanted to be with Justine every second and Justine just went out shopping and left her alone like it was nothing.

If I don't say anything, she might get upset.

"I do." Which the absolute wrong thing because it sounded like she was speaking at a wedding. Maybe Justine didn't catch it? Maybe they did it differently in America?

Justine laughed. "To have and hold." The way she said it was not the way you would say it in church. Worse, this looked like a prelude to more talking. Vienna raised her head high enough to kiss Justine because maybe that would stop another lecture. It was like hitting a switch when a room went from mysterious dark to blinding light with nothing between. Suddenly Justine's hands were tight on Vienna's hair pulling her closer.

The rest followed from that and Vienna only had to play along. First on her back, then on her stomach, which Vienna didn't think she would like but did. Squeezing the pillow under her head as tightly as she could because all of her muscles seemed connected. Her hands came free, which she thought might be cheating, but she kept them tangled in the shirt anyway because asking Justine to reset the knot would only lead to more talking.

She returned Justine's love as well as she could, and she must have been getting better because Justine whispered to her. "Such a good girl." Her breathing loud and shallow. The machinery of heaven. A star hidden among planets. "Such a good girl." Her fingers tangled in Vienna's hair. That felt exactly like Vienna thought it should. Like Justine wanted her more than headlines or houses.

Avarice for nothing but Vienna, and it was more astonishing than anything Vienna had ever imagined.

Until it ended. Because she was wide awake, even as Justine crawled under the covers. "I did most of the work and had more to drink," Justine explained. She sounded oddly defensive.

"May I look at your BlackBerry?"

"Sure." Justine recited a nonsensical ten-character password. Vienna wrote the sequence down, then tore it up.

All of twelve minutes to find what David Andries had hidden. Fourteen numbers that could have saved his life. So obvious.

Vienna's thoughts fractured into a thousand directions. Everything moving too fast and she was trapped inside the Hunter S. Thompson book.

I think I see the pattern. This one sounds like real trouble. You're going to need plenty of legal advice before this thing is over. And my first advice is that you should rent a very fast car with no top and get the hell out of L.A.

Sweaty anxiety crawled inside her. Get the hell out. It made her not want to tell Justine anything. And Thompson kept talking.

This blows my weekend, because naturally I'll have to go with you—and we'll have to arm ourselves.

25

Vienna

Adelina had modified Justine's reservations at Hotel Sacher Wien to accommodate Vienna. She'd also arranged for airport pick-up via a larger than normal limo. Justine couldn't decide if the car was supposed to be a publicity boost, or one of Adelina's arcane social comments. Vienna loved it; spying through tinted windows. "Look! That woman walks funny."

How quickly celebrity makes us assholes.

Justine stopped the limo six blocks from the hotel; shooed Vienna out in front of her.

She realized her mistake even as the hulking car pulled away to deliver their luggage. In the face of what should have been a constant reminder, she'd forgotten the city's murky temper.

Paris and New York and even Rome, in the end, had been bridled by fast food and case-lots of cheap jewelry. They were denizens of the flat earth, anchored to stale shoals of brand names and the bland expectations of tourists. But Vienna remained separate.

The glittering display cases were here, clotted inside the tourist-rich vein linking St. Stephens to the Staatsoper, but they never coalesced into anything beyond shades of glass and light. Step into a narrow side street after sunset and a thread of hoary magic remained. Wagner breathing from the stones. Echoes of empires fallen to darkness. Goths and Vandals and Magyars and Franks.

Justine lifted her gaze to a dark strand of green to the west. The trees of the Wienerwald pushing tight against the city. She imagined a scream cut off by a single shot. Prince Rudolph under the trees, his lover already dead, his gilded world soon to follow. Powerless to do anything beyond pen an epitaph for a dying age. *You are now rid of my presence and annoyance.*

The forest seemed to lean over the city. A serrated loop of history cut free by the Star of Memphis. She saw Vienna, somehow already dead under arched branches. Tangled hair across fallen leaves, tawny eyes empty.

For a breathless second, she couldn't look. "You okay, Vienna?"

"Yes." Vienna stuttered her stride to make certain she stepped on each crack in the sidewalk. Justine heard her counting under her breath. "One-one, two-one, four-two, eight-three, sixteen-five, thirty-two-eight . . ."

The nightmare vision twisted through Vienna's compulsive counting, spreading to places that were nothing more than dates on the BlackBerry's calendar: the Hot Dragon promo in Thailand and the accessories show in Madrid. *I see her with me.* Walking under Buddhist chedis of Ayutthaya or through the Real Jardín Botánico. *I've written her into my future.* When had that happened? *I can't lose her now, not when there's so much yet to share.*

"Vienna?"

The girl stopped. "Yes?"

"After Clay to Flesh is over, we have to buy you new clothes for Spain."

The expected pause. A frown. "Vienna?"

"It has to be green for Spain."

Justine wondered at the logic behind the proclamation, but didn't doubt it was perfectly valid. "We can do that."

The frown deepened, and Vienna whispered to herself. Justine waited. "What if I lose my toothbrush and call to the desk and everyone finds out we're in the same room?"

"We'll just have to hope your reputation remains intact."

A short laugh and a whisper that sounded like "Warm feet." Vienna turned away and continued her broken-step counting.

I am in her future, too. Justine looked beyond the city's stone ramparts, up to the watercolor overcast. *I won't sit by like Prince Rudolph did.*

The blunt geometry of Hotel Sacher's interior lay in wait to ambush Vienna. But Ghost Girl was folded inside herself, not accepting input from anything as trivial as reality. She floated on small steps, passing through the warm browns and deep reds of the lobby.

Only when Emily Holt appeared around a marbled corner did the girl look up. "Hey!" Emily said, "My favorite dysfunctional couple." She gave Justine a European cheek kiss and shot Vienna a cross-eyed look. Vienna glanced at Justine before breaking into a stifled gasp of laughter.

"What are you doing here?" Justine asked.

"Technically I'm at Moana Beach, Bora Bora, helping my brother photograph a gaggle of freakishly rich Barbies." She paused as if considering something. "The weather is nice and the men are very tan. Altogether a great place to be."

"And who got stuck in Austria, braving the chill breeze?"

"That would be Michael Flores. Pegged for shooting the last chapter of the much anticipated Clay to Flesh folio."

"So I remember being told." Something was wrong. "And your brother?"

"Never pays attention to his schedule. Anyway, he likes working with you. He goes on about catharsis, 'strictly in the Greek context of overwhelming emotional empathy.'"

"I make him cry?"

"Or get sexually aroused. Hard to tell with men."

Justine lowered her voice. "We need to talk."

"Yes, we do."

Justine's suite had a balcony overlooking Philharmoniker Strasse and the Staatsoper. "The opera house got terrible reviews when it was built," Emily said as they sat. "One of the architects was driven to suicide."

"Eduard van der Nüll," Vienna said. "He hanged himself in 1868. His design was called a sunken box." Vienna's pupils slid side-to-side as she tracked a new source. "It's an early Renaissance design, influenced by French architectural elements." She looked at Justine. "I don't think that's important."

Justine took her hand. "Not everything has to be important to be worth hearing."

Vienna nodded. "The original centerpiece of the foyer was an orrery by Franz Linz. It showed the planets, covered in hammered metals to represent their ancient alchemical affiliations. Copper for Venus and iron for Mars." Her eyes opened a fraction wider. "For Mercury—which would have required quicksilver—Linz was going to use nickel polished to high reflectivity. But it was too expensive, and the project was canceled. Linz went on to design . . ." Her voice trailed off in a blush.

Emily clapped. "She's amazing. I'll buy her from you. I have information to trade."

"Deal."

"Heather!" Vienna's voice quivered.

"Vienna, this could be important."

"You would give me away?"

"Well, not so much 'give.'"

Emily interrupted before Vienna could break into full storm. "Vienna, did you notice how Justine was walking with you?"

A long pause as Vienna tried to follow the shift in topics. "What do you mean?"

"She was a few inches off your shoulder. It's not the way friends walk."

"It's not?"

"It's a particularly effective piece of body language, though we rarely notice it on a conscious level. She's telling the world that you're spoken for—that she's your lover."

"I don't care. It was a mean joke."

Emily shook her head. "I'll share a secret with you."

"Okay."

"Justine has two older brothers. She adopted a masculine form of affection display: she teases. You have to accept her quirks. Whatever your perception, there has to be trust beyond the simple parsing of words."

Justine looked at Emily. "A bit of a psychologist, are we?"

"Master's in Applied Behavioral Analysis, Cornell. And to answer your next question, my brother needs me and I love traveling."

"Which brings us to why you're here instead of a tropical beach," Justine said.

"Sometimes my insomnia and I look through my brother's e-folios late at night. Would you like to know what his pictures show?"

"I would."

"A brown-haired man with dark sunglasses mirroring the world. He was at our departure gate at Heathrow as well as San Francisco International. He turned up in the background of your London photo shoot no fewer than three times." Emily reached into her purse and pulled out five photos. All showed the same man; one photograph had him in black motorcycle boots that must have been auctioned by an '80s hair band. "You wouldn't know him, would you?"

Justine shook her head. "This is why you traded places with Flores?"

"Humans are the only animals that run toward danger instead of away from it."

Justine exhaled softly. "Back in Brussels, I saw Sinoro snapping pictures of the crowd. I bet he was looking for this spook."

"We'll never know. But Mr. Sunglasses was following us and all I did was talk to you."

"Still, if he was with you, he wasn't in Iceland to kill Haldor Stefansson."

"Already thought of that. He's nothing more than hired help, which means a good deal of money is being spent keeping track of you and your acquaintances. I would bet Sunglasses has your room number, your itinerary, and probably your room service bill by now."

"Great."

"There's more." Emily gathered the photos. "The owner of the Vienna manikin is a huge fan of yours."

"I remember James saying she wanted to meet me."

"Like the ocean wants to meet the shore. She has every picture ever published of you, each one painstakingly cut from magazines and dry mounted in scrapbooks."

"How do you know this?"

"I spent three hours yesterday talking to her. She's an ex-pat, San Diego born and raised. Heiress to a fortune made in organic produce. She moved to Vienna seventeen years ago, after her husband died. The core of her Justine Am obsession dates to when she put her daughter up for adoption. She thinks you're her."

Justine closed her eyes. "Can this get any better?"

Emily brushed it aside with a backhand wave of her hand. "Her condition is more deserving of pity than anything. But she refuses to let anyone other than you have access to the manikin. She's wealthy enough to make it stick. I counted five video cameras panning her estate and I'm no security expert. I doubt she'll share Haldor Stefanssons's fate."

"Doesn't sound like it," Justine said. "When I offered to quit back in Brussels, Igor Czasky doubled my pay. He needed me to gain access to the last manikin. Vienna guessed it was something like that from the very start."

"Where might Czasky be found these days?"

"Kvaisi. As long as he avoids the Georgian political mess—he's wealthy enough to—he's out of reach."

"Still, he must have connections here. You suspect Lord Davy?"

"Davy is of the right social strata, he has plenty of money, and he was in contact with my dear departed boyfriend."

The sky went acrylic purple, releasing a flurry of cold rain. Vienna ran inside. Emily tilted her head a fraction of an inch, silently asking Justine to remain. Justine opened the parasol in the center of the table.

"Do you remember the 'JD' initials in Sinoro's notebook?" Emily asked. "Julian Dardonelle. A talented and recently deceased sculptor, coincidentally seen talking to Vienna after you left her apartment."

"You possess a great deal of information." *An impossible amount.* Was Emily part of this?

"One of Vienna's Lower Town neighbors was a sour old widower. He keeps a diary of suspicious characters—meaning everyone. It describes Julian spot on. Dardonelle handed Vienna a piece of paper, which she threw away the moment he was gone. The police would very much like to know what was on said paper, but Vienna is being protected from high up. No warrants have been issued."

"Emily, how do you know all this?"

"I'm sleeping with a Scotland Yard detective."

"And here I was assembling Machiavellian plots. At least that solves the mystery of your access to Sinoro's police file, as well as his cryptic doodles. I won't ask how this romance came to be."

"It's no secret. He has a tight ass and abs like sand ripples on the bottom of a fast stream."

"Cheers to that."

"My turn to ask about your love life."

Justine smiled despite herself. "I guess you'd have to say she has a tight ass, too."

"So I imagine. And in bed?"

Justine crossed her eyes, sending Emily into a fit of laughter. "Sorry about that," Emily said. "A photo I showed Vienna from your London shoot. You were looking at something that almost caused your eyes to cross—probably a fly or bee buzzing too close. You see that sort of thing more often than you'd think when you look at hundreds of pictures. Still, here was the beautiful Justine Am caught looking like a dork."

"You made her laugh," Justine said, "which is no mean feat. I've seen plenty of embarrassing rejects. It happens."

"Not to high-end fashion models it doesn't, at least not that most will admit."

"Ex-fashion model."

"You've decided to quit after all?"

Justine slid her fingers over the table. "It's just so . . . I mean, where can we go from here? Lipstick lesbians are two girls faking it on the couch for the next line of coke."

Emily leaned back. "She's left a hole in your confidence, if nothing else. My brother spotted that. He says your new vulnerability makes you more beautiful. You marginally topped his A-list a few weeks ago; now he thinks you're miles above everyone else."

"Small price for sleepless nights."

Emily shook her head. "You know George and I had an older sister? Married for three years before black eyes and bruised arms starting showing up. A year after that, she smashed her kitchen window and jammed a shard of glass in her neck. Scored a direct hit on the trachea." Emily took a deep breath. "You can't always choose where your love falls. You made out all right."

"I'm sorry. I must sound conceited."

"You have to be, to be who you are. You're also one of the most thoughtful girls in the profession. Vienna could have done far worse as well."

"At least until my career comes crashing down."

"Don't hold your breath. Have you read about the boycott of Carrie Limited? Not a huge one, but enough to give them a headache for firing you. The nutbars on the right are vilifying you, but that's only adding to your cachet."

"Which seems to be hawking computer cases." She told Emily about the Hot Dragon offer.

"You're missing the point. The Jordan Farquars of the world are going extinct. Twitter and Instagram and YouTube are the new kings and they love you. There's a boutique in Seattle printing 'How is it you sleep at night?' T-shirts. For an extra two bucks it comes with a rather suggestive picture of you. A few have been spotted in L.A. and New York. The Internet is coming of age, and even as a child its strength is unmatched by the old-school media. Why do you think Hargrave took you back? He's no fool."

"I hope you're right."

"Trust me. And enough derailing the subject."

"Can I pretend to have forgotten what we were talking about?"

"No. Whatever you think Vienna might mean to your career, it's obvious you're in too deep to care."

Justine closed her eyes. "Have you ever kissed a girl?"

"I'm from a very conservative Rust Belt town. Of course I have."

"The thought never occurred to me," Justine said. "What did you think of the experience?"

"The problem with kissing a girl is that we kiss like girls."

"Exactly. The right guy is all warm pressure and rabid desire." Justine laughed. "Vienna kisses like a trembling violet."

"There are people who take pleasure in such innocence."

"But it's not an act with her. She really is a wet kitten in a dog pound."

"So are you one of the people who likes kittens?"

Justine gave her a sharp glance. "You going to charge for this session?"

"I don't want the worry lines you're working on to ruin my brother's pictures."

Justine leaned back into her chair, gazed over the green roof of the opera house. "She's done everything she can to encourage me. I wish I knew if she understood that."

"You're asking for mutually exclusive things—for her to be aware of what she is doing while remaining innocent of it."

"Which makes me think I should stop."

"Why?"

"She'll do anything I suggest."

Emily slid her chair further under the umbrella's protective arch. "Certain sexual behaviors—especially submissive ones—can point to any number of emotional issues, many of which Vienna has filled out in triplicate. But, as the textbooks never tire of reminding us, the overriding factor in mental health vis-à-vis sexual relations has always been found in the discrete causes of arousal."

"No wonder people hate shrinks. In English?"

"If fear is part of Vienna's motivation then you have serious issues. Thing is, Vienna has no mechanism for emotional compartmentalization. If she were afraid of you, she would take one look at you and burst into quaking tears. The more realistic alternative is she enjoys playing student to your teacher. It allows her a wide array of sexual expression with minimal risk of exposing perceived defects, most of which have been internalized to a horrifyingly unhealthy degree."

"That was English?"

"Vienna has found a stunningly beautiful lover who encourages her sexual advances. What shy soul would turn away from that? Sounds like paradise to me."

"It's not her sexuality that concerns me."

"The real issue at last." Emily pointed at Justine. "Did you think your personal issues were any less pervasive than hers? You're in a back-stabbing career where success is defined by everyone except yourself. There are people out there who would tear you down out of jealousy or anger or just for the hell of it, and there is not a damn thing you can do about it. In the midst of this, you've discovered a place where sincerity will never be an issue. Why wouldn't you go to her? Why wouldn't she feel like joyous freedom?"

"Because it may not be right for her and there's no one but me to stop it."

"Melodrama aside, your notion of free will is antiquated. Hurting Vienna is inconsistent with your internal programming. Something you can't change any more than she can." Emily was silent for a moment. "Look, you're worried about the wrong thing. If Vienna was the type to turn cartwheels, she'd be dizzy by now. You want to lose sleep over something, you should consider all the people dying around her."

"I know."

"You should fold up shop and get your girl out of here."

"Now who's being melodramatic?"

"Justine, you can't pretend the danger isn't real."

"You tell me where we can go that Sunglasses won't find us, and I'll listen."

Emily swept the question away with a wave of her hand. "Fine. So what was on the paper Julian showed Vienna?"

"She never told me. I suspect it was the weights of four metal cylinders and four gold slugs. They came from inside the Clay to Flesh manikins in Prague, Paris, Budapest, and Rome."

"What does it mean?"

An eight-ton capacity loader. "It means I need your help."

"Yes?"

The vision returned. Vienna's empty eyes. *Something to save her.* Something to create confusion. A few seconds might make the difference, somehow. Give her a chance to escape.

"A jewelry box, watch-sized. A rock inside and the lid glued shut. It has to look very old—late nineteenth century. Is that possible?"

"I'm used to odd shopping lists. You would be depressed to discover what trinkets photographers think they need to accent the perfect picture."

It won't be enough. A shard of glass . . . "And one of those two-pronged landscaping stakes from that tent you use for wardrobe. I need it by tomorrow."

"Deal, as long as my brother gets to shoot you and Vienna for an independent project. He gets first rights. You get to pick the clothing, the content, and the setting."

"What on earth for?"

"I told you already. Your banter with Sir Davy back in London was caught on an iPhone. Several million hits on YouTube last I saw. If the project makes no money that's my issue."

"Who am I not to make the same mistake Vienna did? I'm trusting you to be kind."

"I get the idea from my undercover detective that Vienna has major connections. Even if I didn't care for her, I wouldn't risk upsetting the powers that be."

"Wise girl."

Emily hugged herself. "It's getting cold."

"The forecast is for snow by the end of the week."

"So, you got any particular badass vampire in mind for the tent stake?"

"Anson Davy."

"Dear God, Justine, I was joking."

Justine forced a weak smile. "So was I."

"Right. So now I'm more scared for you than her," Emily whispered.

26

Contour lines rippled across the map, flowing in uneven waves. Vienna's mind struggled to force them parallel, but they invariably narrowed or wavered apart. A series of Reimann sums dissecting undefined curves. Impossible calculus. Vienna tried to ignore them, searching the map's edge for latitude and longitude.

She'd found a hiking shop on Kamptner Strasse and managed to convey to the clerk that she wished to see topographic maps. *I don't even speak the language of my homeland.*

Justine was off with Emily and George Holt, setting up for the last Clay to Flesh shoot. They were working without the statue, the owner refusing to release it until she got to meet Justine. So Justine was posing solo on the grass tiers of the Belvedere.

. . . built in the eighteenth century for Prince Eugene of Savoy. The Belvedere was coveted by the Habsburgs, who in . . .

No time for Eugene or the Habsburgs.

Vienna's gaze slid down and then across the map, connecting latitude with longitude. N48° 14'079; E 16° 15'031. Near the edge of the Wienerwald. The Place of Righteous Murder. The numbers that killed Justine's boyfriend.

David Andries must have thought the coordinates had some power to protect him, or that they could be traded for money. He hid them in that sailboat picture on Justine's BlackBerry. *How could Justine have ever thought forty-eight degrees north was in the tropics?* But it didn't matter because it all went wrong. Andries had forgotten the numbers. That wasn't very smart, because it chained him to Justine's phone, and the one time he really needed it, it was gone. So someone shot him straight in the face.

The topographical map showed a structure at the coordinates.

The last thing Prince Rudolph and von Vetsera ever saw. Vienna slid the map back into its oversized drawer. She bought a compass with money she had taken from Justine's wallet.

Out into the crowd, the Star of Memphis spinning through her thoughts. A giant gemstone with a thousand shimmering facets. Hidden in the forest all these years. But where? She knew the place of Righteous Murder, but what was she supposed to do from there?

"Miss Vienna."

She looked up into the weathered eyes of James Hargrave.

"I didn't know you were here," she blurted. "I can tell you where Justine is."

"She is at the Belvedere, Miss Vienna." He sighed. That was all wrong. Vienna tried to think of him as Justine would. He wasn't the sort of man who would sigh. "This is complex," he continued. "Would you share lunch? Give me a chance to explain?"

"You don't like me."

"That's not true." He held his arm up in a crook; a motion Vienna had seen other men make. She put her hand on his arm. *Is this what I am supposed to do?* Justine would be happy if they were friends. She looked under his coat to see if he had one of those old-fashioned six-shooters in a leather holster. Nothing but a phone clipped to his belt.

"I'll buy lunch. You name the place."

"The place?"

"A good restaurant."

"I don't know any."

"Then we'll walk along with the tourist herd and read menus."

"Okay." He smelled faintly of steely cologne.

Several blocks north of Vienna's chosen route home, they stopped at a street-side café that served pasta. Vienna ordered olive oil and garlic over linguini. *Aglio e olio is the one classic dish all fanciers of Italian cuisine should prepare at least once. . . .*

"Not much of a lunch. You sure you don't want something better?"

Vienna shook her head.

Hargrave had chosen to sit outside despite the breeze. He spoke of his growing realization that he'd misunderstood his client's personal needs and how unfair that had been to Vienna. But the tablecloth was all starbursts of crisscrossed lines and they were pointing everywhere and—

"Vienna, please listen. I'm trying to do the right thing."

She closed her eyes. "Why aren't you telling this to Justine?"

"I've been hovering over her since that foolishness with the manikin in Prague. She's sick of it and I don't blame her. Better if she thinks I'm in New York. But I'm still worried, especially after Iceland. I've grown rather fond of her over the last few years. So here I am, close enough to come running, but far enough away not to crowd her. Useless as far as I can tell, but I want to help if I can."

Vienna squinted at the tablecloth. She imagined that one of the lines pointed at Justine.

Hargrave leaned forward and put his hand around her wrist. Not tight, but Vienna flinched away. Hargrave held on a second longer before letting go. "Did you see anything that might give us a clue as to what's happening? We have to protect Justine."

"No." How had he found her out of all the people in the city?

"I spoke to Justine over the phone. She said something about cylinders of metal." He wasn't looking at her anymore. He was watching people walk by. Who was he looking for?

"Nine grams of gold and fifty-seven grams of tin," Vienna said.

"Does that mean anything to you?"

"No."

He glanced at his watch. "I hate logic puzzles. Maybe the numbers themselves are important?"

Vienna blinked. "Nine times fifty-seven is 513. Eight cubed plus one cubed." No reason to cube one, but the equation fit better that way.

He shook his head. "It's probably nothing."

Hargrave spent the remainder of lunch telling stories that made him seem foolish. He laughed as he wound through them.

Vienna thought she should be laughing as well but she still didn't like him. He ate quickly and then flagged a waiter down for the check, placing cash on the bill before the waiter could leave for another table. That made the gratuity way too large, but that was an American thing, too. "I don't know what the hell I'm doing." He smiled and Vienna hated that, too. "But the trip was worth it, to let you know how sorry I am for the things I did."

"How did you find me?"

"I was on my way to your hotel when I spotted you."

"Okay."

"Can I take you back to the Sacher?"

"No thank you."

"Then this is good-bye for now, Miss Vienna."

"Okay."

Hargrave stood and gave her shoulder a squeeze. Vanished down a set of stairs for the U-Bahn. Why had he been in such a hurry? Not that it mattered. *I'm glad he's gone.*

Vienna sighed at the day, looked at the crumbs left on the table. Which was a mistake because the lines on the tablecloth began to spread, extending into a dense web. Right off the table, like ice crystals covering water. She backed away too fast and caught her feet under the chair, tumbling to the sidewalk. She rose, careful not to look at the table, or at all the people she knew were staring at her.

Away from the restaurant, she closed her eyes. A deep breath and she could see the route back to the hotel. It was okay. All she had to do was follow the map.

She'd covered less than a block before the clouds sank through the stone buildings. Vienna imagined herself walking along the bottom of an ocean trench. Down below the fish, in the darkness where nothing lived. Where everything was peaceful. A few steps more brought the first raindrops.

She sought shelter in an entryway identified as the Gemälde-galerie of the Kunsthistorisches. She remembered the last word as meaning "museum." No chance to buy a ticket before she was carried into the main gallery by a swarm of British tourists anxious to stay dry. It would be too embarrassing to return to the tellers and admit what happened and they would never believe her anyway.

She found herself in a circular atrium, set off by a ring of marble pillars. Shops around the circumference sold expensive coffee and cheap mementoes. The space was too big and it didn't fit right and if she didn't make it work now, it would never go away. She bought an English language pamphlet that had a map of where everything was, as well as an overview of the museum's history. Back to a small plastic table, conspicuously cheap among the beautiful pillars.

But she was still thinking of Mr. Hargrave and the cylinders of metal she'd found in Iceland. *How many of the gold cylinders would fit in a pillar?* And just like that, the nearest pillar went transparent in Vienna's thoughts. It began filling with slugs of gold.

Vienna recognized the dangerous pattern, but she was tired and the demon in her mind raced through the pillars, mesmerized by a recursive stream of geometry. They were not all the same size. This one fits inside this one, just like the manikins. Which was the smallest?

The pillars twisted and shifted together, warping the room like smoothly folding fabric. The shops unhinged and flowed around her in dizzying circles, still attached to the pillars. She compared slight differences in radii as the pillars overlapped in the origami room. Then there were only circles within circles.

The appearance of the wheels and their work was like unto the color of a beryl.

Wheels within wheels. A prophet's vision of heaven.

Her heart was racing. It was all numbers and it didn't fit inside her and it tasted like blood in her mouth and acid in her throat and it slithered through her stomach like a nightmare except there was never any waking up because it was real and no one ever really understood that.

Vienna didn't feel the rain on her face, didn't know she was outside. Didn't see the man standing behind her in the crowd; sunglasses in the rain. There was only a starburst of thoughts, cutting and terrible.

It's a love letter.

Start with the Sun and in the order of the planets and always as the planets move. One to measure distance one to measure time.

Circles within circles.

Her foot caught with a familiar tug.

My shoe is untied. I'll trip.

She kneeled down to tie it.

Let all be made level.

Seven planets. The alchemists' celestial guide. Quicksilver for Mercury, copper for Venus, silver for the moon, iron for Mars, tin for Jupiter, lead for Saturn. Gold for the sun. Metal cylinders hidden in manikins.

My shoe is untied.

She kneeled down.

Wheels within wheels. One to measure distance. One to measure time. Orbits arcing through space.

My shoe is untied.

Crouching to tie her shoe she saw the diagrams for Linz's orrery set across wet cobblestones. She followed the dizzying path of gears, spinning in long chains from the motor. She turned the motor and the Earth moved. The planets in an orrery traveled anticlockwise.

The machinery of God.

To have and hold.

"You're supposed to say they're not real."

I better tie it.

A dusty geography manual from Bath: . . . *it may have been Ptolemy who gave us north as the zero angle of maps. . . .*

I'll trip.

She took the laces in her hand.

A physics textbook published in 1903: *The Convention du Mètre,*

establishing the metric system was signed by eighteen countries on
May 20, 1875. These were France, Germany, Austria . . .

My shoe is untied.

A star hidden among the planets.

Untied.

A shirt of endless tunnels. "I couldn't approach while the limo
was here. They would have recognized me."

I'll trip.

"That book is too boring for our little princess. Here is one on
knights in shining armor."

But I want to read about Sisi and the Star of Memphis.

"They would have recognized . . ."

"Knights in shining . . ."

"How far to that light?"

My shoe is untied.

"They would have . . ." More than one. Another man in Justine's limousine back in Brussels. Pointing at Vienna and laughing. "She walks funny."

Wet pavement under her hands. *I'll trip.*

"They used gold to tint the windows red."

"Au" for aurium. The shining dawn. Enough for a plane ticket
home, so far away.

Gold to measure distance.

Metal to measure time.

Start at the sun and walk north to Mercury. Each gram of gold
translated into a meter. Then each gram of quicksilver stepped
off anticlockwise in an orbital arc. Time recorded in the movement of the planets. Then out to Venus . . .

My shoe.

". . . have recognized . . ."

The alchemy of the planets.

My shoe is untied.

She bent down to tie her shoe. "Will the unicorn be willing to
serve thee, or abide by thy crib?"

"You never saw a unicorn."

My shoe
My
My Little Storm Cloud
Justine?
You're just like her.

And the forest was full of ghosts; acolytes of a forgotten goddess, drowning in the lake by the Cart House. She felt water on her face.

Know ye not this parable? And how then will ye know all parables?

help me help me help me

Justine smiled. "You are now rid of my presence and annoyance; be happy in your own way." Dying under the boughs of the ancient forest. The thick smell of pine. Winter wind through the trees. The dark shadow of the Cart House, warm lights in the windows.

"They were wrong to abandon you, my Lady. But I am forever your knight." And it sounded like Lord Davy, but his hair was deep brown and there was no scar on his face. All around him were walls covered in pictures and diagrams and riding crops and medals. And there was blood dripping all over her and she cried and cried.

It's the rain that made you this way.

And that had to be true because the blood became cold rain, reaching her even though she was under all the pillars filled with gold.

A small crowd gathered around the girl in the courtyard. Her torso twisted as she rocked back and forth, her fingers clawing at the air. But no one was a doctor and no one felt safe touching the girl. It was obviously a seizure of some sort. Moving her might hurt her, and then who knew what the lawyers might do? The museum's eaves were keeping her dry, and she didn't seem to be in immediate danger.

A man tried to calm her with a reassuring stream of words. His companion thought he recognized her. "Wien."

27

The museum courtyard was a gloomy mine shaft sunk in a massive outcrop of stone buildings. Vienna sat on the far side, a marionette slumped over tangled strings. Her hands jerked over cobblestones, working an impotent spell against whatever ripsaw vision had severed her from reality. A museum guidebook beside her, drinking rainwater and pissing a dark smear of ink. Meaning slipping to entropy.

The police held the crowd back. No one approached the girl. Her mouth half-open, torso rocking over collapsed legs. Her fingers grabbing at nothing.

Justine was escorted by the same officers who'd snatched her from the Belvedere and given her a heart attack ride through the Innere Stadt. Their car's two-tone siren a screeching echo of Vienna's ancestry, reaching out to protect the girl.

Then why leave her here, pinned to the wall by gawkers? It didn't make sense. *Unless this was a shadow of her ancestry as well?* Prince Rudolph had been caught in the woods with no witnesses to record his fate. No worry of that here. Cameras clicking at the girl, images flashing to Facebook and Flickr. Had the danger become so great that shame was her only shelter?

Would the same protection have been extended to me?

The wind shifted, kicking rain over Vienna.

Justine went to her, kneeled down. "Vienna?" It came to her that Vienna was tying shoelaces. Fingers winding together and pulling a bow tight, despite wearing flats. Justine cupped her hands over the girl's frantically working fingers. "Vienna?" It wasn't the textbook way to handle such a case. It wasn't what she would have tried back in the wards of Felton Gables.

Vienna slowly looked up. Through the rain, Justine could see tears filling her eyes. Her gaze held nothing of the place around her; pupils searching for a reset button she couldn't find.

"Vienna. It's time to go home." Justine tightened her grip, stopping Vienna's fingers. The best thing would be to let Vienna lie down, but the pavement was sinking under a growing lattice of puddles.

"I'm a good girl," she whispered. Justine remembered the words from their lovemaking. Fought back her own tears.

"You're a beautiful girl."

"My head hurts."

"I know." Justine moved her right hand to Vienna's head, brushing back wet hair. "Can you stand?"

"The sky is spinning. Circles in circles. The machinery of God. Day into night into years. Prince Rudolph couldn't stop it and it ate him up."

"We can sit longer, if you need to."

"Did you know that carbon tetrachloride was first synthesized by Henri Regnault in 1839?"

"I didn't."

"It's raining."

"It is."

"Petrichor."

"Vienna?"

"The smell of water on soil. It's what makes everything seem fresh when it rains." She was back, making eye contact for a heartbeat. "Do you think it made me the way I am? The rain?"

Justine tried to smile, knew it came out wrong. "Then let it rain."

Vienna gathered her feet under herself and slowly rose, Justine holding her arm. "Vienna? Are you okay?"

"It's cold." She threw her arms around Justine and held her with trembling strength. "I dreamed you were dead."

"It's okay. I'm here." Justine held her tightly for several seconds and then gently pried her loose so they could walk.

They made their way to the crowd. Hushed applause, as if Vienna had made a difficult chip at Augusta. People stepped forward, holding umbrellas over them. Justine thanked them with a half smile. She heard, among the strings of Austrian words, both her name and Vienna's.

But not everyone was helping. Justine saw Mr. Sunglasses from Emily's photographs, barely glimpsed as people stepped closer. Her world turned sickeningly, ugly thoughts pivoting on growing realization. Shift a little and new reflections appear.

Lord Davy still had access to the Cart House and all its noble, dusty history. He wouldn't have had to deal with Andries to uncover the estate's secrets, much less kill him. Even so, that didn't erase Grant's phone number from Davy's phone. Was there no one left to trust?

Justine quickened the pace as much as Vienna could handle. Protecting her head as she sank into the backseat of the police car.

In front of the Hotel Sacher, Justine assured the officers that Vienna would be fine. Once in their suite, she stripped Vienna down, held her in a warm shower, and toweled her dry. "Off to bed with you," she finished.

"I'm not sleepy."

"Doctor's orders."

Vienna crawled under the covers, propping herself up on a stack of king-sized pillows. Justine went to the kitchen. The dissected remains of her Sony laptop were spread across the counter. Straight rows of tiny screws arranged by size. Letters popped off the keyboard and laid out alphabetically. Circuit boards evenly spaced over wet spots. *She held the components under water.* The hard drive had been taken from its spindle and bent almost in two. *She must have stomped it against a floor board.*

"Vienna? What happened to my computer?"

"I wanted to see how it worked."

Two weeks ago, it would have fit expectations. *She thinks I'll write it off to her condition.* Not a chance.

"I see." Justine looked at the twisted hard drive. Something stored on the computer's disk.

"Are you mad?" Vienna asked.

All those pictures of the manikins changing. No proof of it left. *At least I have none.* What had Vienna discovered?

"No." Too scared to be mad. Justine poured a glass of cold water and returned to Vienna. "Drink if you can."

"It doesn't matter."

"What do you mean?"

"We're at the last statue. They'll kill us."

"Who?"

"Lord Davy. Or one of his friends."

"Not going to happen. I promise."

Vienna shifted. Her voice slow and careful. "We should open the last statue and tell everyone what's inside." She paused, lips moving over the next words.

Getting more lies straight.

"It might save the woman who owns it, maybe," Vienna continued. As if guessing that was the right thing to say.

She knows! She has the answer to the coded riddle. The Star of Memphis. She only needs to see the cylinders inside the last manikin. But how? *The BlackBerry.*

"Vienna, did you find anything on my BlackBerry?"

"No."

"Vienna, you had to—"

"I hate how you never believe me." Tears starting again.

Shit.

Vienna would know the solution before the killer. Every step she took would be watched. Mr. Sunglasses would see to that. His boss would shoot Vienna the second she succeeded. There was no other way to keep the secret.

With the evidence on my computer destroyed, I might escape. She's trying to save me, but she can't save herself.

Except . . . the killer was like David Andries in one respect. He would never run from a woman. He would never believe one was a threat, not on a level that mattered.

"Doesn't that make sense?" Vienna asked. "To take it apart before it's replaced?"

"It won't be replaced. There was never a chance to make a duplicate. The owner won't let anyone see it but me."

Vienna shrank under the covers. "I didn't think of that."

"The only chance to get the cylinders would be to fake an accident serious enough to break the manikin open. They could drop it during unloading and grab the goods in the resulting chaos."

Vienna remained silent. *Constructing a new argument to get to the manikin.*

Justine brushed her fingers through Vienna's hair. "It never made sense to me—how we started in Budapest and skipped over Vienna—the closest city. But this had to be the last manikin. The thieves knew they'd have to destroy it with no duplicate to replace it. They couldn't do that and expect the other owners to give them access."

"We still need to take it apart." No reason given—none left except that Vienna needed the last piece of the puzzle.

The killer will go after her.

"I'm certain the owner will let me see it first. We can take it apart tomorrow morning, if you feel up for it."

"Okay."

He'll never see me coming after him.

28

Vienna didn't like the old house. The furniture was spindled wood and no padding. Antiques from when people had stronger arses.

The woman living there was broken. She thought Justine was her daughter. She kept on calling Justine "dear" and "sweet child."

"Look at me," said Miss Havisham. "You are not afraid of a woman who has never seen the sun since you were born?"

It made Vienna self-conscious.

The lady showed them to a domed library that held the manikin. "It's such a cute piece, and it looks so much like you, Heather." It didn't look anything like Justine. "If only the pose were more dignified."

The manikin wore a dark gray hobble skirt and a matching top. Vienna thought the dress was a sad attempt to conceal the impish pose of the doll; bent at the waist and her back swayed in open invitation to explore everything south of the shoulder blades. Standing on tiptoes. *Some anthropologists speculate that wearing high heels mimics lordosis behavior, observed in cats and other . . .* She blushed, remembering the last night in Iceland. Justine's hands on her back, the answering arch of her spine.

The manikin's hands were close to her chest, palms open, as if she were leaning on a high counter. She had long, curled hair, seductively dark. Her glass eyes were deep brown.

"She's very pretty," Vienna said.

"But in poor taste. I'm putting her up for sale when this is over," the old lady said. "I only kept her because I knew someday Heather would want to see her."

"Very kind," Justine said. "May we take it apart?"

"By all means, sweetie. I had no idea it even came apart!"

They removed the clothes, Vienna folding them on a spindled chair of polished mahogany. Lowering the statue to its side was easy with Justine's help. Vienna went to the feet, seeing the expected star, bowl, and horn. The other foot was branded with the statue's name: Theodrada. A forgotten queen, known as little more than dame to her king.

Women are nothing but machines for producing children. Napoleon. That French bastard who invaded Austria. *My home.* She liked the way that sounded. My home.

Vienna twisted the big toe lightly, stopping at a slight click. She began to dismantle the manikin.

"Shouldn't you label the pieces?" the old lady asked, alarmed at the growing pile of wooden parts.

"Vienna is an expert," Justine assured her.

Thirty minutes later, Vienna held up a tiny disk of gold and a small cylinder of stone.

"It's marble!" she said, delighted with the beauty of it. The Earth had no alchemical metal associated with it, so Bell had used marble. It was perfect. She guessed at the dimensions. "Five grams of gold." The density of marble was harder to find, but the *Chemical Rubber Company Handbook of Chemistry and Physics* had it. "Marble has a density of 2.563, assuming this is solid, which I think it is." She did the calculation in her head and added five grams. It would throw the final calculation off by meters. *I will never let them get it!* "Twenty-six grams."

"What does it mean?" asked the lady.

"Weights for balancing the machine used to make the manikin," Justine answered.

"They used gold for such things?"

"It could be precisely measured." A ridiculous answer, but there was no change in Justine's voice, no way to tell she was lying.

"How nice," the lady said.

"I'm sure historians of such things will be pleased," Justine said. "Let's get it back together."

Vienna worked faster than in Iceland, taking delight in the

ingenious way the pieces slid together. She listened to Justine instruct the old lady how to lie. "I don't want anyone to know we took the manikin apart. You know how these photographers are. Once something is studied it's no longer art. We'll record the contents on a note and slip it into the skirt pocket. That way, everyone can discover it for themselves."

It won't matter. Vienna had all she needed. It was beautiful. Circles within circles. Treasure hidden among the planets.

Star light, star bright, first star I see tonight.

29

The girl was a ghost once again. Rising from bed the instant twelve flashed blue on the bedside clock. Of course Vienna would start a nocturnal quest precisely at midnight. It was a function of who she was. Across the floor with the preternatural grace of the socially traumatized. *No one notice me. I'm not here. Leave me alone.*

Justine feigned sleep on an anthill of caffeine pills. Belatedly realizing that anxiety would have kept her awake.

Vienna dressed from a stack of folded clothes left on an oversized chair. Shoes on, she hesitated. "I had a dream," she whispered, "which was not all a dream." Justine imagined Vienna's eyes scanning over words only she could see. What meaning did they hold? An exaggerated sigh, and she was gone. Justine sprang from the bed, dressing from her own ready stash.

A lone man in the lobby, his face hidden behind the latest edition of *Der Kurier*. Blue jeans over black motorcycle boots. Justine wondered if he still had the sunglasses on.

How many other people had taken note of Vienna's flight? None of them could doubt her destination. The great forest at the edge of the city. Justine's phone showed the distance to be roughly eight miles from the hotel. The obvious plan would be to hit the front desk for access to the business center. Call up Google Earth and print a map of the area. Then ask the valet to flag a taxi. Show the driver your map and you're off. All it required was interaction with three or four strangers, most of whom would not speak your language. Easy to see how that'd play out in Vienna's world. They'd be angry at being disturbed by such stupid questions. They would laugh at you because you're such an idiot. They might even take you to the wrong place and then what would you do? So much safer just to walk. It would take less than three hours if Vienna kept a good pace.

The girl stepped into the night, hunched down in a black Pringle of Scotland sweater she'd found in a boutique off Stephansplatz. It would keep her warm enough as long as she kept moving.

Following was effortless. Vienna never looked to either side, let alone behind. Apprehension manifest in her broken stride; skipping over lines or tightroping along cracks in the sidewalk. Justine trailed a half block behind, her steps lost in the low drone of nocturnal traffic.

So how easy would it be to follow me?

She stepped to the side and quickly turned around, expecting to see Sunglasses. It was worse. Fifteen people close enough to see their faces. Was the man in the blue jacket familiar? Had he been at the hotel? A useless surge of adrenaline. Maybe in the elevator? Now what?

Justine turned away and quickened her pace to keep up with Vienna. Past a black-windowed bar, Jimmy Buffet absurdly spilling into the night. *"God I wish I was sailin' again . . . "* The staccato pulse of a UV light from the second floor. Impossible to imagine what for.

Justine's thoughts spiraled inward. So many mistakes. *I'm no better than Lina Zahler—a wink and a calculated flash of skin.* All that scheming in Iceland, and the only thing to show for it was Haldor, dead in his geodesic dome. *To what end?* Cut loose on a cold night, no one to trust beyond the girl she followed.

Her thoughts were scattered by the flaps-extended whine of a passenger jet passing to the southeast. Searching for the safe harbor of Flughafen Wien before the coming storm.

She turned again. Fifteen new faces behind her. They all seemed to have come from the hotel. A glimpse of black boots stepping into a nightclub. *Was that him?* Justine looked ahead and saw Vienna had already crossed to the next block; suddenly hidden behind a stopped bus. *I'm going to lose her.* She dodged through the crowd. The bus pulled away in a cloud of exhaust. Vienna's slender frame almost lost in the maze of people. *Idiot! Keep her in sight!* Justine crossed the street against a red light.

Vienna turned on Thalia Strasse. A long climb, the city unfolding below them. Left onto Hertlgasse. Silver fog crawled from the Danube, smearing streetlights into spectral haze. The barbed spire of Saint Stephens sank under the dark tide. Traffic thinned.

Two hours and forty minutes after leaving the hotel, Vienna reached a shadowed corner. A tube of yellow light over a bus stop. Savoyen Strasse and Johann Straus Strasse. She crossed the street and paused under the black eaves of the Wienerwald.

Justine wanted to rush to her; take her away from this place. But running from the forest wouldn't change anything. Wouldn't stop the murders. *I chose to be here. I have every advantage that Prince Rudolph did not.* Her fingers closed around the aluminum tent stake in her pocket.

Vienna turned on a penlight. A single step into the forest, and then she stopped. Another step, this time placing her right leg forward, across her left. Shoulders back, toes pointed forward. Justine recognized a stuttered imitation of her own runway walk. Vienna took only four steps before knocking ankles midstride and almost tripping. *How many times did I do that when I was learning?* She stopped and regained her balance. The short, exhaled giggle, so incongruous on such a night.

Justine held her breath as several seconds ticked by. Vienna's shoulders bunched in one of her long sighs, and she was off again in her normal walk. Justine paused long enough to glance down the street behind her. No one. Far worse than the crowded sidewalks. She turned and followed Vienna. *Just as Marie von Vetsera followed her lover.*

The waning moon backlit thickening bands of cirrus, its light dimming in the failing weather. The girl stayed on a path marked by placards nailed to trees. Red and blue stripes in Vienna's light, then yellow and red. Every so often, shouts came from other parts of the forest. College kids partying. Or worse.

The feeling of alienation returned. This was the heart of the city, more than Saint Stephens ever would be. Ancient trees that had witnessed the coming of the Celts, heard the cadence of Roman legions, and the battle cries of Magyars. Knotted branches stretched across the sky in claustrophobic arcs, calling out the latest invader. Leaves fell through the breeze, snared by the groundcover's tangle of decay and rebirth. Justine breathed in the timeless perfume of wet loam.

A rasping sigh, directly behind her. Justine whirled to face an empty path. A skewed tree whispered to the breeze, banners of lichen hanging from lower branches. Long seconds spent searching the tree's canopy, silhouetted against faint moonlight. *Just the wind.*

Justine turned back. The path was deserted. *Vienna!* Justine bit back the urge to shout out. Too many ears in the forest. *She can't have gone far.* Justine jogged up the path. Nothing.

She's left the trail. Justine backtracked and looked to her left. Only a thin row of trees separating the path from a meadow. No sign of the girl. The other way was dense forest.

She has to be this way. Justine stepped off the path, ducking under low branches. Nothing. Five steps. Ten. *She has to be this way.* Justine crouched low and pushed her way forward. Her foot slipped into the trace of a stream and she went down, her palm sliding through cold mud. Her left side instantly soaked. No traction to get her feet under her. Hands out, clawing into grass. Back up and pushing through another thicket.

There! A narrow beam of light dancing across the ground. Justine closed the distance, trying to catch her breath from the fall.

Ten minutes in the woods brought them to a chain-link fence, long fallen into disrepair. Vienna stepped through a truck-sized hole cut in the metal weave.

Justine heard water bubbling downhill.

The Dornbach.

The forest grew close, and then opened to the ruins of a pergola. Only a loose circle of decayed columns remained, centered around a marble bench. The stone seemed to glow in the diffuse light of the cloud-covered moon. The seat had collapsed under its own weight, lying shattered on the ground. The back remained; a blazing sun engraved into the center.

Starting with the sun . . .

The Place of Righteous Murder.

Vienna removed a small, flat object from her pocket and put it under the flashlight. A compass. She aligned herself northward and took several careful steps. She turned to her left, taking several more steps. Justine saw that she wasn't walking in a straight line, but in an arc around the bench. She stopped and whispered, "Mercury."

After a slight pause, she turned directly away from the bench and started walking. Enough steps to carry her beyond the columns. Then another turn to her left and another curved march. "Venus."

As the planets move . . .

Vienna stopped. Her eyes closed, her fingers twitching at her side. She began to tonelessly hum, recalling the weights of metal and gold found in each manikin. Justine couldn't remember any of them, despite having talked about them several times. Had it been fifty-two grams of tin in the Iceland manikin? Forty-seven? By comparison, Vienna had only briefly glimpsed most of the numbers, given to her on a scrap of paper in Brussels. Utterly meaningless at the time. Her ability to conjure them in this freezing forest seemed less a trick of memory and more a curse of the gods. She pirouetted, almost slipping on the damp ground. "Thou hast spoken right, 'tis true." It sounded like Shakespeare, recited too loudly on this dark stage. "The wheel is come full circle," the girl shouted. "I am here!" Justine realized that Vienna had grown bored with stepping out each planet's location. She'd begun to calculate the complete shape of David Bell's imaginary solar system.

You don't need shortcuts!

Vienna opened her eyes and surveyed the landscape. Her hands stopped; a complex series of geometrical equations solved. She clapped softly and skipped into an uneven run toward the unseen brook. Forty feet brought her to an ancient oak. Justine hunched along a parallel course.

After a complete circuit of the tree, Vienna's light found a depression between fingered roots. She dropped to her knees and started digging. In less than a minute she gave a soft exclamation of delight. She reached down and pulled a small metal box from the ground.

So anticlimactic. An unremarkable box at the base of an unremarkable tree. It would have remained hidden forever.

The girl gave a hushed laugh of delight. She didn't see that she was no longer alone. James Hargrave stepping from the bushes. A triumphant leer twisting his handsome features.

"A long chase," he said. He turned on a flashlight, picked out Justine in the trees. "Come out, Justine."

Vienna stood in shock as Justine approached.

Justine realized on some level she'd known the truth since that last dinner in London. The geometry of his watch. The travel hand mirroring the main hour hand, both pointing straight down. Hargrave's watch had already been set for travel. Not for New York, five hours behind London, but for Keflavík. In the same time zone. Always one step ahead. He'd reached Iceland first. He had been there when Haldor died.

Hargrave turned to Vienna. "Give me the box."

"That's not it," Justine said.

"I saw her dig it up, and you didn't come here last night. I've had you followed."

"The dipshit in the sunglasses and motorcycle boots. I spotted him days ago. That's why I had Emily Holt fetch the star. I knew you no longer had reason to watch her."

"I doubt that's true."

"Don't ever sell me short." She began walking to them, as if concerned for Vienna. No reaction from Hargrave, beyond a patronizing smirk. "You're a mess, aren't you? All because of this pathetic 'tard. What do you see in her?"

Justine kept walking.

"Close enough." He pulled a squat handgun from his coat. No doubt he'd hidden it somewhere in the metal suitcases. Disassembled into something innocuous and reconstructed during murderous layovers in Belgium, London, and Iceland. *All because I said a manikin moved. All my fault.* The gun's blue-black mouth remained only half raised.

He must not point it at her.

Justine stalled. "I'll tell you if you give Vienna and me five minutes together." She resumed walking toward them.

"Not unless I know where it is."

"In my pocket."

"Show me."

Justine removed Emily's small box and shook it. The rock inside rattled. She stopped five feet from Hargave.

"Very good." He flashed a tight grin. "You have five minutes, just as Rudolph and Vetsera had. You'll have a lot less if you call out or run."

She reached into her pocket, dropped the box, took the stake by its blunt end.

Just like Lina Zahler. Meeting old friends in the woods.

Her fingers closed around the stake and she saw words, as if flawlessly conducted by the cold metal. An oath memorized on the sunny lawns of Stanford. Washing through her in perfect fidelity. Exactly how she knew Vienna saw such things.

I swear by Apollo, Asclepius, Hygieia, and Panacea . . .

With a twist of her wrist, the stake flipped upward, the points brushing the soft skin of her wrist.

. . . to consider dear to me, as my parents, him who taught me this art . . .

Hargave still smiling, not yet sensing what was happening. The gun loose in his hand.

. . . I will prescribe regimens for the good of my patients according to my ability . . . .

She saw that he was a manikin, too: a collection of parts

carefully fit together. Only this time, she was the one who held the secret to take it all apart. An ancient trick, relearned by countless medical students slicing through cadavers in anatomy lab.

. . . and never do harm to anyone . . .

Justine flexed her knees and uncoiled, thrusting the stake to his throat. She had to generate enough force to penetrate the cricoid.

I will preserve the purity of my life and my arts . . .

Pray the thin metal doesn't bend.

In every house where I come I will enter only for the good of my patients . . .

The stake took him just above the jugular notch, below the thick thyroid cartilage. The metal held, the blunt end biting painfully into Justine's palm. Hargrave had no time to react. No time to run from a woman.

. . . keeping myself far from all intentional ill-doing and all seduction . . .

Once the tip was through muscle, Justine felt only slight resistance as it punctured Hargrave's trachea. Blood welled around the wound. She released the stake, stepping away.

All that may come to my knowledge in the exercise of my profession I will keep secret . . .

Only a fraction of a second for Hargrave's smile to slip. No air to fill his lungs. He dropped the gun and scrabbled desperately at the stake with his right hand. His left arm was no longer working. The stake must have bent after all, slicing the brachial plexus. Justine kicked the gun away as hard as she could.

If I keep this oath faithfully, may I enjoy my life and practice my art . . .

Hargrave collapsed as the stake slipped free. A terrible sucking sound filled his throat.

. . . but if I swerve from it or violate it, may the reverse be my lot.

No pressure to power his voice box. No way to scream. Vienna did it for him, her shrill cry piercing the night. From the forest behind Hargrave, Justine caught a split second flash of red laser light, reaching from the trees to connect to the back of his sinking head.

Justine grabbed Vienna's hand. "Hush. We don't want to attract attention."

As if on a switch, Vienna went quiet. Justine pulled her away from the writhing body of her agent. Wet gasping and the rustle of legs kicking uselessly at fallen leaves.

He will see the ruins in his last breath, just as Rudolph did. And I will walk away just as Lina did.

But I will not get as far.

30

Vienna followed Justine to the edge of the forest. The city below was all hazy and it was so cold that each breath added its own wispy cloud to the night. Justine headed toward Saint Stephens, but too far north for their hotel. Vienna was afraid to ask what their destination was because Justine had just murdered her agent and it didn't make any sense because there was no way Justine had the Star of Memphis. Vienna had it in her pocket. She grabbed the box to assure herself it was there.

Justine kept walking until Vienna's legs felt like melting lead. They'd covered at least thirty kilometers and she just wanted to sleep and the sun had to be coming up soon and she couldn't stay warm any longer. *Where is she taking me?*

Justine stopped at the edge of a park. Vienna noticed for the first time that her side was muddy and wet. *She must be freezing.*

"Wonderful," Justine said, in that way she said things that meant the opposite of what the word meant. "Vienna, what's the quickest way to the hotel. I thought we were on the right track."

"No." Vienna pointed to a massive tower that loomed before them, visible as a silhouette of concrete decks and steel rails. "It's a flacktürme."

"What?"

"The Augarten is the oldest baroque garden in Vienna, having been established in 1712. It did not gain its most distinguishing features, two enormous flacktürmes, until World War II. Built by the Nazis starting in 1943, these towers were to serve as housing for anti-aircraft guns as well as self-contained fortresses for thirty thousand troops. They included their own munitions factories as well as hospitals and—"

"Come, then, my tour guide. Let us cross the Augarten and find our way home. I'm too tired to take a single step more than I must."

They were halfway across the park when a black SUV pulled up on the street in front of them. Vienna looked at her internal map and found the street: Castellezgasse. A man stepped from the car. He made no move to come after them, but it was clear he was waiting for them.

Justine sighed. "Ah. Well, it was a long shot. I should have called a taxi. Had to try though."

"What's happening?"

"Doesn't matter, Vienna." She took Vienna's hand. "I want you to do something for me."

"Okay."

"I want you to give me the star."

Vienna backed away. "Why? I found it! I have every right to keep it!" She set her arms across her chest.

"More than you know, but I want you to give it to me."

"Why should I?" *How dare she ask after all of this?*

"Because five people are dead from it. I don't . . ." Justine swallowed. "I don't want you having such a venomous bauble. Anyone but you. I can't explain more than that. Anyone but you. Please."

Vienna was stunned to see that Justine was crying. Tears streaming down her face.

You have to trust her. *It's your turn to stop her tears.*

Vienna took it from her pocket. "It would sell for a lot, yeah? If I sold it, I would have enough money not to depend on you."

"I know."

Vienna handed the box to Justine. "Eight people. Prince Rudolph and Vetsera and Sisi died, too."

"True."

Justine took the box and slipped it into her pocket. She took a moment to compose herself. "Shall we see what the fates bring?"

"You think that man by the car is going to kill us, don't you?"

"No. But I wouldn't bet the farm on it."

Whatever that meant.

Justine offered her arm, and Vienna slipped her hand inside Justine's elbow. "It's cold," she said, not knowing what to talk about, but knowing silence was unbearable.

"It is," Justine said.

"It was very clever of me to find the star, don't you think?"

"I do. Will you tell me how you did it some day?"

"I will."

They were close enough now to see the lean grace of Sir Anson Davy. "Not much of a surprise," Justine said under her breath.

They stepped up to him.

"The Talmud cautions never to meet a stranger in the night, for he might be a demon," Lord Davy said.

"If you are, I'm too tired to run," Justine answered.

Davy nodded. "Would you like a ride to your hotel?"

"Is that where the car will take us?"

"Yes, my colonial friend." He was standing unnaturally still, his arms folded in front of his waist, his hands visible. "I had David Andries's number on my cell phone because he'd called to coerce me with the threat of harm to Vienna. He wanted access to a place where he was no longer welcome. His father and I had been friends, long ago. I didn't even suspect you knew I had his number until Olifur told me a few hours ago."

"But he has known for days."

Uncle Anson removed his suit jacket and draped it over Justine, even though it would get muddy. "He was forming the same suspicions you were. He kept several things from me. I can't blame him."

"But you arranged for Vienna to go to Holler," Justine said. She pulled the jacket close around her shoulders.

"I had no way of knowing Andries was one step ahead of me. He wished to demonstrate how easy it would be to get close to Vienna. Ironic that he set you two up as a warning shot. He took the first step, but you took the dance."

"Speaking of warning shots, your lackey in the forest could have been faster."

"He arrived too late due to my stupidity, and his orders were to act only as a final resort." Uncle Anson, left without a jacket, didn't look cold at all. "He was not ready until events had progressed beyond the need to interfere. He reported you acted with courage and intelligence. High praise from such a man."

"Better if he had saved me a lifetime in an Austrian prison for murder."

"Murder? My man reported that Hargrave shot himself in the neck with a gun pulled from his coat. He will testify to that fact and even take a polygraph test should anyone be foolish enough to put stock in such chicanery. I don't think it will come to that. I wager Hargrave's weapon is the same one used to kill Andries and Sinoro, and likely Haldor Stefansson as well. He even left a suicide note."

"As did Prince Rudolph."

"Undying are the echoes of history."

"You know how scary that is, that you can just . . . arrange these things?"

Lord Davy didn't smile or frown; his voice as lifeless as the moon. "The ballistics will speak for the dead."

Justine shook her head. "Why did Hargrave kill Grant?" Vienna wondered why Justine still called David Andries by his assumed name.

"We'll never know the whole story, least of all how your agent and your boyfriend became aware of the star in the first place. Andries must have come across whispers of it long ago and solved some of the mystery—enough to see a connection to your Clay to Flesh project. He contacted your agent, and the scheming started. As for his death, it is the nature of thieves to turn on each other. We can construct a thousand plausible scenarios. The most obvious would be a double-cross involving Gary Sinoro. The photographer had many connections. The others were killed to cover tracks."

"You can add a man named Julian Dardonelle to the list, and it's not finished. Hargrave had someone watching us."

"A loathsome compatriot of yours, wanted by your FBI. He's on a flight to Dulles; thinking he's free but landing to a different reality. He will give us the names of any others involved in this mess. How did you know he was with Hargrave?"

"He was bush league." She looked at Davy. "It gave James away, you know, when I spotted him lurking near Vienna. I knew your minions would never be seen."

Davy ignored that and turned to Vienna. "My lady, you aren't coming back to London?"

Vienna grabbed Justine's arm through the jacket. "No."

"Will you visit?"

"Okay."

"I would like that very much. So would your foster father. He loves you deeply." Davy turned to the car and opened the door. "I understand why you didn't trust me, Heather Ingles. But I hope I am good for a ride home."

"One second," Justine said.

Davy turned back. "Yes?"

"Why haven't you asked about the Star of Memphis?"

"Keep it hidden. Attempting to sell it will cause trouble."

"Don't you want it?"

"The Austrian Empire has lived a century without it. I doubt the sun will fail to rise if another century passes before they see it."

Justine held the box up. "I asked Vienna to give it to me. I don't want her having it. Do you understand?"

"So would we all spare our lovers from the sorrow of the world," Lord Davy said.

Justine nodded. "I'm giving it to you."

Davy took the box. He pried the rusted top off by pushing the side across the top of the open car door. He reached inside and produced an irregular rock. It looked like nothing so much as a clod of dirt, smaller than the width of his palm.

"It's a flipping rock!" Vienna said.

Davy's lips arced slightly upward. "The star was never cut.

There was not a craftsman who dared face the wrath of an angry emperor should it be split by a badly aimed blow."

"But it's ugly." Vienna felt as if she should be kicking something. The car, Uncle Anson, anything.

Davy turned the stone in his hand. "See this flatter side? Hold it to your eye and look at the white light topping the flack tower. If the histories are right, it should explain the stone's renown."

Vienna put it to her left eye, seeing a reddish smear of light.

"Move it around," Davy said. "Rotate it."

She did this, and suddenly the light was a clear point of blood red. Around it appeared concentric circles of red shot through with brilliant flares of bluish and violet light. Her breath caught. "Circles within circles!"

Vienna saved the pattern in her mind. "You have to see it!" She handed the stone to Justine. The American turned it before her eyes until a soft gasp told Vienna she had witnessed the vision as well. "It's beautiful." She lowered it. "How did this stone end up in ancient Egypt?"

"I don't know," Davy said. "We couldn't even find it once it was here. You and Vienna proved more clever than five generations of amateurs who had set themselves to the hunt, myself included. I assume it had something to do with David Bell? The son of the man who made the manikins? I've been saving everything I could of him."

"You put his obituary in that book my foster father has!" Vienna said.

"Yes. Grayfield was interested in the problem as well. We spent many a pleasant evening kicking through the facts. I have no idea how you solved the riddle. It's a story I would hear when this night is a distant memory."

Justine held out the star.

"Wait," Vienna said. "I found it. You have to give me something in return. It's only fair."

"Yes?" Davy asked.

"I want to go back to the Cart House and I want Justine to be there. I want her to see the forest and the lake and the pictures covering the walls. And I want her to see the people dance."

"Vienna, you are welcome in the house, but there are rules—"

"I don't care. Promise me."

"Why do you want this?"

"Because it's part of me and I want Justine to understand what it means and because it's beautiful and I want to share that with her because that is what lovers do."

Davy looked at Justine. "Lario's Cove."

"I'm not even going to ask how you know about that."

Davy reached for the star. "Perhaps you could put in a word for me. I could use a break from this weather."

Vienna kicked at the ground. "Promise I can take Justine to the Cart House."

"I'll arrange it."

"Promise!"

"I promise."

Davy took the stone and placed it in his coat pocket. "We'll fashion a display at the Kunsthistorisches to illustrate the star's amazing properties." He held the SUV's door and motioned Vienna to get in. After a nod from Justine, she slid onto the long seat. But not so far that she couldn't hear Davy talking to Justine.

"He would have put the muzzle to Vienna's head and he would have pulled the trigger. Then he would have done the same to you."

"I know," she answered.

"Any hesitation on your part would have led to struggle with an uncertain conclusion. My agent was good, but people of his training know that success is often as much luck as skill."

"I know," she said again. "But there was me before tonight and me after tonight, and they will never be the same person."

"That is the way of such things. Understand that had we known your agent was the villain we would have acted prior to this. Feel regret if you must, but never question the necessity of your actions. You saved Lady Vienna's life, for which I am forever in your debt."

"I'm too near what happened to know what I think. And too tired."

"Then it is time for that ride home."

Justine slid next to Vienna.

"One more thing," Davy said, his hand on the door. "I understand your suspicions of me, and why they compelled you to keep everything from the police. I am aware that I inadvertently caused much of this. Perhaps I am broken in my own way. Suspicion is a harsh mistress, but in my life she rules all and forgives no tardiness. What happened in Iceland is more my shame than yours. What few amends I can make to Haldor's memory, I will."

Uncle Anson paused, his head bowed. When he spoke his voice sounded sad to Vienna. She had never heard him talk like that before. "I know Igor Czasky, as you no doubt guessed. We met here in Vienna, years ago. Back then, Czasky was chasing an obscure work by an even more obscure impressionist. He's somewhat of a treasure hunter, you see.

"I spoke with him at length this morning. He is innocent of any of this. He has never been to the Cart House—doesn't even know of its existence. He kept you on because he counts you the most beautiful woman in the world. His only thought was to possess that beauty, if only through a book. Another treasure for his collection. A woman might find this offensive, but I find it easy to understand. He would never have wished you harm."

Justine nodded. "I appreciate his opinion, but the honor is not mine."

Davy's smile was as sad as his voice. "Strange that you and I have the same eyes." He closed the door and walked around to the driver's seat.

Vienna looked ahead. The first glow of sunrise. Tiny crystals of ice falling on the windshield.

31

Freezing rain over gray cobbles. Silver-black pools collecting Vienna's twilight. The crowds were gone, flying south on tidings of snow. Shop awnings furled tightly over dark windows. The air had the clean smell of winter.

Justine held off rain with a black umbrella. Her thoughts nothing more than shadowed undercurrents and fleeting images. Too much, too fast. *This is how Vienna perceives the passing of emotion.* Impossible to focus on anything. *Maybe I've caught her disease after all.*

"My father used to call it dream walking. Everything turned inside, until the outside fails to register."

Startled, Justine looked at the man who had fallen in step next to her. He looked like—

He smiled. "Let's assume for once that appearances are not deceiving." He gave a gentle nod, directing her sight around them. Justine was suddenly aware that they were surrounded by a loose web of men. Black earbuds and loose jackets moving with a single purpose. A fleeting image of social insects protecting their leader.

"I apologize," Justine said. "I didn't know, your High—"

He cut her off with a wave. "In Britain we will stand on formalities, Miss Am. Here they would only get in the way."

Justine found her voice. "To what do I owe this honor?"

"I bring sad news. Your agent, James Hargrave, was found dead this morning by joggers in the forest. Circumstances point to suicide. He left a note, which will be made available after the inquest. It appears he had an unhealthy obsession with your personal life."

"And the truth?"

"That is the only truth I've been told. I suggest you and Lady Vienna treat it in the same light."

"I'll tell her. Please give my regards to Lord Davy." Was that too informal?

He gave a silent laugh. "Anson Davy may appear cold, but I believe if he were thirty years younger, you would have a rival."

"That might've been better for everyone."

"Even you?"

"I don't know. This isn't exactly what I imagined for my life."

"Which was?"

"The perfect man, I guess. The handsome prince on a galloping charger, rushing to—" She blushed. "I can't believe I just said that."

He smiled. "I get that now and then."

"I imagine so."

"You must credit me with the perception to discern when a shy lady is in love. Lord Davy, for all his talents, would have lost this contest. It's as true as the sky is blue. Well, a different sky, anyway."

Justine angled her umbrella against the strengthening wind. "She barely hangs on, one glimpse away from the next seizure. Only . . . I think sometimes I see her the way she really is." She felt heat on her throat. "Clear and bright through the tears."

"Then be with her. Someday your perfect man might come along. But dwelling on the future never wins the present."

A camera flash popped. "The numpties have found us," he said.

"I'm sorry."

"Dear Lord above, you're beginning to sound like her. So I am seen with the most beautiful of women? Let them spin headlines. They will never guess the subject of our conversation."

"You care for her, too."

"I don't know her entirely well, but my extended family is large. There's an old man in London: Arthur Grayfield. He is not well known outside his charity work, as he has taken some care to conceal his genealogy. At one time or another his ancestors sat on every throne in Europe. He is distantly related to Vienna—just as I am—grand uncle or the like, several times removed. He has been watching her since her own parents abandoned her. He cares for her more than for the sun rising in the east. I respect him too much not to follow his lead on the matter."

"She has friends in high places."

"Not one of whom can give her what you can."

"Perhaps."

"There is no doubt, if you love her."

Justine paused. She looked down; caught a glimpse of her broken silhouette in a puddle. "There is no doubt."

"Yet your voice holds it."

She tried to frame words without betraying Lord Davy's trust. "A lot of what happened is my fault. I don't see how I can ever feel right about it."

"To walk in the shadows does not make you part of them. Lord Anson Davy understands this better than anyone. He speaks highly of you."

"I hope you're right." *Now that was too informal.* "I didn't mean—"

He laughed. "I'm so right that I give you and Vienna the blessing of the House of Windsor, for what it's worth to an American."

"It's worth more than I can say. But Vienna will never know?"

"In time, perhaps. Whatever happens, she will never lack. Grayfield will see to that. I as well, should it become necessary."

"Thank you."

"And after all this is what you wanted, with only the smallest deviation. Princess, not prince."

Justine laughed.

"I have been told that Lady Vienna has a strong sense of rhythm, as well as a good ear for music. I understand it's not uncommon for a woman of her talents."

"Yes?" *Where was this going?*

"She would make a fine addition to the right dance card of her beloved Cart House. Waltzes are easily tamed."

Justine bristled. "I doubt the sight of women dancing together would be appreciated in such a place."

This brought forth another laugh. "My dear lady, if you wish to reside in the company of a princess, you must learn to exist above the base attitudes of the masses. Who Vienna chooses to dance with may matter out here, but it will not in the Cart House."

Justine smiled. "She told me she wanted to learn to dance."

"Then I will forward a schedule of events."

"Thank you, but I only require the most important one."

"Oh?"

"If I am to dance with Vienna, it will be in the central spotlight of the biggest affair of the year. She is an outstanding catch. I have every intention of showing her off."

He nodded. "I am relieved that you already possess the instincts needed to flourish within Cart House society. You have two choices. The house celebration of Fasching is the largest event, held the weekend after the Vienna Opera Ball. I believe it is late February this coming year. Strictly white tie. But the Mōdraniht Masquerade might be the better choice. Very exclusive, just before Christmas. I will have Anson forward the particulars for both."

"Thank you."

He leaned close. "Lord Davy sends a message from Shakespeare: 'If thou remember'st not the slightest folly that ever love did make thou run into, thou has not loved.'"

"I'm not familiar with the passage. He will be delighted to have foiled me."

"I suspect Lady Vienna could find it quickly enough."

"I'm sure she could."

"And I suspect Shakespeare has the right of it."

"I bow to your wisdom."

"Then Godspeed, Heather Ingles. It may be we will never meet again, though who can say? I should like to witness Lady Vienna's waltz. In either event, may you find joy."

"You as well." She gave a deep curtsey, not knowing what was right. The camera flashed again.

And he was gone, stepping into a black SUV. Dark windows and too much mass to be anything other than armored. Justine stood alone in the rain for a minute before moving on.

Time to go home.

Up to the warm suite atop Hotel Sacher. Vienna bunched up in a chair, lost in a book. *The Crystallography of Gems.* Justine logged onto her BlackBerry and opened the e-mail from Hot Dragon. She put her hand over the lizard tattoo, as if coaxing arcane prophecy from its sleek lines.

You always said you wanted adventure.

> I am interested in your offer to the point I would like to discuss it further. As I am temporarily acting as my own agent, please send details to this address.
>
> Justine Am

She checked the phone's clock. Subtract six hours for Georgia. So many things to talk about. She pulled up her parent's number and stretched out on the suite's couch.

32

One in the morning and the red-light, green-light breathing of traffic. Rain cut by snow. Laughter from somewhere outside. Vienna lay on her side of the bed, crowded by Justine. Impossible to sleep. Somehow it was the night before Christmas only this time she got it right.

Emily had taken her to her room, two floors down, and put her in a school dress from one of those manga books everyone used to read back in London. A red and black skirt that was full of squares inside squares. Vienna felt her mind slipping into the pattern, but the skirt was short enough to render geometry trivial. White socks and those white shoes with black laces and a black band of leather over the top. "Saw this yesterday and had to get it for you," Emily said. "It fits well enough, though you can have Justine get it tailored. If she's like her peers, she'll be a wardrobe Nazi." She put two tails in Vienna's hair, holding them with pink bows.

"Why does everyone want to dress me up?"

"Because you let us," Emily said. "Didn't you ever play with dolls?" She fussed over the white blouse and short tie. "The glasses are already perfect. Now go to Justine and see what happens. If she asks, tell her hello from me." Emily stretched. "I'm off to London tomorrow morning for my own rendezvous. Remind your girl she owes my brother a photo session."

Your girl.

Justine laughed when Vienna walked into the room. But it was a quiet sound and her cheeks were red.

"Tell me no one saw you in that."

"No. Emily says hello and that we owe her brother some pictures. I hope not with these clothes."

"Not with those clothes."

"What does this mean?" She brushed her hands over the too-short skirt. "It makes my legs look skinny."

"It means our friend Emily has been to Akihabara Electric Town—a very strange and strangely alive place. I'll take you there someday."

"And people dress like this?"

"A few, but most only dream of being with someone who looks like you."

"It's pretty?"

"It's you telling me it's okay to share love any way we please."

"I told you that in Iceland."

"I don't have your memory."

How can I love someone so annoying?

"Emily said she even got the panties right." She lifted the skirt, revealing sky blue horizontal stripes on white cotton. They covered far more than the silk underclothes Justine bought for her. That made them useless for what Vienna wanted and that was just stupid because—

"Come here, Little Storm Cloud." And it was there again: the *pressure* that Justine projected. Except now Vienna knew what it was. It was standing above Sellfoss, hypnotized by that exact point where turbulence flattened to rushing clarity. And do you dare take the next step?

Girl moving.

Miracle of miracles, Justine shut up except for when she wanted Vienna to do something a certain way. And maybe she was just trying to be clear, but Vienna thought maybe some caged part of Justine was free, and the more Vienna appeared slightly confused or even shocked, the more fierce this thing became. Vienna liked that, even if lovers weren't supposed to be confused or shocked. She made a mental note to ask Emily about this, appended with a reminder to appear eager but mystified during sex. It was simple enough, and Justine had said Vienna was perfect and it would be "wonderful to continue the lesson in New York."

Vienna thought it must be something about how Americans made love. Hunter S. Thompson or Mark Twain would have understood.

Except now she couldn't sleep. They were flying to New York to have dinner with someone named Simone in—she looked at the clock—eleven hours. Justine said she needed advice. Then off to Thailand. Then Spain, and then London at Vienna's request. Justine should meet Grayfield because that was proper. Then Georgia in the United States because "Mom and Dad will love you." And then back here, which surprised Vienna.

"The forest fits you," Justine had said. "All beautiful and wet."

Vienna couldn't decide if that was a reference to her crying or to a comment Justine had made during their lovemaking. Was that something to be embarrassed about?

"I owe you a dance at the Cart House," Justine added. "We'll have to get gowns and find a stylist in Vienna."

That would be perfect because the people at Cart House would never let two women dance together, so they could go into the ballroom when it was empty and the lights were down and no one ever had to know that Vienna couldn't dance and maybe they could make love right there in the ballroom.

Her mind stuttered and stumbled in a thousand different directions.

You know this is dangerous. Concentrate on one thing.

She saw an article from the *London Telegraph*—a column that had come out the day after Justine and Lord Davy had their public exchange.

"In a world of coy semi-disclosures, how refreshing to see American supermodel Justine Am publicly proclaim her love for a wisp of an orphan named Vienna. It's too much to hope it will last, but even that small hope is new."

Everyone saw it but me.

The night twisted on its silent axis. The machinery of God

pushing rain to snow. Another hour passed. She heard Justine's breathing; timed it by the clock on the nightstand. How many breaths would she take in one year?

Stop it!

She uncurled slightly from her tuck. The bottom of her foot brushed against Justine's shin. Her skin was smooth and warm. *What does this mean?* It means she is here, my foot touching her. That was enough.

The laughter outside faded.

It's a thing lovers share.

She ran to a familiar place. *The phenol group is defined by the presence of a hydroxyl as well as an aromatic hydrocarbon. . . .*

Shelter in a storm. But she could see beyond it.

The world was moving, she was right there with it.

At last.